TERENC_

# CYBER
## COUNTDOWN

RIVER GROVE
BOOKS

Published by River Grove Books
Austin, TX
www.rivergrovebooks.com

Distributed by River Grove Books

Design and composition by Greenleaf Book Group
Cover design by Greenleaf Book Group
Cover images ©iStockphoto.com/JosephJacobs.
©Snaprender; ©13Imagery; ©u3d. Used under license from Shutterstock.com

Publisher's Cataloging-in-Publication data is available.

Print ISBN: 978-1-63299-160-7

eBook ISBN: 978-1-63299-161-4

First Edition

*For Mom, Dad, JoAnn, Tom, Barbara, Joey, Michelle, John, James, and Jordan.*

When written in Chinese, the word "crisis" is composed of two characters. One represents danger and the other represents opportunity.

—JOHN F. KENNEDY

# ACKNOWLEDGMENTS

My wife, JoAnn, for her love, patience, and trust;
My children, Joey, Michelle, and John, for being there;
Mercy and Jeanne for their patient editing and instruction.

# 1

Dimitri Vasin observed the expensive houses and their glittering Christmas lights and decorations outside his parked SUV. With temperatures in the mid-seventies, it seemed more like September than early December. This winter was predicted to be the warmest for the DC area in years. In Grozny, Chechnya, where Dimitri was born and had grown up, he'd never experienced winters this warm. The climatologists claimed that the earth was warming and was doomed. He thought they might be right, but not because of the weather.

Christmas was a time of year that Dimitri had loved while growing up in Grozny, but now dreaded. While most Americans celebrated the season and looked forward to being with family and the gifts they'd get, Dimitri was reminded of what he'd lost. His family and many friends had been slaughtered during the Second Chechen War, in the winter of 1999.

Dimitri had come from a prominent Russian family, was well educated, and had been on his way toward becoming a surgeon. The outbreak of war had changed all that. Instead, he left medical school and learned a new trade when he joined the local Christian militia that fought alongside the Russian Army. They taught him how to kill easily, stealthily, and savagely when necessary.

The horrible death and savagery that Dimitri witnessed and experienced during the war changed him. He began to think of his life as a Greek tragedy in which dire circumstances reshape the lives of characters who inevitably suffer a brutal death in the final act. Tragedy seemed inevitable for Russians like him, who were born Christians in a Muslim Chechen Republic that was governed by an agnostic Russian empire. Dimitri remembered the words of a professor of Greek literature that he found prophetic: *Life is a tragedy and death is the final act.*

Like many other Russian Chechens, Dimitri decided to utilize his new skills after the war ended. There were governments and criminal organizations that would pay well for his talent. It was also much easier than saving lives and was a bigger growth industry than medicine. He thought it was an indictment of the human condition that a highly trained soldier like him was often more valuable than a skilled surgeon.

The US government and those in Europe had been his best clients, and they paid well for his services, but not as well as the "Big Man" he'd worked for over the past three years. Dimitri had never met the Big Man, as his representatives called him. This made him feel vulnerable, but he accepted it as a tradeoff, since his current position was much more lucrative with fewer hours and less risk than the work he'd performed for his government clients. He also didn't need to worry about changes in management and available opportunities with each new government.

The arrival of the red Jaguar interrupted his thoughts.

"Time to go to work," Dimitri growled to Chin, his young Chinese cohort sitting in the passenger seat. "There's his car, right on schedule."

"Wow, you didn't say he drove a Jaguar convertible," Chin replied. "Can I have it after we're done?"

"We'll see. Looks like he's alone. Look to see which lights go on after he goes in."

"Okay, but do I get to do the wet work?"

Chin had only been in the country a short time and was already using American crime movie slang. *Ah, the pervasive evils of Western culture*, Dimitri thought.

"There's no wet work on this job," he said. "We're just here to question him and to take some of his things."

"What things?"

"That's not your concern. Just do your job."

Dimitri preferred working alone, but this Chinese punk was a necessity for this job. Not for the reasons the psychopath sitting next to him anticipated, however. One of the reasons Dimitri had selected Chin for this job was because he had a reputation for performing burglaries without leaving clues.

The Big Man's representative had made it clear that the target was high profile. Dimitri understood what that meant. The job had to be done right, without leaving any clues behind other than the ones Dimitri wanted to leave.

"He's been in there a while, Dimitri. It looks like the only lights that are lit are on the first floor."

"Okay, put on your ski mask and go through the trees on the right to get to the back of the house," Dimitri directed. "There's a sliding glass door near the pool that you can jimmy. Remember, disable the alarm on the back door first, and then enter and disable the target. Don't harm him. I need to talk with him. I'll follow when you signal everything's okay."

"Don't worry, no one will see me. There are no other houses nearby, and the trees will hide me from anyone driving down the street. I've done this lots of times."

Dimitri waited about ten minutes until the lights turned on and off three times: Chin's signal. He put on a pair of custom-made latex gloves and his ski mask, and he unsheathed his Russian combat knife as he walked through the trees to the back of the house. Entering through the back door, he went down the hall toward the living room. From the display cases that lined the hall, Dimitri could see that the occupants of the house had a taste for Chinese art and antiquities. They were beautiful, but he didn't believe they were real. Genuine antiques would require a better alarm system than the house appeared to have.

When he entered the living room, Dimitri found their target sitting in a leather lounger with his hands tied and a gag in his mouth. Chin was sitting across from the target on a matching leather couch, smoking one of the target's expensive cigars. *What an idiot*, he thought, but a useful one, as Lenin would say.

"Untie him and take the gag out of his mouth," Dimitri growled. "Hurt him if he screams or tries to escape." He could see his captive's eyes widen, so he knew his words had the intended impact.

"Where's your safe? Tell me and you won't get hurt."

"In the master bedroom upstairs."

"Show me," Dimitri ordered as he pulled the man to his feet.

Dimitri followed his captive up the stairs. As they entered the master bedroom, Dimitri looked around and said, "Where is it?"

"Under the carpet. It's built into the floor."

"Open it."

The man removed the carpet and the floor panel above the safe and then walked toward the phone on the end table next to the bed.

"Don't touch the phone," Dimitri warned.

"The phone's keypad is the mechanism for opening the safe. I need to enter the pass code and then correctly respond to an audio challenge."

"Okay, go ahead," Dimitri said. "But if the safe doesn't open or there's an alarm, I'll shoot you. Is that clear?"

He nodded and entered a nine digit number, and then responded to the audio challenge question with a verbal pass phrase. The red light on the safe turned green as the lock unlatched.

"Stand back," Dimitri said. "I'll open the safe."

Dimitri opened the safe and found a large amount of cash, some legal papers, and some technical documents, which he quickly viewed.

"What's in the documents, Philip?"

"How do you know my name?" asked his captive, Philip Wu, with a surprised look on his face.

"I'll say it just one more time," Dimitri warned. "What's in the documents?"

"They describe a research project my company is involved in. A plan to enhance cybersecurity for our customers."

"Is any of this information classified?"

"No," Philip said. "My company doesn't sell its products to the federal government, only businesses."

"That's good, because I wouldn't want to break the law," Dimitri said with a laugh. "Tell me—does any of this relate to Project Backfire?"

Philip Wu flinched and nervously said, "I've never heard of that project."

"I know that's not true, Philip. Now tell me, does this research project relate to Project Backfire? If you don't tell me, I'll get my answers from your colleagues and family."

"My colleagues and family know nothing and my research isn't related to any government project. You should know that my company doesn't sell its products to the government, since you seem well informed."

"I'm very well informed, Philip. Now tell me where I can find the documents that describe Backfire. If they're not in these papers, where are they? I don't have all night."

"You're wasting your time taking those documents."

"Then why don't you tell me what the goal for Backfire is."

"Project Backfire is very technical. I doubt you'd understand."

"Just keep it at a layman's level, so even I can comprehend it," Dimitri said with contempt.

"I'm sorry. I meant no offense," Philip replied.

"None taken. Answer my question."

"We're implementing a new technology that will make our cybersecurity systems more adaptive to new threats."

"How are you doing that?" Dimitri asked.

"We're using artificial intelligence. The exact mechanism is very complex."

Dimitri considered his options and decided there was nothing of use that could be gained from Philip Wu without the necessary technical knowledge, which he didn't have.

"Okay, but I think I'll take these technical documents anyway. Put the cash and papers back in the safe and we'll go see how my little friend is doing. He really likes your cigars."

When they got downstairs, Philip Wu took his seat across from Chin, who was lighting another cigar. Dimitri almost laughed at the sight of Chin attempting to light the cigar without setting his ski mask and face on fire.

"These are really good cigars. Are you sure you don't want one?" Chin asked.

"No thanks, our masks are flammable, and I like my face the way it is. I have a few more questions for Philip, and then we can leave with some of his things."

"Philip? Is that his name? What things are you talking about?"

Dimitri gave Chin a long and silent stare, and he immediately stopped talking. He then turned to Philip Wu and asked, "Do you have a PC or laptop or any portable data storage devices in the house, Philip?"

"My laptop's in my briefcase by the hallway entrance, but there's no information on it about Backfire."

"I warn you, don't lie to me," Dimitri said. "I know that you sometimes keep confidential information on important projects at this residence."

"Who told you that? I'm afraid you've been misinformed."

"Our information is from a reliable source."

"What source?" Philip asked.

"If I told you that, my friend here would have to kill you," Dimitri said flatly. "I really don't want to do that. You're a brilliant man who's done a lot of great things, and I admire you and your success."

"I think you'll kill me anyway," said Wu. "I won't help you, no matter what you do to me."

Dimitri walked directly in front of Wu and bent over so they were face to face. He then took out his knife and pressed it into Wu's neck. Wu didn't flinch. Dimitri pressed harder until small droplets of Wu's blood began to appear on the blade. He continued this for more than a minute until Wu said, "I'm ready to die. Just end it."

"You know, Philip, I believe you," Dimitri said. He then turned to Chin and said, "Watch him while I check his briefcase."

Dimitri had just started to go through the contents of the briefcase when he heard Chin and Wu speaking loudly in Chinese. Suddenly, he heard a loud thumping, grunts, and then abrupt silence. He ran back to the living room. Chin was straddling Philip Wu's body while removing his bloody stiletto from under Wu's rib cage. Blood was surging from the wound. Dimitri kicked Chin in the head so hard that it rolled him off Wu's body. Chin was gasping for air and Dimitri saw blood flowing from his ear as he ripped off Chin's ski mask.

"You idiot, I didn't tell you to kill him," Dimitri shouted.

Chin looked up at Dimitri with tears in his eyes. "Please don't kick me again, Dimitri," he cried. "Wu tried to get away, and we were going to have to kill him anyway."

Dimitri removed his ski mask and threw it at Chin. "Wu's death was never part of my plan, and it wasn't your decision to make. I still needed him to describe what's in his briefcase. You should've just restrained him."

"I was angry. He called my mother a prostitute."

Dimitri composed himself and remembered why he liked working alone.

"Take Wu's car," he ordered. "I'll meet you in the parking lot at the marina we passed on the way here. I need time to check the house for the information the client is paying us for."

"Can I keep Wu's Jaguar?" Chin asked hopefully.

"I doubt Mr. Wu will be needing it," Dimitri spat. "You made sure of that. I'll bring some of Mr. Wu's more valuable things after I'm done here. Take your cigars with you—they could be evidence. When you drive Mr. Wu's car past the security post, keep your head down. There might be security cameras."

"Okay, I know how to do that. How long will you be?"

"I don't know. Just stay there until I arrive. Is that clear?"

"I'm sorry about what happened, Dimitri," Chin said quietly.

"Just get out of my sight," Dimitri replied.

Once Chin was gone, Dimitri set to work. He searched the entire house, including Wu's office, for more than two hours, but found nothing of interest. His detailed search of Wu's briefcase revealed a small laptop computer, a portable USB drive, some personal and legal papers, and Wu's corporate and government ID badges.

*Well, maybe we've found what we are looking for,* thought Dimitri.

Dimitri put the technical documents from the safe into the briefcase and went back to the master bedroom to make sure nothing looked like it had been disturbed. As he entered the bedroom, he noticed that the light on the safe door was red. He remembered the light being green after Philip Wu had closed it earlier. Frowning, he opened the safe door and carefully reclosed the door again. The light was green, indicating that the safe was locked. He tried to open the safe door but couldn't; the safe was indeed locked. Dimitri sat on the bed and watched. After about fifteen minutes, the light turned red again, and the unlocked door opened easily when he tried it. He realized that the safe wouldn't remain locked and there was probably another sequence of numbers and possibly another vocal challenge question required to lock it. Those were things only Philip Wu knew.

*Very clever,* thought Dimitri. Chin had killed Philip Wu; he wondered if Wu had goaded him into it, knowing that the inability to close the safe would provide evidence that it had been breached. Dimitri knew the Big Man might be upset about this, if he knew. He needed to hide his involvement from the authorities. Dimitri closed the safe and covered it with the flooring and carpet so it would look like Wu had just forgotten to lock his safe. He prayed it would work.

Dimitri also took some small Chinese antiquities from Wu's display cases and wrapped them carefully in newspaper. He then placed them in a large plastic shopping bag he found in the kitchen and checked the house to make sure he had not left anything behind that could connect him to Wu's death. Dimitri then left the house with Wu's briefcase and the shopping bag through the same door he had entered and placed everything in the SUV.

When Dimitri and Chin had arrived at Wu's house earlier that afternoon it was sunny, warm, and dry. They had driven the SUV through the woods over rough and hilly terrain to avoid the security gate for the gated community where Wu's house was located. Now it was raining and the ground was soft from the warm temperatures.

Dimitri knew the drive out would be treacherous so he drove very slowly until he finally reached the main road. The drive to the marina took another forty minutes. He hoped Chin hadn't left with his new red toy before he arrived. That would ruin everything.

Dimitri was relieved when he saw Wu's red Jaguar. It was the only car in the empty marina parking lot. The lights in the marina were off, and there appeared to be no one nearby. Just to make certain, he used a set of binoculars to observe the parking lot but didn't see anyone near the Jaguar or, for that matter, anyone in it, either.

Dimitri cautiously drove the SUV to a concealed spot about fifty feet behind the Jaguar and watched. He could hear music coming from the car but saw no sign of Chin. Dimitri grabbed the plastic bag with the antiquities and walked slowly toward the Jaguar with his combat knife unsheathed. He looked all around the area as he approached the car.

When he was within ten feet he could see that the driver's-side window was down and smoke was streaming out the window. Then he saw the top of Chin's head as it bobbed with the music. Chin was smoking a cigar and had the driver's seat all the way back. Dimitri quietly approached the car until he was near the open window. He reached into the window while holding the plastic bag, and dropped it into the young psychopath's lap.

Chin screamed and then said, "You scared me! Did you find what you needed?"

"I'm not sure," Dimitri said. "Give me the car keys so I can put this bag with Wu's property in the trunk."

Chin relaxed and smoked his cigar while Dimitri put Wu's Chinese art treasures in the trunk of the Jaguar. Dimitri quietly closed the trunk, took a deep breath, and walked back to the driver's side of the car. He looked down at Chin smoking his cigar, gazing at his smiling face for a few seconds. Then, in one incredibly swift action, he grabbed Chin's long hair, slammed his head back on the headrest, and sliced his combat knife savagely through Chin's jugular veins, carotid arteries, windpipe, and almost through the neck bone.

Dimitri could see the look of surprise in Chin's face as he had less than thirty seconds of life remaining. He quickly took a picture with his cell phone.

"That's for my friend Yuri and his sister Marta who you brutalized, Chin. Maybe you remember them."

Dimitri then spit on Chin's face and watched his blood spew all over the front seat and windshield. He threw the car keys into the bushes next to the parking lot and walked back to the SUV. His clothes were stained with Chin's blood spatter so he used a rag and some cleaning solvent to remove as much of it as he could. He donned a full-length raincoat and sat in the SUV for a few minutes to unwind from the adrenaline rush after killing Chin.

As Dimitri drove back to DC, he thought about his mistake in allowing Chin to murder Wu. It could be disastrous if someone figured out the message Wu had sent by preventing the safe from being locked. At least Dimitri could take some satisfaction in Chin's death. He'd selected him as the scapegoat because he was known as a brutal killer who enjoyed hurting the weak and helpless. No one would miss him. Dimitri justified Chin's death as a public service that would save lives.

The next day, Dimitri called one of the Big Man's legal representatives.

"Meet me at the seafood restaurant in Reagan National Airport at six."

"Okay, Mr. Vasin. I'll be wearing the usual clothing."

The Big Man's law firm had contacted Dimitri three years ago about a job. He was hired as a security consultant and was retained on an annual basis to provide his services to the Big Man. The firm also provided any required legal services, so Dimitri was also their client. This was for their mutual protection, since the Big Man's legal representatives were required to keep all client transactions private, in accordance with their legal oath.

Dimitri arrived at the airport during a rainstorm and walked directly to the restaurant, where he recognized his contact. He was wearing the usual blue suit, white shirt, and a red-white-and-blue tie. Dimitri sat down across from him and said, "Here's what you wanted."

The attorney opened a small duffel bag and looked through the contents.

"Have you examined the materials and the files on the drive and the laptop?"

"No, the technical documents and papers are above my skills, and the laptop hard drive and portable drive are definitely encrypted."

"Okay, the Big Man has people that can evaluate them. We'll get back to you if we need more."

"Tell the Big Man that if the materials he wanted aren't in this bag then getting them from Wu's company files will be much more difficult. The costs will be much higher," Dimitri said, with a grin.

"I'll let him know."

The attorney left, and as Dimitri sat there drinking a vodka, he noticed a special report on the TV. The reporter said that the co-founder and CEO of Virtual Security Incorporated, also known as VSI, had been found dead in his summer house by one of his colleagues. His wife had been informed and had flown back from a retreat in San Diego, California. Their son had also been contacted and was flying back from a vacation in Maui.

The reporter stated that the cause of death appeared to be a knife wound from an intruder and that the crime probably occurred the previous evening during an apparent burglary. There was no report of any witnesses, nor was there any mention of the hidden safe. Dimitri was pleased; the Big Man wouldn't know of his mistake. The report ended with the most interesting information, at least as far as Dimitri was concerned.

"The information from the Maryland State Police indicated that there was a possible connection to a murder that took place on the same evening in the parking lot of a marina in St. Mary's County," the reporter said. Dimitri smiled and thought to himself that once again he'd managed to elude the final act.

# 2

"What a view," James Jordan said, as he sat at a table looking down at the Potomac River and in the distance, the Washington Monument.

"Yes, she's beautiful, but a little young for you, isn't she, James?" joked James's dinner partner, a Washington lobbyist.

James glanced at the next table where a beautiful blonde woman was standing while talking to some male customers.

"Very funny, Fred. Don't get any ideas. Her boyfriend is the head chef here. She owns this place."

"You're kidding. I guess that would make her Michelle?"

"That's her, and I do agree with you, she's beautiful. But her boyfriend is jealous and is very good with knives. So if you don't want to be castrated, I'd concentrate on the Washington Monument and take your eyes off her ass."

"Okay, but being a legislative advocate is very stressful. I need to occasionally relax and enjoy the sights."

"Legislative advocate? You lobbyists are certainly kind to yourselves, Fred," James said, as he laughed.

"It's a job. You've certainly redefined the responsibilities of your position as Federal Chief Information Officer, James. It's a lot more powerful than it was during the previous administration. How'd that happen?"

"When President Meredith offered me the job, I said I'd consider it only if I was also his direct advisor on all cybersecurity issues. That included those involving national security. The president agreed, but he had to twist a lot of arms in the Department of Homeland Security, the FBI, Cyber Command, and especially NSA."

"Yeah, I heard that it ruffled a lot of feathers in the national security community. I also heard that your background as the former CEO and co-founder of VSI was not accepted very well."

"That's true, Fred. They didn't like the fact that VSI was known for not selling its products to government agencies. It wasn't political. We just didn't want to deal with the federal government bureaucracy."

"That's somewhat ironic, isn't it, James? Your current position requires you to deal with that bureaucracy every day. I thought it was because your primary investor, George Solomon, wasn't a US citizen. That would bar VSI from all classified government work."

"That wasn't it at all. George agreed to sell his interest in VSI if we ever wanted to pursue federal work."

"Okay, if you say so."

"I do. What was so urgent that you needed to meet with me tonight, Fred? JoAnn isn't going to be very happy that I canceled on a home cooked meal at her place. Nor am I, since she's infinitely more attractive and personable than you are."

"She sure is. You lucky dog," Fred said, as he tossed down the last ounce of an excellent pinot noir. "Listen, James, I need to know if you're in favor of the pending senate bill that would implement large trade penalties against China for the recent increase in their alleged cyber attacks."

"Actually, I'm not in favor of the current legislation in the senate, nor is the president. But he's getting a lot of pressure from some influential donors."

"I know. Many of those donors would like to see the current Chinese government replaced with some of the younger members waiting in the wings."

"I agree with that view, Fred. The younger crowd in China grew up after Mao and are certainly more sympathetic toward us evil capitalists."

"Do·you know who's leading the charge against the current Chinese government? It's your former partner, George Solomon."

James's face reddened as he raised his voice. "George has been a large part of the success of VSI, but don't think for a moment that I'd allow that friendship to influence me in my current job. I'm no longer running VSI, and all my stock is held in a blind trust, so my only loyalty these days is to the president and the American people."

Fred put up his hands and said, "Whoa, calm down, James. I'm not accusing you of anything, and I'm not saying that the president or you would be influenced by George. But you both could be on the opposite side of the fence from a very powerful billionaire who has close ties to the both of you. Can you handle that?"

"We can, and will, if necessary. I really have to go, Fred. JoAnn is waiting for me."

Fred smiled and in a much lighter tone said, "You're one lucky SOB, James. You have it all: looks, wealth, power, and a gorgeous senator for a girlfriend."

James's phone suddenly rang.

"I have to take this, Fred. It's JoAnn." James shook Fred's hand and answered the phone. "Hi, baby. I know I'm late, but I'm on my way."

"James, did you see the news this evening?" asked JoAnn.

"No, we're at Michelle's, and there are no TVs here."

"Philip Wu is dead, James. He was murdered in his summer house."

It was like someone punched James in the stomach, and for a minute he couldn't breathe. "What do you mean, who did it? When did it happen?" James gasped.

"They don't know yet, but the Maryland State Police think it was a burglary gone bad. Philip's car was found at a marina with a dead body, possibly the burglar. They haven't officially connected it to Philip, but some reporters have speculated on a possible connection. I'm certain the press will want to talk with you about Philip."

"Okay, I'm on my way to your place. No one would look for me there."

James took his check up to Michelle and handed it to her with his credit card. Michelle looked at him sympathetically and said, "Is there anything wrong, Mr. Jordan?"

"I just got some very bad news."

"I'm so sorry to hear that. I thought maybe that sleazy lobbyist had pissed you off."

"No, he was just doing his job. Goodnight, Michelle, and say hello to Daren for me."

"I'll do that, and the same to JoAnn."

James got to his car just as it started to rain. He opened the driver's side door and slumped into the seat, thinking about Philip. He suddenly felt exhausted, and it was an effort just to start the car. The rain began to subside as James drove his Corvette out of the parking lot to JoAnn's house in Georgetown.

James really liked JoAnn, more than any woman he had met. She was as independent as he was and had done well in her previous career as the successful manager of a hedge fund in Minneapolis. He felt comfortable with her since he knew she wasn't interested in him just because of his wealth or political position. He thought JoAnn felt the same way about him and for the same reasons.

James arrived at JoAnn's house and exited his car into a torrential downpour. He slowly walked through her front patio and up the steps to JoAnn's door, where he rang the doorbell. James was totally drenched by the time JoAnn answered, wearing a bathrobe and a towel around her head.

"Oh my God, James. You look wetter than I do. Why didn't you just use the key I gave you?"

"I don't want to scare you in case you don't hear me come in. I also know you have a gun, and I don't want to get shot."

"All right, then let's compromise. Ring the doorbell and then use the key."

"That makes sense. I guess I'm still in shock. Is there any more news about Philip?"

"Not really, except that his wife is already back from her vacation and his son is flying back to Maryland as we speak. Oh, Karen from your office called here and asked you to call her back. It sounded urgent."

"Okay, I'll call her after I get out of these wet clothes."

James walked up the stairs to the bedroom to change. He came back down wearing sweatpants and a tee shirt and smiled when JoAnn handed him a drink.

"Thanks, baby, you must've read my mind," he said as he kissed her. James downed the first scotch and immediately poured himself a second.

"Slow down, cowboy, or you'll be sleeping down here on the couch. I can't carry you up those stairs."

James smiled as he picked up the phone to call Karen.

"Hi, Karen. I hope I didn't wake you."

"No sir, I was waiting for your call. I'm sorry about your friend. The president asked me to pass on his condolences."

"Thank you, Karen. Is there anything else? JoAnn said you sounded like it was urgent."

"Yes, sir. Shelly Brockner from the FBI called and requested that you call her at your earliest convenience."

"The FBI director called? Did she say what it was about?"

"No, sir, but she definitely wanted to talk with you."

"Did she leave a number where she can be reached?"

"Yes, sir, I forwarded it to your cell phone."

"Thanks, Karen. Goodnight."

James found the message with Director Brockner's number and called.

"Hello?" a woman answered in a somewhat dazed voice.

"Is this Director Brockner?" James asked warily.

"Yes it is. Who am I talking to, please?"

"Director, this is James Jordan. I'm returning your call to my office."

"Oh, thanks for calling me back, Mr. Jordan. Can you meet me at my office in the Hoover Building tomorrow morning at ten? I'd like to discuss Philip Wu's murder with you."

"Can I ask why the FBI is involved in this case?"

"You can, and I'll provide an answer to that question when we meet tomorrow. Don't worry, Mr. Jordan, you're not a suspect. However, this case has serious national security implications that require your help. Can I expect to see you in my office tomorrow?"

"Yes, ma'am, I'll be there. Goodnight."

"What was that all about?" JoAnn asked.

"Nothing much. The FBI Director wants to interrogate me in her office tomorrow morning."

"You're kidding, right?"

"No, I kid you not. She wants me in her office at ten to discuss Philip's death."

"That doesn't make any sense. I'd think the jurisdiction would be limited to the county and state where Philip was killed. Do you think you'll need a lawyer?"

"No, she made it clear that I wasn't a suspect, but she did say that there are national security implications."

"What does that mean?"

"I haven't a clue, but I guess I'll find out tomorrow. Have you ever met her?"

"Yes, I did. The senate is required to approve the appointment of all FBI directors. Didn't you know that?"

"I really didn't, but then again, I'm a political novice. What's she like?"

"Well, she was a successful state's attorney and federal district court judge before being appointed to be the director of the FBI. Personally, I liked her. She seemed firm but fair and wasn't afraid to show her femininity."

"What do you mean by that?"

"Some women who work in organizations with large male populations often try to hide their femininity and become one of the guys."

"Well, you certainly don't do that, and most of the senate is male."

"Yes, and it sometimes reeks of testosterone, but I'm comfortable in my own skin, and it's apparent that she is, too."

"Any advice for me tomorrow?"

"Just treat her like any other powerful woman."

"Like you?" James asked.

"Yes, but not exactly like me. She's very attractive and single."

"You have nothing to worry about. That's the last thing on my mind."

"I know. I was just trying to lighten your mood, James. Philip was a dear friend, and he'll be missed."

"I can't believe he's gone," James said. "He's been my best friend since high school."

"Is that where you met?"

"Yeah, I met Philip at the sailing club during our freshman year at Ryken High School. Other than sailing, we seemed to have little in common."

"So how did you become so close?"

"The sailing coach partnered us, and we worked well together. While sailing we began talking about our ambitions. We realized that we had common interests in computers and programming."

"How did that lead to your work together in cybersecurity?"

"We programmed a computer worm that won first place in the county science fair. Our worm could identify specific software configuration flaws and report on their location. We both studied cybersecurity in college, him at Caltech and me at the Naval Academy. After my shortened career in the navy, we reconnected while I was at NSA and decided to start VSI twelve years ago. I can't believe he's gone. It's like I've lost a part of myself that I can never replace."

The next morning, James arrived at the Hoover Building and walked through security showing his White House badge. A young intern took him to Director Brockner's office. The director came out of her personal office and greeted him with a big smile and handshake.

*So far so good*, he thought. Director Brockner was very tall with auburn hair and green eyes and was probably in her mid-forties. She guided him to a couch and sat down across from him in a matching armchair. The furniture was very attractive, clearly not standard GSA issue.

"It's so nice to finally meet you, Mr. Jordan. The president speaks very highly of you, and your history as a decorated naval officer and brilliant entrepreneur speaks for itself."

"Thank you, Director, and please, call me James."

"Okay, James. I guess you're wondering why I asked you to meet me here today."

"Yes, I'm puzzled as to why Philip's murder would have national security implications. I thought it was just a burglary that went wrong."

"Fair enough, so let me explain. Philip Wu was found dead by the Maryland State Police in his house with a single knife wound to the chest that pierced his heart and killed him instantly. The house appeared to have been ransacked, as if someone was looking for something. There was a very high-tech safe in the floor of the master bedroom that was hidden under the flooring and a rug. The safe was closed but unlocked, and contained a large amount of cash."

"What kind of safe was it, Director?"

"I'll get to that, James. The Maryland State Police found Mr. Wu's red Jaguar in the parking lot of a local marina with the driver's throat cut. He was male and of Chinese extraction, like Mr. Wu. There were items in the car that clearly came from Mr. Wu's home. They were identified by his wife last night. The police were going to rule it a burglary, with the burglar being killed by someone he knew or by local thugs. I was asked by the president to have the FBI assist with the investigation as a courtesy to Mr. Wu's family and friends, including you, which is the reason for this meeting."

"Why would the FBI have any jurisdiction, Director? It seems like a burglary and a homicide that would fall under local jurisdiction."

"Mr. Wu was working with NSA and Cyber Command on some highly classified projects. The fact that his safe was opened gives the FBI jurisdiction based on national security. What do you know about what your partner was working on at VSI?"

"Philip and I never discussed business after I left the company to become Federal Chief Information Officer. We both felt it was best, in order to avoid any potential conflict of interest."

Director Brockner stared at him for at least ten seconds like a predator sizing up its prey. James knew she was trying a tactic he'd seen lawyers and law enforcement use to unsettle a witness or defendant. He was amused, and a smile formed on his face and then on hers as well. She realized he wasn't easily intimidated and softened her approach.

"Okay, James, I'm not trying to determine if you violated any legal obligations. I need to determine the actual motive for your partner's murder."

"Do you think it wasn't just a burglary?"

"Let's just say, I have some suspicions based on the facts."

"How so, Director?"

Director Brockner stood up to her full height, which James guessed was equal to his at six-foot-two. She began speaking as if she were making a final argument to a jury.

"The safe in Mr. Wu's house wasn't large. Its high-tech design indicated it was the type of safe used for securing valuables or secrets. Mr. Wu's wife, who had access to the safe, said her husband used it to store corporate documents and emergency funds, which she thought was about fifty thousand dollars. When the safe was examined after the murder, it contained fifty thousand dollars in cash and some papers. The police believe that the deceased burglar didn't know about the safe because it was hidden by a carpet."

"So what'd he take?" James asked.

"The police found some Chinese antiquities in the trunk of the Jaguar that were similar to those found at the Wu residence. Mrs. Wu identified them as coming from their house."

"I doubt they're very valuable, Director. Philip liked to collect Chinese art, but he didn't want to spend a lot of money. They're probably just very good reproductions."

"Yes, we know that, James. However, the police think the burglar didn't know that. The man found in Mr. Wu's car was a Chinese national who was in this country illegally. He was a suspect in a number of small-time burglaries and violent assaults in New York. The burglaries all involved relatively inexpensive electronics."

"Were any electronics missing from Philip's house?" James asked.

"No, Mrs. Wu said everything was there. The only things taken were the antiquities. This whole thing doesn't make sense," the director said while shaking her head.

"What do you mean, Director?"

"The burglar's murder while sitting in Mr. Wu's car is suspicious, to say the least. The parking lot is concealed, and there's nothing there that would attract anyone at that time of night. Why was he even there?"

"Maybe he was waiting for someone," James answered.

"That's what the police think, James. They believe he had a meeting with a fence to sell what he'd stolen and that there was an argument that resulted in the burglar's death."

"You don't?" James asked with a puzzled look.

"The burglar was from New York; I doubt he'd know any fences in southern Maryland. Also, that area is not exactly a hotbed for fencing such goods, and fences aren't usually this violent."

"Maybe the burglar just pulled into the marina to rest or relieve himself and someone tried to steal the car. It's an expensive car, Director."

"Yes, James, that's another theory that the police suggested. I don't buy it. He was armed with a handgun and should've been able to see anyone approach the car, since he had a clear view for at least a hundred yards in every direction."

"Maybe he was tired and was asleep in the car when he was attacked, Director."

"Very good, James. That was also suggested by the police. It's certainly possible, since the seat was reclined. But if that was true, why were the car keys found in some bushes ten yards from the car? They weren't well hidden and would have been easy to find. The police found them within ten minutes of arriving at the scene. Someone who wanted the car bad enough to kill the driver could've easily found the keys after they were thrown, and driven away."

"What do you think happened, Director?"

"I think he was waiting for an accomplice who was at the scene of Mr. Wu's murder. My gut tells me that the accomplice killed him and probably picked the marina for their rendezvous because it has a history of violence by gangs that used the marina for drug smuggling. The brutal decapitation of the burglar is a method used by some local gangs."

"Did the police find any evidence that someone else was at the house?" James asked.

"No, everyone's fingerprints from the house were accounted for, including the dead burglar's. His were the only suspicious fingerprints found, along with his DNA on the cigars from the house that were found in the car. The interesting thing is that his prints were only found on the first level of the house. He never went upstairs, which seems odd."

"Why is that, Director? Do you have a theory?"

"I believe the crime scenes at the house and the marina were staged by an accomplice," the director explained.

"Is there any tangible proof, Director?"

"Not so far, but there are some things that can't be explained. There's camera video of someone other than Mr. Wu driving his Jaguar past the guard post and out of the protected community where Mr. Wu's house is located. The police believe it was the deceased burglar, since a hidden camera located in a tree to the right of the guard post caught his image as he turned away from the cameras he was aware of on the left. The police believe it to be proof that he was the only burglar."

"That does seem fairly conclusive, Director."

"Maybe, but why is there no camera footage or record of a driver entering the gated community on the evening of Mr. Wu's murder that matched the known burglar's description? So how'd he get in? The only possibility is to bypass the guard post by taking an off-road vehicle or hiking over some very difficult terrain to get to a location that allowed access to the Wu residence. The suspected murderer was found wearing expensive loafers and dress slacks and shirt with no evidence of wear, so he didn't hike in. I believe there was another vehicle used by at least two burglars to get into the community. It had to be an SUV if it avoided the guard post."

James thought for a few seconds about what he just heard.

"If the deceased burglar was alone and was recorded on video driving Philip's Jaguar past the guard post on his way out, what happened to the SUV?" James asked.

"Exactly. There had to be at least two people at the crime scene. One of them would need to drive the SUV out the same way it came in, since all community resident vehicles were accounted for by the guard force records and cameras. The FBI is searching to find any evidence of SUV tracks near the Wu residence. The recent warm weather should leave the ground soft enough to leave such tracks, if the rain hasn't washed them away."

"Something you said bothers me, Director. You stated that Philip was working on classified projects for the federal government, but that's not something our company ever did, at least not while I was there.

Neither VSI nor Philip ever worked with the federal government. As far as I know, VSI only sells its products to commercial entities. What was Philip working on with the government?"

"According to Theresa Killian, Philip was developing a type of advanced worm or Advanced Persistent Threat, as she called it. I assume you know her, since she worked for you at VSI. She was very reluctant to discuss it, but did so after getting permission from the NSA and Cyber Command at Fort Meade—after I brought the president into it. If you want to know more, I suggest you contact NSA directly. They expressed the most concern over Mr. Wu's violent death. In fact, it was their high level of concern that first triggered my suspicions over the nature of Mr. Wu's murder. I've one last question, Mr. Jordan. What do you know about high-tech safes?"

"Philip and I designed the electronics for the high-tech vault at VSI. What do you want to know?"

"The safe at Mr. Wu's summer house was installed about eighteen months ago. His wife said he used it to secure VSI intellectual property. It also had some legal papers related to the company, and cash for emergencies. She had a combination that was separate from his. I found that very strange. Why would Mr. Wu's wife have a combination to their safe that was separate from his, even though they both had access to the safe? She said that her husband insisted on it. Do you have any idea why he'd do that?"

"None that I can think of, Director. Was there anything of value in the safe besides the money?"

"No, nothing. The fact that it contained all that money and wasn't locked was also strange. The police believe that Philip forgot to lock it. There's something else about the safe that seems unusual. In order to lock it, you have to close it and then enter a second combination within a short period of time or the safe remains unlocked. Do you have any idea why a safe would have such a feature?"

"Yes, I do. That feature would be used for what we call in the cybersecurity business 'intrusion detection.' If the safe isn't locked after it's closed, it could mean that the person who closed it didn't have the knowledge required or the capability to lock it. It's either an indication of an unauthorized intrusion or a forgetful owner who forgot to lock his safe. I know that Philip wouldn't fall within the second category, since he was the most meticulous person I've ever known. He would never have failed to lock his safe unless he was distracted or disabled. Your theory about the murderer being something other than just a common burglar might be true. If the safe was unlocked, they were obviously looking for and possibly found something more important to them than the money."

Director Brockner smiled. "That's exactly the type of information I was looking for, James. It indicates to me that he was targeted for a different reason than money and that national security is an issue that's still on the table. I believe that someone had that safe opened to find something that was of much more value than the amount of money in your partner's safe. If we can find the vehicle tracks, we might be able to determine the type of vehicle from the tires and its footprint. That could be very useful in identifying the driver. It's a long shot, but it's all we have right now. Oh, one last thing, I've assigned a special agent to this case from our Cyber Division. He's very bright, and a former US Navy SEAL. His name is Rick Tanner, and he'll probably be contacting you after he gets up to speed on the case. Please keep him in the loop if you come up with anything that could be relevant."

"I will, Director."

"Thanks. Good day, James."

As James drove back to his office, his head was spinning. Why would Philip suddenly go to the dark side, as they used to call it? Throughout their careers they both had reveled in the fact that they were developing cyber defenses to stop cyber threats. It was part of their core beliefs. They were white hats, not black hats, as the cyber community referred to defenders as compared to the offenders. What caused Philip and the company to develop malware? Not just malware, but APTs, the most insidious of all cyber threats? Also, why would he be working with the federal government when their corporate by-laws specifically barred such work by VSI? Violating that requirement could trigger significant penalties.

James wondered if he really knew his partner and best friend as well as he thought.

# 3

Kim Kwon-Mu was happier than he could ever remember. He was a North Korean who'd been accepted as a student at one of the best technical universities in the world in a city that was one of the most modern in China. He was also one of an increasing number of foreign exchange students from North Korea selected to attend Chinese technical schools. Kim was selected by Harbin Institute of Technology to study Information Warfare Technology and was looking forward to learning and applying the advanced cyber warfare skills taught by HIT.

As Kim was walking toward the arrival area of Harbin Taiping Airport to meet the person who would be his contact in Harbin, he observed a tall and very attractive middle-aged Korean woman approach him.

"Hi, Kim, I'm Lee Park, and I'll be your advisor while you're a student in Harbin. I have a car, so let's get your luggage and I'll take you to your new apartment."

"I don't have much luggage, Ms. Park. Everything I have is in this duffel bag I'm carrying."

"Please call me Lee. Follow me to the car. It's parked in the visitor area."

When Kim saw the car, he was amazed. It was beautiful and much more modern than the vehicles he saw in North Korea.

"Is this your car, Lee?"

"Yes, it's a Buick. Do you like it?"

"It's gorgeous. I've never seen anything like it in my country," Kim said, as he got into the front passenger seat.

"I'm glad you like it. I don't know much about you, Kim. Could you fill me in on your background?"

"What exactly do you want to know?"

"I'm curious why you're the only North Korean student in China who has been selected for special treatment by your government."

"What do you mean?"

"All the other North Korean students in China are assigned to dormitories monitored by North Korean intelligence. Yet you have been assigned to me, a Chinese citizen who escaped North Korea over a decade ago."

"Who contacted you about this assignment?"

"An admiral's adjutant from the North Korean Western Fleet."

Kim smiled. "It must've been due to my uncle. He's the fleet admiral of the North Korean Western Fleet. The admiral has watched over my mother, sister, and me since his brother, who was my father, was killed in an accident at a Nampo shipyard when I was twelve."

"That explains it. So should I believe the resume I received about your accomplishments from the admiral's adjutant, or was it all fabricated based on your uncle's influence?"

"Show me the resume and I'll let you know."

"I have it my pocket. I was reading it while waiting for your flight. Here it is."

Kim scanned the resume and smiled.

"The resume is accurate. I did graduate secondary school when

I was sixteen at the top of my class and was accepted to the Marine Patrol Academy."

"I'm not familiar with that school."

"It's the top school for naval officer training in North Korea. My uncle attended the school, as did the current senior naval staff. I graduated first in the class with no assistance from my uncle."

"Are you certain of that?" Lee asked in a challenging tone.

Kim could tell that Lee was trying to test him and also inject her authority. He had seen his superiors attempt that tactic throughout his career, and he was prepared.

"I am absolutely certain. My uncle may have watched over my well-being, but he's known for not suffering idiots or fools, even if they're family."

"Yes, I've heard that he's much different than the senior North Korean leadership in that respect."

Kim thought it was strange that Lee knew about his uncle, given the way the admiral always avoided publicity. He had warned Kim that notoriety in North Korea was often fatal, since the Supreme Leader was the only one who was allowed that honor.

"My uncle is different. He values competence and real achievement based on measurable results. I can assure you that I earned my record of promotion during my two years in the submarine service as an electronics communications officer, followed by two years as a North Korean SEAL. The admiral never interfered, other than attempting to talk me out of being a SEAL due to the high mortality rate."

"I see you graduated at the top of your class during SEAL training, but there's not much in the resume about your short two-year career as a SEAL. Why's that?"

"Largely because the missions were highly classified. My career as a SEAL was also shortened by a diving accident caused by faulty equipment."

"So then you transferred to the North Korean Reconnaissance General Bureau as a military intelligence agent?"

"Yes. That was a very unhappy period in my life."

"Why?"

"I got to see firsthand the poor conditions of our people outside the cities and how many were starving and rioting because of it. Many rioters were arrested or killed by the police and the army."

"Were you part of that?"

"No, my group only monitored the overall political situation and turned in reports to the Korean People's Army. They were the enforcers."

"Yes, the KPA. I remember their reputation when I lived in North Korea. How did you feel about spying on fellow citizens?"

"I hated it, but we never reported on individual citizens, just the local community as a whole. My job was electronic intelligence. I used computers to analyze and correlate reported incidents and information and then provided my overall analysis to KPA headquarters. My communications and computer training and experience allowed me to finally extract myself from that assignment."

"So you enrolled in Huichon University of Telecommunications for training in cybersecurity after only fourteen months in military intelligence?"

"Yes. The government was looking for qualified individuals for cybersecurity training to participate in the global cyber war between the East and West. I applied and was accepted. I desperately wanted to get out of military intelligence, but I also wanted to develop skills that would demonstrate my capabilities in a real war, the cyber war. Of course, that was before the US economic sanctions on North Korea."

"It says you received numerous commendations for using your new skills against North Korea's enemies."

"Yes, I implemented many successful attacks against the South Koreans and Taiwanese over the past two years. However, I knew I needed better skills to successfully attack the Western democracies, and especially the United States."

"So you hate the Americans?"

Kim hesitated for a second since he was not certain why Lee was asking the question. "Do you?" he asked.

"No, I have no reason to hate them. I left North Korea for a better life and to also get away from the oppression of the government," Lee said. "If you're worried that I'm trying to trap you, I promise you that I'm not. I believe your uncle selected me to be your contact because he knew about me. I was a trainer for the North Korean Olympic Team in 2000 and attended the games that took place in Australia. I'm quite certain it was your uncle who influenced someone on the South Korean team to help me defect to South Korea."

Kim learned how to judge someone's responses during his training and work as a military intelligence agent. He was very good at it, and he believed Lee.

"How did you get to China after you defected to South Korea?"

"I'll answer your question if you first answer mine, Kim. Do you hate the Americans?"

"I probably should hate the Americans after their severe economic sanctions on North Korea. They were starving our people."

"Then why don't you?"

Kim hesitated for about a minute and then said, "No one has ever asked me that question, Lee. It's not a topic you would discuss in North Korea, as I'm sure you know. I did have an initial reaction of hatred after the American sanctions. Then I remembered the government propaganda when I was in primary school. They politicized the supposed massacres of thousands of North Koreans by the American Army during the Fatherland Liberation War in the 1950s. The claimed atrocities were documented in horrible photographs that we were required to view at the nearby Sinchon Museum of American War Atrocities. They claimed thirty-five thousand North Korean civilians were massacred by American military and buried in mass graves near the cities of Nampo, Sariwon, and Sinchon. It was all a lie—like our leaders' lies to the US government that enabled the sanctions. Our leaders are at fault, not the US."

"Thank you for sharing that, Kim. If what you're saying is true, why would you want to attack the Americans using cyber warfare?"

"Because they're the best. They invented cyber warfare, and I love the challenge of trying to beat them at their own game. Also, no one is actually killed during the attacks."

"I see. Is it just to satisfy your ego?"

"Possibly. Does it matter?"

"It doesn't really. I'm just trying to gain some perspective on your personality to see if I can trust you."

"And what have you concluded?"

"Based on what I have learned from this resume and our brief conversation, I think I can trust you. I believe you have a good moral compass and would do anything to protect those you care about, especially your family. What bothers me is that you never mentioned any friends or lovers. Do you have any?"

Kim smiled. "I keep my private life private," he said. "That's often difficult in North Korea, as I'm sure you know, Lee. The government knows about my family, but the admiral has protected them. That protection wouldn't extend to friends or lovers, so I have kept that to a minimum since personal attachments create vulnerabilities. However, I have a few friends and have had a number of female lovers."

"You're very attractive, Kim, and unusually tall for a North Korean. I'm sure that will draw attention from some female students at HIT, but you must be careful. Some Chinese tend to think of North Koreans as barbarians, and even the local Korean population could be hostile. Your government sometimes monitors North Korean students. They have even paid Chinese students to spy on them. You should keep a low profile and avoid unnecessary attachments."

"I've been taught to analyze personal motives, Lee. I'm quite good at it. I plan to concentrate on my studies, but I can't guarantee that I'll remain celibate."

"Understood. Just be careful."

"I will, but you still haven't answered my question. How did you get to China after defecting?"

Lee smiled and said, "You are certainly persistent, and I'll answer you, but you must keep this confidential. People I care about could be hurt."

"I promise, Lee."

"Okay. When I arrived in Seoul, I was provided with a new identity as a South Korean national and was provided a job with a real estate developer. I found out that it was all set up by the South Korean and American governments. After I learned the real estate business, I was moved to Harbin, where I partnered with a Chinese national to do real estate development here. My partner was an American spy, and I was his courier. I took information to and from the South Korean embassy and sometimes to South Korea on business trips and vacations."

"Are you still a courier, Lee?"

"No, I was relieved of those duties after my partner died five years ago."

"So now you work for the North Koreans?"

"No, they just pay me to find places for their VIPs to stay when they're in China and to provide private communications that they don't want the Chinese to know about. They hired me because I speak their language. I'm not a North Korean agent, just a real estate agent who gets paid well by her clients. That building in front of us is one of my properties, and it's where you'll be living. I'll take you up to your apartment and brief you on the local area."

Kim was amazed by the building. Its architecture was like nothing he'd ever seen. It seemed more European than Asian, and it looked to be in excellent condition.

"This is an unusual-looking building, Lee."

"Yes, it was built in the early twentieth century by the Russians as a military staff building during the war between the Russians and Japanese. You'll see a number of buildings in Harbin with this classic

Russian architecture, including some at HIT. The inside is as beautiful as the outside since I had the entire building refurbished."

"So you own this building?"

"Yes, I've been quite successful in my business ventures in Harbin."

Lee led him onto an old-style elevator with a metal chain gate that took them to the sixth floor.

"This is your apartment, Kim. There's a fully furnished living room with a modern large-screen TV. There's also a dining room and a kitchen with a refrigerator, stove, and oven. The bathroom has a bathtub and shower. All are fully stocked with whatever you need, including food, soap, shampoo, and toiletries. I also provided a new cell phone with my phone number preprogrammed and a laptop computer with all the applications you'll need for school. You'll be able to connect to China's version of the internet. There's also a new bicycle in the bedroom for your short journey to HIT and home. What do you think?"

"I've never had any accommodations as nice as this. It's more than I ever dreamed of."

"Great, let's discuss a few more things you need to know. The winters in Harbin are brutal, so you'll need to buy warmer clothes."

"I know. I read that Harbin was called the Ice City."

"Don't wait too long, Kim. Temperatures today were in the mid-seventies, but this is late August. In December and January it will be continually below freezing. Temperatures more than one hundred degrees colder than today are a definite possibility."

"I understand, but how will I pay for everything? My current salary won't go very far in Harbin."

"I know." Lee handed Kim an envelope. "There's a bank card in this envelope that you can use. It should cover all your daily expenses, including food, clothing, and local transportation. It should also cover any educational needs. You can use it at any bank in Harbin to withdraw cash. If you need more, let me know."

"What type of local public transportation does Harbin have?"

"Mostly taxi, but there's also a subway that's partially completed. It doesn't go everywhere in the city but there are some stations near HIT."

"Thanks, Lee. I'll call you if I have any problems."

"I'll also check in on you to see if things are going well. There's one last thing I need to tell you. I'm sure you already know this, but your government expects you to report on any cyber attacks against the Americans or other Western countries that the Chinese are planning."

"Yes, I know. I have no problem with that, since learning about any such exploit would be educational in itself. I'd like to see how the Chinese do it and how effective they are. I was briefed by my superiors on how the Chinese government often uses the best students at their universities to assist in such attacks. My understanding is that they even recruit talented students from friendly countries. If I come across anything like that, I'll certainly report it to my superiors. Thanks for everything, Lee."

Kim's daily routine consisted of going to class and returning to his apartment to eat his meals and study most of the evening. He traveled the same route from the apartment to HIT and back by bicycle every day, but he did take some time to see the city before winter set in. Kim used his bank card to buy some warmer clothing. The climate in Harbin was definitely colder than he was used to.

For his first few months as a student at HIT, Kim felt totally isolated and lonely. Even though he was fluent in the Chinese language, Kim's North Korean accent caused some of the local Chinese and even the large Harbin ethnic Korean population to fear him. It was as if he'd been posted to another planet, not just a city that was only about five hundred miles from Nampo.

As Kim became more acclimated to his environment, he began to take notice of his fellow students, especially the women. He noticed several of the female students smiling at him in class. One of them was a tall Chinese girl with beautiful green eyes who sat across from him in his networks class. Her name was Cai Chan Li, and in addition to being gorgeous, she was also very smart. She frequently was called on by professors to answer the toughest questions, and she never failed. Her work in the technical labs was also superb.

As the first semester was coming to an end, Kim felt confident that he'd adjusted to his environment and the university. He had studied hard and done extremely well in all his classes and his semester final exams. After finishing his last exam of the fall semester, Kim was approached by one of the male students in his class who he'd never talked to.

"Hi, Kim. My name is Shen Wei. How do you think you did on your exams?"

"Okay. How about you?"

"Not sure about this last one, but I believe I did well on all the others. The network security architecture question was difficult, and there were multiple options. I just hope I selected the correct ones."

"I wouldn't worry about it. I don't think there was one single correct answer. You just need to select the network systems and security architecture that you believed worked best and then justify your selection."

"I guess I'll find out. By the way, there's an end-of-semester celebration tonight with some of our classmates at the Ice and Snow World. It's part of the Harbin Ice and Snow Sculpture Festival that takes place every winter. You can go with me and some friends if you like."

"Sounds great. Where should I meet you?"

"I'm going there now and I have a car. You can ride along."

"Okay, but I don't have much money on me right now."

"No problem, I have it covered."

Shen Wei did definitely have a car, a red Mercedes-Benz E-Class sedan that smelled like it was still brand new. Kim had never seen or ridden in anything like it.

"Is this your car, Shen?"

"Yes, I just bought it. We need to stop off to pick up some friends, okay?"

"Sure, no problem."

Shen drove for a short distance and stopped at a brightly lit four-story corner building that every student knew as the Harbin Xinhua Bookstore. It was well known for its classic Russian architecture and wide variety of books. Two warmly dressed girls immediately came out of the store and jumped into the rear seat. Kim recognized both girls as students in his class, but especially took notice of the taller one, Cai Chan. The other girl was clearly Shen's girlfriend, since she gave him a kiss immediately after she got in the car.

"Kim, I'd like you to meet Cai and my girlfriend, Lian."

"Hello," Kim said, as he stared directly at Cai.

She smiled back at him and said, "Hello, Kim, how are you?"

"We need to get going, Shen. Do you know where to park?" Lian asked.

"I've a friend at the Shangri La. He gave me a valet parking pass, and the hotel has transportation to the park. I also brought some Russian liquid heat to keep us warm. It's in the bag on the floor—take a look, Lian."

"Russian vodka? Where'd you get it?"

"It's really good stuff. I got it at the Russian market for a hundred yuan. I also have wool caps, scarves, and gloves in a backpack in the trunk. We need to make sure we get them before the valet takes the car. It'll be really cold at the festival."

As they drove, Kim noticed that traffic was almost at a standstill.

"Is traffic always this bad, Shen?" Kim asked.

"No, not usually. It's only during December through February when the festival is open. The festival is one of the biggest events in China. It attracts many international tourists to Harbin."

"How far away is the Shangri La?"

"Three miles, but at this rate it'll take us almost fifteen minutes."

Twenty minutes later, Shen pulled up to the valet parking line at the Shangri La and popped the trunk on the Mercedes. He grabbed the backpack and threw the keys to the valet. As they walked into the lobby of the hotel, Shen opened the backpack and handed it to Lian, saying, "Ladies first."

"This place is amazing, Shen," Kim said.

"It's my favorite five-star hotel."

"It's like a palace. Look at the lush peacock-colored carpet," Cai said.

"I know," Kim replied. "The chandeliers and white pillars are incredible."

"It's nice," Lian said, "but Shen and I have been to better hotels."

Shen and Lian went to the concierge desk to arrange for transportation to the festival as Kim and Cai sorted through the backpack.

"How do you like HIT, Cai?" Kim asked.

"The school is great and the education is first rate. I'm extremely lucky to study here. The campus has everything I need. There are restaurants, supermarkets, and the Xiyuan Hotel on campus that will allow my parents and friends to visit."

Shen and Lian returned and said that the van to the festival would be there in about five minutes. When the van arrived, they all boarded quickly, with Shen and Lian sitting next to each other and Kim and Cai sitting behind them.

"Where are you from, Kim?" Cai asked.

"I'm from the city of Nampo in the northern part of Korea."

Cai laughed. "I know you're North Korean, Kim. You don't have to hide anything, at least not from me."

"I'm not ashamed of it, but some of the people in Harbin seem nervous when they find out I'm from North Korea."

"It isn't a problem for me, Kim."

"Where are you from, Cai?"

"I'm from Qufu. It's a small city in Shandong Province, south of Harbin. It's the birthplace of Confucius."

"Yes, I know. Confucius was a brilliant philosopher."

Cai smiled and then pointed at the lights from the park as they crossed the bridge. "It's incredible, isn't it, Kim?"

Kim was stunned. He'd never seen anything like it, and it took him a few seconds to catch his breath and respond.

"It's the most beautiful thing I've ever seen, present company excluded."

The words came out so fast there was no way for Kim to take them back, but he really didn't want to.

Cai looked at him and smiled as she kissed him on the cheek. "That's one of the nicest things anyone has ever said to me, Kim."

Before getting out of the van, everyone put on extra clothing.

"I can't believe how cold it is, even with these winter clothes. Have you ever experienced anything like this, Kim?"

"It was this cold in Tumen at the very northern tip of North Korea. Thankfully, I wasn't there very long."

"I'm already shivering, Kim. Lian and Shen must be used to this."

"They've probably lived here all their lives. I'm sure they're used to it. Do you mind if I put my arm around you? It might help."

"Sure, but let's not lose Shen and Lian. They have our tickets, and they both seem to know the area like the back of their hands."

As they went to the entrance, Kim overheard some Americans complaining about the price to get into the park, over two hundred dollars. Shen went up to the entrance with four tickets in his hand, and they were immediately let in at what seemed like a VIP entrance. Apparently Shen had some connections. Kim made a mental note that Shen was someone he needed to know better.

"All those full-size buildings and statues were made from blocks of crystal-clear ice," Shen said. "They are three to four feet thick and were taken directly from Harbin's Songhua River."

"How are they sculpted and fitted?" Kim asked.

"With chain saws and hand tools," Lian said. "Different colored LED lights are used to provide the rainbow of colors. The ice sculptures are buildings and monuments of different architectural types and styles. There are also ice figures, including animals, people, and mythical creatures."

"Look over there, Cai. There are slippery dips and ice slides as well as tricycles that people are riding on the ice."

"There's also a miniature train and zip line that would be fun if I weren't so cold," Cai responded, in a stammering voice.

Kim could see that Cai wasn't adjusting to the cold, and her shivering was getting worse.

"Shen, Cai is freezing. We need to get her out of this cold."

Shen looked at Cai. "Okay, follow me."

Shen and Lian led them to a large food tent.

"You girls sit at that table over there while Kim and I get some hot drinks and snacks."

"Hurry, Shen, Cai looks very weak," Lian said.

"We'll be right back, Lian."

Kim and Shen returned with hot cocoa, coffee, and hot food, which they all rapidly inhaled.

"Cai is looking better, but I think we should leave soon, Shen."

"Okay, Kim. I'll call the Shangri La to request the van to pick us up."

The van arrived in less than fifteen minutes, and they all jumped in, along with some tourists staying at the hotel. After they arrived, Shen went to the front desk and set up a dinner reservation for four at the hotel's Shang Palace restaurant.

Shen pointed to a brightly lit bar in the corner of the lobby and said, "We have about an hour to kill. Let's go to the Lobby Lounge and get a drink while we wait."

As they walked in, Shen was greeted by the bartender. "Shen, Lian, where've you been? I haven't seen you for weeks."

"Lian and I needed to study for our final exams, as did my two friends. The usual for me and Lian and whatever my friends want."

Cai ordered hot coffee, as did Kim.

"Do you want anything in it?" the bartender asked.

Cai smiled. "Do you have any Bailey's Irish Cream?" she asked.

"Sure, any particular flavor?"

"No, just regular, and could you make it with extra whipped cream?"

"No problem, I'll even add a cherry to match the color of your beautiful face."

Cai smiled. "Thank you," she said.

Kim thought for a second. "I'll change my coffee to an Irish double espresso, if that's okay?"

"Sure thing," the bartender said.

"How can you afford all this, Shen? Is your family rich?"

"Actually they are, Kim, but that has nothing to do with me. My father cut me off a while back."

"Then how can you afford the car, and everything you paid for tonight?"

Shen smiled. "I've developed a talent that's in high demand right now. It's actually a talent that got me into some minor trouble with the authorities and is the reason my family exiled me."

"Can I ask what that talent is?"

"Well, it's a talent that everyone sitting at this table has and may also have used. I'm getting paid by some very influential people to hack into commercial enterprises in the United States."

"Does this have anything to do with why you took us out?"

"I wasn't planning on discussing it with you tonight, but since you asked, now is as good a time as ever. Lian is already working with my team and has demonstrated her skills. I've observed both you and Cai in class, and clearly you're both very talented. I just want to know if you're interested in making some money and if you've ever done any hacking before. If you're not interested, just forget I said anything."

Kim decided quickly that it would be best not to show too much enthusiasm, so he let Cai answer first.

"It's something I've done before, but never for money or on my own behalf," Cai whispered. "I once hacked into the computers at my secondary school to change a grade for a friend who needed to get accepted to a school she was applying for. I set the hack up so that I had admin privileges, and then after I changed the grade, I embedded a script that changed the grade back after the grade transcripts were sent. The script also removed any evidence of the new admin account and its use and then erased itself."

"Did it work?" Shen asked.

"Absolutely. I'd never do anything like that unless I knew it would work."

Kim was seeing a side of Cai that surprised him.

"Okay, Kim, how about you?"

"Yes, I've done some hacking. It was part of my work and it wasn't illegal. That's all I can say."

"Then my next question is, are any of you interested in learning more about what Lian and I are doing? Remember, if you say yes, there's no turning back. Also, be aware that what we're doing isn't something that the Chinese authorities are against. They simply look the other way as long as no one gets caught and it doesn't harm China. The Americans are doing the same thing to the Chinese. I'm sure they're also doing it to North Korea, Kim."

"I know they are," Kim said.

Their drinks came and everyone stopped talking. The bartender asked if there was anything else, and they all said "no" in unison.

When their dinner reservation was called, they all walked over to the restaurant in dead silence. Everyone was considering the change in their relationship from classmates to fellow conspirators against the most powerful country on the planet. After they sat down and ordered their meals, Cai asked the first question.

"Would we only be hacking into private businesses and not into American government systems?"

"Yes," Shen said. "The goal is to obtain financial information, trade secrets, and intellectual property. We won't be stealing money or interrupting business operations in any way. There's no national security interest at all, since our attacks will not target the US government or the companies that support their government."

"Who's funding this effort, Shen?"

"I don't know, Kim. Nor do I want to. Even if I did, I wouldn't tell you until after I know if you're in or out. There's one other requirement. All individuals must have a valid passport that I'll need to make a copy of, for identification purposes. I was told that it was to ensure none of you are Americans, which I assume you're not."

Kim and Cai both laughed. "That's not a problem. I just hope the Chinese government is okay with it," Cai said.

Lian quickly responded. "I wouldn't be doing this if there was a possibility of being prosecuted by the Chinese government. After all, they do it to other countries and foreign businesses. I look at it as legal free enterprise, since we're just supporting Chinese industry against competing American interests while being paid for our efforts as capitalists."

"Mao would either be rolling in his grave or laughing if he knew that we were using Eastern capitalism to attack the Western capitalists," Cai said, as they all laughed.

Even Kim saw the irony and said he was in, followed by Cai.

# 4

George Solomon was livid, although no one except Nadya Murin, his longtime assistant, could tell.

"The senate majority leader is going to ruin everything I've been working for, Nadya. That fat bastard's bill will never pass; and even if it did, the president would veto it. He's just doing it to get re-elected and is wasting time that the country doesn't have."

"You need to calm down, George. This meeting today with Barbara Chang is crucial to passing the foreign cyber-attack bill you've been trying to get approved for the past eleven months."

"You'd think the millions of dollars I've spent in getting politicians elected, including the president, would guarantee it. I need this legislation, Nadya, and so does the country. We need to punish those foreign bastards for hacking into American businesses."

"I know, George, but the president is worried about the backlash from what the press is calling 'draconian penalties' in the senate version of the bill. It would have a major impact on the Chinese, who have had their lobbyists working overtime to kill it."

"Yes, and if the senate version does pass, the Chinese could also respond by using their military to threaten our Far East allies. It's the reason I'm meeting with Barbara Chang, as distasteful as that is for me. I need to derail the senate majority leader's efforts to pass his bill."

"His bill will never pass in the house, George. Even if it did, the president would never sign it."

"I know that, Nadya, but its passage in the senate would delay passage of any bill until the next session of Congress, which works against my plans. I also hate kissing Barbara Chang's ass and she knows it. She would prefer that no bill is passed. At least the president is on our side. He realizes that most American voters believe the Chinese are skinning us. That's why he made the bill a campaign promise."

"You need to be calm and polite when you talk with Barbara about the bill. The two of you clashed frequently when she was the CEO of that large technology conglomerate."

"She's an extremely smart businesswoman, but I won more of those battles than I lost, Nadya. It was that stupid business magazine that nicknamed her the 'Dragon Lady.' Her staff claimed I gave her that name and that it was racist. We both know it isn't true."

"I know, George. The name was created by a reporter she knew."

"Probably at her request. Barbara fools a lot of adversaries, since she is petite, and that cute round face and smile make her look completely innocent and unassuming. I know better, as do many of her victims."

"I worked with her once on a charity fundraiser. She's a lot like you, George. Very innovative, with an ability to quickly analyze a situation and implement a winning strategy. Unfortunately, she also has a long memory and will never forgive you for trying to convince the president not to select her as his chief of staff."

"Yes, that was a mistake. She kept me away from the president for almost a year after the election. I've always hated her holier-than-thou attitude because she ran successful businesses, while I merely bought and sold them. She thinks that puts her on a higher ethical plane."

"You need to forget all that when you meet her. The problem isn't her. It's Senator Thompson and that onerous legislation he's trying to push through the senate."

"I never thought he'd get anywhere with his bill, but he's surprised me, Nadya. His constituents love it, and so do many of the voters around the country. He's just using it to curry favor for his upcoming election."

"It could work, George. His bashing of the Chinese has erased the accusations against him of marital infidelity, drunkenness, and allegations of influence peddling. His arm-twisting in the senate seems to have gotten him the votes he needs."

"I still have a few cards to play. It's not over yet."

George arrived at the White House and was ushered into Barbara Chang's office. The office always amazed George because it always looked the same. Nothing ever seemed out of place. It was as if it was never really used.

"So good to see you again, Barbara. You look wonderful, as always."

"Thank you, George. I assume you want to discuss the pending foreign cyber-attack legislation."

"Yes, I want to make it clear to both you and the president that I don't support the current senate bill. I believe if we work together, we might be able to get the legislation that we can all support."

"The president agrees with the concept of the foreign cyber-attack legislation. I have my doubts that it could be implemented without initiating a trade war with China. However, it would be in the country's best interests with respect to national defense if the final legislation looks like the house bill instead of the abomination in the senate."

"I'm in total agreement, Barbara."

"What do you propose, George?"

"I believe I have some influence with the senate majority leader, and I'd like to approach him about softening his position."

Barbara knew what that meant. George either had some dirt he could sling, or he'd make Senator Thompson an offer he couldn't refuse.

"You realize that the president and his administration will not be involved in any dealings with the majority leader."

"Actually, that's exactly what I'm requesting, Barbara. I want to make sure that after I have my meeting with Senator Thompson tonight, the president doesn't provide him any help with the predicament he may find himself in."

Barbara knew immediately that George was going to use the stick and not the carrot. She didn't mind, since Senator Thompson was a buffoon and an embarrassment to the president, the senate, and their political party. Everyone would be happy when he was gone, or at least removed as the majority leader.

"That's a deal, George. I'll inform the president when I meet with him later today. I have to go, as I have a meeting with the Chinese ambassador."

"Give the ambassador my regards."

Barbara smiled, knowing that George was not and had never been a friend of the Chinese government, and the Chinese were quite aware of that fact.

George arranged for a meeting in a private conference room at a hotel in northern Virginia. He knew that the hotel he selected was where the senator often had his sexual rendezvous with his aide and would know why George selected it. It would send a message that should make Senator Thompson uncomfortable. George had used that tactic before during difficult negotiations.

He scheduled the meeting for seven in one of the hotel's banquet rooms. The senator was known to be a man who lived his life in excess with respect to eating, drinking, and extramarital sex. George decided to let him indulge at least two of his vices by having a high-quality buffet and an open bar set up in the room.

The majority leader was already in the banquet room when George arrived. He had apparently already tried some of the food and poured himself a drink, as well as another for a very attractive blonde who he introduced to George as his aide, Carla Allen. Senator Thompson turned and gave her a big kiss. "I'll see you later, dear. I need to take care of some business. Drive carefully."

George realized the senator wasn't intimidated by his reputation, which would make the negotiations much tougher.

"Good evening, Senator Thompson, I can see you've already started without me." George poured himself a vodka and tonic and sat down across from him. "How's your wife and family, Senator?"

"They're fine, George, and how's your fiancée? Have you set a date yet?"

"No, not yet, but there's no hurry."

"Will she be your third or fourth?"

George smiled and ignored the question. He decided it was best to just get down to business.

"Senator, I'm concerned that the proposed foreign cyber-attack legislation in the senate will trigger a trade war between the US and China that would have disastrous consequences for our economy and theirs."

Senator Thompson smiled. "Are you here on behalf of the president, or yourself, George?"

"I'm here on behalf of the American people, including your constituents, Senator."

"That would be a first for you, wouldn't it? After all, the only thing you ever cared about was your own self-interest."

"I'm not here to point fingers. I just want to do what's best for everyone and avoid an ugly confrontation with the Chinese that could get entirely out of hand. Wars have been started over trade and commerce issues like the one we'd be precipitating with your bill. I also don't believe it'll help you in your bid for re-election next fall."

Senator Thompson laughed at the last comment.

"Are you kidding, George? Have you seen the political ads I've been running in my state? Those Chinese devils have killed my state's industrial base and have undercut our manufacturing so that it's less than a third of what it was ten years ago. The actual unemployment rate in my state is over twelve percent and rising. My constituents hate what's happening to them, and I'm telling them why, every day, twenty-four seven. By the time I'm done, they'll think the Chinese chairman is Satan himself, and I'm their savior. Look at the polls in my state; they've already turned in my favor. Give me one reason why I should stop."

"Senator, I can see from your actions earlier with your very attractive aide that you believe you're shielded from any scandal."

The senator smiled with his big, toothy campaign grin.

"My wife knows about Carla and other past indiscretions. She hasn't cared about me or what I do for the past ten years, as long as I get re-elected and provide her with a good life, which I have. The people in my state don't care about sex scandals or political favors as long as I'm working hard for them to improve their lives. The days where those things mattered ended with Bill Clinton. They have little impact as long as the wife and family is supportive and the scandal isn't too public, and isn't with the same sex. So I guess you could say I'm somewhat shielded right now."

George could see that the stick wasn't going to work, so he decided to use the carrot with this jackass.

"What if I could improve your state's economic condition by moving some of my businesses into your state? That would help your constituents in a more substantive and immediate manner."

"That would always be appreciated, George. But my daddy always told me never to change horses when you're ahead, and I'm definitely ahead."

George could see there was nothing he could offer, so he resorted to one final ploy.

"Senator, if you don't remove your bill, I'll have no choice but to use my resources to work against your re-election. I'll make your life miserable and see how bulletproof you really are."

The senator smiled. "I knew it might come down to that, and I'm prepared to respond to your threat with one of my own. If you go after me or my family in any way, I'll let the world know about your gay illegitimate son and how his mother died in a highly suspicious manner, to say the least."

George was rarely flustered or at a loss for words, especially during a negotiation, but he was totally stunned by the senator's threat. "How—who told you about that? It's not true! You'll regret it if any word of this leaves this room or becomes public!"

The senator leaned toward George and said quietly, "Please, George, calm down. This will go no further as long as neither you nor the president take any action against my interests."

George composed himself and said, "It's clear that you have your goals and I have mine, so goodbye, Senator," George said, as he headed for the door.

"Good luck to you as well, George. Give my regards to your son when you see him."

George was furious. As he left the hotel he made a quick phone call.

"I need to meet with you in my office as soon as possible."

Barbara Chang had just finished briefing the president in the Oval Office on her meetings earlier that day with George Solomon and the Chinese ambassador. She had tried to determine what the president was thinking, but she knew from experience that trying to read his reaction was a fool's errand. He was well known for being able to hide his feelings.

President Joseph Meredith was forty-six years old, tall and athletic, and had movie-star looks with blond curly hair, blue eyes, a square chin, and a wonderful smile. He'd been a very successful attorney and Maryland state senator before running for the senate on a business growth and tax reduction platform. While in the senate, he sponsored cybersecurity insurance legislation for American businesses. When he ran for the presidency, Joseph Meredith included protection against foreign cybersecurity attacks on American businesses as part of his platform. After getting elected, he made foreign cyber-attack legislation one of his highest priorities.

The president asked one question after Barbara had finished her briefing. "Does George understand that my administration cannot take any part in his efforts to persuade the majority leader?"

"Yes, Joe, I made that very clear. He agreed that he was on his own, and he wanted it that way."

"Yes, that's pretty typical of George. He loves the role of the lone gunfighter. Okay, let me know if he was successful. Now let's discuss your meeting with the Chinese ambassador."

Barbara frowned. "It didn't go as well as I'd hoped. Ambassador Yang was very upset about the legislation in the senate. He believes that it'll lead to a trade war and possibly worse. The ambassador made a strong claim that the Chinese government has eliminated cyber attacks by their military and intelligence organizations against US government agencies."

"That's not entirely true, Barbara. We still see them probing our government information systems to find weaknesses for future attacks. They only stopped their attacks after we identified and indicted a number of their military hackers for attacks on our key industries. They weren't aware that we could do that, so they backed off."

"Those were their military hackers, Joe. Ambassador Yang made it very clear that the Chinese government doesn't have control over civilian hackers and that Chinese companies do it against each other. He also stated that it's on such a large scale that they don't have the resources to control it, just as we can't control our civilian hackers."

"Well, there's an element of truth in that, since the Chinese don't even try to curtail civilian hackers. We try, but, unfortunately, aren't very successful. In addition, their businesses get direct support from the government in implementing defenses against foreign hackers, while our laws don't permit us to do the same."

"It's also clear that our businesses are less cybersecurity conscious than theirs, Joe. Some would rather rely on cyber insurance to correct for their laziness, carelessness, and outright malfeasance."

"I know that, Barbara. That's why I worked hard when I was in the senate to implement a cyber insurance program that encouraged lower insurance rates for companies that implemented better cybersecurity practices. So based on your analysis, what do you think the Chinese will do after the proposed foreign cyber-attack legislation becomes law?"

"It depends on how severe the penalties will be on Chinese companies. If the legislation looks more like the senate bill than the house bill, we could have some real trouble with the Chinese leadership. They or their North Korean surrogate could start flexing their military muscle against Japan, Taiwan, and South Korea, which could lead to severe consequences. If the legislation looks more like the house bill, it'll be painful but not catastrophic. They could retaliate with some trade measures of their own; but since the trade deficit is so heavily weighted for them and against us, they'd suffer much more than we would. My hope—excuse me, *our* hope—is that it could trigger some needed attitude changes by the Chinese. It might even encourage more cooperation that would bring in some new and younger leaders who are more willing to provide fairer trade practices. That would be good for the US and the world. But there's no guarantee that will happen, so we must be prepared for something worse."

President Meredith was so glad that Barbara was his closest advisor. She had no problem telling him what others were afraid to.

"I understand, Barbara. But I believe we have to do something. This legislation is necessary to change an untenable situation with the Chinese that's been going on far too long. I promised the American public I'd do what my predecessors were afraid to do. Our embargo against North Korea slowed China down a bit, but North Korea has not gone away. China has been increasingly helping North Korea to become a very competent cyber threat, even if it has derailed their nuclear program. I have no doubt that North Korea will be their cyber-attack surrogate, just as they were their nuclear weapons surrogate."

"I know, Joe, and I agree that something has to change. I just hope we get a bill with the right balance so the Chinese leadership doesn't overreact. We have the upcoming combined naval-training exercise with the Japanese, Taiwanese, and South Koreans at the Senkaku Islands that could provide them that opportunity. The Chinese ambassador has been very vocal about their leadership's objection to the exercise. I'm certain they'll have their ships monitoring our ships, and I'm worried that something bad might happen. With that many ships in one area, anything is possible."

"We can't cancel the exercise, Barbara. The Chinese would see it as an act of weakness, and the Japanese would look at it as a violation of our Treaty of Mutual Cooperation and Security. Both countries have had recent confrontations over those islands. If we pulled out, our allies in that region could start militarizing. With Japan's technology base they could have a nuclear weapons program very quickly, followed by South Korea and Taiwan. That could destabilize the whole region."

"I agree, Mr. President. I just hope the Chinese also understand the danger. I'm sorry, Mr. President, but I have to leave to meet my fiancé for dinner. I'm already late."

The president knew that Barbara never called him Mr. President unless the First Lady was nearby, which was the case. He knew that Barbara believed such informality in front of the president's wife wasn't proper. The First Lady walked in just as Barbara was leaving. "Goodnight, Barbara," Sarah Meredith said.

"Goodnight, Mrs. Meredith. Please make sure he gets some rest. We have a big week ahead of us," she said as she left.

"What'd she mean by that, Joe?"

"Oh, she's just worried that we could soon be in a war with the Chinese."

"Are you serious?"

"I don't think it'll get that serious, but she's very worried, Sarah."

"It's that bill in the senate, isn't it?"

The president closed his eyes and nodded. "You know, honey, the president of the United States is supposed to have more power than anyone in the world. I've discovered that isn't the case at all. I'm often in the middle of situations I have no control over. I actually feel powerless more often than powerful. I can't even control some corrupt politician in my own party who can't keep his fly zipped and may trigger a war just to get re-elected."

"You can't control evil, Joe. You can only try to keep it at bay."

"I'm so glad you married me. You could've probably done a lot better, had the career you deserved, and a normal life with someone who worked a forty-hour week and was home for dinner every night."

"I wouldn't change a thing. I have two wonderful children and a husband that the columnist from the *Washington Post* says any woman would kill for."

The president laughed. "Let's take Barbara's advice and go to bed."

"Great idea. I have that new negligee you bought me in France," she said, as she smiled coyly. "We can have some fun before the world ends."

# 5

Dimitri Vasin wasn't a religious man. His mother made him and his sister go to St. Michael's, the only Russian Orthodox church in Grozny, every Sunday for the divine liturgy, but any religious beliefs he might've had were destroyed by his experiences during the war. He'd witnessed the atrocities that were often done in the name of religion, including the destruction of St. Michael's and the massacre of his mother and sister.

He wasn't a man of habit since habits made one predictable, which wasn't a good trait for someone in his line of work. Nevertheless, Dimitri always attended services at the Russian Orthodox Cathedral in Brooklyn whenever he was home. It was not because he was trying to regain the faith he had lost. He simply found the services soothing and a way of remembering the times that were once so joyful with a family that no longer existed.

Today, however, it was more than that. He'd been contacted by one of the Big Man's representatives for a meeting early the next day. That was unprecedented in the years he had worked for the Big Man. He was never contacted and asked to provide services so soon after a previous job. It was done that way to allow the dust to settle and make sure that there were no mistakes in the last assignment that could be traced to Dimitri before assigning him to his next job.

Dimitri was worried that the Big Man had discovered his error about the safe and that his life could be in jeopardy. Although he didn't believe that praying would really help, it couldn't hurt, and the church helped to calm him and focus.

After the services ended, Dimitri followed the normal process he used to prepare for an important assignment. He went home and worked out for several hours. Dimitri then took a long hot shower, ate dinner, and went to bed.

The next morning, Dimitri dressed, ate a light breakfast, and took his briefcase with a notepad and pencil. It was one of the first really cold days of the season, so he wore an overcoat with a concealed and sharpened plastic knife in an inside pocket. Dimitri had used the knife on previous assignments that required him to go through a metal detector. It was made of hard plastic and was disguised as the easily removable handle of a hard plastic comb that he could carry in a pocket or briefcase.

Dimitri took a taxi to the building where the meeting would take place. After going through security without incident, he was met by an escort who took him to a conference room on the tenth floor. A single individual was sitting on the opposite side of a large conference room table. He was rather small, overweight, probably over fifty, and definitely didn't look like an assassin. Regardless, Dimitri didn't relax. He kept his eyes glued to the man's every move.

"Did you have any problem finding the office, Mr. Vasin?"

"No, I've been to Manhattan before, but never to this building."

"Fine. I have a very high-priority contract for you that needs to be completed as soon as possible, no later than this time next week. I'm also authorized to inform you that your fee will be tripled for this particular assignment. The assignment is described on the encrypted USB flash drive I'll give you. To decrypt the drive use your eight digit date of birth, which I believe is 07231977. Is that correct?"

"Yes, that's correct."

"The file has an embedded script on it, Mr. Vasin. It'll only allow you to access the read-only file one time. The file and everything else on the drive will erase thirty minutes after the file is opened, or if you log off before then. It also can't be copied. Any attempt to copy it will destroy the file. Be prepared to take and then destroy any written notes you might need and the drive as well. Please be aware that you only have thirty minutes after the file is opened."

"I understand. And I don't need notes, I have an excellent memory."

"So I hear. In fact, I was told it was eidetic, what they used to call a photographic memory. Here's the flash drive. It has all the information on the target and a contact number if you need anything more. Good day, Mr. Vasin. I think we're through, unless you have any questions."

"No questions. Thank you," Dimitri said, as he followed a young woman who escorted him back down to the lobby. He flagged a taxi, but didn't relax until he arrived at his house in Brighton Beach. Dimitri knew that letting one's guard down, believing you're no longer in danger, is the worst thing you can do. He had often relied on creating a false sense of security to make a target more vulnerable.

As he walked into his apartment, he was greeted by Putin, his African grey parrot.

"No final act today, Dimitri."

It was a greeting Dimitri had taught Putin, but it still made him laugh. "Yes, Putin, no final act today."

Putin was a gift from a colleague whose life Dimitri saved while working for the American government in Afghanistan. He wasn't thrilled at first, but after he saw how smart it was and how quickly it learned to talk, it became his companion and confidant.

"I have work to do, Putin."

"Dimitri works too much."

"Eat your food, Putin."

"Food tastes like crap."

Dimitri turned on his laptop and switched off the wireless network connection to eliminate any possibility of hackers. He inserted the flash drive in his computer's USB port and opened the file while he monitored the time displayed on his computer. He began reading the files describing the target who was to be eliminated.

"This is going to be the most difficult assignment I've ever implemented. Do you know why, Putin?"

"Why, Dimitri?"

"Because of the microscopic scrutiny it will undergo after it's done. Do you know why, Putin?"

"Why, Dimitri?"

"Because the target is a very important and well-known politician. I'll need to set up the attack so that it is absolutely deadly and can never be traced back to me. What do you think, Putin?"

"Putin thinks Dimitri is smart."

Dimitri read through the file carefully. It stated that his target was a severe diabetic who was badly overweight and a heavy drinker. He also had a young mistress who appeared to be in very good shape in more ways than one. It was obvious to Dimitri that the target, Senator Lee Thompson, was a dead man walking who could die of natural causes at any time.

*Hell*, Dimitri thought, *I could probably just show up at his house and scare him to death.* As he read through the file further he saw that the senator was no friend of the Chinese. Dimitri realized that could be used to his advantage in implementing his assignment. He knew the optimal outcome would be for it to appear as if the senator died from the effects of his diabetes and overall poor health.

Dimitri also knew that if that failed and the actual causes became known, he would need an alternate suspect. He knew that the Chinese government's harsh criticism of the senator and his bill could make them a possible suspect. If Dimitri's primary plan failed and the senator's death was found to be a murder, he would need to make the Chinese look like the prime suspect. He thought that's why the information about the Chinese was included in the file.

Dimitri read from Senator Thompson's files that he used insulin shots from Humalog mix 75/25 insulin pens to control his Type II diabetes. He apparently wasn't very serious about testing his blood sugar levels, since his recent tests showed levels well above normal. His blood pressure was equally as bad, and he was taking statins for high cholesterol. Dimitri knew the senator's behavior was a menu for death, and that he just needed to select the correct dish.

As a medical student, Dimitri had learned that excess insulin can lead to a coma and death in rapid succession. He also knew that, if administered correctly, it wouldn't be detectable in even a normal person. In a severe diabetic such as Senator Thompson, accidental overdoses weren't uncommon. *He's using insulin to compensate for his excess eating and drinking. The possibility of taking an overdose if he was drinking is likely*, Dimitri thought.

Dimitri read the rest of the file and left the drive in his computer after logging out of Word as instructed. Just to make sure the file had been erased, Dimitri logged back into the drive and verified the file was no longer there.

*Okay*, Dimitri thought, *now the hard work begins*. Dimitri needed to develop a plan that would allow him to gain access to the senator in a location that was private and that Dimitri could select and control. He remembered that the senator had a house in Georgetown that he used when Congress was in session, but that his wife never used. The file had provided a complete description of the house, including its location, size, layout, and alarm system. A big smile erupted on Dimitri's face when he realized that the senator's house was within walking distance of the Chinese embassy.

"I'm done. I have a plan, Putin."

"Putin thinks Dimitri is a genius."

The plan had come together in Dimitri's head, but he still had to arrange for some outside help from the Big Man. He called his contact, and a woman answered.

"What can I do for you, Mr. Vasin?"

"I need to meet tomorrow morning as early as possible."

"Fine, same building at nine."

Dimitri arrived at the office in Manhattan the next morning and was escorted to a conference room. He waited for about ten minutes when a tall, athletic-looking young man entered and sat across from him.

"What can I help you with, Mr. Vasin?"

"I need three Humalog mix 75/25 pens, a cold travel case, and a fast-acting bacterial serum that will cause severe nausea for twenty-four to forty-eight hours. The serum must be loaded into a very small and sharp painless syringe like the one I was provided for a previous assignment. In addition, I need to know the target's schedule in the DC area for the next three days, the home address and cell phone number for his mistress, and twenty authentic business cards in a card holder for a high-level Chinese intelligence agent currently assigned to the Chinese embassy in DC."

"We can get a real card and then reproduce the twenty you need on the same stock and with the same type and style used by the embassy. Is that acceptable?"

"Yes, as long as I have them by tomorrow afternoon. I also need my usual weapons, military grade night vision goggles, and a high power EMP gun like the one I used during a previous assignment. Please deliver all of these items to the storage locker in Arlington."

"Please wait here while I verify our delivery schedule."

Dimitri waited for about thirty minutes when the man returned to the conference room.

"We can have all the items delivered to the storage unit by nine tomorrow morning. Is that acceptable?"

"Yes, thank you."

After the meeting, Dimitri returned to his house to get the erased flash drive. He took the drive to the electronics shop where one of his hacker friends was working.

"Hi, Yuri, I need your help."

"Sure, Dimitri, what do you need?"

"I want you to examine this flash drive to see if all the files were completely erased."

"Sure, follow me to my lab in the back so I can check it with the digital forensics tools on my laptop."

Yuri worked for thirty minutes and said, "The information was written over using a sophisticated algorithm that writes digital data patterns to the drive seven times. There's no recoverable information on this drive."

"Thanks, Yuri, but how would I destroy the drive so that it couldn't be reused, just in case?"

"That's easy. Some people like to use an electrolysis tank to fry the drive's electronic components by applying a voltage to the drive in a solution of baking soda and water. That works, but I just use this sledgehammer. Do you want to try?"

Dimitri took the hammer and hit the drive three times as hard as he could, breaking it into very small pieces.

"Looks like a dead drive to me," Yuri said with a smile.

"Thanks, Yuri. I have a present for you."

Dimitri gave Yuri the envelope with the bloody photo he had taken of Chin.

"Is this what I think it is?"

"Yes. Please let Marta know that her attacker is dead and will never bother her again."

Yuri hugged Dimitri and said, "If ever I can do something for you, just ask."

"There's one thing. Please destroy that photo when you're done, along with the remaining pieces of that USB drive."

"I'll do that, but I still owe you."

Dimitri walked home and packed. The taxi to JFK arrived on time, and Dimitri boarded his flight to Reagan National Airport in DC. He arrived at his hotel in Arlington and went up to his room, unpacked, and turned on the TV. There was news about Philip Wu's funeral, scheduled for the next morning at eleven at the Universalist National Memorial Church near Dupont Circle in DC.

The reporter described how many local and national dignitaries planned to attend, including the president's chief of staff, Barbara Chang, the Federal CIO and Wu's former partner, James Jordan, billionaire investor George Solomon, some prominent and unidentified federal legislators, and several Maryland state delegates. Dimitri decided to attend the funeral, at least from a distance, to see if his new target would also be there as one of the unidentified federal legislators. He took some notes on the location of the funeral and the names of some prominent attendees and then switched off the TV and went to sleep.

The next morning, he immediately called down to the front desk to arrange for breakfast and a rental car. After having a quick breakfast in his room, he went to the lobby and signed for his car. Dimitri then drove to a nearby storage unit, where he removed a duffel bag and put it in the trunk. He drove back to the hotel and took the duffel up to his room, where he removed the insulin pens and syringe in the cold travel case and put them in the refrigerator.

There was also a large manila envelope with the requested business cards in a leather card holder and a USB drive. The cards were for a Zhou Ming who was listed as a senior commercial attaché at the Chinese embassy in DC. Dimitri plugged the drive into the USB port in his laptop and examined the files, which included Senator Thompson's schedule for the next several days and the local addresses for the senator and his aide. He was happy to see that the senator was going to be in DC for the next week.

Dimitri used his laptop to do some quick internet research on the funeral attendees of interest, and programmed the GPS app on his cell phone with the senator's and his aide's local addresses. He also programmed the address of the church near Dupont Circle where Philip Wu's funeral was being held.

It was time to go, so Dimitri grabbed his binoculars and camera.

He drove to Dupont Circle, parked, and then walked to a location where he could observe the funeral attendees. He watched as the limousines pulled up to the church and let their passengers out. He recognized both Barbara Chang and James Jordan, who arrived together in a limousine that was led by a large black SUV with tinted windows. *Well, I guess the Secret Service is here*, Dimitri thought. An extremely attractive brunette also got out of the limousine and walked with James Jordan as they entered the church.

Shortly after, a large black Mercedes limousine dropped off a tall, white-haired man whom Dimitri recognized from his research as the billionaire George Solomon. Mr. Solomon was surrounded by several muscular individuals, definitely his bodyguards.

Right before the funeral was to start, a Lincoln Town Car pulled up to the cathedral. A pretty young blonde woman jumped out, followed by Senator Lee Thompson in a long black overcoat that couldn't hide his considerable girth. Dimitri watched as his target struggled to get out of the car with the help of the woman who was obviously his aide and mistress. Dimitri laughed to himself; bringing his mistress to a funeral with so many dignitaries certainly showed that he had balls. *The senator would have made an excellent Russian premier*, Dimitri thought.

Dimitri had taken pictures of all the attendees. Seeing Senator Thompson in the flesh was useful, since the pictures he was provided by his employer didn't do the senator justice. He was at least thirty pounds heavier than the pictures in the file he was given. Dimitri knew that he'd have to adjust the dosage to compensate for the senator's actual weight.

After observing the attendees, Dimitri returned to his car and drove to the target's home in Georgetown, less than five miles away. He drove slowly by the senator's home, a detached two-story townhouse on a small lot with many trees. He was pleased, as the trees would provide cover and there were no connecting walls for neighbors to hear anything. Dimitri also made a mental note of the closest power transformer to the house, a nearby area where he could safely park, and the best exit routes if he had to leave quickly. He then returned to his hotel, had lunch, and reviewed his plan one last time.

Dimitri needed to take care of one more task before implementing his plan. He drove to the apartment building in Old Town, Alexandria, where the senator's aide lived, and he walked in with a small group of people. After looking around the lobby, he went to the clerk at the front desk and said, "Can you call Carla Allen's apartment and tell her that a friend is waiting for her downstairs?"

He called her number. "There's no answer, sir. She may be out."

"That's fine, I'll wait."

Dimitri took a seat on a couch at the rear of the lobby near the elevator, since it provided a clear view of the entrance. He'd waited for about thirty minutes when he saw a black Lincoln Town Car pull up to the entrance and Carla Allen jump out.

Dimitri quickly checked the syringe and then cupped it in the palm of his hand with the needle slightly exposed. As Carla Allen approached the elevator, she removed her keys from her purse and headed toward the mailboxes to pick up her mail. Dimitri jumped up from his seat and purposely ran into her as she approached. He quickly injected her as they both fell down.

"Oh, I didn't see you, I'm so sorry," Dimitri exclaimed. "Are you all right?"

They both got to their feet and she said, "I think so, are you okay?"

"Yes, I believe I am, and I'm really sorry. I guess I was in too much of a hurry to get to an appointment."

"That's okay, I hope you make it."

"Me, too. Goodbye," Dimitri said as he hurriedly went out the front entrance. She seemed like a nice girl, too nice for her ogre of a boss. Dimitri felt sorry for what she was about to endure. At least she'd survive.

The serum would take a couple of hours before she started feeling the effects, so Dimitri returned to his hotel and watched TV. At six he used a burner phone to place a call to Carla Allen.

"Hello," Carla said in a weak voice.

"Hi, I work for a news media organization and I was wondering if you could do a survey on the accuracy of the reporting on the cable news networks."

"I'm sorry, I normally would, but I feel really ill. Can you call me some other time?"

"I'm sorry to hear that. We'll call back next week. Thank you."

Dimitri knew that the first phase had worked and that the senator would be alone that evening. Now he needed to prepare for the next phase.

Dimitri waited until about nine and then got dressed in dark clothing and a dark navy pea coat. He took the duffel bag and stuffed the business card holder, flashlight, lock picks, insulin pens, and plastic gloves in his coat pockets. The traffic was light and his drive to Georgetown took only fifteen minutes. As he drove by the senator's house, he could see that the lights were on and the senator's car was in the driveway.

He found a parking space a block from the senator's house and less than fifty yards from a power transformer. Dimitri waited until most of the nearby house lights were out and then grabbed the duffel bag and walked to a point directly beneath the transformer. He removed the EMP gun from his bag, set the power at maximum, aimed the gun, and pulled the trigger. The lights in the neighborhood flickered several times and then went out.

Dimitri quickly walked to the senator's house. He donned his night vision goggles and walked through the trees on the property. Dimitri aimed the EMP gun at the front and back doors to disable any house alarms that might be on emergency battery power. He then walked to the back door, removed his latex gloves and lock picks from the duffel bag, and used them to open the door. There were some emergency lights on in the living room, and Dimitri could hear someone talking. It was the senator in his pajamas. He was talking on his cell phone and he clearly sounded drunk. Dimitri smiled. *That will make things so much easier,* he thought.

After the senator finished his call, Dimitri removed the Glock, attached the silencer, and sneaked up behind the target. He put his left hand over the senator's mouth and his right arm around his neck.

Dimitri whispered in the target's ear, "If you want to live, be quiet, or I'll shoot you. Do you understand?" The senator nodded and Dimitri slowly removed his hand.

"Please sit on the couch and don't try to escape. I have a gun. Is there anyone else in the house?"

"No, I'm the only one here. What do you want? I don't keep much money here, but I'll give you what I have."

"I just want some information," Dimitri said, trying to make the senator feel more comfortable.

"How'd you get in? I activated the alarm when I got home."

"That's my secret. Let's have a little chat, Senator. I have a few questions I'd like to ask."

"Can I pour myself another drink first?"

"Sure, where's the bar? I'll have one with you."

"There's a bar in the dining room."

Dimitri pushed the senator toward the dining room where a few emergency lights made it easy enough to see.

"Sit down, Senator, while I mix our drinks. What would you like?"

"Bourbon and water."

Dimitri took off his goggles and poured their drinks, making sure the senator's drink was much more potent.

"I hope you like your drink, Senator."

Senator Thompson lifted his glass and took several big gulps. "I don't know who taught you to mix drinks, son, but you're my kind of bartender. Go ahead and ask away, I'll tell you anything you want."

"Okay, what's your relationship to Philip Wu?"

"None at all, I only met the man once."

"Then why were you at the funeral today?"

"I know some of the others at the funeral, and was just paying my respects for their sakes. It's just the nature of politics—you never know who you may need a favor from down the road. Can I have another one of those drinks?"

Dimitri poured him another drink, even stronger than the first.

"Thanks, son. Are you working for Whitey? Did he put you up to this, or was it those Chinese devils?"

"Who's Whitey?"

"Whitey's a bastard. He was pissed off that I knew about his illegitimate son and how he probably murdered his son's mother. There's a lot of rumors about Whitey. Some say he has connections to organized crime. He threatened me if I revealed what I knew."

Dimitri was now intrigued. *Was this man Whitey the Big Man?* It was a shot in the dark, but Dimitri believed that a man with the senator's influence and contacts might recognize the nickname. If he did, it would be Dimitri's first real link to his employer's actual identity. Dimitri could see that the senator's eyes were drooping and he was badly slurring his words. He decided to ask a few more questions before finishing it.

"Senator, do you know of anyone called the Big Man?"

"No, I don't, son."

"Is Whitey a big man?"

"Yeah, he's very tall."

"How tall?"

"Much taller than you. Can you help me to the couch in the living room? I need to lie down."

Dimitri almost had to carry the senator to get him to the couch, which was no easy task given his excessive weight. The senator quickly passed out and started snoring heavily.

Dimitri went to the refrigerator in the kitchen and found what he was looking for. There were insulin pens just like the ones he brought with him. He decided to use them instead of his, since they might have the senator's fingerprints on them and it would avoid any possible discrepancies in the insulin that was used. Dimitri attached one of the needles he'd brought with him and set the injection amount on the pen to what he knew would be a lethal dose. He knew from his medical training that most diabetics injected their insulin in locations that were easily accessible and created the least amount of pain. The thigh was the most popular option.

Dimitri rolled up the senator's right pajama pantleg since he was right-handed, and saw evidence of very recent injections. He injected the senator with the insulin and left the pen by the senator's side. Dimitri then gathered up everything he'd brought with him, along with the glass he used, and put them in the duffel bag. He left the senator's glass on the table.

About twenty minutes after being injected, the senator's body spasmed several times and went limp. Dimitri checked for a pulse and found none. He turned his night vision goggles on, grabbed his duffel bag, and exited by the back door. As he walked toward the street, he took out the card holder and gently threw it and the business cards near the bushes on the senator's property.

On the way back to his hotel, Dimitri stopped at the storage locker and left the duffel bag, which contained all the items he had used. When he got back to his room, he called the front desk and informed them that he was checking out the next morning and would drop the car off at the airport. Dimitri then sent an email to his contact with a single word: "Done."

# 6

James Jordan hadn't attended many funerals during his life. Other than his father, who had died in an automobile accident, he'd never lost anyone really close to him. Philip wasn't family, but James was probably as close to him as any family could be. Going to Philip's funeral would be incredibly difficult under any circumstance, but it had been made much worse by the unusual circumstances surrounding his death. Circumstances that created doubt in his mind about whether Philip was developing cyber threats and if he really ever knew him like he thought he had.

Barbara invited James and JoAnn to ride with her to Philip's funeral in one of the White House limousines. She was going as the president's representative, since she knew both James and Philip well from their careers in the information technology industry.

James liked Barbara. As former CEOs now working for the president, they were kindred spirits, and close friends. James put that friendship to good use whenever he needed to discuss an important issue with President Meredith.

"I need to talk with the president, Barbara. Could you arrange it for tomorrow?"

"Can you tell me what it's about?"

"I need a short leave of absence to address the issue of Philip's successor. There are also some circumstances about his death that are rather strange. I believe both the president and you should be aware of them, if Shelly Brockner hasn't already briefed you."

"This is news to me, James. I'm not aware of any strange circumstances surrounding Philip's death, and I doubt that the president is, either. I can arrange the meeting, but I'd like you to brief me before we see the president so I'm prepared. Let's discuss this further after the funeral."

"Sure, Barbara, we can talk at the reception at the Wu residence. Were you planning on going?"

"Yes. I need to talk with my least-favorite billionaire and your partner in VSI, George Solomon."

"I could sell tickets for that match," JoAnn said, as she smiled.

"Oh, he isn't that bad once you get to know him," James said. "Just think of him as a big teddy bear."

"More like a hungry grizzly bear," Barbara said, as she rolled her eyes.

The funeral lasted more than ninety minutes, and James gave the eulogy at Ann Wu's request. James emphasized what an intelligent, innovative, honest, and kind person Philip was, and how he was a great colleague and friend, and a wonderful husband and father. Many guests shed tears, but James was totally stoic. He wasn't sure how much of what he said was true.

As James and JoAnn were walking out of the church with Barbara, she waved to George Solomon, who completely ignored her. "Oh, that doesn't look good," mumbled Barbara under her breath. As they arrived at the Wu residence, Barbara rocketed out of her seat. "I'll meet you inside, I need to talk to someone first," she said, with a concerned look. Barbara made a beeline for George Solomon.

"I wonder what that's all about," JoAnn said.

"I don't know, but it doesn't look good based on Barbara's body language," James responded.

"I heard that those two have a long history of bad body language. Is that true, James?"

"You could say that. George can be difficult to deal with."

"How'd George become involved with VSI?"

"President Meredith introduced him to Philip and me when he was still in the Maryland state legislature. George was interested in cybersecurity, and Maryland State Senator Meredith convinced him to invest in VSI when we really needed the money. It turned out to be one of the best investments George ever made."

"Philip seemed very respectful around George."

"As am I, but with Philip it was more than respect. In fact, he seemed almost afraid of George."

"Why would Philip be afraid of George?"

"I don't know. He never said."

"I heard that George and his foreign citizenship prevented VSI from selling its products to the federal government."

"Yeah, I heard that, too, but it isn't true. Philip and I made that decision. It had nothing to do with George."

"So do you like George? I've seen you irritated after meeting with him."

"George isn't someone I like to socialize with. You worked for him at his investment firm. You must know how he is."

"Yeah, egotistical, selfish, and self-centered."

"All true, but I've had only one major dispute with him."

"What was that, James?"

"He requested that VSI hire a recent college graduate as a design engineer. The guy was smart and had good grades from a great school, but he clearly didn't have the necessary experience we were looking for. At that time, VSI was very small. Hiring anyone who might be dead-wood could be disastrous."

"How'd you get out of that, James?"

"We didn't. George offered to directly pay the salary out of his own pocket. Actually, it was one of the best deals we ever made. He became a brilliant engineer and is now the Chief Technology Officer at VSI. He'll probably be here today, since he worked directly with Philip for years. His name's Chris Hoffman. I'll introduce you if I see him."

As they walked in, JoAnn went over to talk with some of the politicians she recognized, while James went immediately to Ann Wu and expressed his sympathies.

"How are you, Ann?"

"I'm okay. I have to be for my son's sake. He thinks I'll fall apart without Philip. Sometimes I think so, too."

"I think you'll do fine. You're a lot stronger than Jim realizes."

"I hope so. Are you going to take back the VSI CEO position?"

"No, I plan to finish out the president's first term. I promised him that when I took the job."

"Who do you think will become the new CEO, James?"

"I think we have several options, including Theresa Killian, Christopher Hoffman, and Tom Allen."

"I hope it isn't Theresa. Philip thought she was a great engineer and had a talent for product development, but he never trusted her business judgment. She thought VSI needed to move their products into the government sector to increase sales and innovation."

"I wasn't aware of that. That could be a problem. Anyway, you'll have some say in who the next CEO will be since you inherited Philip's stock and his vote."

"Actually, Philip asked that I provide a voting proxy for all his shares to you if anything should happen to him. It's even in the will. I do have one favor to ask."

James was totally shocked by her news about the proxy but tried not to show it.

"What's the favor?"

"Jim is graduating from Georgetown Law School, and I was wondering if VSI could find him a job with their intellectual property division."

"I'm sure we can, Ann. It would be a real catch for VSI to have a patent attorney who's the son of one of its founders. Jim also worked for us as an engineering intern and knows the technology."

"Yes, I know, and he really loved engineering; but his father insisted that he not go into the same field that he was in. Philip was concerned that Jim would be compared to him, and he didn't need that burden."

James saw JoAnn looking for him, so he waved to her. She joined him and he introduced her to Ann.

"Ann, I'd like you to meet Senator JoAnn Young, a close friend of mine."

"You have my sincere condolences, Mrs. Wu. I met your husband on several occasions, and he was as nice as he was brilliant."

"Thank you, JoAnn. Philip said you weren't only smart but gorgeous, and I can see he was right. James deserves someone who's very special."

"Thank you. I'm very lucky to have met James."

"Okay, let's not go there," James said. "I'm not a saint, as both of you well know."

"Maybe not," Ann said, "but you're listed as one of the most eligible bachelors in the DC area. Not only tall and attractive, said the article in the *Washingtonian*, but also brilliant, rich, and a decorated former naval officer. You really need to settle down and have kids of your own."

"Thanks, Ann. You sound like my mother. I do plan to do that, maybe sooner than later," James said, as he looked at JoAnn, who was blushing.

"Jim will be here later with his fiancée. Maybe you could talk with him then."

"I'd enjoy that," James said, as he noticed Barbara walking toward them.

"Mrs. Wu, I'd like to offer my condolences to you for your loss on behalf of the president and myself," Barbara said. "The president wanted me to tell you that the entire country is poorer for his loss."

"Thank you, Barbara. And, please thank the president for me."

"I will, but if you don't mind, I need to talk with James for a moment."

Barbara grabbed James's arm and forcefully led him to a more private area of the room.

"James, I need to meet with the president immediately on an important issue. I'll arrange our meeting with the president for ten tomorrow morning. Does that work for you?"

"Yes, thank you, Barbara."

"Oh, do you have transportation? I'm taking the limo back."

"That's not a problem. JoAnn and I can catch a taxi."

James returned to Mrs. Wu and JoAnn as they watched Barbara sprint out the front door. JoAnn shook her head and laughed. "Wow, she looked like her hair was on fire, James."

"Yes, she did, and that isn't normal behavior for Barbara. She's known for always being very calm and collected. Something must be happening, and it probably isn't good."

James saw the VSI senior management standing together in a group by the bar.

"Will you excuse us, Ann? I'd like to introduce the senator to some former colleagues."

As they approached, James noticed that the group seemed to stiffen and stop talking. He walked directly toward Chris Hoffman, since James had known him the longest.

"Hi, everyone. I'd like to introduce you to Senator JoAnn Young. JoAnn, this is Theresa Killian, the VSI Vice President for Product Development and Support, Christopher Hoffman, the VSI Chief Technology Officer, and Tom Allen, the VSI Director of R&D."

They all smiled and returned his salutation, but James could still sense their nervousness.

"Relax, everyone. This is a sad and stressful situation, to be sure, but I'm certain all of us and VSI will survive this terrible incident. This is a day for mourning our loss, but I plan to have a meeting at headquarters tomorrow to discuss our future plans together. Is everyone okay with that?"

Theresa, the newest and most gregarious member of the management team, responded first.

"We'll all be there, James. We're just all stunned by Philip's death."

Tom, the youngest and probably the most brilliant member of the team, said, "It doesn't seem like VSI anymore with the both of you gone, boss."

"I'm not gone, Tom. I'll be back, maybe sooner than you think."

Both Theresa and Tom smiled, while Chris seemed totally detached, as if he wasn't there.

From across the room James saw Ann talking with a young couple, so he and JoAnn walked over to join them. As James got closer, he realized that the young man was Jim Wu, Philip's son.

"Jim, how are you? I haven't seen you since your graduation from engineering school at Johns Hopkins. You look great."

"Thanks, Mr. Jordan," Jim said, as he reached out his hand.

Instead James gave him a hug. "You don't have to shake my hand, Jim. You're my godson, or have you forgotten?"

"No, sir, I haven't, especially since I was named after you."

"Who's this beautiful young lady, Jim?"

"I'm sorry, this is my fiancée, Margaret. She's also a law student at Georgetown."

"Yes, I heard that you plan to go into patent law. VSI could certainly use an in-house patent attorney who's familiar with our technology. Please come see us before you take any other offers."

"Thank you, I'll certainly do that," Jim said, with a huge smile on his face.

"JoAnn and I have to leave now, Ann. I have an early meeting tomorrow with the president that I have to prepare for. Can you recommend a taxi service I can call?"

"I won't hear of it, James. You can take my car. It's in the driveway. I hardly ever use it."

"Thanks. I'll have someone from VSI return it tomorrow."

JoAnn and James left after waving goodbye to everyone they knew on the way out.

"Your place or mine?" James asked.

"Let's go to your place this time. My place is such a mess."

"How'd that happen?"

"I had a messy house guest the other night."

"I know. I'm a typical bachelor, not yet housebroken."

James drove to his condominium in Crystal City, and they took the elevator to the fourteenth floor. He had bought the three-bedroom condo a year ago from a former senator who had lost his re-election bid. It was much closer to DC than his home in Maryland.

James got out of his suit and changed into jeans and a sweatshirt, while JoAnn put on some clothes she kept in the closet of one of the guest bedrooms.

"Do you want to go out for dinner or eat in, James?"

"How about we just keep it simple and order takeout? That way we don't have the hassle of cleaning up. We can just relax and talk."

"Fine with me, but one of these days I want to try out that fancy kitchen of yours."

"That would be great, since I never have time to use it."

James ordered pizza, and they enjoyed it with a bottle of wine that he knew JoAnn liked.

"Did you enjoy your reunion with your former VSI management team?" JoAnn asked.

"I have mixed feelings. I enjoyed seeing them again, but I believe they expect me to come back and take over the CEO position now that Philip is gone."

"Is that what you're going to do?"

"No. I made a commitment to the president as Federal CIO, and I intend to keep it. Cybersecurity is a major theme of his administration, and he needs my help with the foreign cyber-attack legislation."

"I'm glad you're not leaving, but who will run VSI?"

"There are at least three people in the company who have the experience and capability to step in and run the day-to-day operations. You met them earlier, and as of today I have majority voting status to select who I want."

"When did that happen?"

"Ann told me earlier that she's giving me a permanent proxy to vote her husband's shares. She also told me that of the three candidates I suggested to take over as CEO, Theresa Killian wouldn't be a good choice."

"Why?"

"Ann believes Theresa would try to expand the VSI market into the federal government sector, which would be a bad move."

"Why is that, James?"

"We'd have to submit the VSI products that we wish to sell to the feds for testing so they can be validated or certified for government use. Commercial security products are required to go through a validation under test requirements defined in a standard called the Common Criteria. The alternative would be certification testing by NSA or the Defense Information Systems Agency."

"What's wrong with that?"

"The required testing would reveal some elements of our products that we wouldn't want known and that aren't described in any of our documentation or patents. They're essentially VSI trade secrets. Since they aren't in our patents, we have no protection if another company discovers them and steals the technology."

"Isn't it against the law for the government to reveal such proprietary information?"

"Yes, but the feds contract with commercial companies and labs to do most of the testing. We couldn't be certain that the technology wouldn't be discovered and stolen by the lab or one of their employees. Philip and I referred to the trade secrets as VSI's 'secret sauce.' Other than me, only Tom, Chris, and Theresa have any knowledge of those secrets. Only Philip and I know all the technical details, seeing as we developed the technology."

JoAnn knew that she wasn't a technologist and she had no desire to know VSI trade secrets, but she was curious about the technology and why it was so successful and highly regarded.

"Could you give a simplified layman's explanation about the technology without describing the secret sauce?"

"Sure, it's not all that complex if we don't get into the technical details. VSI sells boundary protection systems such as firewalls and intrusion detection systems for the protection of corporate information technology systems that use virtual machine technology. A boundary protection system looks at incoming or outgoing data traffic for an information system or network. It determines if there's any suspicious data or anomalies that should be blocked from getting in or any protected data that shouldn't be allowed out."

"I understand everything you said except what virtual machine technology is."

"A virtual machine, or VM, is essentially a software program that performs the operations of physical data-processing systems such as servers and personal computers or hardware systems used to control network traffic, such as network switches and routers. VM technology became popular in the last decade because it's very efficient and reduces costs. It allows designers to create operational networks and component systems quickly and cheaply via software that runs within a physical data-processing system. The data-processing system can be a server, personal computer, a laptop, or even a tablet."

"So, you're programming a virtual information system within a physical computer and calling it a virtual machine, correct?"

"Yes, except we aren't really programming it. The VMs that we need can be created from a commercially available software application that will create what you want when you specify the requirements. Designers can create an entire virtual data-processing enterprise that emulates the operation of a physical data-processing enterprise much more quickly and at a lower cost."

"Okay, I understand that, but where does VSI fit in all of this?"

James smiled. "Here's where it gets a little complex, but I'll keep it as simple as possible."

"Thank you. Keep in mind that I majored in business, not engineering."

"I'll try. Virtual systems need to be secured against many of the same threats as physical systems. They also have an additional feature that physical systems don't have called the hypervisor, which is the basis of all VM technology. Just as software applications, such as Microsoft Word, depend on the operating system software such as Windows to operate within a computer, the operating systems within a VM depend on the hypervisor. The hypervisor is their connection to the physical hardware processing system or computer on which everything operates. It connects with and controls all the VM operating systems. Because it's connected to all the VMs, any vulnerability in the hypervisor could allow attacks on all the connected VMs and their operating systems and applications, which could be disastrous."

"I have a question. Is the hypervisor an operating system?"

"Not exactly. It's more like a monitor that supports and controls all the VMs that connect with it. The important thing is that VSI creates security systems to protect the hypervisor. Our systems are the hypervisor firewalls or hypervisor intrusion detection and protection systems that protect the VMs, including operating systems and applications. It's more complex than that, but that's essentially what VSI does. Any questions?"

"Yes. Are the hypervisor security systems you mentioned the secret sauce?"

James smiled and said, "No, there are numerous companies that use hypervisor technology. It's not new, since it was invented in the 1960s. However, our secret sauce is what makes the VSI security technology superior, and I can't talk about it."

"Because if you told me, you'd have to kill me?" JoAnn asked with a smile.

"Something like that," James said, as he laughed.

"Well, you sometimes talk in your sleep, but I promise not to listen unless I overhear another woman's name."

"I need to prepare for my meeting with the president and Barbara tomorrow. Maybe you can lend me some of your political expertise now that I've finished my security lesson."

"Okay, but before we start I need another glass of wine. I'll be right back."

JoAnn went to the kitchen to get more wine, and noticed a red light flashing on the kitchen phone.

"James, do you know that there's a message on your phone?"

"Yeah. I'll get it later."

"That would drive me crazy. What if it's important?"

"If it's going to bother you, then play it." James was slightly annoyed because he hated being tethered to a phone twenty-four hours a day. He and JoAnn listened to the message.

"Hi, James, this is Special Agent Rick Tanner from the FBI. I'm calling to tell you that we have found evidence of SUV tracks leading to and from Philip Wu's home that bypassed the gatepost at the entrance. We ran the tracks through the FBI's TreadMate database, and they look like they might be from a Ford SUV. We're checking with local rental agencies using the picture of the Chinese suspect found dead in Philip Wu's Jaguar. Please contact me when you can."

James quickly finished his wine. His meeting the next day had just become a lot more important.

James showed up for the meeting with the president at the White House thirty minutes early. He wanted to tell Barbara about the message he'd gotten from Rick Tanner prior to the meeting. Barbara was talking with her secretary when she saw James enter her outer office.

"You're earlier than expected, James. The meeting isn't for another half hour."

"I need to discuss a message I got from FBI Special Agent Rick Tanner last night, since it could reopen Philip's case."

"Let's go into my office and talk."

James entered Barbara's office and she closed the door.

"The FBI found proof that indicates Philip was targeted and that his death probably had nothing to do with a burglary."

"What evidence leads you to this conclusion, James?"

"Are you aware that Shelly Brockner believes Philip was targeted, and that there were at least two assailants?"

"Yes, I was there when she briefed the president, but her analysis was based on circumstance. As I recall, there was no actual evidence of a vehicle entering and leaving the community and making its way to Philip's house without passing through the checkpoint at the entrance."

"I was informed by the FBI last night that they found that evidence. They think the vehicle might be a rented Ford SUV and are checking the local rental car agencies that rent that model. We're hoping someone can identify the dead assailant."

"Okay, we can discuss it with the president at our meeting. I also have some bad news. It looks like the foreign cyber-attack bill in the senate is going to pass and will be sent to the house."

"Who told you that?"

"George Solomon. He met with Senator Thompson two nights ago. He informed me yesterday at the funeral, which was the reason I left so fast."

"Does the president know about this?"

"He does. I briefed him last night, and he was angrier than I've ever seen him. Let's walk over to the Oval Office before we're late. I'm sure he's going to also want to hear your news."

The president was sitting at his desk as they walked into the office. He stood up and greeted both Barbara and James.

"Good morning, James. I assume Barbara has briefed you on the status of the cyber-attack legislation."

"Yes, she has, sir. Is there any possibility that the majority leader will change his position?"

"I don't know. I called his office to arrange a meeting for later today, but they said he wasn't in yet."

"What can we do?"

"Absolutely nothing. We just need to let this play out. Your buddy George thinks the majority leader has a messiah complex and that his brain is pickled, which is probably true. Hell, half the politicians in this town hate Lee Thompson, and the other half are scared to death of him. We all know the senate bill will be tabled when it gets to the house and that months of hard work will go down the drain. There are no options at this point except to pick it up again after the midterm elections. It's obvious that Senator Thompson is just using this to propel himself into another term in office. He'll ride it as long as it helps him."

"The delay of this legislation will certainly make the Chinese happy," Barbara said.

"Maybe I should use that point with Senator Thompson. He hates the devils, as he refers to them. I'll let you know what happens after my meeting with the senator. I suggest we look to see if there's anything I can do as president through regulations or executive orders while we wait this out. My predecessors seem to have used that avenue quite a bit. Maybe I can as well."

"We can look at that, but it isn't very popular in Congress or the courts these days. Congress and the electorate have become very suspicious of presidents who try to go around the legislative process. I'm not certain that we should take on that fight in your first term, Joe."

"You mean if I do, it could be my last term?"

"Something like that."

"Is there anything else we need to discuss, Barbara?"

"Yes, it looks like the Philip Wu murder was premeditated, and that he was targeted and killed by at least two assailants."

"My God, to what end?"

"We aren't certain sir," James said. "Shelly Brockner believes he could've been targeted because of the work he'd been doing with NSA and Cyber Command. The FBI found evidence of an SUV that bypassed the gatehouse to get to and from the Wu residence where he was killed. They're also checking rental car agencies where the vehicle could've been rented."

"That's terrible. We need to give this investigation our highest priority."

Just then the president's secretary buzzed his phone. He listened for a few seconds and his eyes widened before he said, "Get the details, and please make sure Shelly is notified immediately. Has anyone notified his family? Thanks, Andrea. Please get me his wife's phone number and find out the arrangements when they're made."

After hanging up, the president turned to James and Barbara.

"Senator Lee Thompson was found dead at his home by one of his staffers this morning after missing an important vote. It looks like a heart attack brought on by excessive alcohol consumption. His body has been taken for autopsy by the DC medical examiner."

Everyone was stunned. Barbara broke the silence. "I'll put together a respectful press release, Joe."

"I'm sure that'll be difficult, Barbara. But we need to respect the office, if not the man, and give this the deference it deserves. Please determine which candidates are likely to take Senator Thompson's place as majority leader. I'll need a complete dossier on each by tomorrow morning."

"Sure, Joe. I guess this will change all of our priorities."

"Yes, it certainly will. I hope there's nothing more we need to address today. I have things to do, and I'm sure the both of you do, too."

James momentarily thought about telling the president about his leave of absence, but decided it was not the right time. The evidence indicating that Philip may have been murdered and the sudden death of Senator Thompson had just changed everything.

# 7

George Solomon was in his office when he got a call from one of his lawyers.

"Good morning, George, this is Jason Fisher."

"Hello, Jason. How are you doing today?"

"I'm fine. Have you seen the news?"

"Not since earlier this morning. Has something happened?"

"Senator Thompson was found dead in his home this morning. They believe it was natural causes. It's on every news channel."

"Thanks, Jason. I'm turning on the TV. I'll talk with you later."

As the TV came on, George said, "CNN," and the TV displayed a reporter doing a live report from Georgetown. He listened as the reporter said, "Senator Thompson was found dead in his home this morning by his longtime friend and campaign manager, Alex Travon, when he didn't show up for a vote on the senate version of the foreign cyber-attack bill. Mr. Travon had a key to the house and found the senator on a couch in his living room. The death has been listed at this time as being due to natural causes, and the vote has been postponed because of his death."

George locked his office door and poured himself a glass of champagne to celebrate. *The country, his state, and his family were better off without the bastard*, thought George. He buzzed his assistant, Nadya Murin.

"Have you heard the news about the majority leader, Nadya?"

"Yes, George. How could you miss it? It's all over the media."

"I need to talk with you. Please hold all my calls and come to my office."

"I'll be right there."

George was scanning through the news channels on his TV when Nadya walked into his office.

"Close the door, Nadya. We need to develop a plan on how we can take advantage of this turn of events."

"If you're planning on making a statement to the press, I suggest you don't. The majority leader had friends and associates that you don't want to alienate."

"I doubt he had any real friends, just sycophants and dependents. But that's not what I wanted to talk about. We need to determine who the front-runners are in the senate to replace him and who the White House is backing. I need to know if it's someone we can work with, and the best way to do that."

Nadya breathed a sigh of relief. "Okay, the first part will be easy. I'll have a list of the top five likely candidates to you along with dossiers in two hours. Finding out who the president will back is much more difficult, George."

"I know. The president and Barbara Chang will never tell me anything, given our current relationship. We need to find someone else who might know."

"What about James Jordan? As Federal CIO, he's a senior member of the White House staff and also a close friend of the president. He might be able to find out."

"I doubt the president would discuss it with him since it has nothing to do with James's position as Federal CIO. Even if he did, James would never tell me, and I have nothing on him that would allow me to coerce him into finding out."

"True, but you did introduce James to his current girlfriend, Senator JoAnn Young. I hear that she's very close to James, and is also well respected by her senate colleagues. She could be involved in the selection process."

"It's a possibility, but JoAnn is very independent. She left our firm to start her own very successful hedge fund, even after I offered her a vice presidency and a ton of money to stay."

Nadya frowned. "I remember that. You offered her more than I was making. I also recall that you sent her a lot of customers when she was struggling in her first year. She owes you, George."

"Okay. I'll call James and see if he and JoAnn will meet me for dinner tonight at Michelle's. They seem to love that place."

George called James's office and was told that he was out for the rest of the day. He then tried James's personal cell phone, but it went directly to voice mail, so he left a message. George also thought about calling JoAnn but rejected that idea, since he heard the senate was in caucus after the death of the majority leader. *The whole government is probably on hold because of the death of such a useless bastard as Senator Thompson*, George thought.

After his meeting with the president, James went back to his office and turned on the TV. The local stations were still just reporting the basic facts of the majority leader's death, but Fox News was interviewing a doctor who was describing a possible cause. James listened intently as the doctor said, "The majority leader was rumored to be a severe diabetic and used insulin to control it. I believe that's likely, based on his weight and known family history. Alcohol can cause blood sugar to become seriously elevated; and if the senator was very intoxicated, he could've accidentally taken a lethal overdose of insulin. It's been known to happen with diabetics after drinking alcohol." *Here we go with the rumors and conspiracies*, James thought.

It was twelve thirty, and James needed to be at VSI by two p.m. He grabbed two energy bars out of his desk drawer and headed to his car. James walked into VSI a few minutes early and showed his identification. He was escorted into the large conference room on the first floor with a huge oval conference room table. Theresa Killian, Christopher Hoffman, and Tom Allen were sitting on one side of the table. James thought they looked nervous as he took a seat on the other side. After some small talk, James started the meeting.

"The other day I was called into the FBI director's office to discuss Philip's death. During the discussion she said that she contacted VSI for information and was told that Philip was working with NSA to develop an Advanced Persistent Threat. When the hell did VSI start working with the government to develop cyber weapons?"

Christopher was the first of the group to respond.

"VSI wasn't involved at all in those projects. They were outside projects between Philip, NSA, and Cyber Command; we know nothing about them. They were awarded to him, not VSI, on a sole-source basis as 'black projects.' The funding line items are themselves classified. No one at VSI has the clearance to know what they're about. Theresa had to be cleared for top secret just to access Philip's schedule at Fort Meade. She was also provided a secure cell phone to contact him while he was there."

"Thanks, Chris. When did this happen, and why wasn't I told?"

"It happened about two months after you left VSI to become Federal CIO," Tom said. "Philip made it clear to all of us that it was his personal business and that no one, including you, was to know about it or be part of it. I've no idea why he was working with the feds. I'm sure he wasn't enjoying it. We all believe he was being coerced, but we don't know how. Philip doesn't seem like someone with skeletons in his closet. You knew him better than we did, boss."

"No skeletons that I know of, Tom. Philip was about as straight up as they come. Who in the federal government is running these projects that Philip was involved with?"

"All we know is that it's someone high up in NSA or Cyber Command," Theresa said. "We have no names, but I'm sure you could get that information from the president. If you do, don't tell us. Whoever it is, we don't want to know."

"Don't worry, Theresa, this conversation is private. I promise all of you that it goes no further than the people in this room."

"Or the people bugging this room," Tom said, as he frowned.

"What do you mean by that, Tom? Do you believe that someone is electronically monitoring this facility?" James asked in a challenging manner.

"We aren't certain, but we all have the feeling that it might be happening. There have been a number of unusual events. We believe someone was trying to gather information on our technology. I have no evidence that they succeeded," Tom responded.

James slowly stood up, and with his palms on the table he leaned toward Tom with a concerned look on his face.

"What events? When did this occur? Why wasn't I informed?" James asked, raising his voice.

Tom was startled. He'd never seen James that angry. Tom gathered himself and said, "It started right after you left. Our corporate network administrator, Tony Maxwell, was offered a government job at the Pentagon. The weird thing was that he said that he never applied for the job. He took it because the salary was about the same as here, but it was much closer to his family and friends. We hired a replacement who was here about a month, and then he just disappeared. I was suspicious, so I looked at the network logs after he left and found evidence of attempts to get information beyond his authorization level. He was denied access by our security systems."

"Did you inform Philip?" James asked, in a calmer voice.

"Yes, and he was not happy. I asked him if you should be informed. He said no, and that he would take care of it."

"Did you find out what happened to Tony's replacement?"

"He doesn't exist. We checked out all his personal contacts and none of them were real. His name and social security number belonged to a guy in North Carolina whose identification was stolen."

"Thanks, Tom," James said, as he shook his head.

"That's not all of it, boss. After this guy disappeared, our wireless intrusion prevention system picked up a very sophisticated soft rogue access point on a laptop in your old office. It was apparently transmitting to a wireless access point outside the building. The system tracked the location of the wireless access point to a white van parked nearby. We asked one of our engineers to casually walk by the van to see if it had government plates. It did, but as you know, government plates aren't unusual down here. Government vehicles are used by the navy guys at Pax River right next door."

"Do you think it was the government doing this, Tom?"

"I don't know, but when we disconnected the rogue access point, the van left. We decided to do an inspection of the entire network. Our techs found some unauthorized connections to the serial ports on some of the VoIP phones. They were apparently being used to monitor our voice communications. We checked all the phones and disconnected the serial ports. It's clear that we were under attack by someone, but it seemed to stop after Philip went to work with the guys at Fort Meade."

"Philip and I designed and developed all of VSI's security systems and procedures when we started the company. I'm confident they would've kept all of our sensitive data secure. Our corporate proprietary data is stored off-line in a security vault that isn't accessible via the network. As far as I know, there are only a handful of individuals, including Philip and myself, who can access that data. I assume the missing network administrator wasn't added to the list, or was he?"

"No, he wasn't, boss. He had no physical or network access to privacy act information, corporate financial records, or proprietary data such as patent applications, copyrights, and trade secrets."

"Do you all think these attacks stopped because the attackers were able to coerce Philip into providing what they wanted?"

"We aren't certain," Theresa said. "But about a month after the attacks stopped, there was a big meeting here on a Sunday between Philip and several senior military officers."

"Was any one of you, or for that matter, anyone from the VSI staff here during the meeting?"

"No one other than the guards, Philip, and his guests," Tom said. "It was the day of the big Redskins-Ravens game. The facility was empty since both teams were playoff contenders, and all employees received a memo saying that the network was being worked on that day and that VSI would be closed. I only heard about the meeting from one of the guards who told me he was specifically instructed by Philip that the guests didn't have to log in and sign the visitor journal. That was unprecedented. You know as well as I do that logins are a corporate requirement for every visitor. It was mandated by both Philip and you. I have no idea what it was all about."

"Okay, I think we've beaten this to death, and I appreciate your input. This helps me a lot in determining what happened after I left, and why Philip would suddenly start working with the feds."

"Well actually, you were both working with the feds," Theresa said.

"That's true, Theresa. But I was working on cyber defense, while it appears Philip may have been working on the development of cyber threats. I hope I'm wrong."

"Since you were both working with the feds, does that mean that VSI will start selling our products to the government?"

"Not as long as I have anything to say about it, Theresa. There are reasons for my and Philip's decision to only sell VSI products to the commercial sector. Even though Philip and I were working with the feds as individuals, that requirement hasn't changed. It can't change without the unanimous approval of the VSI board of directors."

"I understand, but the government market is huge, and they have a lot of interest in our products. The board should consider the opportunities and revenue we are missing."

"We have looked at it, Theresa. I also want to let everyone know that I still plan to continue working as the Federal CIO. I made a promise to President Meredith that I wouldn't abandon him during his first term. Since I won't be available to run this company, I'll need to select a successor. I'll do that over the next week or so. It'll definitely be someone in this room. I won't pick an outsider, unless all of you decide you're not interested."

"I'd like to remove my name from consideration, since I don't agree with the restriction against federal business," Theresa said.

"I would like you to reconsider your withdrawal and delay your decision for a couple of weeks, Theresa. Will you do that?"

Theresa stammered for a few seconds. "Okay, I'll do it for you, James."

Theresa walked with James to his car. He'd always liked Theresa. She was extremely intelligent and very attractive but could alienate those around her by her forceful personality and aggressive temperament.

"I hope you can forgive me, James, but I think this company can be so much more than it is now."

"It's doing very well, Theresa. Please don't become discouraged." James smiled and kissed her softly on the cheek.

When James got in his car, he immediately checked his phone for messages. He listened to one from George requesting a return call and decided that he'd better call him back. James knew George got irritable if he was ignored. *Probably most billionaires would*, he thought. He dialed the number and George answered immediately, which was unusual.

"Hello, James. Where are you?"

"I'm just about to leave VSI. What can I do for you?"

"You and your beautiful girlfriend could meet me at Michelle's for dinner tonight."

"I'd need to see if JoAnn is busy, but if she isn't, I see no reason why we couldn't. Let me call her and get back to you."

"Okay. She's never turned me down before."

James called JoAnn and she answered immediately.

"What's up?" JoAnn asked.

"Well, if you're not busy, your former boss and my business partner just invited us to dinner at Michelle's."

"That sounds good. What time do you want to meet me? Or should I drive separately?"

"I can pick you up. Where are you going to be in about an hour and thirty minutes? It'll take me that long to get back to DC from here."

"Meet me at my house. You can take a shower and wear one of the suits you have here. It's about four, so tell George we can be there by seven."

"Do you have something else planned? I was thinking more like six."

"Think of something we can do in an hour, baby."

"Okay, I'll be there even earlier."

James called George and smiled as his Corvette accelerated and he hit almost no traffic. He made it to JoAnn's house a little after five. He rang the doorbell and then let himself in with his key. He was surprised to see JoAnn walking down the staircase absolutely nude.

"Got home earlier than expected," James said.

"I see that. You're lucky you didn't get a ticket. Let's go to the bedroom," JoAnn said, as she started walking up the stairs.

"We could start with the sofa down here."

"Not tonight, sweetie. Just follow me."

James did as he was told and started removing his clothes while walking behind her. He couldn't get used to how incredibly beautiful JoAnn was and how unaffected she was by her appearance. From the first time they met, he was mesmerized by her statuesque appearance at almost six feet tall, and with a figure that a Greek goddess would envy. He thought her long, wavy black hair, beautiful green eyes, wide full lips, and alabaster skin were almost hypnotic.

James watched as she lay down on the bed and grabbed his hand to pull him toward her. After forty minutes of incredible passion they were both exhausted. James looked at JoAnn and then kissed her on the lips.

"Will you marry me?" James asked.

JoAnn was so surprised she couldn't say anything. He stared at her and said, "I think that deserves some response, don't you?"

JoAnn smiled and said, "I fell in love with you the day George introduced us, James. Saying it now would almost be anticlimactic, but my answer is yes."

They lay in bed together holding hands.

"What's next?" James asked.

"Well, I guess we should get up, shower, and get dressed. You know how George hates it when people are late."

"That isn't what I meant, and you know it."

"Well, what do you think is next, James?"

"I asked you first."

"If you're referring to marriage, both of us are no longer kids and have never been married. I think I'd like to have a family, wouldn't you?"

"Very much so."

"What does that mean? I'm thirty-one and don't have many child-bearing years left. So let's think small, maybe two kids, and drop the 'very much so,' okay?"

"Okay, two kids would be fine, a boy and a girl."

"Children aren't something you can order, James. You get what you get, and there are no returns."

"I know that, baby. We can talk about this later. We better shower and get dressed, or George will be angry."

James walked into the shower and turned on the water while JoAnn walked in behind him. She turned the temperature down since it was starting to steam. After they showered, James grabbed a towel and went downstairs and shaved in the other bathroom, then got dressed in a navy blue suit. James knew it always took JoAnn longer, so he turned on the TV to the local news. He saw a news conference with the Washington, DC, medical examiner, Pamela Robinson, who had been assigned to Senator Thompson's autopsy.

She seemed much too young and attractive to be a medical examiner. James had always seen them played on TV by grumpy old men. She was definitely neither. The reporters kept asking questions she couldn't or wouldn't answer, such as whether she saw any indications that the death wasn't due to natural causes.

"The senator's cause of death hasn't been determined," she said. When asked about his excessive drinking and obesity, she acknowledged they could've been contributing factors. She went on to say that they were still examining the body and were waiting on the toxicology report. The reporters asked when the autopsy would be completed. "When I'm satisfied that we have all the answers," she responded and then walked away from the podium.

JoAnn walked down the stairs in a silver dress, blue scarf, and diamond earrings. James thought she looked like an angel. They drove to Michelle's, and as they walked into the restaurant, Michelle personally led them to their usual table overlooking the Potomac.

"Would you like anything to drink?"

"I'd like a vodka martini, heavy on the olives, and I'm sure my fiancé wants his favorite single malt scotch."

Michelle smiled. "When did this happen?" she asked.

"About forty minutes ago," James said.

"Congratulations to you both. I'll be back with your drinks."

"I have something to tell you, baby. I plan to take a few weeks off from my Federal CIO position to assist with the selection and transition of the new VSI CEO."

"I expected that. Who do you think it'll be?"

"I hope it's one of the senior management."

"How'd your meeting go with them today?"

"Not good. Theresa announced that she doesn't want the job, and there's been a lot of strange things happening since I left. Tom thinks the VSI network was under attack."

"By who?"

"They think it's the military and that Philip was coerced by someone at NSA or Cyber Command into working with them. I need to determine the relationship Philip had with the military and what he was working on after I left VSI. Can you find out anything? You're on the Senate Intelligence Committee."

"Getting such information from the military, especially NSA or Cyber Command, on projects they're working on is very difficult, James. Even Congress has problems getting that information."

"Yeah, I guess they would," James said.

"I wonder if George is bringing his new fiancée. Her name's Astrid Von Steuben, and she's supposed to be a really tall and beautiful redhead. Have you met her, James?"

"No, but that's definitely George's type. All his past girlfriends were tall redheads."

"Well, this one has a brain and a fortune of her own. I wonder what she sees in George."

"I wonder what any of them did. The abuse is not worth it. Just ask Nadya."

"Nadya Murin was once George's fiancée?" JoAnn asked.

"Yes, about twenty years ago. He couldn't buy her off like the others. She was originally an employee, and she knew too much about George's companies and their operations. That's why she's the manager of George Solomon Enterprises. What's weird is that I think she still loves him."

"That's got to be difficult for her, working so close to George and seeing all those women in his life. That poor woman."

"She seems to handle it well."

"I think I just saw George walk through the door, and it looks like he did bring his new fiancée."

Michelle led George and Astrid to the table and took their drink order. George introduced Astrid as his fiancée and then introduced James and JoAnn to Astrid.

"James is the Federal CIO and former CEO of VSI, a very successful company I helped fund. JoAnn is a US Senator and successful entrepreneur, and a former employee of one of my investment companies."

"I'm certain they had a lot to do with their own success. You can't take all the credit, George, now can you?" asked Astrid.

George's face flushed. "Of course not," he said in a very low voice that could hardly be heard.

James liked her immediately. So did JoAnn, who always considered George something of a pompous ass. Nothing slowed George down, and he immediately moved on to his reason for dinner.

"Do you know who the president is supporting as the new majority leader, James?"

"When I left the president this morning he was planning on having his staff provide a list of possible candidates. I assume he'll meet with the senate leadership to determine who they think is the best choice. As far as I know he has no favorite."

"Thanks, James. Do either of you know who the senate leadership favors?"

JoAnn knew it was her turn to answer.

"The most likely candidate will probably be Senator Hopkins from South Carolina, since he's the assistant majority leader. However, he may not want it, as his health is failing and he was considering retiring when his term is up in about a year. If he passes on the job, the next likely choices are Senator Castro from Florida or Senator Domingo from Texas."

"Of those three, who do you think has the best chance?"

James jumped in. "JoAnn's vote is privileged information, George. She won't even tell her future husband, the current Federal CIO."

George knew when he'd been had.

"Congratulations to the both of you. When did this happen?"

"Today, George, less than an hour ago. But I'll need to get JoAnn a ring to make it official."

"I can help you there. I have a lot of friends who are jewelers. They created Astrid's ring."

"Thanks, George. I'll let you know."

As James drove JoAnn home, he said, "I hope I wasn't too presumptuous by saying we're officially engaged. I haven't gotten the ring or officially asked you while getting on one knee."

She looked at him affectionately and said, "James, I'm on cloud nine tonight. If you hadn't told them, I would have. I love you so much."

"I love you, too, baby, but I don't think George should be involved with the engagement ring. Did you see that iceberg that Astrid had on her finger? It was the gaudiest thing I've ever seen."

"I want to thank you for saving me from having to tell George where to get off when he asked me how I might vote. I didn't like Lee Thompson, but I don't want to discuss his successor before the poor man is even in the ground."

"Yeah, he certainly has always lacked sensitivity. George can be as cold as that diamond on Astrid's finger."

# 8

Kim couldn't believe his good fortune. He'd been sent to China to learn Information Warfare Technology and to support cyber warfare opportunities against America. A great opportunity that would allow him to do both, and also get paid for it, had fallen into his lap. He couldn't have asked for anything more, but first he needed to call Lee Park.

"Hi, Lee, I'm at the apartment and I need to talk with you. It's very important."

"I'll be there in an hour, Kim."

Kim was excited to tell Lee, which was obvious to her when she arrived at his apartment.

"What's so important, Kim? You're acting like my son when he gets a new toy."

"That's about right. I have an opportunity to participate in cyber warfare against the Americans. It includes some of my classmates at HIT. Here's a report I put together for my superiors. It looks real, Lee."

"Okay, I'll forward this to my contacts in North Korea and let you know when I hear something. In the meantime, be careful who you talk to about this."

Kim didn't tell Lee that he'd already committed to the project, but it didn't matter since Lee met with him two days later to brief him on the response.

"You certainly intrigued my contacts, Kim. I've never seen them respond this quickly."

"They must be really interested."

"They are. Your orders are to proceed with caution and determine who is behind the attack."

"I'll see what I can find out, but everything I've seen indicates this isn't a trap."

Kim was amused at how the North Korean government was hard-wired to believe that nothing was ever what it seemed and that any opportunity was a potential trap. Before Kim had left for China, his uncle advised him to make the most of his training at HIT. The admiral warned him that life in North Korea was going to get much worse, since the leadership was becoming desperate. North Korea's economy had worsened even after the worldwide economic sanctions were removed. It seemed as if his uncle was telling him to look elsewhere for his future.

During Kim's meetings with his friends, it was apparent that Shen, Lian, and Cai's attitudes were different than his. Their frequent discussions began to influence him as did the money he was getting paid, which allowed him to sample Harbin's feast of goods, services, and personal freedom. His growing affection for Cai was by far the greatest influence.

The project meetings and training were conducted after class and were run by Shen. He emphasized network and system penetration skills and identified the specialized hacking tools that they would be using. Kim's training sessions only included Cai, Lian, and Shen, but he knew there had to be other hackers based on the large range of targets.

At the conclusion of each week of training, Shen handed everyone an envelope with cash that was normally around 1500 yuan, more than 250 US dollars. That was an exorbitant sum by North Korean standards. He decided not to inform his superiors about that detail. The money could be used to help his family.

Kim decided to use some of the money to invite Cai out to dinner at the Shangri La. It would be their first official date. He approached Shen after the training session.

"Hi, Shen, I need some help."

"What could you need help with? Your hacking skills and penetration tactics are the best I've seen."

"No, not with the training. I want to ask Cai out for a date at the Shangri La. Can you set up a reservation for this weekend?"

Shen laughed. "No problem, but you better ask her first."

"I'll ask her tomorrow."

"She'll say yes. Lian says she really likes you."

"Thanks, that makes it easier."

The next day after class, he approached Cai.

"Do you have any plans this weekend, Cai?"

"Yes, we have our normal weekend training with Shen and Lian. Have you forgotten?"

"I meant after the training is over on Saturday evening."

"Are you asking me out on a date, Kim?"

"Yes, I have reservations at the Shang Palace in the Shangri La Hotel."

"Oh you do—so you assumed I'd say yes?"

"No, I was hoping you'd say yes."

Cai smiled and said, "Relax, Kim, I'd be happy to go with you. Did you book a room at the hotel as well?"

"No, I didn't." Kim hesitated and then asked, "Were you expecting me to?"

"Of course not, but I wanted to see your reaction."

"Did I pass?"

"You did. What time do you want to meet?"

"I could meet you at your place at six, if that's okay."

"Meet me in the lobby of the hotel at six. We can have a drink before dinner at the pub. I love their Irish coffee."

"I'll be there," Kim said with a huge smile. He was glad that hurdle was over.

The next afternoon, Kim approached Shen after the training session.

"Have you made the reservations, Shen?"

"Yes, everything is prepaid, compliments of our employer. Here's the envelope with your Shangri La priority card. Give it to the concierge before setting up your dinner reservation."

"Is this part of the agreed-upon payments or is it an addition?"

"It's a bonus for superior performance during training."

"But I haven't demonstrated my capabilities yet."

"I know, but I talked with your Korean friend the other day, and he said you were one of the best cyber warriors in North Korea."

"My friend? What's his name? Where'd you meet him?"

"He approached me after class and didn't give me his name."

"What'd he say?" Kim asked nervously.

"Just that he was a friend and that you were selected for this school because you were at the top of your class at Huichon University in North Korea. Don't worry, he said that he was just checking to see how you were doing at school."

"Why was he talking with you, Shen?"

"I was wondering about that, too. He said that he just wanted the opinion of a fellow student on your progress and that he saw us talking and decided to ask me directly. I told him you were one of the brightest students in the school."

"Thanks. Please let me know if he contacts you again."

Kim walked away with a concerned look on his face. He wondered if he was being monitored and what he'd done to warrant such attention. *This was completely unnecessary*, Kim thought. He'd done everything they'd ever asked and done it well throughout his career.

The next day, Shen approached Kim.

"Is everything okay, Kim?"

"Everything's fine, Shen."

Kim was still concerned but he didn't want to alarm Shen and become a possible liability. He changed the subject.

"Do you know where I can go to find some dress clothes for my date?"

"Meet me after class. I'll take you to where I buy my clothes."

"Okay, but don't buy anything for me. You've done enough."

"More than you know," Shen said, as he laughed.

"What does that mean?"

"Nothing. Just enjoy your date with Cai."

After his last class, Kim walked out the front entrance of the main building at HIT and saw Shen sitting with Lian in his Mercedes. *Why is Lian there?* he thought.

"Hi, Lian," Kim said, as he got in the rear seat.

"Hi, Kim. Are you wondering why I'm coming along?"

"I assume you're also shopping."

Lian laughed. "Yes, I'm going to assist you. Shen has horrible taste in clothes. I pick everything he wears, even his underwear."

"I have underwear. I just need some dress slacks, shoes, and a sport coat."

"I can help with that, especially since I know what Cai likes."

Shen drove to the Hongbo Century Square shopping mall, one of the largest in Harbin. Lian took Kim through several stores where they selected some dress shoes, several pairs of dress pants, and a sport coat. It only took about an hour.

While shopping, Kim thought he saw a young Korean man following them through the mall. He couldn't confirm it without alerting Shen and Lian. Kim thought he saw him again as they were leaving.

The next training session on Saturday ran for about six hours and was getting into the details on how the attacks on the dedicated targets would be implemented. Kim understood the basic methodology, since he'd used it many times. It was based on the Information Systems Security Assessment Framework. The framework was the model for all penetration methodologies used by hackers to penetrate IT systems and networks. Normally the framework included a probing phase consisting of information gathering, target discovery, target identification, vulnerability analysis, and social engineering. Shen had eliminated social engineering, since the target was in America, which required English-language skills that most of the hackers didn't have.

The probing phase would provide information on the target systems and their vulnerabilities. It would be followed by an exploitation phase in which identified targets were hacked. The exploitation phase would include initial target hacking and the identification of valuable data and assets. This was followed by more advanced hacking that allowed continuous access to the most valuable data and assets.

Kim saw some problems with the project schedule, and he talked to Shen about it.

"The plan for the attack seems too short and overly optimistic to gain the desired results, Shen."

"Why do you think that, Kim?"

"Based on my past experience, the probing of these systems has to be done delicately and slowly so that it isn't detected by the target's intrusion detection systems. That generally requires many weeks or even months of effort before a successful attack of this size can be implemented. The current schedule limits the probes to a few weeks, and the actual exploitation to a few days at most. I also don't understand why there's no apparent emphasis on continuous access. It seems like a hit-and-run attack."

"Don't worry about it. It's not our problem. Just enjoy the money."

Kim took Shen's advice since he didn't want to rock the boat. After the training session was over, Kim walked out with Cai.

"Are we still meeting at six, Cai?"

"Of course. Why do you ask? Are you worried that I'll stand you up?"

"No, I wasn't worried about that. I was just checking the time so I'm not late."

"Good, because I'm looking forward to it. What do you think of the plan for the cyber attack? It seems like the schedule is much too short."

It was as if Cai were reading his mind.

"It seems like a very optimistic schedule. But maybe they'll have us use some new techniques and hacking tools that I'm not aware of."

"That could be. I don't have the depth of your experience. Nor does anyone else on the project, according to Lian."

"Why did she say that? Does Lian know every member of the project?"

"No, but Shen does, and he told Lian that you're the best. Everyone at HIT knows about your skills, Kim. That's probably why those two men have been watching our class from the back of the lecture hall. I think they're probably recruiters for a local company."

Kim tried to keep his cool.

"I never saw them. What'd they look like?"

"They were wearing black overcoats and were fairly young, probably in their mid- to late twenties. They looked like twins."

"Were they Chinese or Korean?"

"They spoke fluent Chinese, but they could've been from Korean ancestry. There's a large population of ethnic Koreans in Harbin who are Chinese citizens. Are you worried they might be from North Korea?"

Kim didn't want to alarm Cai. "No, probably just recruiters. There'd be no reason to monitor North Korean students in Harbin, unless my country thought I was going to defect, which I'm not."

"Too bad, I was hoping you might stay in China."

"You never know what might happen. Though I doubt the Chinese would accept a North Korean as a defector."

"There are other options. Maybe we should save that discussion for another time."

"Yes, maybe we should. I'll see you at six."

"Don't be late," Cai said with an alluring smile.

Kim decided to walk home, even though it was about three miles away. He purposely walked very quickly down streets that he knew wouldn't be crowded to observe if anyone was tracking him. For a moment he thought he saw someone in a black overcoat following him, but the man quickly disappeared and Kim didn't see him again.

When he got home, Kim did some hapkido exercises to take away the tension. He then took a shower and a short nap before getting ready for his date. He dressed in his new clothes and took a taxi to the Shangri La, arriving about ten minutes early. Kim immediately saw Cai in the lobby. She was dressed in a long black leather coat over a gorgeous red dress with black stiletto heels that made her almost as tall as Kim. She was the most beautiful woman he'd ever seen.

"You look absolutely gorgeous," Kim said as he approached Cai.

"You look incredible yourself, Kim."

"Before we go to the pub, I need to arrange our reservation for dinner at the Shang Palace."

Kim walked up to the front desk with Cai and handed the card Shen had given him to the woman at the concierge counter.

"What time would you like to have dinner?" the woman asked.

Kim looked at Cai. "Is seven okay?" he asked.

"Absolutely."

The woman booked the reservation and then handed him a plastic card. "Here's your room key."

"What room key? I didn't reserve a room."

"The priority card you gave me was set up for dinner and a large luxury suite with a river view."

"I don't need the room. There must be a mistake."

Cai interrupted. "I realize you had nothing to do with this, but keep the room, Kim. I'd like to see what the room is like. I bet it's fantastic."

"Are you sure?"

"I didn't say I was going to stay the night, but I would like to see it."

"Okay. I think we should get a drink. I know I need one."

As they walked into the pub, the same bartender who they'd seen the previous time waved at them.

"Kim, Cai, so happy to see you again. What can I get you?"

"A coffee with Bailey's Irish Cream, whipped cream with a cherry, and an Irish double espresso."

"Same as last time?"

"Yes. You have a good memory," Kim said.

"It's an occupational requirement."

Kim and Cai walked back to the same table where they'd sat when they were in the pub with Shen and Lian.

"I'm sorry about the room, Cai. I think Shen must've thought I'd like it," Kim said after an awkward silence.

Cai pulled him closer and kissed him on the lips.

"I'm sure you would and so would I. But I think we should wait a little while. Is that okay?"

"I can wait for as long as you like. I really like you, Cai."

"I like you, too, but you need to know I'm not completely inexperienced, in case that's what you're looking for."

"No, neither am I."

They both laughed, and as they sat there, a man walked in who immediately caught Cai's attention.

"That's one of the men who was in the classroom, Kim."

Kim looked over her shoulder and saw a husky man less than six feet tall who looked to be Korean.

"Are you certain?"

"I'm absolutely certain."

"It's probably just a coincidence."

Kim really didn't believe that, but he didn't want to scare her.

"This is a popular hotel. He may just be staying here and wanted a drink," Kim said, as he crouched a little lower in his chair.

Cai and Kim relaxed when the man left after buying some cigarettes.

"Does the North Korean government monitor their citizens outside their country, Kim?"

"They do. They're notorious for doing that and a lot worse."

"Why would they be monitoring you? You're just a student."

Kim hesitated for a few seconds, struggling with how he should respond. "You need to know that I'm not just a student, Cai. I'm a lieutenant commander in the North Korean Navy and an intelligence agent. The North Korean government trained me to hack into

Western military computer systems and businesses. I hope you're not upset with me for not telling you earlier, but I could be executed if my superiors knew."

Cai smiled and said, "I appreciate you telling me, Kim. I kind of suspected that you were more than just a student. Did you ever think about leaving North Korea?"

"They don't allow you to just leave, but if I did find a way, it would have to include my mother and sister."

"If China won't give you asylum, where would you go?"

"To one of the countries in Western Europe. Where would you go if you left China?"

"Probably America. I have family there. They escaped to Taiwan and then to New York after the nationalists lost to Mao decades ago. One of their children came to Qufu to find my family. She told us how wonderful America was."

Kim and Cai finished their drinks and walked out of the pub. Cai suddenly grabbed Kim's arm and pulled him back to their table.

"What's wrong, Cai?"

"The man we saw earlier was standing by the front desk."

"I've had enough of this," Kim said, as he walked over to the front desk where the husky man was standing.

"Are you looking for me?"

"Commander, I need to talk with you."

Kim pulled him away from the front desk, and said in a low voice, "Don't call me by my rank. How'd you know I was here?"

"We've been following you for over a week, sir."

"Why have you been following me?"

"To determine if your contacts on this hacking project are Western agents. Our superiors are worried they might be luring you into a trap that would embarrass both you and our homeland."

"Have you seen anything suspicious?"

"Nothing to indicate it's a trap, which is what we've reported to our superiors. We were told to make contact with you. Our superiors want to determine if you need any assistance in identifying who's behind the project."

"I actually may need some help, but it'll need to wait until tomorrow. I have a date with an eager young lady, if you know what I mean."

"Yes, sir. We can meet at your apartment tomorrow."

"Okay, meet me there at one."

Kim watched the agent leave the hotel. He then walked back to the pub to inform Cai as to what was going on.

"So they weren't really spying on you?" Cai asked.

"Oh, they were definitely spying on me. Otherwise I would have been informed about the surveillance. Their primary goal, however, was to determine if any of my contacts in the project were Western intelligence operatives."

"So they were also spying on me?"

Kim nodded. "Probably Shen and Lian as well," he said.

"They seem very paranoid."

"Paranoia is the national pastime in North Korea. Are you ready for dinner? Then we can see the room."

"We could just have dinner sent up to the room."

"That sounds even better."

They took the elevator to the top floor of the hotel and were both stunned when they walked into the suite.

"This suite is magnificent. It's at least four times larger than my apartment."

"It's incredible," Cai said. "The bedroom is huge and there are two bathrooms."

"There's also a kitchen and a separate dining area with a bar."

"Let's order dinner. Here's the room service menu, Kim."

"Okay, select what you want, and I'll call in the order."

Kim ordered dinner and joined Cai, who was looking out the window at the Songhua River.

"This is a fantastic view, Kim. It's where the Ice Festival was held."

As they stood together looking at the river and the sparkling lights on the boats, Kim put his arms around Cai's waist and pulled her close to him. He kissed her on the lips and neck passionately and slowly. He could feel her tense up and then relax in his arms as she kissed him back. Kim couldn't believe this was all taking place. He never would have dreamed when he first came to Harbin that he'd be kissing the most beautiful woman he'd ever seen in a luxury suite that was probably meant for celebrities and rich executives.

They heard a knock on the door and they knew dinner had arrived. The dinner consisted of an assortment of dim sum, Cantonese dishes, and some local Heilongjiang dishes such as cooked wild pig. Both the food and the champagne were exceptional by any standards but were truly magnificent compared to what Kim was used to eating. During dinner they discussed the project.

"Who do you think is funding us, Kim?"

"I have no idea, but my superiors really want to know."

"I think Shen is working with a foreigner. Lian says Shen was given a special phone for the project with encryption capability and that Shen was speaking English to someone outside of China."

"That's what I assumed. I don't believe the funding source would be someone who lived in China. The potential risk would be too large if things didn't go well. The Chinese government would be in a difficult position if this was a plan that originated with one of their citizens. It would look like it had their backing."

"I'm concerned that the only people we know on the project are Shen and Lian. Doesn't that seem strange?"

"It looks like the project organization has been broken into separate cells. It's a technique used by terrorist and intelligence organizations. It allows a large organization to be run without raising much attention while also being insulated from surveillance. No one except the funding source and his representative knows who's involved outside of their cell. The representative is clearly Shen."

"I think you might want to perform some surveillance on Shen to see if you can identify who the funding source is."

"My thought exactly, and that will be my next assignment for the North Korean agents who I'm meeting with tomorrow."

"Great. Now to more important matters such as our plans for the rest of the evening."

"Did you want to go home or stay here and enjoy the room?"

"I want to stay, Kim. But first I need to get out of this dress and into one of those bathrobes in the bathroom."

Cai smiled and then stripped off her dress slowly in front of Kim, exposing her breasts, which were as perfect as the rest of her. He watched as she slowly walked to bathroom while looking back at him. He could hear her turning on the shower, so Kim took off his clothes and joined her. It was a very long shower.

Afterward, they both got into the huge bed and talked about themselves.

"How big is your family, Cai?"

"It's just my father, mother, and me. My parents have been happily married for twenty-four years. What about your family?"

"My father died when I was young, so it's just my mother and sister."

"It must have been difficult to lose your father."

"It was, but my uncle took his place. He's a fleet admiral for the North Korean Western Fleet, and he's been my mentor for as long as I can remember."

"Do you like being an intelligence agent?"

"I like the cybersecurity part, but I hated spying on our citizens."

"What are your future plans, Kim?"

"Finish school, and find a way to get my family out of Nampo."

"What about you? Do you think you'll go back to North Korea?"

"It's my country. I hate our government, but it could be a great place to live, if . . ."

"You said you can't defect to China, but what about another country, like America?"

"It would be difficult to get there and even if I could, I'm not sure they'd accept me."

"I think they would," Cai said. "With your knowledge of North Korea and its military, you'd be highly valued. We should go there together. I have relatives in New York."

Kim and Cai fell asleep in each other's arms and awoke in the same position the next morning. Cai kissed Kim, and said, "Let's call for breakfast and then shower."

"Sure. What do you want?"

"How about an American-style breakfast with eggs, bacon, hash browns, toast, orange juice, and coffee. It'll prepare us for our future trip to New York."

"Sounds like a great idea."

After eating breakfast and enjoying another long and sensuous shower, they got dressed and took the elevator to the lobby. Kim asked the front desk to call them a taxi and if there were any charges.

"No, sir, everything was paid for."

"Can I ask who paid for all of this?"

"I can't tell you that, sir. He wants to be anonymous."

"Here's three hundred yuan, can you tell me now?" Kim whispered.

"Wait here, I'll be right back," the clerk said, as he grabbed the money and quickly put it in his pocket. When he returned, he handed Kim a business card with the name Sean Flaherty, Esq., of Fisher and McGowan in New York City.

Kim went over to Cai, passed the card to her, and whispered, "It looks like our benefactor might be an American working in the same city as your relatives."

"New York is a huge city, and none of my relatives are named Flaherty, Fisher, or McGowan."

The taxi finally arrived. She was dropped off first, since her address was closer to the hotel.

"You live in a nice neighborhood, Cai. Do you live alone?"

"No, I have a roommate. Her name is Mei. I have to go, Kim. I'll see you in class."

Cai gave Kim a kiss and then quickly ran into her apartment building, which Kim found curious.

Kim arrived at his apartment at around noon and changed into his normal weekend clothes of blue jeans and an HIT sweatshirt. At one, the North Korean security officers arrived.

"Come in and please introduce yourselves and show me your credentials."

"I'm Lieutenant Park and this is Ensign Park. Here are our credentials."

Kim looked at their identification cards. "The both of you look very much alike. Are you related?"

"Yes, sir, we're brothers."

"From now on, neither you nor I will refer to each other by military rank, is that clear?"

"Yes, sir," both agents said simultaneously.

Kim shook his head. "No, you can't acknowledge my rank in any way. That means you can't call me 'sir.' No one is to know that I'm an officer in the KPN."

"Should we just call you Kim?" Lieutenant Park asked.

"Yes, that's fine. I have someone in my class at HIT that I want you to follow. Report back on everywhere he goes and who he meets. One of you already met him at HIT, so make sure you aren't seen. He's smart and he drives a Mercedes-Benz, so you'll need a car to follow him. His name is Shen Wei."

"We can get a car."

"This individual is from a very prominent Chinese family, so don't harm him in any way and don't get caught. Is that clear?"

"Very clear."

"Good. Report back to me immediately on anything you find out. Make sure you have a good digital camera to take pictures so you can email them to me. Don't send the pictures to anyone else until after I've reviewed them. I need to determine if they're just his friends or someone we need to take a closer look at."

"Will you come along too?"

"No, he knows me too well. I'm in his class at HIT, and he'd get suspicious if he saw me tracking him. I also have to go to school, and if I started missing class it would look suspicious."

"We understand. We'll start immediately."

"Good. Keep me informed."

After they left, Kim called Cai on her cell phone.

"Hi, it's Kim. Are you okay? You ran into your building after we said goodbye. Were you sick?"

"I'm fine, Kim. But my roommate is dating someone I detest. I try to avoid him since he's very crude."

"What's he done?"

"He asks if I'd want to have a threesome with him and my roommate. He also takes advantage of Mei by constantly borrowing money. He's even tried to borrow money from me."

"Is he a student?"

"No, I think he washes dishes at a local restaurant."

"Has he threatened you or Mei in any way?"

"Not yet, but I'm thinking of moving out."

"I can talk with him, if you like."

"No, you could get in trouble. Maybe we could find a place together if things get really bad."

Kim knew his superiors would never allow that.

"Yes, maybe we could. What's his name?"

"My roommate calls him Woo Lei, but I'm not sure that's his real name."

"Thanks. I'll see you in class tomorrow. I love you, Cai."

"I love you, too, Kim."

# 9

When James got to his office the morning after his meeting at VSI, he immediately drafted a letter to the president and then called Barbara Chang.

"Hi, Barbara, do you have a minute?"

"Actually, I have more than a minute. The president's over at the Hill meeting with some senators about the majority leader's death. What do you need?"

"As you know, I was hoping to talk to the president at yesterday's meeting about a possible short leave of absence. Unfortunately, the death of the majority leader delayed that, which I entirely understand. My situation has changed since then. I'm couriering a letter to you requesting an indefinite leave of absence so that you can give it to the president."

James didn't hear anything and he thought he'd lost the connection.

"Barbara, are you still there?"

"Yes, James. What has changed that would require an indefinite leave of absence?"

"I had a meeting with the VSI senior management after our meeting yesterday, and I was informed of some corporate problems that are very serious and need to be addressed. After thinking about it last night, I've decided that these problems will require more of my time than I originally thought."

"This is a very bad time for you to be gone, James. I hate to put it this way, but with the senator's death, the roadblock preventing the passage of the foreign cyber-attack bill has been removed. You had more to do with defining the requirements for that bill than anyone else."

"I appreciate that, but VSI needs me now that Philip is gone. I didn't realize how much, until yesterday."

"Okay, James, I'll get the letter to the president. When do you think you'll be leaving?"

"I need to tie up some loose ends and brief my staff so they can take over. Maybe two weeks."

"That soon. Okay, can we at least call on you if something comes up?"

"I'd be upset if you didn't. I won't be that far away."

"Well, that's good."

"Give the president my regards."

"Will do."

James then called Shelly Brockner.

"Good morning, Director. I'd like to meet with you this afternoon to discuss some news that relates to my partner's murder."

"Sure, James, how about one thirty at my office? I'd like to have Special Agent Tanner there."

"Great. I'm looking forward to meeting him."

James quickly checked his favorite news sources from his laptop to see if there was any more news about the majority leader's death. The big story of the day was the DC medical examiner stating that her office needed at least a week or two to complete their examination. This was questioned by many of the political reporters, who claimed that examinations of most deaths by natural causes are completed in a few days. James wondered how long it would take if the causes weren't so natural.

After looking at a few more news articles about Senator Thompson's death, James pulled up the latest version of the senator's foreign cyber-attack bill on his laptop. He began marking the areas of the bill that would need to be removed or changed for it to look more like the house bill. At one p.m. he called for a car to take him to the Hoover Building for his meeting with Director Brockner.

During his drive, James noticed two texts from Tom Allen asking him to call. That was unusual, since Tom rarely contacted James after he'd left VSI. Tom had developed a special bond with James, who hired him from Caltech. While Philip used Christopher as his right hand, James had relied on Tom, who had proved himself as a brilliant design engineer. He thought Tom felt betrayed when he left VSI to become Federal CIO. James was happy to see Tom reaching out to him again and immediately called him.

"Hi, boss," Tom said. "I texted you because I found some information that could help identify the military officers Philip met with. The car they were in was in a fender bender on the way to the meeting. Their SUV got rear-ended while stopping at a light near the Lexington Park sign as you enter town. The guard at our front desk remembered what time they arrived and that the driver was pissed at how long it took the state police to respond to the accident. Apparently the brass in the car were very upset that they might be late for the meeting. I looked up the date that the Ravens played the Redskins, and I can estimate the time of the accident from what the driver said to the guard."

"How does that help us determine who they are?"

"The driver would have had to file an accident report with his guys at Fort Meade. If we can get the information on the accident that day, we could probably get the license and registration for the car as well. The accident report should also identify the driver and the passengers."

"Thanks, Tom. Please email me the information."

*That was a start,* thought James as he entered the Hoover Building. He checked in through security and was met by Special Agent Rick Tanner. James expected a SEAL to be built like most swimmers he knew, tall and lanky. Instead, Rick was built like a fullback, standing no more than six feet with a barrel chest, broad shoulders, and huge biceps that almost bulged through his suit jacket.

"Great to finally meet you, Mr. Jordan. I assume you got the message I left on your home phone."

"I did. Please call me James."

The director was waiting for them when they walked into her outer office.

"Please come in, James," she said. "I'd like to ask you if you could help Rick with the investigation of your partner's death. I hope you don't mind."

"Not at all, I was actually going to ask you if I could assist the FBI in your investigation. He should know everything I know if we're going to work together."

"I agree, and I think you'll find Rick to be one of the best young agents we have at the FBI. He's also very computer literate. Rick graduated from the Naval Postgraduate School with a master's degree in Cyber Systems and Operations, with a specialization in cybersecurity."

"Better be careful, Director. Some IT company like VSI might try to hire him," James laughed.

Neither Shelly nor Rick laughed. James quickly got down to business.

"Has there been any progress on Philip's case?"

"You know that we found the SUV tracks we were looking for near Philip Wu's home, right?" asked Shelly.

"Yes, Rick left me a message to that effect. But can you be absolutely sure it was the murderer's vehicle?"

"Nothing is ever absolute in this business," Rick said, jumping in. "It's clear that the tracks start outside the protected community where your partner lived and led directly to his house. The same is true for the tracks from the house to the main road that adjoins the community. I'd say that someone was definitely seeking a specific house and was probably using a GPS to get in and out."

"Have you found the agency where the vehicle may have been rented?"

"Not yet, but we did get some video from a security camera near the marina that recorded the deceased assailant driving Mr. Wu's Jaguar. We also found another video taken a few hours later of a black Ford Escape leaving the marina parking lot. That fits the approximate time of the Chinese assailant's murder. We have a picture of the license plates, but unfortunately they trace back to plates that were stolen from a 98 Buick in Brooklyn several months ago."

"Can you identify the driver of the Ford from the video?"

"Not really. The driver had his head to the left and was looking down as if he was trying to avoid the camera."

"Do you plan to release any information to the public?"

"No, we don't want to alert the suspect, and we don't have sufficient information for an ID."

"Do you have anything you can add, James? It seemed like you wanted to discuss something when you called my office earlier to set up this meeting."

"Yes, I do, Director. I had a meeting with some of the senior management at VSI yesterday, and I learned some interesting things."

James described the strange circumstances surrounding the cyber attacks on the VSI networks and the meeting between Philip and the military officers. He included the information Tom had told him earlier about the car accident.

"We know the date, time, and location of the accident. Couldn't the FBI request the information from NSA on who was involved?"

Shelly looked at him sternly. "I probably could, but I'd need a damn good reason. Have you got one I can borrow? I haven't heard anything so far that comes close. The cyber attacks on VSI are suspicious, and our Cyber Division could've investigated them. But it was over a year ago, so that trail is cold. The meeting at VSI may look suspicious to you, but it could easily be explained by security requirements for a highly classified project that we know Mr. Wu was working on."

"There must be something the FBI can do," James said, hopefully.

"I have something," Rick said. "If the accident was reported by the police, I might have a way to identify the driver and the vehicle. That could lead us to the passengers. All I need to know is who took the accident report."

James interrupted. "Tom Allen told me it was the Maryland State Police who were at the scene and took the report."

"Then they'd have a copy of the official accident report. They'd keep it on file for at least as long as the statute of limitations remains in effect, and maybe longer."

"That's fine, Rick, but how would you obtain the report?" asked Shelly.

"I worked with the Maryland State Police on the Wu murder, Director. They really appreciated the fact that I didn't release the information to the press on the crime scene and the SUV. It would've shown that they were wrong about their analysis. Their lead investigator, Captain Drew Michaelson, thanked me and said he owed me one. It's time to collect."

"Okay, Rick, you can run with it. But if it looks like it could rebound on us, cut it loose as fast as you can. I don't need any more headaches than I already have."

Just as she said that, Shelly's secretary buzzed her and said that her next meeting had arrived and was waiting. Shelly escorted Rick and James out the door and greeted her next visitor. James was surprised when he recognized her as the DC medical examiner.

As they left the director's office, Rick turned to James and said, "I'd like you to work with me on this, James. We need to put together a strategy."

"Okay, I'll talk to Tom and get the information on the exact date and time that the meeting at VSI took place and the location where the accident occurred."

"Good. I'll contact Captain Michaelson to see if he can provide us with a copy of the accident report, which should have everyone's names. I have friends who can tell us who they are and what they do. Can you get me the information that I need by later this afternoon?"

"I might be able to get it right now, Rick. Let me check my email to see if Tom sent it. Yeah, here it is. I'll forward it to your email account."

"Thanks. Do you mind if I call you later if I find out anything?"

"You'd better call me on my personal cell phone since I'm not certain I'll be home." James handed Rick a card. "The card has all my numbers and email accounts."

As James drove back to his office, he turned on the news and heard that the DC mayor was going to hold a short press conference to address questions surrounding the delay in the DC medical examiner's report on Senator Thompson. It was scheduled for seven that evening, and the medical examiner would be there to address all pertinent medical questions.

James thought the medical examiner must've found something unusual for her to schedule a press conference. He also found it intriguing that Philip and the senator had died within five days of each other. James doubted that Philip really knew the senator, but he did wonder if they'd ever met.

When James got back to his office, he immediately called Ann Wu.

"Hi, Ann, how are you doing?"

"I'm okay. What are you up to?"

"I'm working with the FBI on Philip's case. Did he ever meet Senator Thompson?"

"Yes, I believe he met the senator when he toured Cyber Command at Fort Meade last summer."

"Do you know who Philip worked with or reported to on the project he was working on at Fort Meade?"

"I don't, James. Philip would never talk about the project or anyone he worked with. At first I thought it was because of security, but I think he really hated working there. It was like he was in prison and couldn't wait to escape."

"Do you remember anything that he and the senator had in common?"

"Nothing, other than they both knew George. The senator told

Philip that George was a Russian SOB, and that VSI shouldn't trust him with any corporate secrets. Philip wasn't surprised about him calling George an SOB, but he didn't know George was Russian. Why are you asking this now?"

"It's probably nothing, but if it becomes something, I'll let you know."

"Goodbye, James. Keep in touch."

James didn't know George was Russian or if it was relevant to the investigation. The fact that both Philip and Senator Thompson knew George wasn't particularly surprising, but he was concerned about the accusation from the senator that George might be compromising VSI technology.

James was wondering how George could possibly compromise VSI's technology when he had no access to it. His thoughts about that were interrupted when he got a call from Rick Tanner.

"Hi, James. It looks like our plan is working. Captain Michaelson talked to the two state troopers who were at the scene of the accident. They remember the one officer as being a navy captain who was tall, thin, and had wavy gray hair. The other officer never got out of the car, so they didn't have a good description of him."

"Do they have their identities?"

"It's on the accident report. Captain Michaelson said he'd fax it tomorrow morning."

"That's great work. Call me tomorrow after you get the fax."

"Will do, James. Goodnight."

When James got back to JoAnn's house, he was exhausted and hungry. She gave him a big kiss and walked him into the dining room where she had place settings for two. There was also candlelight and his favorite dish, chicken marsala with garlic, ginger, and peppers.

"Thanks, baby. My favorite dish, made by my favorite dish," he joked.

"I can always tell when you're tired, James. You start making those corny jokes. Let's eat and have some wine and go to bed."

"I can't. I need to watch a press conference, and if I drink any wine, I won't make it."

"This will be your last home cooked meal until I get back from my trip to Minnesota, so let's enjoy it."

"I'm sorry, baby, I forgot you had those constituent soirées this weekend. What's the subject this time?"

"Nothing important. Just the impact your foreign cyber-attack legislation will have on world peace."

"I may have drafted the technical parts of the bill, but the current senate bill is nothing like I intended. As a senator, the ball is more in your court than mine."

"From what I'm hearing, the senate bill probably died with the majority leader."

"Then let's have a very small glass of wine to celebrate world peace and see what the medical examiner has to say."

At seven all the local news stations were focused on the mayor's office. The mayor made a short statement on the history of outstanding performance by the office of the chief medical examiner. He then invited Dr. Robinson to the podium.

"As DC medical examiner, this has been one of the most difficult cases I've ever worked on," she said. "My team found no evidence of physical abuse, and there was also no evidence of drug abuse or foreign substances of a toxic nature other than alcohol. I can say that the senator was inebriated at the time of his death. This case was made difficult by the fact that the deceased was diabetic and used insulin by injecting it via an insulin pen, which I have here in my hand."

The medical examiner demonstrated how the pen worked and how the needles were removable. She then said something that James found startling.

"Based on information from the senator's doctor, the needles that were prescribed were four millimeters in length. You can see how short that needle is from the one in my hand. All the needle marks on the deceased's right thigh, where he injected himself, were made by a four-millimeter needle, except for one. The freshest needle mark on the deceased's thigh appears to have been made by a longer needle, probably twelve millimeters in length. When my office checked with the deceased's doctor and his family, they said they weren't aware of him having used such a needle. We also checked his Georgetown residence; and while there were several boxes of four-millimeter needles, we could find no evidence of any twelve-millimeter needles. Although this doesn't constitute proof that there was foul play, I'd have to conclude that further investigation is warranted."

James thought that it was a very skillful and professional performance. It was also clear to him that Dr. Robinson believed that the senator was murdered, even without saying it. He knew that many in the news media would also come to that conclusion. James was glad he didn't have Shelly Brockner's job. She was going to be managing a certain criminal investigation based on Dr. Robinson's findings under some of the most intense scrutiny that any FBI director ever experienced.

As soon as the news conference ended, James's phone rang. He recognized Rick's number.

"Hey, Rick. Anything new?"

Rick laughed. "I guess you could say that. I assume you saw the press conference."

"I did, and I assume it's what your call is about."

"Sort of. Director Brockner called me after I talked to you earlier. She informed me about what the medical examiner was going to say. The director wants yours truly to determine if there's a link between Senator Thompson's suspicious death and your partner's murder. I'm going to need your help, James."

"Okay. I'll see you tomorrow in your office."

James arrived at Rick's office the next morning at ten.

"Good timing, James. I just got a fax from Captain Michaelson.

The passengers in the vehicle were identified as Navy Captain Michael Kinsley and Army Colonel Frank Carpenter, both of whom live near Fort Meade. Apparently the driver of the other vehicle was under the influence, had no auto insurance, and was arrested for those offenses."

"That's great. Now we know their names."

"Yeah, I can use my contacts at the base to find out what organizations they're attached to, and possibly more."

"How do you have contacts at Fort Meade?"

"Many of my missions as a SEAL were highly classified covert operations that involved support from intelligence personnel at NSA. Their support saved a lot of lives, including mine. After I left the SEALs, I was reassigned to NSA. That's how I got involved in cybersecurity. In fact, my supervisor at NSA was the one who sponsored me for the Naval Postgraduate School."

"Great. Is there anyone still there that you know and is high enough in the chain of command to be helpful?"

"You might say that. There's a navy admiral who knows just about everything that goes on at the fort. We have a meeting with him at noon at the Fort Meade officer's club. We'd better leave now in case we hit traffic. He doesn't like people wasting his time."

Rick drove his Mustang GT. They got there with twenty minutes to spare, which they needed to get through security.

"How's the food at this club, Rick?"

"I don't know, I haven't been here in almost three years, and it really isn't an officer's club anymore. All ranks are allowed in, as well as civilians."

As they walked through the door, Rick pointed to an older man in uniform sitting in a booth and waving.

"Good to see you, Rick. Where'd you find this rascal?"

"This is James Jordan, sir."

"Yes, I know. How've you been, James? It's been a few years."

"About fifteen to be exact, Admiral. The last time was in your class on naval history and tactics at the academy."

Rick stared at James with a confused look.

"I didn't know you went to the naval academy."

"It's worse than that, Rick. I also spent two summers right here working with NSA before graduating and three more years after that as a naval officer."

"Gentlemen, you can swap war stories later," the admiral said. "Tell me what this is all about, and since we know each other, just call me Paul."

"Okay, Paul. There were two officers from Fort Meade who were at a meeting at VSI in Lexington Park more than a year ago. James is the former CEO of the company."

"Yes, I know. I've been following his career. Might even ask him for a job after I retire."

"I hope you do, Paul. I'm sure VSI could use you. Right now we need to know if you can tell us anything about the officers who attended the meeting."

"What're their names?"

"Navy Captain Michael Kinsley, and Army Colonel Frank King."

"Real spooks, in every sense of the word. Captain Kinsley is a zealot and a hothead who I had to reprimand more than once. He cuts corners and goes around regulations any chance he gets. The captain has gone as high as he'll go in this man's navy, and he knows it, so he isn't worried about his image or future promotions."

"Can you tell me what organization Captain Kinsley is attached to on the base, sir?"

"He's assigned to Cyber Command on a special project that's highly classified. Rumor has it the project concerns advanced malware."

"What about the colonel, sir?"

"Since he isn't navy, I don't know that much about him. He seems to be a highly respected officer who has a master's degree from MIT in math, I think. I met him once. He's very quiet and kind of a nerd. But unlike Kinsley, he's not a head case."

"Do they work together?"

"Almost certainly. I see them together a lot, and I know they're not gay, or at least Kinsley isn't. Can I ask why the FBI is involved with investigating two military officers?"

"The FBI isn't really investigating them for any specific offense, sir," Rick said. "We think they may be involved with some strange circumstances involving cyber attacks at VSI. I got involved after the murder of Philip Wu. I'm sure you heard about it on the news. James was Philip Wu's best friend and partner."

"I did hear about the murder. But as much as I dislike Captain Kinsley, I believe murder is a little out of his league, Rick."

"We do too, sir. James and I are just going down every path. The FBI director believes Mr. Wu's death could have national security implications."

"Okay, gentlemen. Please keep me in the loop on this and let me know if there's anything I can do to help."

"There is something, Admiral. I'd like to have your permission to interview them on their relationship with Philip Wu."

"I can't help you with the colonel, Rick. He's outside my chain of command, but I can order Captain Kinsley to cooperate. I'd like to talk with him first. When and where would you like to meet him?"

"Anytime within the next few days at FBI headquarters. Just tell him we're interviewing people who knew Philip Wu as part of the murder investigation."

"No problem, Rick, but you should know that he's an arrogant SOB. If he feels threatened, he'll try to intimidate you."

"I don't think that'll be a problem," Rick said with a smile.

"No, I guess not. Just don't rough him up too much."

"Yes, sir, and thanks for your help, Admiral."

"You're both welcome. Now let's get something to eat. I'm starving."

While driving back to DC, Rick and James discussed how they'd interview the captain.

"We shouldn't let the captain know that you have any connection with VSI," Rick said. "That might make him suspicious and totally defensive."

"I can't guarantee he hasn't heard my name during his meetings with Philip. Maybe I shouldn't be there at all."

"No, I need your insight about VSI and Philip if this is to work. I have an idea. We can do the investigation in an interrogation room with a one-way mirror. They have those facilities at the Hoover Building for interrogations that are witnessed by undercover agents or confidential informants. I'll do the interrogation and ask a set of questions pertinent to the case. I'd also like you to put together some questions you think I should ask based on your knowledge of VSI and your partner. You'll be able to prompt me through my earpiece."

"How long will that take to set up?"

"I'm not sure. I'll contact technical support when I get back to arrange everything we need. After Kinsley starts talking about your partner, you can tell me if you think he's lying."

"I like it. Just hope it works."

"Yeah, me too. So James, why didn't you tell me you were an Annapolis grad?"

"Didn't think it was important. It has no relevance to what we're working on."

"Why'd you leave the navy?"

"After graduation from the academy, I was assigned to NSA to work on a special project. It was based on a cybersecurity paper I had written during my second year at the academy. It was also the basis of the work I did with NSA while at the academy."

"Must've been a pretty good paper to get NSA's interest. What was it about?"

"It described how a network worm could be used to disable military weapon systems, including US Navy systems. The navy didn't allow its publication and classified it as top secret."

"It isn't anymore. There have been lots of articles on the internet about that subject in the last couple of years."

"Yes, but this paper was written almost fifteen years ago, and it went into detail about possible attacks on US Navy systems."

"I see. It certainly explains NSA's interest."

"Yes, as well as other high-level government research organizations."

"Looks like it made you a naval celebrity. So what's the problem?"

"It ruined my naval career."

"How?"

"I wrote the paper as an incentive to develop defenses against the coming threat. Instead, they were only interested in building cyber weapons based on my idea. Then maybe a defense, if they had the funding. If it wasn't for the accident, I would have spent my entire five-year naval commitment on that project."

"What accident?"

"Do you remember that 688 fast attack boat that crashed into the bottom and killed several sailors while seriously injuring forty more?"

"Yeah, that was more than ten years ago."

"I was on that boat. We were testing the effectiveness of one of the network worms we developed against the sub's fire-control system. It disabled the fire-control system, but it unexpectedly also disabled the dive-control system. I was one of the injured, and it cost me multiple broken bones and six months in a body cast."

"That got you out?"

"It did, after I brought my boss into it."

"Your boss? Who was that?"

"Now, he's the president. But back then he was Congressman Joseph Meredith, a senior member of the military appropriations committee. He was the one who nominated me for the academy."

"I see. So what went wrong with the worm?"

"The exact details are still classified. However, I can say that the worm was designed to attack and disable a specific type of data-processing component based on its software. I was told that the target data-processing component only existed in the sub's fire-control system. Unfortunately, a recent upgrade to the dive-control system had added that same component and software. The worm caused that system to also be disabled, which caused the sub to hit the ocean floor at flank speed. The cause of the accident was found by the navy review board to be a mistake in the information we were given. After that I decided to never work on weaponized malware again."

When they got back to the Hoover Building, Rick saw an email from Admiral Mancini that also copied Captain Kinsley.

"Looks like Captain Kinsley has agreed to be available anytime tomorrow. Does tomorrow afternoon at one work for you, James?"

"That's fine."

"Great. I'll let them know. Now all I need to do is meet with the technical support folks to get everything set up."

Rick called technical support, and James could see he was upset after he got off the phone.

"What's wrong, Rick?"

"They said that interrogation rooms and monitoring systems require twenty-four-hour notice."

"Did you tell them how important it is?"

"I did, but they didn't care. Maybe they'll care after I tell the director."

Rick called Director Brockner, and after she interceded, Rick was informed that he'd have everything he needed for the scheduled interrogation.

"I'm going home to prepare my questions for Kinsley. I'll see you tomorrow, Rick."

James put his questions together and sent them to Rick in an email. He was exhausted and fell into a deep sleep. The next morning, he was awakened by a call from Rick.

"Hi, sleeping beauty. Are you still coming to the meeting?"

"I guess I overslept. Did you see my email?"

"I did, and I think it's a good idea to eliminate him as a murder suspect at the beginning of the meeting so that he relaxes when we get to the tough stuff."

"Great. I should be there by eleven thirty."

When James got to Rick's office, two techies were fitting Rick with a hidden earbud. It was linked to a wireless transmitter that James could use on the other side of the one-way glass.

Kinsley got to the office for the meeting shortly before one and was taken into the interrogation room where Rick was waiting. James sat in a darkened room on the other side of the one-way glass.

"Good afternoon, Captain," Rick began. "I'm going to ask a series of questions. Please answer with a yes or no, but you can elaborate if you want. Okay, first question. Did you know Philip Wu?"

"Yes. I was very sad to hear of his death."

"Were you involved in any way with his murder?"

"No. I was attending a retirement party at the Naval Academy Officer's Club with at least one hundred other guests when it took place."

"Did you attend a meeting at VSI headquarters with Philip Wu?"

"Yes."

"Did you request Philip Wu to approve the sale of VSI technology to the US government?"

"Yes, but he refused."

"Did you request Philip Wu to work as a consultant for the US government?"

"Yes. He refused."

"Did Philip Wu later consult with Cyber Command and NSA on the development of advanced malware?"

"Yes, he did."

"Did you or anyone else in the US government coerce Philip Wu into providing VSI product information to the government?"

"No."

James communicated with Rick from behind the glass and asked him to present the questions he'd emailed.

"Is VSI technology currently being used by the government?"

"No," Kinsley said, as he removed his glasses.

"Was Philip Wu coerced into working on the development of advanced malware?"

Kinsley looked down. "No," he answered.

"Was Philip Wu coerced by anyone at NSA into developing such malware?"

"No," Kinsley said, after some hesitation.

"Have you ever taken any action to coerce Philip Wu into developing malware for the government?"

Kinsley shifted in his chair and said, "No, I did not."

"Okay, Captain, we're done. You can go."

Kinsley got up and quickly walked out without saying a word. James came out from the room and said, "I think you really shook him up on that second set of questions. It was obvious from his body language that he was lying—too bad we don't have any tangible proof."

"Actually, we do."

Rick removed a small black box from underneath the conference room table.

"What's that?"

"It's a wireless polygraph. It recorded Kinsley's pertinent physiological indices used to detect lies, such as respiration, heart rate, blood pressure, and vocal patterns. Some of the sensors are in this box. Others, such as hidden thermal and optical cameras and microphones, are built into the walls of the interrogation room. They connect to the black box via Bluetooth."

"Why didn't you tell me about this yesterday?"

"Because I only found out about it this morning when the technical support guys set it up. It's a gift to make up for their poor response yesterday and to soothe the director. It should provide a complete report of the interrogation in about thirty minutes. All I need to do is get them to pick it up and analyze the recorded data."

Rick called technical support and two technicians removed the black box. Fifty minutes later, a single agent showed up with three hard copies of the report and a DVD.

"How accurate is the polygraph?" James asked the agent.

"It's generally been more accurate than wired polygraphs, because the subject doesn't know they're being tested. This prevents them from trying to trick the machine. We tried to keep the technology secret, but unfortunately the internet and websites like YouTube have prevented that. It's still experimental, and like other polygraphs, the results aren't admissible as evidence."

The agent went through the report and provided a summary of the results.

"The subject was being truthful when he answered the first seven questions. He wasn't truthful about whether technology developed by VSI is being used by the government. The subject also wasn't truthful on all of the remaining questions, except the question on whether the captain knew if Philip Wu had been coerced by anyone at NSA into developing malware. He may not have been lying, but he seemed uncertain of his answer."

"Well, this shows Kinsley did lie about whether he personally coerced Philip into developing malware for the government."

"Yes, Rick, but we don't know how he was coerced. There are also some answers that don't make sense. Kinsley truthfully answered 'no' to the question on whether Philip was coerced into providing information on VSI products to the government. However, the polygraph also said Kinsley lied when he denied that technology developed by VSI is currently being used by the government. That would mean VSI technology is being used by the government, but Philip wasn't coerced into providing it. Philip wouldn't do that unless he was coerced."

"There's another possibility, James. The information could've been provided by another source."

"I have no idea who or what that would be. The technology being used in our products is locked away in an off-line storage system. Only Philip and I had access to that information, given that we developed it together."

"Maybe we should visit the crime scene at your partner's house to see if the investigators missed something."

"Yeah, but we need to bring Ann and Jim Wu. They know the house better than we do. I believe we're missing some information and I believe Philip would've left behind some clues. We just need to find them."

# 10

Dimitri was at a bar in Brighton Beach when the news conference about Senator Thompson's autopsy came on the TV.

"Put the Knicks game on," said Gustav, a well-known neighborhood bully. He was big and burly with tattoos all over his body.

"Don't change it," Dimitri said. "I want to see the news conference."

"Sure, Dimitri, whatever you say," the bartender responded.

Gustav grabbed the bartender and lifted him off the ground so they were face-to-face.

"I said I want to watch the Knicks game. I suggest you listen to me and not pretty boy over there. Is there anything you'd like to say to me, pretty boy?"

Dimitri probably seemed to be an easy target, since his boyish face and tall but slight stature didn't appear to be very menacing. That was an error that many adversaries had committed in the past, to their regret.

"Let him go," Dimitri ordered. "I asked him for the news."

The bully released the bartender and walked to where Dimitri was sitting. He put his large hand on Dimitri's shoulder, and looked down at him.

"Look, asshole, I've got money on that game. I suggest you leave before you're carried out."

Dimitri stood up and said, "You can watch the game after the news conference is over."

The man took a swing as Dimitri moved quickly under the punch while wrapping his arm around the man's neck from behind. The bully struggled to get free, but Dimitri held him tight and increased the pressure. He finally lost consciousness and Dimitri gently dropped him to the floor.

Everyone in the bar stared at Dimitri, talking quietly about the incident and how Dimitri disabled Gustav so quickly. All, that is, except the owner of the bar, a longtime friend of Dimitri. He was a *pakhan* or "godfather" in the Russian Bratva, the brotherhood that outsiders often called the Russian Mafia.

"Dimitri, let me buy you some good Russian vodka while my employees remove this piece of shit," Marat Chubais said. Marat had been a friend of Dimitri's father in Russia before the Chechen mafia killed him when Dimitri was only seven. Dimitri and Marat had served together during the fight against the Chechens, and both had emigrated to the US after the war ended. The pakhan was a stocky man with huge hands that had killed many Chechens back in Russia.

"How are you, Pakhan, and how's your family?"

"They're all doing well. I just need to find husbands for my daughters so I can have some peace in my house. By the way, my oldest daughter, Anya, is still unmarried. You two were close once."

"That was a long time ago. How's Anya doing?"

"She finished up her residency at Stony Brook Hospital and is now a practicing surgeon. She still comes home to visit at least twice a month. I'll invite you for dinner next time she's in town."

"Thanks, but I'm sure as beautiful and smart as she is, she could do much better than me."

"Nonsense. You could've been a great doctor if it hadn't been for the Chechens. She was devastated when you left medical school to fight them."

"I didn't have much choice after what happened to my family, Pakhan."

"I know. I loved your mother and your sister as I loved my family. Their deaths and the deaths of my sons were avenged many times over by the Bratva during the war, but that's over now."

"Pakhan, I was wondering if you could answer a question for me. Have you ever heard of anyone associated with the Bratva nicknamed the Big Man?"

"I've never heard that name, but I'll see if anyone else has."

Dimitri nodded as he picked up his glass of vodka and said, "*Na sdarovie*, my dear friend," and drank the entire glass. He then slapped the pakhan on the back and said, "*Do svidaniya*," as he walked out of the bar.

When Dimitri got back to his house, the news conference had finished, but the controversy created by the autopsy results was all over the news. He was disappointed that he'd used the wrong needle, but there was no way to do anything about it now. There was nothing in the senator's medical records that identified the needle he used, only the medication. It was really the fault of the Big Man and his contacts. They had provided the needles.

Although Dimitri knew he couldn't have anticipated this problem, he'd allowed for the possibility of a mistake by creating a diversion toward the Chinese embassy. There was no mention by the press of the business cards being found, but he was certain they must've been.

Dimitri needed to know whether the diversion worked before he could feel comfortable. He knew the best way to do that was to check it himself. That required surveillance of the Chinese intelligence agent whose identity he placed in the crosshairs. Dimitri contacted a representative of the Big Man by email to request a meeting. The response set it up for nine the next morning.

After being escorted to the conference room, one of the Big Man's representatives asked him what he needed.

"I need to determine if the Chinese intelligence agent is being investigated for the senator's murder."

"We have no way of knowing that, Mr. Vasin. Trying to find a contact in the federal government right now, given the nature of the case, would be much too dangerous. It could draw suspicion instead of diverting it."

"I know that. I plan to monitor the agent myself. I'm going to DC tonight to determine if he's being questioned by the police or federal agents."

"I need to contact the Big Man to see if that's acceptable."

"Okay, I'll wait."

The man came back in thirty minutes.

"It's okay, as long as no overt action is taken against anyone and the surveillance is covert so you can't be observed. We also want someone to assist you on this."

"Why? I can handle it."

"The target was very high profile and the job didn't go exactly as planned. We realize that our choice of needles was a mistake, and we also sense your frustration about that. The Big Man just wants to make sure your frustration doesn't cause you to be careless."

"I'm never careless, but if that's what the Big Man wants, then so be it. Where will I meet my assistant?"

"Her name's Irina and she'll meet you at your hotel. Email us your itinerary."

"Fine, but I'll need a GPS tracker to perform the surveillance. Please leave it in the storage locker in Arlington. I also need the address where the Chinese agent resides, the type of car he drives, and the license plate number."

"You'll have everything, including an encrypted email with the information you requested and your travel arrangements. Good day, Mr. Vasin."

After arriving in Arlington and picking up his car and requested equipment, Dimitri drove to his hotel. While checking in, he saw an alert on the TV describing breaking news about the senator's death. He went to his room, turned on the TV to the same news station, and waited.

A breaking-news banner suddenly appeared on the TV and a reporter made an enthusiastic reference to a "reliable rumor" that the DC police had identified a foreigner as a potential suspect. The reporter also included a statement from the DC police chief denying it. Dimitri knew he would need to be careful during his surveillance of the Chinese agent. It wouldn't be good if he was detected by the police following the prime suspect.

The next morning, Dimitri unpacked the tiny GPS tracker while waiting for his assigned assistant. The thought of having to work with an assistant—or rather, a spy, as he viewed it—made him angrier the longer he waited. He inspected the tracker to relieve his tension.

Dimitri was familiar with the technology, having used it during previous assignments. This one was much smaller and it had a magnetic base so it could be attached to a car. He was very impressed when he saw it also had a remote self-destruct capability.

He began syncing the tracker to his cell phone, when he was interrupted by a knock on his door. He opened the door and was greeted by an extremely attractive young woman.

"Hello, Dimitri, I'm Irina. The Big Man sent me. Can I come in?"

Dimitri pulled her in the room and looked up and down the hall to make sure she had not been seen.

"Did anyone ride up the elevator with you?"

"No, I ran up the stairs."

"All fifteen floors?"

"Yes, I wanted to make sure no one was following."

Dimitri smiled. "Well, I guess you're in good shape. Where are you staying?"

"At the Marriott in Crystal City. I got in last night. What's your plan for today?"

"First, show me some ID."

Irina took out her driver's license and handed it to Dimitri, who laughed. "Your last name is Putin?"

"I'm not related to the Russian president, if that's what you're thinking."

"No, I was laughing because Putin is my parrot's name. Okay, what do you know about the assignment?"

"Only that we're to determine if the authorities have identified a Chinese diplomat named Zhou Ming as a suspect in the possible murder of the senate majority leader."

"Good. I have the address for Ming's residence. Do you have a car?"

"Yes, it's in the garage."

"Okay, you drive. I need to finish syncing this GPS tracker to my phone."

Irina and Dimitri drove to Zhou Ming's residence. It was an upscale apartment building in Georgetown that had been converted into residences for the Chinese diplomatic staff.

"Park near the residence parking area," Dimitri ordered.

Irina found a place to park on the street, and Dimitri exited to find Ming's car. He was back in fifteen minutes.

"Did you have problems with the tracker?" Irina asked.

"No, I had a problem finding the car. Seems like the Chinese like the car model and color that Ming drives."

"How does the tracker work?" Irina asked.

"You just install the tracker where it can't be seen, like the inside of a fender, and turn it on with the cell phone app. It tracks the target car's location and speed and transmits the information to my cell phone."

Dimitri showed Irina the app on his phone.

"Your app show's that his car is moving," Irina said.

"Yeah, I see that. Looks like we got here just in time. It's that blue Lincoln that just pulled out of the parking lot exit. Don't get too close."

They followed Zhou Ming over the Key Bridge and into northern

Virginia. Twenty minutes later they arrived at a mall near Tysons Corner and parked close enough to the Lincoln to watch while not being seen.

"He's just sitting there," Irina said.

"No, I think he's talking to someone on his phone."

"You can see that from here?" Irina asked, obviously impressed.

"Yes, good eyesight is an occupational requirement. He's getting out of the car. I'll follow him, you stay here."

"No, Dimitri. I was ordered to stay with you."

"Okay, Irina, try to keep up," Dimitri said with a smirk.

Irina smiled and said, "No, you try to keep up," as she sprinted past Dimitri.

They closed the distance on Ming, and observed him entering a coffee shop. The both of them followed him in, acting like a couple.

"Get us some coffee, Irina. I'll find a table."

Dimitri watched as Ming bought a coffee and sat at a nearby table. Irina returned with two coffees and said, "It looks like he's waiting for someone."

"Yeah. Ming's staring at that tall guy in the expensive overcoat who's fixing his coffee at the condiment station. That's interesting, the tall guy just left his newspaper."

"Yes, and Ming just took it," Irina said.

"Looks like a dead drop to me. Ming is definitely a Chinese spy."

"Let's go, Dimitri. We need to follow Ming."

"No, let's follow the tall guy. He went into that men's room over there. We need to find out who he is and if he just gave Ming intelligence information."

"That's not part of our assignment, Dimitri."

"It is for me," Dimitri whispered. "If we can get evidence that Ming is a spy, it could be used to prove that he might also be capable of murder. Besides, we can track Ming on my phone and see everywhere he goes while also following the tall guy."

Dimitri knew his rationale wasn't without merit, but it wasn't the real reason he wanted to identify the tall guy.

"Okay, it's your neck if we blow this," Irina said with a deadly stare.

"I know. This is my op, Irina. I'd take the blame even if it was your idea."

"Okay, okay, let's go. Your tall guy just walked out of the men's room."

Dimitri and Irina got in their car and followed the tall man to a large building with a huge American flag.

"Your GPS says this is a technology park," Irina said.

"Yeah, with all the antennas on the roof and the flag, I'm guessing it's a federal government contractor. I'm taking a picture of the company's name and logo as well as our target's car and license plate and emailing them to New York. They should be able to identify him."

"Great. Let's find Ming before we lose him."

"Don't worry so much. It will age you, Irina. It looks like he went directly back to the embassy after completing his dead drop."

"That's good. I'm hungry. Let's get some lunch."

"Okay, I know a place in Georgetown that's good."

They were five miles from Georgetown when Dimitri saw Ming's car leave the embassy.

"It looks like Ming is heading right toward us and is only a mile away."

"Where's he at?" Irina asked.

"He just stopped. The GPS says it's a restaurant. Looks like we'll be able to get lunch."

"Great. I'm starving."

Ming was giving his order to a waitress as Dimitri and Irina walked into the restaurant. They took a nearby table directly behind him. The same waitress then took their order. After Ming finished his meal, Dimitri noticed that Ming started looking around the room to see if anyone was watching.

"Take out your phone, Irina. I think Ming is about to make his move. We need to record this."

"Okay, let's both record him."

Ming quickly took his billfold from his coat pocket to pay the check along with a thick letter-sized envelope that he deftly stuck to the underside of the table. He then left.

"Did you get that, Irina?"

"Yes, I have photos of everything. What about you?"

"I got several frontals of Ming at the table and then a video of him putting the package under the table. Let's stay and see who's picking it up."

Seconds later a guy wearing army fatigues walked in and moved toward the table Ming was sitting at.

"He looks like a really nervous soldier," Irina said.

"Yeah, I think he's Ming's contact."

Dimitri used his phone to zoom in on the soldier's nametag.

"His nametag reads 'Koenig.' We need to record this," Dimitri said.

Dimitri and Irina recorded Koenig reaching under the table and taking the envelope.

"It looks about the right size for cash," Dimitri said.

"Yes, we've got what we need. Where did Ming go?"

"Here's my phone. You can track him yourself. I need to use the men's room."

Ten minutes later Dimitri returned. "So where's Ming?"

"At his residence."

"Okay, then let's follow Mr. Koenig. It looks like he's leaving."

Dimitri and Irina followed Koenig for about thirty minutes until he entered Fort Belvoir, which Dimitri recorded.

"Well, I guess that's it, Irina. You can take me back to my hotel. I'll even buy you a drink."

Irina smiled and said, "Sounds good to me."

After some dinner and several drinks, Dimitri went with Irina up to his room and downloaded the photos and videos from his phone onto his laptop and encrypted the file.

"I'll provide all these files with the encryption key to you, Irina. I'd also like the pictures you took."

"Sure, Dimitri. I'll show you mine if you show me yours."

"Not tonight, Irina. Business before pleasure. I'll just load your files from your phone onto my laptop, and then I'll send mine to your email."

"No need, just load your files and encryption key on this," Irina said, as she handed him a lipstick with a USB port. "I never go anywhere without it."

The next morning, Dimitri checked his email and saw the response from New York identifying the tall man's license plate from the day before as belonging to an Alexander Buehler. He then picked up Irina at her hotel and drove toward Ming's residence. Suddenly the GPS tracker alarm went off, indicating Ming's car was leaving.

"Where's Ming?" asked Irina.

"He's approaching Georgetown and heading toward us. We should be able to cross the Key Bridge before he gets there. I'll park by that liquor store at the DC end of the bridge and wait for him."

"There's a lot of police cars on the Georgetown side of the bridge, Dimitri. Do you see them?"

"Yeah, it's a roadblock and I believe I know who they're after. Let's get out and watch and take some pictures for the folks back home."

Dimitri and Irina saw Ming's Lincoln stopped on the bridge and watched as the police dragged him out of his car. They both recorded Ming resisting the police and being thrown to the ground and handcuffed while being read his rights. Ming was yelling at the police about being mistreated when he was forced into a police car and taken away.

"Looks like he's on his way to jail," Dimitri said.

"Yeah, and he's definitely not happy about it. We need to get this video to New York."

"Okay, but first I need to destroy the tracker on Ming's car."

Dimitri entered a phone number in his cell phone, and pressed send. The tracker received the call and initiated an exothermic chemical reaction, destroying any evidence.

"Let's go back to your hotel room and send these videos to our friends in New York. I'm sure they'll be interested," Irina said.

"Sure, we can also turn on the news to see what they're reporting about the arrest," Dimitri replied.

Dimitri and Irina returned to his hotel room and turned on the TV. There was no news of the arrest for most of the day until a local station reported that a foreign national had been detained for questioning about the death of Senator Thompson. Dimitri and Irina both smiled and booked flights home for the following morning.

"What're you going to tell them when you get back, Irina?"

"That you were great and had everything under control."

"Thanks. How long have you been working for the Big Man?"

Irina smiled and said, "I don't work for any Big Man, Dimitri. I work for a law firm."

"You're a lawyer?"

"No, a private investigator. I used to work for the feds."

Dimitri smiled. "So did I."

"I know. What would you like to do for the rest of the evening, Dimitri?"

"Whatever you want."

Irina smiled as she took off her clothes and said, "Sounds good to me."

When Dimitri arrived at his house in Brooklyn the next afternoon, he found an envelope under his door with a note written in Russian. It said to come to the bar in Brighton Beach at seven that evening. He entered the bar and as he took a seat, his favorite Russian beer appeared in a large mug in front of him. It was a beer that he couldn't find in the US, but somehow the pakhan was able to import it, probably illegally.

At seven, the pakhan came into the bar and asked Dimitri to follow him to his office. He led him through a back door and then down a creaky, well-hidden stairway under the floor. They entered a large musty room with an expansive oak conference table, expensive leather chairs, and a very well-stocked wet bar. The pakhan poured himself a diet soda and sat down across from Dimitri.

"My doctor said I need to stop drinking to save my liver. So now I'll live longer but I'll be miserable. Such is life."

"Are you okay, Pakhan?"

"Yes, I'm being treated by a very good doctor—my daughter Anya. I followed up on your request to find the Big Man and got some information. It seems that there was an individual who was sent to New York from Moscow as a member of the Russian UN delegation. His family apparently had connections in the Politburo. He quietly defected, requesting political asylum in 1978. The US government obtained important information from him and allowed him to relocate after changing his name and his appearance with minor plastic surgery. His last name was Sokurov, but his code name was the Big Man."

"Is this information reliable?"

"Very reliable. It was provided to me by a close friend who's helped me in the past."

"How can I repay you for your help?"

"You can be at my house this Saturday night for dinner. Anya will be there, and she's really looking forward to seeing you again."

Dimitri hesitated for a second. "Okay, what time do you want me there?"

"I think six would be good. We'll be having some good Russian food cooked by my wife and daughters, so don't be late or it'll all be gone."

Marat laughed, and Dimitri realized there was no way he could get out of this without insulting the pakhan, which was never good.

Dimitri knew someone who could help him identify the Big Man based on the information provided by the pakhan. His name was Frank Green, a friend and colleague from when Dimitri worked for US Intelligence. Frank was a former member of the US Marine Corps Force Recon, a Marine Corps special operations group similar to the Navy SEALs. Dimitri had saved Frank's life in Afghanistan by taking out a group of terrorists who were getting ready to ambush him.

Frank didn't have a published phone number, as that wasn't permitted by his employer. Instead, Frank had given Dimitri his parent's phone number in Quantico, Virginia. Dimitri called the number and a woman answered.

"Hello?"

"Can I speak to Rick Green?"

"Who's calling, please?" a woman asked.

"I'm a friend of Frank Green. We used to work together."

There was a pause and then a gruff voice answered.

"This is Rick Green, what can I do for you?"

"Mr. Green, my name is Dimitri. I used to work with your son and I'm trying to find him."

"Oh, Dimitri, he mentioned you. You're the Russian who saved his ass in Iraq, right?"

"No sir, it was Afghanistan."

"Just needed to be sure. Frank's traveling right now, Dimitri. He should be back in a couple of days. Can he call you?"

Dimitri gave him the number of a burner phone and hung up. He turned on his burner phone and waited. In about thirty minutes, he got a call.

"Is this Stalin?" Stalin was Dimitri's nickname when he worked with the feds.

"How are you, Frank?"

"I'm well, how about you, Stalin?"

"Fine, but I need to meet with you. When are you going to be back in town?"

"Tomorrow afternoon. We could meet at Dulles Airport at the sushi restaurant at one thirty?"

"I'll be there, Frank, looking forward to it."

After he hung up, Dimitri booked a flight from Kennedy to Dulles for the next day.

Dimitri's flight was early, so he went to the restaurant and waited. At the scheduled time, he saw a muscular African-American man whom he recognized instantly as Frank Green. Frank had a big smile on his face and embraced Dimitri.

"How are you, man? Are you getting fat on that cushy job of yours?" Frank asked.

"It's not as cushy as it used to be. I need some help from you to identify my employer, Frank."

"Let's get some sushi first. I just got off a long flight with no food, and I'm starving."

After getting their food, Frank asked what Dimitri needed.

"I've been working for my employer since I left the feds several years ago, Frank, and I still don't know who it is. The pay is great and the workload is a lot less than it was with the feds, but without knowing the person I'm working for, I feel vulnerable."

"So what do you need from me, Stalin?"

"Recently, a friend was able to find out some information about him. He's in his sixties, was born in Moscow, and worked at the Russian diplomatic mission at the UN in the 1970s. I also know that he defected to the United States in 1978. His last name was originally Sokurov, but his nickname is the Big Man. He's obviously very wealthy."

"What do you want me to do?"

"I need you to find out who he really is. You have access to intelligence databases for mission planning."

"That'll be difficult. You know we only have access to those databases based on mission requirements. I'd need to justify why such a search is necessary."

"I know, but they always gave us broad latitude in our research, since we never knew the exact requirements of a mission."

"That changed, Dimitri. The current administration placed stricter controls on our access due to previous abuses. Maybe I can fit it into one of my searches for my current mission. Research on a defector could set off some alarms, but since it was thirty years ago and relates to an enemy that no longer exists, it might be okay. I'll see what I can do."

Dimitri laughed. "You Americans are so naive. It wasn't the Soviet

Union and the Communists that were the enemy; it was and continues to be the Russian power structure, which hasn't changed. It's just
reemerged with a different mask, like a wolf in sheep's clothing."

"I guess we are naive, and I hope we still are. If they're more diligent
than you think and my search sets off some alarms, I'll need some cover."

"I'll be there if you need me; I've never let you down before."

"I know that. I owe my life to you. When are you going back?"

"Immediately. I have a dinner date this evening in New York with
a beautiful woman from my past."

"That sounds like fun. Maybe you'll finally be settling down."

"It would be fun, if her mother, father, and her sisters weren't also
going to be there. Her father is also one of the biggest Russian mob
bosses in New York."

"Well, your personal life is certainly a lot more exciting than mine.
How's that parrot I gave you?"

"Putin's well, and his vocabulary keeps getting bigger. I have to go,
Frank. My flight leaves in forty minutes. If you find anything, call me
on the phone number you used previously."

Dimitri got back to Kennedy and took a taxi to his house. He
took a shower, shaved, and put on some dress pants and a sweater. He
got to the pakhan's home early and rang the bell. The pakhan's wife,
Antonina, answered the door.

"Dimitri, come in. It's been much too long."

Antonina took his coat and announced his arrival to her daughters. It took Dimitri's breath away to see Anya again. She was no longer
the young girl he knew in medical school who never wore dresses.
Anya was now a full-grown woman, and one of the most beautiful he'd
ever seen, with dark hair, bright blue eyes, and a spectacular figure. She
was definitely the prettiest and smartest of the pakhan's daughters, as
well as her father's favorite.

She'd once told Dimitri that he was too pretty to be a boy. He
remembered how angry she got when he told her she was too ugly to
be a girl. As they got older, Dimitri noticed her more and they became

lovers at the Chechen State University. They both ended their medical studies when military action destroyed several university buildings. Marat had sent his wife and the two younger daughters to America to stay with family, while he and his sons fought against the Chechens. Anya had also stayed and worked as a nurse until the war ended.

Anya walked over to Dimitri and kissed him on the cheek.

"You're still too pretty, Dimitri."

Dimitri smiled. "You're gotten even more beautiful than I remember, Anya."

"What are you doing in America, Dimitri?"

"I came here after the war. Where's your father?" he asked, to avoid Anya's question.

Antonina responded. "Marat has always been late. He was even late for our wedding, but I'm sure he'll be here soon. Come, Dimitri, let's all sit and talk so we can catch up."

Marat finally arrived and kissed his wife and daughters as he took off his coat. He sat with them to enjoy the tea and cakes. After talking for a while, Antonina asked her daughters to help with serving the dinner and Marat led Dimitri to the living room.

"Have you found out anything more about the Big Man?" Marat asked.

"No, nothing yet, but I'm working on it. Thanks for your help."

Antonina and her daughters had prepared a marvelous traditional Russian dinner. It consisted of a beef solyanka soup, a kabob dish called shashlik, pelmeni dumplings, and beze pastries for dessert. After dinner, the two younger daughters went out to meet their friends, and Marat and his wife left Anya and Dimitri alone to talk.

"I hear from your father that you're a surgeon. Do you enjoy your work, Anya?"

"Most of the time. I hate it when I lose a patient. What do you do, Dimitri?"

"I'm a security consultant for a law firm. I don't enjoy it, but it pays well."

"Father said you're not married. Are you involved with anyone?"

"No, I don't have time right now," he lied.

Dimitri couldn't tell her that his romances were mostly one-night stands like the one with Irina.

"Have you been serious with anyone, Anya?"

"Not since you. I'd like to see you again. Maybe you could spend a weekend at my house in Stony Brook."

"I'll try, but my schedule is very difficult." Another lie.

Anya moved closer to him on the couch. Dimitri didn't respond, even though he was still very attracted to her. He resisted until she pulled him closer and kissed him passionately on the lips. He kissed her back, and for a moment he thought that maybe she could change his life. Then he realized he'd hurt too many people to ever feel worthy of a woman like Anya.

"I have to leave, Anya."

She kissed him again. "I have something for you," Anya said.

She handed him a small envelope with photographs of the both of them when they were lovers in medical school. She even had the dates and some inscriptions on the back. There was one photo of them standing with Dimitri's sister, mother, and Marat, taken in happier times before the war.

"Thank you, Anya. This is the best present I've ever gotten." Dimitri kissed her again, and put the envelope in his coat pocket.

"My card with my address and phone numbers are also in the envelope. Call me, Dimitri. I still care for you."

# 11

FBI Director Shelly Brockner was between a rock and a hard place, and she knew it. The investigation into Senator Thompson's death was definitely not within the FBI's jurisdiction. It belonged to the DC police, at least until it was proven to be a murder. Evidence of potential foul play triggered a deeper investigation that uncovered the business cards of a Chinese diplomat on the senator's property. The victim had been the leading proponent of the senate version of the foreign cyber-attack bill, and he had been running ads in his state that were definitely anti-Chinese. Both could've made him a potential target of the Chinese government.

While Shelly didn't think the Chinese would ever do anything so stupid as to murder the majority leader of the US Senate in the capital of the United States, she had to admit that the pieces fit perfectly. She requested a background check on the Chinese diplomat, Zhou Ming, who was identified as an employee of the Chinese Ministry of Commerce. Shelly knew that was a cover often used by intelligence operatives. The Chinese had the motive to kill the majority leader, and the evidence pointed to Zhou Ming. The case read like a damn James Bond novel, and she knew the American people might buy it.

Her only possible play was to discredit any evidence of murder presented by the medical examiner, while hoping the Chinese could provide evidence that exonerated Zhou. Shelly Brockner knew that if the Chinese embassy refused to cooperate and claimed diplomatic immunity, the relations between the US and China could be irreparably damaged. She decided to request that the senator's body be transferred to Walter Reed National Medical Center in Bethesda for further examination. That would surely be objected to by the DC government, which had temporary jurisdiction. It would also upset the senator's family, who demanded the release of his body for burial. She knew that a second autopsy was their only chance of avoiding an international incident.

Shelly had precious little time before the situation went public and the proverbial shit hit the fan. So far, she'd convinced the DC police chief not to bring any charges, and just detain Zhou without releasing his identity. While the chief was a friend, she couldn't delay much longer once the DC mayor got involved.

The mayor was no friend of the president. Joseph Meredith had publicly criticized the corruption in the DC government when he was in Congress. The mayor would take great joy in having his police make the arrest of a Chinese agent that the US government seemed to be protecting.

Shelly left for her meeting at the White House and went directly to Barbara's office. She greeted Barbara, who was talking with her secretary.

"Hi, Shelly, how's your day?" Barbara asked as she smiled.

"It's been interesting, to say the least. I'm sure it'll be a three-martini evening."

"I bet," Barbara said as they walked to the Oval Office. They were ushered into the office as the president finished a phone call.

President Meredith smiled at both Barbara and Shelly and said,

"Ladies, please sit down and make yourselves comfortable. Can I get you anything to drink?"

Barbara laughed. "Not right now, but Shelly was just saying how she might have a few adult beverages later. I may join her."

"Okay, Shelly, where do things stand with the investigation of Senator Thompson's death?"

"I assume you've been briefed on the possible Chinese intelligence agent being detained by the DC police."

"Yes, I have," the president said. "But do the DC police really believe he murdered the majority leader? Until we know for certain that Senator Thompson was murdered, this is still just an investigation into the cause of his death. The Chinese would've had to have lost their collective minds to murder the majority leader."

"In my opinion, the Chinese government has no involvement in the senator's death, and I know Barbara agrees," Shelly said. "Zhou Ming's dossier identifies him as a thirty-five-year-old Chinese national who's married and has two children. He's listed at the embassy as reporting to their Minister of Commerce. We have no proof that he's an intelligence agent, although the Ministry of Commerce is often a cover for their intelligence operatives. It allows them access to our businesses, and in some cases, US government or military personnel who contract with those businesses. The CIA believes he may actually report to their Ministry of State Security."

"Don't we monitor these guys when they're here, Shelly?"

"Some of them, but the FBI doesn't have the resources to monitor all of them. Our primary focus these days is finding and monitoring potential terrorists, which has left us pretty thin in the homeland counter-intelligence role."

"Is there enough evidence to have Ming arrested?"

"There can't be an actual arrest until there's evidence that the majority leader was murdered. In any case, the evidence against Mr. Ming is all circumstantial. There's no physical evidence other than his business cards that were found on the senator's property. I think the case is very weak, but there's enough evidence to have him detained for questioning. At this point, Mr. Ming is just a person of interest. I think the mayor is simply looking to embarrass us."

"I know the senator's death falls under DC jurisdiction, but since his cards were found on the senator's property, couldn't the FBI have detained him on suspicion of espionage, Shelly?"

"Maybe, but it would only temporarily delay a possible murder investigation. If the senator was murdered, jurisdiction is entirely federal and the FBI takes over the investigation."

"Shelly's right, Joe. Also, the FBI detaining the Chinese agent based on possible espionage would suggest that the senator may also have been involved. That would really hurt us politically. You'd be smearing a deceased majority leader from your own party to protect a Chinese intelligence agent from murder charges. I'm sure the opposition would love to run on that in three years, and your party wouldn't be thrilled, either."

"I knew there was a reason I selected you as my chief of staff," the president said as he smiled. "Okay, Shelly, what's your next move?"

"I want to have a second autopsy performed at Walter Reed to determine if the DC medical examiner was correct in her analysis. If we can get Walter Reed to do the autopsy, any indictment for murder would be delayed until there's absolute proof. That would give the FBI and CIA time to investigate Zhou Ming's background. It would also allow the Chinese embassy time to find any credible witnesses who might be able to provide an alibi, maybe someone who can verify where Ming was on the night of the senator's death."

"What do we need to have Walter Reed agree to perform the autopsy?" the president asked.

"You'd first have to personally request the family's permission, sir."

"I'll do that right after this meeting, Shelly. I met his wife when she and the senator campaigned for me when I ran for president."

"You'll also need to tell the secretary of defense that you want the surgeon general to review the autopsy results. Someone will also need to get the mayor to agree to the review of the autopsy. That might not be easy, since it would be putting the competency of his medical examiner in question. He has nothing to gain from that, Joe."

"True, but the mayor also has a lot to lose, Barbara. Without the FBI's help, the Chinese embassy will never provide any assistance. They might just claim diplomatic immunity, since they'll never deal directly with the DC police. The Chinese would consider that beneath them, since they'll certainly see this as a federal matter."

"I agree," Shelly said. "The mayor is in a no-win situation, and we can use that to our advantage."

"Given the fact that the mayor and I don't exchange Christmas cards, I suggest you deal with him, Shelly. Barbara, I'd like you to handle the interaction with the Chinese embassy, since you seem to have an excellent relationship with the ambassador. Looks like we have a plan. Now I need to make my calls to the senator's widow and the secretary of defense, and the both of you have work to do. Please keep me informed."

President Meredith called Senator Thompson's widow at her home. He explained to her the need to be absolutely certain about the cause of death, and she agreed to allow a second autopsy. The president also called the secretary of defense, who agreed to assign the autopsy to Walter Reed.

Shelly's call to the mayor didn't start off well. Merely requesting his help wouldn't work. She knew his type; in fact she'd dealt with men like the mayor most of her adult life. The only thing they understood was power.

"Mr. Mayor, if you don't allow the autopsy results to be reviewed by Walter Reed, the president will hold a press conference. He'll let everyone know that he's granting Zhou Ming diplomatic immunity because his right to a fair review of all the evidence against him was being denied by the DC mayor."

"The evidence is getting a fair review by our medical examiner, Director."

"The Chinese won't see it that way. They'll almost certainly file a claim for diplomatic immunity, and the FBI, the State Department, and the president will support it."

"If they did that, your administration would be dead. Current polls indicate almost fifty percent of American voters believe Mr. Ming was involved in the senator's death."

"Those same polls indicate that almost seventy percent of the voters are also very worried about a possible war with China due to the current situation. I'm sure you wouldn't want the administration to blame you for a possible war with China."

"That's real hardball, Shelly. Okay, you win. I'll agree with your request for a second autopsy."

The Chinese ambassador was surprised when he was told that the DC police had detained Zhou Ming. He assumed it was based on espionage, which was under the jurisdiction of the FBI, not the local police. When he was informed that the police were detaining Zhou Ming for questioning in the murder of Senator Thompson, he became irate. He called the law firm that represented the Chinese embassy and requested that they get him released immediately.

The attorney for the Chinese embassy went to the police station and demanded to speak to his client. When Zhou was brought to meet with him, the attorney noticed that he had a bruise over his right eye.

"Hi, Zhou, my name is Bradley Smithson. I'm your attorney. What happened to your face?"

"The police threw me to the ground when I tried to retrieve my cell phone from my car."

"Did you explain that you only wanted to get your phone?"

"Yes, several times, but they ignored me."

The attorney left Zhou and confronted the ranking officer on the case.

"Why was my client beaten, Officer Garret?"

"He wasn't beaten. He resisted being taken into custody."

"Have any charges been filed against my client?"

"Not yet, counselor. We're still reviewing the evidence."

"Then unless you charge my client, we're leaving right now. I also want all of my client's possessions returned, including his car."

"I need to call the lieutenant."

"Go ahead. I'll wait."

Ten minutes later the officer returned.

"Your client is free to go with all his possessions, counselor."

Ambassador Yang called the White House the next day and was put through to Barbara Chang, who was expecting the call.

"What can I do for you today, Mr. Ambassador?"

"Are you aware that one of our best young diplomats was stopped in his car in Georgetown yesterday morning and detained for several hours? He was also beaten by the local police and treated like a common criminal."

"We had nothing to do with that, Mr. Ambassador. It was entirely a local matter. When we heard the news report, the FBI director contacted the mayor, who agreed that Mr. Ming should be released."

"Why was he detained?"

"My understanding is that he was being questioned in relation to the death of Senator Thompson. His embassy business cards were found on the senator's property."

"Where's the senator's home located?"

"In Georgetown, not very far from your embassy."

"Do you know where the cards were found on the property?"

"No, I don't have that information. You'd have to ask the police about that."

"Our lawyers are already in contact with the police and the mayor's office, Ms. Chang. We'll also be talking with the Department of State about the physical abuse of a Chinese diplomat."

"The president and the administration are very sorry about that,

Ambassador. We have requested that Walter Reed Medical Center review the autopsy evidence from the medical examiner to determine if it's valid. We're also reviewing the business cards found at the crime scene. Any evidence your embassy might have that would demonstrate your diplomat's innocence would be helpful."

"The president's assistance in this matter is greatly appreciated. I'll see what we can do with respect to providing any new evidence. Please keep me informed on anything new related to this regrettable incident."

"I'll certainly do that, Ambassador."

"Thank you, and please give my regards to the president."

Ambassador Yang was very concerned that relations between his country and the United States were starting to unravel. Something or someone was pushing the two nations into a potentially catastrophic conflict. He was worried that the American populace might believe the Chinese were the monsters this situation portrayed them to be; and he was also worried about how the Chinese government might react.

The ambassador knew he needed help from Colonel Sun Yu, an old friend who was legendary within Chinese intelligence. Sun was a tenacious agent who wouldn't quit until he solved any problem he was given. He was excellent at evaluating intelligence data to find patterns and trends with automated tools and was superb with languages and social skills. Sun also spoke fluent English and was well versed in American customs, culture, and law.

Sun Yu arrived at the ambassador's residence late the next evening and immediately was escorted into his private office.

"Sun, old friend, how are you? It's been a few years."

"I'm well. But I miss the fieldwork, and I'm bored. These days I'm in charge of developing training materials for students at the institute. I hope you've got something interesting."

"I do. I need you to investigate who's framing one of our agents for the possible murder of the US Senate majority leader."

"I heard about the death of the senator but didn't know it was a murder."

"Actually, that hasn't been determined yet. The business cards of our agent, Zhou Ming, were found at the majority leader's residence in Georgetown, and he's a suspect. Here's the case file with all of the information we have so far. You'll have access to any resources you need."

"I've known Zhou since he was a student at the institute. He's one of the best agents I ever trained, and I'd like him to work with me on this case. I'm sure he's motivated to prove his innocence."

"I agree. Until this is solved we can't assign him to his usual duties anyway."

Sun smiled. "Thanks, Ambassador. This is a huge challenge, compared to what I was doing at the institute. It could even be the biggest assignment of my career."

The next day, Sun checked into the embassy residence and began reviewing the files with Zhou. They started by investigating Senator Thompson's relationships.

"I think we can eliminate the senator's family, since they had nothing to gain from his death," Zhou said.

"I agree, Zhou. But we do need to interview his staff before they scatter after finding new jobs. They might have information on possible suspects."

"We'll need help. The senator had a very large staff. I suggest using the private investigators employed by the embassy's law firm. Most of them are former federal law enforcement and are skilled interviewers."

"Okay, instruct them to interview those who are willing, and to do it quietly. Tell them compensation is authorized for worthwhile information. Emphasize information on possible enemies, confrontations, and unusual incidents relating to the senator or his staff. I've developed a spreadsheet format for the collection of the information. It will allow us to compile and sort the information quickly."

After a week of data collection and analysis, Sun and Zhou met to review the results.

"It seems that the senator had a lot of enemies, Sun."

"Yes, but one name is at the top of the list: George Solomon. I know him well. He's known to be an enemy of our government. I could definitely see him being behind a plot to destroy our relationship with the American government."

"There's also an incident that needs investigation. Carla Allen, the senator's personal aide and alleged girlfriend, was stricken with a serious illness the same day the senator died. She's recovering from a severe bacterial infection and hasn't been interviewed."

"Yes, I saw that. I've contacted the family to see if they'll let us talk to her. I convinced them that we might be able to identify the cause of their daughter's illness. A meeting's been arranged for tomorrow morning at her parent's house. I've also arranged for a local doctor who's an expert in bacterial infections to examine her and a composite sketch artist in case Ms. Allen can describe a possible suspect."

Sun arrived for the meeting with Carla Allen the next day and began asking her questions.

"Do you recall the day the senator died, Ms. Allen?"

"I'll never forget it. It was a horrible day. I'd gone to a funeral with the senator that morning, and afterward we attended a campaign event. Then he dropped me off at my apartment building and went home. I was walking through the lobby to get my mail when I was knocked down by this foreign guy who was in a hurry to get to an appointment. That was the same day I got sick, and I haven't felt well since."

"Has the cause of your illness been identified?"

"No. My doctors said it's a bacterial infection like none they've seen before. It included several bacterial strains that shouldn't exist together. It's almost as if I'd been poisoned, but the only thing I had to eat that day was my energy bars and bottled water."

"How long after being knocked down did you become ill?"

"It was less than an hour later."

"When you fell, Ms. Allen, did you feel any pain in your thigh or legs?"

Carla hesitated. "You know I thought I did, but I assumed I just fell on my mailbox key since I'd just picked up my mail."

"I think it's possible you may have been poisoned by the man who knocked you down. He might've used a small hypodermic needle to inject you with a toxin."

"Why would he do that?"

"I'm not sure. Do you remember what he looked like?"

"He was kind of cute, with dark brown hair and green eyes, and he was over six feet tall. He also had an accent."

"What type of accent?"

"I'm not sure, but he sounded like that Russian president who visited the White House a couple of months ago. I was introduced to him by the senator."

"Would you mind if we arranged to have you examined at no cost? We'd also need you to provide our artist with a description of the man who knocked you down."

"I don't mind, but could we do it here? I don't feel well enough to leave the house yet."

"Certainly. I'll arrange it for later today if that's okay."

"That's fine. I'm not going anywhere."

When Sun finished his interview, he immediately arranged for a doctor and a composite sketch artist to come to the house. When they arrived, he instructed them on what he needed and then left for the embassy.

Later that afternoon Sun received an email from the doctor with an attached medical examination report. The report identified a small puncture wound on the back of Carla's upper right thigh that was surrounded by necrotic tissue. Her blood and urine samples both indicated a massive bacterial infection. The conclusion was that Carla Allen was intentionally injected with a toxin that had caused her symptoms.

Sun also received an email from the sketch artist. It included an attached composite sketch that Carla had verified as an excellent representation of the suspect. He downloaded the sketch, printed it, and showed it to Zhou to see if he recognized the suspect.

"The face looks familiar, but I can't say I know him."

"Those Caucasians all look alike to me as well," Sun said, as they both laughed. "Relax, Zhou. Nobody believes you killed the American senator, not even the American government."

Sun gave a file with the digitized sketch of the suspect to the embassy's data-processing center. He ordered it to be run through their intelligence, criminal, and military databases and to call him immediately if they found anything. Both Sun and Zhou were leaving the embassy to go to dinner when they got a call that there was a match. They hurried back to the data-processing center where the technician had already printed the file on Dimitri Vasin. *There you are. Let's see what you're all about*, Sun said to himself.

"This is very interesting, Zhou. It appears that Dimitri Vasin was an American intelligence operative in Europe and the Middle East. There's no information over the past several years, which could mean he changed jobs. My guess is that he's now working as a private contractor. The senator was too high a profile target for any domestic or foreign intelligence agency to risk his removal. There's no apparent connection to George Solomon, but we may not need that."

"We now have the proof that shows I'm innocent, Sun. We need to show this to the Americans."

"No, we don't share results of our intelligence with anyone. It would provide information on our capabilities. It's not really evidence, anyway."

"I don't understand. This is proof that this man killed the senator?"

"No, Zhou. It's at most circumstantial evidence that he may have attacked the senator's aide and made her ill. It could easily be disputed in an American court of law."

The next afternoon, Sun Yu briefed the ambassador on what they'd found.

"Very good work as always, Sun. But how are you going to find this Dimitri?"

"His current address isn't listed in our databases, which I anticipated based on the work he does. We do know that he has no family
anywhere, since they were all killed in Grozny during the Chechen
wars. I believe a man like this would want to blend in and feel comfortable in his surroundings. He'll probably be living with friends in
one of the Russian communities in the US."

"There are a number of such communities, Sun. We don't have
time to search them all."

"We shouldn't have to, Ambassador. Last night I contacted a friend
in Russian intelligence for information on who sponsored Vasin's immi-
gration to the US and their location. Dimitri Vasin was sponsored in
2005 by Antonina Chubais from Brighton Beach, in Brooklyn. Brighton Beach has a large Russian ethnic population and is exactly the type
of place Dimitri would reside. I suggest we start our search there."

"Okay, Sun, I want you and Zhou to develop a plan for the search
that doesn't put any of our agents or anyone else in danger, nor draw
any attention to the embassy."

Sun met with Zhou after the meeting to discuss how they could
find Dimitri and still meet the ambassador's mandate for safety and
anonymity.

"Finding Dimitri Vasin in a large, tight-knit Russian community
in Brooklyn would be difficult at best for any outsider," Sun said. "For
a Chinese foreign national, it will be almost impossible and dangerous.
The Russian Bratva are very active in Brighton Beach. Based on his background, it's likely that Dimitri is either a member of or associated with
the Bratva in some manner. If he was involved in the murder of Senator
Thompson, he'll also be very cautious. That will make finding him even
more difficult and dangerous."

"How can we do the necessary surveillance and still meet the
ambassador's requirements?"

"I have an idea, Zhou. Meet me at my apartment tonight at nine.
There's a movie we need to watch."

Zhou seemed puzzled. "Why do we need to watch a movie?"

"Because it shows how we can safely find Dimitri in Brighton Beach."

Zhou showed up at nine as ordered, and they both watched a recent historical drama that depicted how the United States had gotten some American diplomats out of Iran during the Iran hostage crisis. After the movie ended, Sun asked Zhou what he thought.

"It's a very good movie, Sun, but how does it help us?"

"Did you see how the Americans were smuggled out of Tehran by pretending to be part of a movie crew? We can do the same thing in reverse."

"I don't understand."

"We can reverse the plan from the movie. Our investigators will pretend to be part of a real Chinese film crew shooting a documentary in Brighton Beach. The documentary will be about the Russian ethnic culture in the Brighton Beach community. We'll do interviews with members of the local population that suffered oppression in Russia and immigrated to America for a new life. Our documentary will focus on their new lives. During the production, we'll hire some of the locals to arrange interviews with Russian immigrants and find locations for filming. We'll also get some information from them in the process. Hopefully information about Dimitri Vasin."

Zhou smiled. "You're a genius, Sun. It could work, but we'll need to get the ambassador involved to find a film crew and arrange for the filming in Brighton Beach."

"I briefed the ambassador before you got here. He's agreed to find the film crew and get the required permits for the filming. I had to assure him that none of the Chinese or Americans involved in this plan will be harmed in any way. It helped that the ambassador is a film buff."

"How hard is it to get permission for filming a documentary in New York?" Zhou asked.

"Dozens of documentaries and TV shows are made in the city annually. The city government actively encourages it as a great source of revenue and publicity."

"All I want is a confession from this Dimitri on his involvement in framing me. Hopefully, he'll also confess to the murder of Senator Thompson?"

"The ambassador said he doesn't care about the murder or who did it, Zhou. That's America's problem. He only wants proof that you and the embassy had no involvement. That'll have to be enough."

"I understand. It'll be enough for me."

"Good, I'm meeting with the ambassador tomorrow morning to discuss the plan."

The next morning, Sun arrived at the ambassador's office.

"Good morning, Sun. I've arranged for a Chinese film crew with experience in documentaries. They'll be in New York after I arrange for the permits."

"Will the permits be a problem?"

"I doubt it. I've met the mayor and I'm certain she'll see this as a political opportunity. The Chinese community in New York City is a large component of her political base. A generous donation from the Chinese government to the New York City Mayor's Fund will also help. I'll arrange it. What will your role be in this production?"

"I'll be the producer for the documentary. I speak excellent English and Russian and have experience with the making of films and videos."

"That's fine, Sun. But don't let it go to your head. You're an intelligence agent first and a producer second. Is that clear?"

"Yes."

A few days later the film crew arrived and began walking through Brighton Beach to find filming locations and hire locals to support the interview and filming process. All local hires were screened at the mayor's insistence by the New York Police Department to make sure they had no ties to organized crime. The mayor also assigned a dozen of New York's finest to ensure that the Chinese film crew was safe and avoided any trouble with the locals.

That didn't seem to be an issue, since the locals were ecstatic, based on the anticipated influx of tourists and revenue. Local merchants were salivating over the crowds that would assemble when the filming began. The potential for jobs in a community that desperately needed them was a boost for morale, as was the possibility of the locals getting their fifteen minutes of fame.

# 12

Kim and Cai were happy that the weekend training sessions were over. They'd have more time to spend with each other before the probing of the targets in the US would begin. Both noticed that the project was taking a toll on Shen. In addition to school, he was managing the training sessions and the plan for the attack.

The two Korean intelligence agents, whom Cai had nicknamed Tweedledum and Tweedledee, were monitoring Shen's activities. They reported that Shen had met with five groups of four hackers each, all students from HIT, Harbin University of Science and Technology, Harbin Engineering University, and Heilongjiang University. Kim thought that there had to be more than twenty hackers based on the size of the target population that they'd been briefed on.

Kim asked Shen to set up a meeting at the Shangri La that evening with their girlfriends.

"We should celebrate the completion of the training, Shen. It'll be fun."

"Yeah, I could use a little fun and relaxation right now. I'll arrange for the rooms."

Kim called Cai.

"We have a date at the Shangri La tonight, Cai. Do you want to go?" Kim asked.

"Do you realize that this is the third time we're going to the Shangri La and you've yet to ask me first?"

"The first time doesn't count. I hadn't met you yet," Kim replied.

"Yes, but not the last two. I hope you're not taking me for granted."

"Never. You know I love you. So can you go?"

"I wouldn't miss it. Does a room come with the offer?"

"Yes, Shen is setting it up. Is that okay?"

"Yes. I just wanted to know what to bring with me."

"Just bring yourself. You won't need any clothes in the room, except maybe the hotel bathrobe."

Cai laughed. "That's not why I asked. I need to know if I have to bring my valuables so my roommate's boyfriend doesn't steal anything."

"Maybe I should have Tweedledum and Tweedledee talk with him."

"No, please don't. I can handle it."

"Okay, Cai. Do you want me to meet you at your place or at the Shangri La?"

"I'll meet you at the pub. It's easier that way."

"Are you trying to protect me from your roommate's boyfriend? I can take care of myself."

"I know that. Actually, I'm protecting him from you so you don't get deported."

"Okay, I'll see you at the hotel."

Kim's taxi got to the hotel a few seconds before Cai's, and they walked into the pub together while holding hands. Shen and Lian were sitting at a table with four empty glasses.

"Looks like you've been here a while, Shen."

"We have. You need to catch up."

Shen ordered another round for Lian and himself.

"This was a great idea, Kim. I really needed to have some fun time."

"You look exhausted, Shen. What's wearing you out like this?"

"This project requires a lot more work than I anticipated, Kim."

"What happened? Were additional targets added or more hackers recruited?"

"Neither. The duration of the attack was decreased, which means the planning got more complex. I'm totally confused about the goals of this project, but nobody seems to care. Someone knows what's going on, but it isn't me."

Kim hesitated as he thought about what Shen just said. He decided to share his doubts and said, "I also have a problem understanding the goals. Can you tell me how many hackers are involved in the project?"

"No one is supposed to know that except myself and Sean, my contact. I already told Lian, so I guess I can tell you as well. There are twenty hackers from several Harbin universities. I report to Sean via a phone he gave to me at the beginning of the project."

"Do you have any idea who Sean is and who's funding this project? It must be enormously expensive."

"I think Sean's an American, Kim. I have no clue as to who's providing the funding. He must be very rich the way he's been throwing money around."

"What's his role in all of this, Shen?"

"I'm not sure. I met with him initially when he first contacted me at HIT several months ago about a research project. He said that it required about twenty Harbin students who were experienced hackers. Sean visits Harbin periodically to identify and address any issues. All our meetings were held at a suite I'd reserve here."

"Were they scheduled meetings or were they random?"

"Definitely random. He'd just reserve a room for himself at the Shangri La and then notify me when he wanted to meet. I think he did that so I couldn't prepare for our meetings."

"Possibly. It definitely gave him the advantage of surprise. So Sean never told you what the goals are for the attack?"

"No. He never has, Kim. I have no idea if the plan is to take down the target systems or steal or destroy the data. If I knew what the goals were, I could focus the training better. Instead I have to consider all the possibilities, which is really difficult."

"I can see why you're so stressed," Kim said. "You should relax tonight and just have a good time."

"We all should. I arranged dinner reservations at the Shang Palace. We should have time for one more drink and then get some dinner."

Kim could see that the alcohol was having an effect on Shen.

"I think we should go now, Shen. We can always order drinks and wine at the restaurant. Cai and I haven't had anything to eat all day."

As they started to walk to the restaurant, Shen stumbled. Kim grabbed him before he fell.

"Do you have your room key, Lian?" Kim asked.

"It's in Shen's wallet. He has the room keys for both suites."

Kim got the keys and then helped Lian get Shen to the room and into bed. Kim and Cai then went to their suite, looked at each other, and burst out laughing.

"I think Shen is going to have one monster hangover," Kim said.

"And one angry girlfriend," Cai added.

"I'm really hungry, Cai. This time you select the food."

"Okay, how about the goose liver terrine as an appetizer and the stir-fried shrimp and steamed cod fish as the main dishes?"

"Sure, what about dessert?"

"Is mousse with blueberry coulis okay?"

"It'll certainly be something I've never had before."

"It won't be the only thing tonight that you've never had before," Cai said with a smile.

"Sounds like the real dessert will be à la carte."

"Yes, and we can have seconds or even thirds."

Cai took a quick shower while Kim called room service and ordered their dinner and a bottle of champagne. Kim walked back to the bedroom and joined Cai, who had put on a hotel robe. He took off his clothes and lay on the bed while she joined him. Kim kissed her and whispered in her ear. "Dinner will be a while. Let's start with dessert."

Cai smiled, and took off her robe as Kim kissed her passionately. They enjoyed each other several times until they were spent. Later, Kim gave Cai her robe while he put his on to answer the knock on the door. Kim signed for the dinner and looked at all the dishes.

"Look at all this food, Cai. The colors are almost as incredible as the aroma. I have never seen anything like it."

"I know. Try the goose liver. It melts in your mouth."

Kim kept staring at the food. "I'm sure it does, but I feel guilty eating this when many in my country are starving."

"Try not to think about that, Kim. Let's just enjoy the moment."

After dinner they both had the mousse with champagne and decided to watch some of the latest movies on the satellite channels.

"Have you ever seen an American movie, Kim?"

"No, the only movies we have in North Korea are based on the propaganda that the government promotes."

"Let's watch an adventure movie. How about *Iron Man*? It's really good."

"Sure, let's watch it."

As they watched, Cai could see that Kim was totally transfixed by the movie. After it ended, she asked him if he liked it.

"It was great. I've never seen anything like it."

"What'd you like best?"

"The Iron Man suit. If I had a suit like that I could get my family out of North Korea. Too bad it isn't real."

"I believe you'll get them out, Kim. You're my Iron Man."

Kim moved closer to Cai and began to run his hands down Cai's thighs as she moaned softly. He deftly moved his fingers up her back and toward her magnificent breasts as she whispered, "I love you, Kim."

"I love you, too, Cai."

Kim picked her up and carried her to the bed. He laid her down softly on the bed and then joined her. They made love until they both were exhausted and fell asleep in each other's arms.

The next morning, Kim was awakened by the sound of the room

phone ringing. He assumed it was the front desk asking if they wanted breakfast. Instead it was Shen, who was talking so softly Kim could barely hear him.

"There was a message on my phone from Sean," Shen said. "He's going to be here this evening and wants to meet with me. We need to talk, Kim."

"Okay, I'll meet you in your suite in about an hour."

Kim and Cai arrived at Shen's suite and knocked on the door. They were both shocked when they saw him.

"Are you okay, Shen? You look like you've had a horrible night."

"That's because I did. Lian left me last night, and then Sean called this morning about this meeting. I'm worried about the project and its goals. Lian keeps telling me not to worry and just take the money, but what if this is a trap? I could be putting everyone in jeopardy."

"Who do you think would want to trap us and why? I don't think it's a trap, Shen. I think there are goals for this project that we're not aware of and probably aren't supposed to know. What do you think, Cai?"

"I agree. We need to get Sean to tell us what the project goals are, if he knows."

"The only way we can be certain is to question Sean. Are you ready for that, Shen?"

"It's the only option left. But how do we do it, Kim?"

"I know just the people who can help."

"Who's that?" Shen asked.

"Tweedledum and Tweedledee," Cai said with a grin.

"Who are they?" Shen asked with a puzzled look on his face.

"They're just Cai's names for some Korean friends of mine who are very good at getting answers. When does Sean get to the hotel?"

"He didn't say, but based on past experience, it'll probably be late this evening. It's a long flight, so he won't contact me until late tomorrow morning or even early afternoon. That's been the pattern in our previous meetings."

"Where do you normally meet?"

"We always meet in my suite and have lunch while we talk. I don't know why, but he always insists on meeting in my room."

"Probably because he's afraid that his own room is bugged. The Chinese government has been known to do that when American businessmen visit China. He's probably just being cautious. I'll need access to this room."

"No problem. Here's my room key, Kim. I need to find Lian and apologize for last night. Who's doing the interrogation?"

"Actually you'll be doing the interrogation, Shen."

Shen looked shocked.

"Don't worry," Kim said. "He'll never know he was interrogated. I plan to dose him with a very sophisticated drug that reduces anxiety. It normally takes five to ten minutes to take effect. The subject will become relaxed and may become very talkative and friendly. You'll definitely see the difference. When you meet, do you order the lunch or does he?"

"I call in the order to room service. He always calls and tells me what he wants before he comes to my suite."

"Good. Instead of calling room service I want you to call me on my cell phone. I'll place the order and have it delivered to my suite where I'll dose his meal. You'll need to tell me what you're ordering so I know which order to dose. I'll deliver the meals to your suite and then wait outside until you call me in after the drug takes effect. Do you understand?"

"Yes. It sounds like you've done this before, Kim."

"I have, and it always works, so don't worry. After he's under, you'll ask him a list of questions that I'll provide to you before the meeting. It's best if the questions are presented as part of a conversation about the project and the issues you're concerned with. Just pretend you're talking to a friend. I have a lot to do, so I'll call you when everything is ready."

Kim left with Cai and went down to the front desk in the lobby. There was a new clerk on duty whom Kim had never seen before. Kim showed the clerk Shen's room key.

"I have an associate who will be staying at this hotel this evening, and I'd like to make certain that everything is set."

"May I ask your associate's name, Mr. Wei?" the clerk asked.

"His name is Sean Flaherty, and this is his card."

Kim handed the clerk the business card that he'd been given during his last visit to the Shangri La. The clerk looked up the name in his computer. "Yes, sir, Mr. Flaherty gets in as a late arrival this evening and he's staying in suite 1084. Should I inform him that you're here?"

"No, I'll call him tomorrow morning. I'm sure he'll be tired from his long flight."

Kim and Cai returned to their suite, where Kim called Lieutenant and Ensign Park. He asked them to meet him in the pub in about an hour.

"I assume you don't want me at that meeting."

"Yes. That wouldn't be wise, Cai. It's important that they not know of our relationship so that they don't tell my superiors. That might get me recalled to North Korea, and we don't want that."

"No, I certainly don't want that. We have an hour to kill, so maybe we could have another serving of dessert before your meeting?"

Kim smiled and began undressing. After dessert, Kim went down to the pub and found a secluded table. Lieutenant and Ensign Park showed up right on time and joined him.

"Good afternoon, gentlemen. Do you want anything to eat or drink?"

"No, we just ate. Is anything wrong?"

"No. I called you because I need to interrogate an American named Sean Flaherty, who's arriving at this hotel late tonight. He can't know he's been interrogated, so I need to use SP-117. Are you familiar with it?"

"Yes, we know of it, but we don't have it with us."

"You need to contact our superiors and let them know that I'm requesting its use. I need to have it by tomorrow morning."

"We'll need to tell them why it's needed."

"I need to ask the American contact for this project about the person financing it and find out if this is a trap. I also want to know if he's a US agent." Kim was pretty certain that the US government wasn't involved, but he also knew that if he mentioned that possibility, his superiors would react faster and provide him everything he needed.

"We'll contact them immediately."

After they left, Kim went back to the room and explained to Cai what he planned to do to get the information from Flaherty.

"Have you ever heard of truth serums, Cai?"

"Do you mean drugs like scopolamine and sodium pentothal?"

"Those were used as truth serums at one time, but were abandoned because they're dangerous and often ineffective. The Russians developed a truth serum with the code name SP-117. It's highly effective and has been widely used by countries in Eastern Europe, China, and North Korea. It has no taste, no smell, no color, and no apparent side effects. The subject appears normal and will talk freely about what he knows as if he was having a conversation. He'll also have no recollection of having been interrogated. If anything, it just seems like he suddenly fell asleep."

"Is this SP-117 classified? I've never heard of anything like it."

"It was classified at one time, but now you can find it described on the internet by searching for truth serums. The Americans have similar drugs that I heard are even better. So do the Russians and the Chinese, who no longer use it. The Chinese provided it to North Korea a few years ago."

"Are you sure it'll work?"

"Yes, it always has for me."

"What do you think about Shen's description of the project, Kim? It seems like we're a little understaffed."

"A lot understaffed, with too little time to accomplish what I think they want. There must be others involved that we don't know about. We don't have all the information, and I'm not certain Sean Flaherty will have what we need, either."

"Well, we've got another whole day together, Kim. What do you want to do?"

"I need to rest a little, Cai. Please forget about any more dessert until later. If you want to take off your clothes, I give a pretty good massage."

"Is that one of those happy ending massages?"

"Where'd you hear about that?"

"My roommate used to work in one of the massage parlors in the Korean section of Harbin."

"Is she a prostitute?"

"Not anymore, but I think she met her boyfriend at one of the parlors where he was a towel boy."

"Great. You need to find another place to live after this is over, Cai."

"I agree. We can decide where later. How about we watch another American movie? They have great movies."

"That sounds good."

Kim and Cai spent the rest of the day watching American action movies. At about eight, Kim got a call on his cell phone from Lieutenant Park. He told Kim that his request had been approved and they'd deliver the medication by two p.m. the next day in the pub. Kim called Shen, who seemed to be in a better mood.

"Hi, Kim. I made up with Lian."

"I can tell. You sound a lot happier than you did earlier."

"I definitely am. What's going on?"

"We need to meet tomorrow afternoon at two in the pub. Tweedledum and Tweedledee will also be there."

"Okay, I'll see you then. Goodnight, Kim."

Kim and Cai had a sensuous and passionate evening and then slept until eleven the next morning. After breakfast, Cai went back to her apartment for clean clothes, while Kim met Lieutenant and Ensign Park in the pub. Shen arrived a few minutes later.

"I'd like you to meet my friends, Shen. They're the Park brothers, and they have the medication we need."

Lieutenant Park pulled out a small four-ounce bottle of a clear liquid from his briefcase. "This is it," he said.

"Why is there so much?" Kim asked. "I only need a half ounce."

"They don't want to send this stuff more than once to the same destination for security reasons. Just use it as you need it."

Lieutenant Park reached into the briefcase again and pulled out a small electronic device that looked like a cell phone.

"This device can transmit, receive, and record conversations. It's activated by the sound of voices. My brother will put it in Shen's room. There's another one in my briefcase that we can use to listen from your room. Is that okay, sir?"

"Yes. My room is unoccupied so we won't be disturbed. Let's go," Kim said.

"Follow me," Shen said, as he took Ensign Park up to his suite.

When they got to the suite, Ensign Park set up the transmitter in the dining room.

"Can you hear me, Kim?" Shen asked.

"We hear you," Kim said from his suite. "I also hear your phone ringing, Shen. It might be Flaherty."

"It is. I'll put my phone on speaker so you can hear the call."

Kim listened to the call and placed the lunch orders based on Shen's conversation with Flaherty.

Ten minutes later, Kim called Shen. "They just delivered the meals to my suite. Are you alone?"

"Yeah, my companion just left to join his brother in your suite. Flaherty just called again to say he's on his way."

"Okay, I'm dosing his meal. You have the sandwich and he ordered the soup, correct?"

"Yeah, no possible confusion there."

The order was delivered, and Kim checked to make sure it was correct. He tipped the delivery boy and asked him to leave the cart. Kim dosed Flaherty's soup with the SP-117 and took the cart to Shen's suite. After delivering the food, Kim went back to his suite and waited until he heard Shen speaking through the device in his suite.

"I think he's ready, Kim. He seems very relaxed, almost tranquil. He's just sitting here and staring at the screen saver on his laptop."

"Yeah, he's ready. I'll be right there, Shen."

Kim entered Shen's suite and saw a thin man with light brown hair who looked to be in his thirties sitting at a dining room table. The man was staring at a laptop computer and took no notice of Kim as he sat down in a chair next to him. Shen sat across from Flaherty and began asking the questions.

"Sean, I have some questions about the project that I hope you can answer. Can you tell me how many hackers are involved and how they're organized?"

"Sure, there are sixty hackers from universities in Beijing, Harbin, and Shanghai. There are five cells in each city with four students to each cell. Each city has one manager."

"Who's in charge of the entire project?"

"Whitey's in charge. I don't know his real name, but he's very wealthy."

"Do you report to Whitey?"

"No, I've never had any direct contact with him."

"What's the target of the cyber attacks?"

"American businesses, but I don't know who they are."

"What's the purpose of this trip, Sean?"

"I have information on your targets, schedules, and reporting requirements."

"Why does Whitey want to attack American businesses?"

"He wants to hurt them."

"For what purpose?"

"I assume it's to help his businesses. No one has told me."

"How many businesses does Whitey own?"

"I'm not sure, but I heard he's a billionaire."

"Are the students or countries such as China and North Korea scapegoats for the attack?"

"There are no scapegoats, Shen. Just targets."

Sean Flaherty yawned as his eyes began to droop and were almost closed.

"I'm very tired, Shen. Is it okay if I take a nap?"

"Sure, Sean."

Kim stood up and took a close look at Flaherty.

"He'll be out for a while, Shen. I might've given him too much serum. It's hard to judge, since everyone reacts differently. At least I know it works well on him. There was no resistance, and he answered the questions without hesitation, which indicates there was no deception. I'm certain all his answers were truthful."

"That's good. How long will he be out?"

"At least thirty minutes, Shen. Maybe even an hour. Let's take the transmitter and go back to my suite and talk."

Both Park brothers were waiting for them at Kim's suite.

"It's apparent from the interview that no one is a scapegoat and there is no trap," Kim said. "Someone in America named Whitey is apparently looking to attack his competitors and is using foreign hackers so he can't get caught."

"We agree. My brother and I are convinced that the project is aimed at American businesses. Good luck," Lieutenant Park said as he and his brother left.

"I'm happy that there are more hackers," said Shen, "but I'm still worried about the schedule. What do you think, Kim?"

"I'm also worried about the schedule. But we also need to find out who Whitey is."

"I agree. I'd better return to my suite before Flaherty wakes up."

"Yes, you better go. Call me after he leaves."

Flaherty was just waking up when Shen returned to his suite.

"Sorry I fell asleep, Shen. I guess the long trip wore me out."

"No problem. What'd you want to discuss, Sean?"

"I have this jump drive for you with the project schedules and targets, and I also need to discuss some reporting requirements."

"What reports do you need?"

"I need grades on all your people by tomorrow, Shen."

"That will be difficult; they're all excellent and I've nothing yet to grade them on."

"Nevertheless, I need those grades by noon tomorrow. I also want to review the information on the targets."

"What are the grades being used for?"

"I don't know, and it's not your problem, Shen."

Shen frowned. "Okay, I'll meet you in the hotel pub tomorrow at noon."

"That's fine. I'm going back to my room. I have a splitting headache."

After Sean left, Shen turned on his cell phone and checked his messages. He saw one from Lian asking him to call. The message came in during his interrogation of Flaherty. Shen called Lian, but it went immediately to her answering service. He then called Kim and let him know about his discussion with Flaherty. As they were talking, Kim received a call from Lian.

"I need to go, Shen. Lian's calling me. We'll talk later."

Kim took Lian's call and immediately heard the anxiety in her voice.

"Kim, something terrible has happened. Cai was attacked by her roommate's boyfriend and is in critical condition at the Harbin Medical University Hospital. I just texted Shen and told him to meet you in the lobby and drive you here."

"I'm on my way," Kim shouted as he ran out of the suite to the elevator. Kim saw Shen in the lobby and ran toward him as he grabbed his arm and almost dragged him into the car.

"Let's go, Shen. As fast as you can drive and don't stop for anything."

"Okay, buckle your safety belt," Shen said.

The tires on Shen's Mercedes squealed as they left the hotel lobby parking area. Shen wove in and out of traffic, hitting speeds over ninety at some points during the drive. Shen pulled into the hospital admissions area and brought the car to a screeching stop. Kim jumped out of the car and ran into the lobby. Lian was waiting for him and she took him to the waiting room.

"Cai was beaten and stabbed, Kim. The police have been here and taken the information from Cai's roommate, Mei." Lian pointed to the woman sitting across the room with bandages on her arm. "That's Mei. She's the one who called the police."

"What happened?"

"Mei said her boyfriend was drunk and he tried to take advantage of Cai. He was calling her all sorts of names. She rebuffed him, and then he shoved her. Cai tried to defend herself, but he hit her hard and she fell. Mei got a kitchen knife but he took it away and slashed her and then stabbed Cai when she tried to help Mei."

"I warned her. I knew this could happen. What do the doctors say, Lian?"

"She's critical, Kim. The knife went into her back and punctured a lung. It also nicked some blood vessels and she lost a lot of blood."

"How long ago did this happen?"

"This afternoon around three. Her roommate called the police and the ambulance. They took Cai into the operating room over an hour ago."

Kim walked toward the roommate, and he could tell from the look on her face that she was scared.

"I'm not here to hurt you, Mei. I just want to know where your boyfriend is."

Mei slowly looked up at Kim with tears running down her face. "He's not my boyfriend. I broke up with him weeks ago, but he won't leave me alone."

"Where is he?"

"He has friends in the Korean section of the city. He's probably hiding out with them. He knows the police can't find him there."

"But I bet you could, Mei. Cai said you used to work there."

"I won't go back there by myself. It's too dangerous."

"I live over there."

"Yes, but you live in the good area, not where he is."

"I'll go with you. I promise you'll be safe. Do you have a recent picture of him?"

Mei showed Kim a picture from her wallet.

"Do you know his real name, Mei?"

"He said it was Woo Lei, but I don't think it's his real name."

Lian called out to Kim. "The doctors are coming back, Kim."

Kim, Mei, and Lian walked toward the doctors and Shen joined them. One of the doctors walked over and smiled.

"Cai is a very lucky young lady," the doctor said. "She's going to be fine, but she'll need to be here for at least a week. Cai lost a lot of blood and is weak. The knife wound, though serious, didn't cause the damage it could have if the entry wound was an inch higher."

Tears came to Kim's eyes for the first time since his father died, and he hugged the doctor.

"You must be Kim. She kept saying your name when she was being wheeled into the operating room."

"Thank you, doctor. I am eternally grateful."

Kim asked Mei if she was ready, and she nodded.

"I need you to take me back to my apartment, Shen. Wait in the car with Mei while I pick up some things I need."

"Can I drop Lian off at our apartment first and kiss her goodbye in case she never sees me again?"

"Sure, but I can handle this. Don't worry, Shen."

After they had dropped Lian off, Kim went into his apartment and put on some dark clothing and sneakers. He put a folding combat knife and a black woolen cap and black scarf in the pockets of his coat. Kim got into the front seat next to Shen, who asked Mei for directions. Shen drove as Mei directed while Kim was repeating the same words, "*pyun yan sho yong haka.*" Mei was staring at Kim with concern as he repeated those words. Shen knew that Mei must have understood what Kim was saying, since she was ethnic Korean. Kim had a hateful look on his face and spoke the words in such a violent manner that it scared Shen.

Mei told Shen to park down the street from an old dilapidated apartment building. She pointed to the second floor and said, "That's where some of his family lives. He's probably in there."

"Drive the car down the street near the building entrance after I get out, Shen. I'll be back shortly."

"Okay, we'll be there," Shen said.

After Kim left, Shen turned to Mei and asked, "What were those words Kim kept repeating?"

Mei looked directly at Shen and said, "He was saying *I will kill you* in Korean."

As Kim walked toward the building, he wrapped the black scarf around his face just below his eyes and put on the woolen cap. He could see lights and movement on the front of the building where Mei had pointed. Kim didn't see any lights in the rear of the building, so he climbed up a drain pipe to the second floor and shimmied across a small four-inch ledge until he reached a window. He used his knife to pry the window open and entered without a sound. Kim allowed his eyes to adjust to the dark and listened. There were sounds from a room down the hall. He moved slowly until he saw a sliver of light from under a door.

A TV was broadcasting a soccer game and he waited out of sight for about ten minutes until a young, slightly-built man came out the door. Kim grabbed him and covered his mouth as he threw him to the floor without making a sound. He could see it wasn't his target, but he needed information so he pressed his knife against the man's throat.

"Where is Woo Lei?" Kim whispered.

The man's eyes grew larger and he started to say something so Kim uncovered his mouth. He pushed the knife against his throat harder. "In the room," the man whispered.

"How many?"

"Two men."

"Thanks," Kim said, as he removed the knife from the man's throat. He then hit him with the knife's handle, knocking him out.

A large man came through the door while calling out for

someone—probably the man Kim had just disabled. The large man reached for a gun when he saw Kim, who quickly reacted by kicking the gun out of the man's hand and into the room. As the man turned and went to pick up the gun, Kim ran toward him and kicked him hard. The large man was knocked into the room. Kim quickly followed him and saw Woo Lei sitting in his underwear in a chair six feet away. He threw his knife at Woo's groin, and Woo began screaming. Kim was grabbed from behind by the big man, who tried to crush his ribs. Kim disabled him by slamming his leg down into the side of the big man's knee while driving his right hand into the man's throat. The big man fell to the floor, gasping for air before passing out. Kim took the gun and walked toward Woo Lei, who was still screaming as blood streamed from his groin.

Kim looked at Woo Lei with contempt. "It looks like you'll need to have your appendage stitched, Woo." Kim then pushed down hard on his knife while pulling it quickly out of Woo's groin.

Woo screamed again. "You cut it off," he cried.

Kim took a pillow and put it over Woo's face.

"Be quiet and listen, Woo. If you ever come near Cai or Mei again, I'll kill you."

With that, Kim hit him with the gun and knocked him out. He then walked down the stairs, out the front door, and got in Shen's car.

Kim called the police and told them there'd been a bad fight and that someone was screaming. He gave them the address and asked Shen to take him and Mei home.

"Did you kill him?" Mei asked.

"No. It was still breathing when I left."

"It?" Mei said, with a confused look.

"Yes. He's no longer a man. Do you have a tissue? I need to clean his blood off my knife."

Mei smiled while handing Kim the tissue.

"Thank you," she said.

Shen drove the car back to the hospital, his eyes as big as saucers.

# 13

James really missed JoAnn. Her trip to Minnesota to visit with her constituents was the longest period they'd been apart. He followed her trip in the Minnesota news and was happy to see that her popularity was soaring due to her successful support for less state and local government regulation, lower taxes, and economic growth.

He was also grateful for her support for the president's cyber-attack bill in the house as opposed to the oppressive bill in the senate.

The local press lauded her support, since Minnesota had almost thirty billion dollars in exports to China the previous year, a growth of more than twenty percent that could be jeopardized by the senate bill. James called her to see if her flight back to DC was also in jeopardy due to a predicted Minnesota snowstorm.

"Hi, baby, is your flight getting out today? Minneapolis is in the path of a huge storm."

"It just started to snow, but we should be leaving on time. I really miss you and can't wait to get home, James. Don't forget to meet me."

"Reagan National, 6:10. I'll be there."

"How's your investigation going?"

"Rick and I made some progress while you were gone. I'll tell you about it tonight."

After getting off the phone with JoAnn, James called Ann.

"Hi, Ann, how are you? How's the new house?"

"Everything's fine, James, but you'll never guess who I'm having dinner with."

"Who?"

"George Solomon. The rich old bastard called me last night and asked if he could meet for a late lunch. I told him only if he comes to St. Mary's County. I don't drive to DC anymore unless I have to. He agreed, and I'm waiting for him at a small restaurant on Solomons Island. I bet George selected it because he probably thinks the island was named after him."

"Possibly, we all know George has a big ego. Try to be nice—he did help the company when we were getting started."

"Yes, I know. He enjoys telling everyone about how he was responsible for the company's success."

"I know. Just let it go."

"I will. Have you ever been to this place? It's called Rick's."

"Yeah, really good food. Try the crab cakes and the key lime pie. Why's George meeting you? Did he say what it's about?"

"Haven't got a clue, but I'll let you know. Got to go, he just walked in."

"Call me back later. I need to talk with you."

"Will do. Goodbye, James."

James was working from home while on his leave of absence. He'd been given the complete report of Captain Kinsley's interrogation and was going through it in detail. He was still puzzled how the feds could've obtained information on VSI's "secret sauce" without getting it from Philip, as indicated by the polygraph.

As James considered the possibilities, the phone rang. He looked at the caller ID.

"How was lunch, Ann?" James asked.

"Lunch was great, but George is still an SOB."

"What happened?"

"He asked me to provide my VSI proxy to him. When I told him that I'd already agreed to provide the proxy to you, he became upset and tried to convince me to change my mind. I believe he even threatened me."

"I can't believe he'd do that. How'd he threaten you?"

"He mentioned something about Philip violating his NDA, but I'm not sure what he's talking about. Do you know?"

"No, I don't, but I need to meet with you and Jim on this and other issues involving Philip. Can you meet me and an FBI agent who's working Philip's case at your summer house tomorrow morning? It's very important."

"I can make it, and Jim's been staying with me since the funeral, so he should be available as well."

"Great, see you and Jim tomorrow morning at about ten."

James quickly ended his call with Ann to answer an incoming call from Rick.

"Rick, I was just talking about you. Where are you? It's noisy."

"I'm driving home with the top down. Really nice weather for this time of year."

"I don't know. I haven't been out all day. So what's up?"

"The admiral called me earlier. Apparently, Captain Kinsley took leave right after our interview."

"You think the two are related?"

"The admiral does. Kinsley listed it as emergency leave."

"I guess we must've really touched a nerve. I'm glad you called. Can you join me tomorrow morning at about ten at the Wu summer house to talk with Ann Wu and her son, Jim?"

"Sure. What's it about?"

"George Solomon and possible extortion by him to gain control over VSI."

"Sounds interesting. Pick me up at my house in La Plata—it's on your way to the Wu house. I'll text you my address."

James suddenly heard what sounded like Rick cursing and the squealing of tires.

"Is everything okay, Rick?"

"I need to go, James. I have a crazy driver trying to race me."

Rick loved everything about his new Mustang GT, with the exception of the idiots it attracted wanting to race. This one was a big pickup coming up right behind him. Rick slowed down and moved to the right lane to indicate his lack of interest. He saw the truck's passenger-side window open and then the barrel of a rifle protruding from the window.

Rick slammed on his brakes and used his phone to take a picture of the rear of the truck as it went by him. The truck also slowed down, and he could see the barrel of the rifle turning toward him. He took another picture as he heard the boom of a shotgun and the sound of buckshot hitting the front of his car.

"This ain't no damn race," Rick said aloud.

Rick pulled behind the pickup and rammed the rear bumper on the driver side in an attempt to spin the truck. The truck wobbled, but didn't spin. Too heavy, Rick thought, as he grabbed his Glock and accelerated toward the truck's passenger side. The shotgun turned toward him again and Rick swerved to the left out of the line of fire as two shots hit the Mustang's passenger side. Rick accelerated and fired several shots into the passenger side of the truck, which veered into the front quarter panel of his Mustang, forcing it to spin off the road.

"Shit!" Rick said, right before he hit the tree.

When James got to the arrival area at Reagan National Airport, he saw JoAnn standing there with more luggage than she left with.

"Hi, baby, I'm glad you're home," he said, as he gave her a big kiss. "It looks like you did some shopping. I hope we can fit it in the car."

"I guess I should've told you to bring the SUV," JoAnn said.

"I'll get it in."

After squeezing everything in, James realized that his beloved sports car was probably doomed after he got married. Maybe even sooner when he saw the look on JoAnn's face as she squeezed herself into the passenger seat.

"You look tired, baby. What do you want for dinner?"

"After eating hot dishes, bratwurst, and deep-fried cheese curds for the past few days, anything would be fine."

"Okay, I'll order Chinese."

"Sounds good. I'll probably just go to bed after dinner. I hope you don't mind."

James smiled. "That's fine. I have an early meeting with Rick tomorrow."

James arrived at Rick's house the next morning and was impressed by the size of the house and its view of the golf course. He rang the doorbell and Rick appeared, followed by a very large Great Dane. Rick had his left arm in a sling and bandages on his left hand and the left side of his head.

"Come on in," Rick said. "I'll only be a minute."

James walked into the kitchen and was greeted by an extremely attractive blonde dressed in a sheer pink baby-doll nightgown.

"Hi, I'm Allison."

James was stunned and just stared at Allison for several seconds before saying, "Uh, hi, Allison. Is this your house or Rick's?"

"It's Rick's house. I'm just staying here to take care of him after his accident yesterday."

"Yeah, I noticed that. Did he say what happened?"

"All he said was that he was run off the road by a pickup truck and hit a tree."

"Was the driver drunk?"

"I don't know. Rick said he took off."

"When did it happen?"

"It must've been around five, since he was driving home. I'm an intern at the local hospital in La Plata where he was taken, and his contact for all medical emergencies."

Rick came into the kitchen with his briefcase and told James he was ready to go.

"Are you sure you're up to this, Rick? I can go without you and fill you in later."

"I'm fine, James. Let's go."

After driving for a few minutes in silence, James finally said, "Are you going to tell me about the accident?"

"It wasn't an accident. But I don't want Allison to know. A pickup truck came up next to my car right after I got off our call last night. The passenger shot at me with a shotgun."

"Was that the crazy driver you mentioned during our call?"

"Yup. I put three shots into the passenger side, and I'm sure I hit someone. The pickup then hit my car and spun me into the woods. The next thing I know, I was being dragged out of my Mustang by the EMTs."

"What do the police think?"

"After looking at the pictures I took and the gunshot damage to my car, they're calling it assault with a deadly weapon. If they find the assailants, it could be elevated to attempted murder."

"So they got away?"

"Yeah, the FBI checked the license plate from the picture I provided. The pickup was reported stolen in New Jersey more than a month ago. They're also checking with the local hospitals for any reports of a gunshot wound. Unfortunately, I never got a good look at the driver or the passenger who shot at me. I think the shooter had long hair and bad marksmanship."

James laughed. "Thank God for that. How badly was your car damaged?"

"It's totaled. Too bad—I really liked that car. I'll probably buy another with the insurance money."

"Do you think it was related to the interrogation?"

"Maybe. I told the agent who took the report about Kinsley's interrogation."

"I have one more question, Rick. Who's the blonde?"

Rick laughed. "She's a friend I met a few years ago when I had shoulder surgery at Johns Hopkins. She was a medical student then. We've dated off and on, but I guess now it's very on. She purposely selected the hospital in La Plata to finish her internship so we could be closer."

"That house overlooking the golf course is really nice. When did you buy it?"

"I didn't. I inherited it from my dad, after he passed away a year ago. It's kind of big for my needs, but it's the house I grew up in, and I like playing golf. And before you ask, Allison isn't living with me yet, although I've asked several times. She likes having her own place, but she ends up spending more time at mine."

"Too bad."

"That may change after she finishes her internship. We're talking about it."

James got to the Wu summer house a little before ten and saw Ann's Escalade in the driveway. Jim met them at the door and escorted them into the kitchen, where Ann was brewing coffee. She handed James a cup the way she knew he liked it and then asked Rick if he wanted a cup.

"Yes, please, black with no sugar."

James made the introductions and could see that Ann and Jim were staring at Rick's bandages.

"Rick was in a car accident yesterday," James explained. "Can you take us on a tour of the house, Ann?"

"Sure, what do you want to see first?"

"We'd like to see where Philip worked."

"He either worked right here at the kitchen table or in the sitting room off the master bedroom."

"Did he have a computer at the house?"

"Just the laptop that he used while he was here. He also had a removable drive that allowed him to transport files to and from the office."

"Is the laptop still here?"

"No, it went missing after the break-in, along with the removable drive. Philip usually put them in his briefcase, which is also missing."

"Maybe the accomplice took it," Rick whispered to James, who nodded.

"Can we see the sitting room, Ann?"

"Sure, follow me."

James and Rick inspected the sitting room connected to the master bedroom.

"Are there any hidden safes in here, Ann?"

"No, there's only the rolltop desk, which is locked."

"Do you have the key?"

"I'm sorry, James, I didn't bring it. It only contains receipts and warranties for household items purchased for this house. I didn't think it was important."

"That's okay, just bring it next time. It's my understanding that the safe in the master bedroom was found unlocked. Does anyone other than you and Jim know about the safe?"

"I doubt it. I also told the police that nothing appeared to be missing, including the fifty thousand dollars we stored for emergencies."

"Yes, I know. You also told them that Philip never stored VSI technical information in the safe. Are you certain about that?"

"That's what my husband told me. Do you know something I don't, James?"

"No, I'm just trying to be thorough. Philip would never lie about that and certainly not to you, Ann. Do you know who installed the safe?"

"It was designed by Philip and built by the same company in Ohio that built the VSI security vault. Some of their people installed it. I have the receipts at the other house, if you need them."

"We might. Do you know why your combination was different than the one Philip used?"

"No, I don't. I asked Philip, but he never really gave me a good answer. I do know that he absolutely required separate combinations in the design. Do you know why, Jim?"

"I haven't a clue, Mom. But it was like dad to have a plan that no one thought of. I'm sure you know that, James."

"I do, Jim. Can you show me the floor safe and the procedure used to open it?"

Jim removed the carpet and the piece of flooring that covered the safe. Ann entered her combination and the verbal passcode from the bedroom phone. The light turned green, indicating that the safe was locked.

"How was it locked without having Philip's combination?"

"He kept our combinations in the safe deposit box at our bank," Ann said. "We did that in case something happened to either or the both of us. Jim was the only other person who knew about the safe deposit box."

"I'll need Philip's combination next time I'm here."

"Sure, James. I'll get it tomorrow."

Ann demonstrated how the safe was unlocked and then relocked, and James watched as the light on the safe went from green to red and then green again.

"I bet the phone has a Bluetooth wireless system to transmit the combination and passcode from the phone to the safe," James said. "Check the phone, Rick."

"Yeah, it looks like it has a Bluetooth antenna, James."

James opened the safe and saw that it was completely empty.

"Do you still plan to use it, Ann?"

"I can't stand to even see the damn thing. Every time I look at it

I get depressed. I'd have it removed if it wasn't embedded in concrete and supported by the house's main beam."

"We know this is difficult, and I don't want to cause either you or Jim any more pain than you're already dealing with."

"I know that, James. You're the best friend Philip and our family ever had."

Ann started to cry, so James changed the subject.

"Jim, do you know if the FBI has done any physical analyses of the safe?"

"I know they had someone examine it, but I don't know what they found."

"That's okay, we'll get the FBI report. Right, Rick?"

"Sure. No problem."

"Was there a duress code for the safe, Ann?"

"No, Philip didn't want one, James. He said there was nothing that important in the safe to risk anyone getting hurt."

"Do you have any documentation on the safe?"

"We couldn't find any, James. Do you want me to get that information from the company?"

"I can do that if we need it. Just email me the contact information."

James reached into the safe and ran his hand around the inside to see if he could find any wires or electronic components. He found none.

"I think the light on the safe door is controlled by a circuit board either within the door or outside the safe wall. It's probably powered from the house's electrical line that runs along the main beam. Hopefully there's a diagram in the documentation. If not, we'll need to get it from the company that installed the safe."

"Some of that information may be in the rolltop desk, James. You can open it with the key when you come back," Ann said.

"I'd like to discuss the situation with George. I'd also like Jim to sit in on the discussion, Ann."

"I do, too, James. Jim's my legal advisor as well as my son."

"Can you tell me why George said he wanted your proxy?"

"He said he only needed the proxy for the board meeting to select a temporary CEO and that it wouldn't be permanent. When I told him I wouldn't do that, he threatened to have the board buy Philip's shares in a forced sale. He said he could do that since Philip had violated his NDA by disclosing VSI proprietary information. I'm certain my husband would never have done that."

"So am I, Ann. I'm going to disclose some information to you from an FBI interrogation that Rick and I participated in last week that may be pertinent. You both need to keep this confidential."

"Sure, James. My mother and I both agree," Jim said.

"Good. The interrogation was conducted by Rick, and the subject's answers were analyzed using a polygraph. FBI personnel reviewed the results and determined that the government had obtained uncoerced information on proprietary VSI technology. Such information could only have been provided by Philip or me, and I've never talked to the government about VSI technology, Jim."

"That doesn't mean my father provided it, James. There must be other sources."

"I can't believe it was your father, Jim. But, it would have to be another source I'm not aware of."

"I read the NDA after Mom found it. It says the evidence must meet the requirements under Maryland law for criminal cases, which is a very tough requirement. Do you think George can do that?"

"No, I don't. The lie detector test is the only indication that VSI proprietary information was disclosed, and that wouldn't be admissible in a court of law. George's evidence would have to be airtight. I can't imagine that he has such information, but if he does, it might provide the reason your dad was murdered and who the murderer was. I suggest we call his bluff."

"I know my mother wants to take George on, but I'm not so certain. If George succeeds in court and she's forced to sell her shares, she'd be outside of the company looking in. She would no longer have any income other than what she got on the sale of her shares. Based on the corporate rules, she'd be an outsider and not a stockholder. That means you couldn't buy her shares and then sell them back to her without George having the right to buy her shares at a higher price. I'm pretty certain George is wealthier than you are and could outbid you. She could end up with no dividends and no increased equity based on the rising value of the company. I have advised her against it."

"I understand, and it's a great legal analysis that I hadn't considered. I can see you haven't wasted your time in law school."

"No, I haven't. There's also another consideration. Although I can't believe my father would've violated the NDA, George is rich enough to fabricate convincing evidence. From what I've heard, he isn't the most honest person."

"There may be another solution, Jim. George is only doing this so he can select the temporary CEO. It would be someone other than him, someone who's technically capable of running the company. He obviously believes that he can scare your mother into giving him her proxy. If I decide to take back the CEO position, which is my right, there's no longer a need for a vote. George couldn't demonstrate that I violated my NDA. He also knows the president and I are close, so I don't believe he'd attempt to bully me."

"That would mean you'd have to resign as Federal Chief Information Officer, which you promised the president you wouldn't do."

"I know that, Ann. But given the situation, I believe the president will understand. I'll inform the president and George tomorrow. I'd like to hear what George has to say."

"So would I. I hope the old bastard chokes," Ann said.

On the drive back to La Plata, James asked Rick what he thought about his return to the CEO position.

"I don't think it'll make that much difference with respect to the investigation. I'm going to keep working the case, and I'm pretty sure the director will still want you in the loop. The question is whether you'll have the time to help."

"I'll make the time, Rick. I believe there's something going on in

VSI that directly relates to Philip's murder, and it might involve George. I need to get to the bottom of it. Unfortunately, I'll need to find a place to live that's closer to VSI. JoAnn isn't going to like that."

"You know you can stay at my house," said Rick. "I have plenty of room."

"You sure that won't cramp your relationship with Allison?"

"Not a problem. It's a big house, and she's not a screamer."

"Too much information, Rick, but I might take you up on that."

"When do you think you might be moving in?"

"I'm not sure. I need to talk with Barbara, the president, and most importantly, my fiancée, Senator Young."

"Well, at least you have your priorities straight."

# 14

Dimitri was happy to have some time to relax after the hectic pace of the past several weeks. He monitored his favorite news sources every day after returning from DC to see if there was anything about the investigation into Senator Thompson's death. This morning he saw reports from multiple news sources that the DC government had requested that Walter Reed verify Senator Thompson's autopsy results.

His experience working for US Intelligence agencies taught Dimitri how federal politics worked, and he knew that this request was based on politics, not forensics. The White House needed to find the Chinese agent innocent in order to avoid a major incident. That meant they needed to have Walter Reed show that the majority leader died of natural causes. Dimitri believed he was off the hook.

Later that morning, Dimitri got a text from Frank Green asking him to call.

"Hey, Frank, have you had any luck?"

"Not yet."

"Do you know when?"

"Yes, but I have to go, Stalin. I'm getting prepared for a business trip. I hear there's a winter storm coming your way. Maybe you should plan a trip down south to avoid the cold."

"Yeah, I think I'll do that."

Dimitri knew that Frank had just sent him a covert message saying that he'd have the information soon since he was getting ready to deploy on a mission and would have access to the databases. The message also said he'd only provide it to him in Quantico.

Later that day Dimitri visited the electronics shop to get a new phone. He replaced his phones several times a year as a security precaution to prevent his number from being traced or the phone being cloned.

"How are you today, Yuri? It looks like business is growing."

"Yeah, it's doing well. What can I do for you Dimitri?"

"I'm here to buy another cell phone."

"Another burner phone? You know it would be cheaper if you just bought a phone with a plan that's flexible. It would also provide more capability."

"I know, but I'm rough on phones. A phone plan would be a waste of money. I only need it for calls, texts, and occasional photos."

Yuri had heard about Dimitri's past, so he accepted the explanation even though he was skeptical of the rationale.

"Have you heard about the new documentary that's going to be filmed in Brighton Beach, Dimitri?"

"No, what kind of documentary?"

"It's going to be about recent immigrants in the Brighton Beach community who suffered tragedy while living in Russia."

"When does it start?"

"In a few days. The Chinese film crew is looking for locations and people to interview."

"What kind of people?"

"People like you, Dimitri. You could be a star."

"I'm not star material, Yuri."

"Yeah, neither am I, but local businesses will really do well. There'll be lots of tourists in the area during filming. More police, too."

"How long are they supposed to be here?"

"Probably two weeks or more," Yuri answered.

Dimitri now had a second reason to leave. After Yuri set up his new phone, Dimitri went home and called a woman he knew.

"Good morning, Claudia. Can I come visit you for a few days? My community is being invaded by a film crew, and I need to escape."

"Sure, Dimitri. I have some vacation time I need to use. Why don't we both get out of New York for a few days?"

"Sounds great. I'll pack a bag and meet you at your house tomorrow night."

"Okay. We'll discuss the trip over dinner."

Dimitri had developed an ongoing relationship with Claudia, who was originally from Cuba but had immigrated to the US during the Mariel boatlift as an infant. Claudia worked as a psychologist counseling patients with behavioral and addiction disorders at a local hospital. Dimitri met her at the Metropolitan Museum of Art three years ago while at an exhibition of Russian artists of the nineteenth century.

The relationship was casual at first and generally included dinner and some discussion of literature, art, and current events. It became sexual after several months, but neither was interested in anything more than that. Claudia was passionate but had bad experiences with some violent men, including her father and her ex-husband, which made her wary of commitment. She knew that Dimitri was also non-committal, which made him the perfect paramour. Their meetings were sporadic and usually initiated by Dimitri calling her. When they stayed together overnight, it was always at her house in Queens. Dimitri never invited anyone to his home except Yuri.

The next day, Dimitri left his house key with Yuri to take care of Putin while he was gone. That evening, Dimitri called a taxi and arrived at Claudia's house. She opened her door as Dimitri walked up the steps and kissed him passionately before he got in the house.

"Either you really like my new cologne or you're really happy to see me. What's going on, Claudia?"

"I just found out my father died. You know I hated him. I'm so happy my mother is rid of the abusive bastard. She gets all his pension money and title to all their property and is giving me half. I can pay off the mortgage on my house and all my bills. Let's celebrate. I'll cook your favorite Italian dinner, veal scallopini."

"Okay. We can also talk about the trip."

"I already know where I want to go. I'd like to visit my mother in Orlando, Florida, and then my father's grave."

"I thought you said you hated him."

"I do. I want to piss on his grave."

Dimitri laughed. "I'd like to see that."

"Better yet, take some pictures. I want to send them to everyone who knew and hated the SOB."

"We can also visit Disney World. I hear it's nearby."

"It is. I'll set up a hotel reservation near the park. My mother's house is small and she has guests, so she has no room for us."

"On the way there I'd like to stop and see a friend. He's someone I worked with that lives in Occoquan, Virginia."

"Where's Occoquan, Dimitri?"

"It's near the military base in Quantico, Virginia. It's on the way."

"Okay, but we should take my SUV. There's a winter storm coming up the coast."

"Then we should leave as soon as possible. I need to get to Occoquan before my friend leaves on a business trip. It's on the same route that we'll take to Orlando."

"Okay, I'll plan the trip," Claudia said.

Claudia estimated that with both people driving, they could make it to Occoquan in about six hours and then to Orlando in another thirteen hours, weather permitting. She had to take care of a few things at work the next day, so it was noon before they left.

Dimitri and Claudia took turns driving and arrived in Occoquan at about six that evening. They found a nice hotel off of I-95 where they got a room, had some room service, then watched TV before going to bed. The next morning, Dimitri got up early and used the hotel's indoor pool and spa as Claudia slept. He also called Frank.

"Hey, Stalin, are you here?"

"Yeah, I got in last night, Frank. I'll text you where I'm staying."

"Great, I'll be there in an hour. I have what you want."

Dimitri was ecstatic and went back to the room to celebrate. As he walked into the room, he could see that Claudia was still sleeping, so he quietly slipped off his shorts and slid under the covers. He began to kiss her shoulder and then her neck. She awoke with a smile and they made love until it was time to get ready for his meeting. Claudia went back to sleep while he got up, took a quick shower, and went down to the lobby to meet Frank.

Frank was sitting in the lobby reading a newspaper when Dimitri got off the elevator. They found a quiet booth in the back of the hotel restaurant.

"I got your guy's name, and you won't believe who it is."

"Okay, Frank, you have my attention. Who is it?"

"He's one of the richest bastards on the planet, and he isn't hiding at all. He doesn't have to. The Russians would never do anything to him, and he knows it. His name is George Solomon, the billionaire investor. He's a friend of the president, even helped him get elected."

Dimitri remembered hearing that name from his research on Senator Thompson, and he had also seen him as the tall white-haired man attending Philip Wu's funeral. He also remembered Senator Thompson's reference to a tall man he had called "Whitey." *Could George Solomon be the Big Man he was trying to find?* Dimitri wondered.

"Was there anything else interesting in his file, Frank?"

"Yeah. He's listed as supporting a number of groups that oppose the Chinese government. He's also a hard-line supporter of the foreign cyber-attack legislation being considered by Congress. His file said his only brother was a Russian soldier who was killed by the Chinese

Army during the Zhenbao Island incident in 1969. He was one of fifty-nine border guards killed when the Chinese ambushed them. That's probably why he hates the Chinese government."

"Did the file say he had connections to organized crime?"

"No, there's no mention of that. I've got to get back to Quantico, Stalin. Do you want to meet me for dinner this evening?"

"I can't, Frank. There's a woman with me. It wouldn't be safe."

"Yeah, I guess not. Another time?"

"Sure, Frank. Thanks for the help. This makes us even."

Dimitri and Frank knew that bringing outsiders into their environment was never smart in their line of work. Claudia could provide a connection between the two of them if the intelligence information on George Solomon was ever discovered to have been compromised.

When Dimitri got back to the room, Claudia had already showered and dressed and was ready to get breakfast.

"I already met my friend in the restaurant for coffee, Claudia. He's leaving the country on business and won't be able to see us."

"Okay. I guess I'll be able to see my mother sooner."

"If we leave after breakfast, we should be there tonight."

"I'll set up a hotel reservation near Disney World."

The weekday traffic wasn't bad, and they made it into Orlando before ten that evening. They checked into their room, and Claudia immediately called her mother. After the call, she joined Dimitri on the couch.

"My relatives are still at my mother's house. I'd like to visit them, Dimitri."

"That's fine. I'm tired. Enjoy yourself."

"I will. If I enjoy myself too much I might not be back until tomorrow morning."

"Okay. Have fun, Claudia."

Dimitri stayed in the room and watched TV. He saw a story on one of the cable news channels about the documentary being filmed in Brighton Beach. There was an interview with the Chinese producer,

Sun Yu, who described their objectives and how well it was going with the community. Sun Yu described how everyone was so friendly and specifically mentioned the owner of a local bar and community leader, Marat Chubais. A video clip of the pakhan's bar described him as a survivor of the Chechen wars who was doing well. Dimitri laughed; they had no idea.

Dimitri called the pakhan. He could hear the background noise from the crowd. The noise dissipated as the pakhan entered his office.

"I just saw you on TV, Pakhan. You're famous. How are things at your bar?"

"My bar is doing well, but I'm miserable. There are lots of Chinese with cameras and thirsty tourists. I pray for these Chinese *mudaks* to leave soon."

"How can you call them 'bastards' when I just saw an interview where the Chinese producer said Marat Chubais was a friendly bar owner?"

"Yes, I saw it, too, and have been reminded about it everywhere I go. I like the producer. He speaks and drinks like a Russian. I haven't seen you for a few days. Where've you been, Dimitri? Why aren't you suffering like me?"

"I'm in Florida. I'm going to Disney World."

"You lucky mudak. I wish I was there."

"You're a celebrity now, Pakhan. When I get back I'd like your autograph."

"Have fun. I'll see you when you return."

Sun Yu's plan to find Dimitri in Brighton Beach was based on a strategy that would locate him quickly, based on his history. He had ordered his production crew to specifically target Russian partisans from Grozny for interviews. The plan began to pay off after the Chinese film crew hired Yuri to help them repair one of their cameras.

One of the crew had family from Russia and became friendly with

Yuri. During a discussion between them about the documentary, Yuri recommended that they interview Dimitri as a hero of the Second Chechen war whose family had been massacred. Yuri was introduced to Sun Yu, who asked him how he could find Dimitri to do an interview.

"I haven't seen Dimitri for a few days. He travels a lot."

"Do you know how I can contact him, Yuri?"

"I sold him a new phone, and I have his number and contact information at the store. I can go get it."

"Please do. It's very important."

"I'll be back in fifteen minutes."

When Yuri returned, he gave Sun Yu Dimitri's cell phone number and address. Sun Yu provided the phone number to the embassy so that they could track it. All they had to do was wait until the phone was turned on.

That happened pretty quickly when a phone conversation took place between a land line in Brighton Beach and Dimitri's cell phone in Orlando. The Chinese located and identified Dimitri's hotel. When the ambassador was informed of the location, he called Sun Yu.

"We found him, Sun. He's near Disney World in Florida."

"That's great, Ambassador, but I think I need to stay and finish the film to avoid suspicion."

"I agree. Do a good job, Sun. You could have a future making movies in Hollywood."

"I'm working hard on this, Ambassador. I want to make it look genuine. Maybe it'll even win some awards."

The ambassador chuckled, but Sun Yu didn't laugh. He was actually enjoying the prospect of making a first-rate documentary.

Claudia returned from her visit to her mother's house early the next morning and found Dimitri asleep in bed with the television on. She quietly undressed and got into bed. After a sexual massage, Dimitri was awake, and they enjoyed each other until they both climaxed. They showered together, dressed, and went to breakfast at the restaurant in the hotel. Dimitri was looking forward to having some fun for a change, something he hadn't done in a long time.

As they waited for a table, Dimitri quickly looked around the restaurant. He requested the patio, since it was an open area that provided a panoramic view of all entrances and exits. As he and Claudia were led to their table, Dimitri noticed several Asian and Caucasian males near each exit, but no families or couples.

Dimitri thought that was unusual for a vacation resort near Disney World. His sixth sense about ambushes had saved his life before. He knew he was under surveillance, but acted totally unaware while preparing for a very dangerous escape.

"I'm going to have the steak-and-egg breakfast, Claudia. What're you having?"

"That sounds good. I'll have the same."

The waiter came over and asked for their order.

"Two steak-and-egg breakfasts," Dimitri said. "We'll need steak knives."

"Yes, sir."

The waiter brought the steak knives, and Dimitri slipped his in his pocket after Claudia left to go to the ladies' room. She returned as the waiter was bringing their breakfasts. Dimitri stood, pulled out her chair, and then kissed her.

"I'm so very sorry," he whispered.

Dimitri ran toward a small fence surrounding the patio, knocking over a table and chairs to slow his pursuers. He quickly scaled the fence and made his way through the surrounding foliage toward the valet parking area of the hotel garage. Dimitri lost all of his pursuers except one Asian male who entered the garage about twenty seconds after he did.

After hiding behind a garage column, Dimitri watched as the man entered the garage and approached the column where Dimitri was hiding. The man didn't appear to be armed, so Dimitri confronted him by attempting to use the same move he had used to subdue the bully in the pakhan's bar. Unfortunately, it didn't work. The man was too fast and was obviously trained in martial arts, but so was Dimitri. Dimitri also had the advantage of size and the steak knife, which he didn't want to use unless absolutely necessary.

The fight that ensued was intense, but went to Dimitri's advantage until Dimitri knocked his opponent down near a four-foot piece of rusted rebar. The man quickly jumped to his feet as he grabbed the rebar and swung it at Dimitri, hitting him in the thigh. Dimitri grunted loudly as he fell to the ground.

As the man approached, Dimitri pulled his knife and tripped him with his leg. The agent fell toward Dimitri, who heard a groan as the agent fell on top of Dimitri's knife. Both Dimitri and his attacker were hurt, but it was clear that the attacker was hurt worse.

Dimitri could hear the gurgle in the agent's chest and saw bubbling blood as he tried to breathe. The knife had penetrated the attacker's lung, which created a sucking chest wound. Dimitri had seen such wounds in combat and knew the agent would die if he didn't quickly get help.

He removed the man's wallet and saw that he was a Chinese national assigned to the embassy in DC, probably as a security or intelligence agent. Dimitri turned his cell phone on and laid it near the victim. He knew that he was being tracked and that his cell phone would quickly lead his pursuers to the injured agent.

Luckily, Dimitri could still walk, but he needed to find some transportation. One of the valet attendants entered the garage. Dimitri waited until he got closer and then grabbed him from behind, disabling him with a sleeper hold. He grabbed the key from the valet's hand and walked through the garage pressing the unlock button until he found a car with flashing lights. He jumped in and drove out of the garage in a direction toward Orlando.

Dimitri drove to the Florida Mall near Orlando and parked. There was an electronics store nearby where he purchased a burner phone, and then limped to the hotel connected to the mall. The pain was getting worse, so he found a quiet area and called the pakhan.

"Pakhan, I've gotten into some trouble in Florida and I need your help."

"Where are you, and what do you need?"

"I'm in the lobby of a hotel in Orlando. It's located in the Florida Mall. I need a car with clean tags and registration that can get me back to New York. Some Chinese agents are after me."

"Chinese agents? Do you think they're the same Chinese that are here?"

"Possibly. Be careful, Pakhan. I was in a fight with one of them and have an injured leg. It's hard to walk with the pain."

"Are the police involved?"

"I assume they are. I stole a car and disabled the garage attendant. I'll need a safe place to stay outside of Brooklyn until things cool down."

"Okay. Stay out of sight, and I'll call back in about an hour."

"Thanks, Pakhan."

Dimitri found a quiet bar and grill and ordered a vodka. He had just finished his drink when the pakhan called.

"I have a car for you. It's a 2016 Ford Taurus in excellent condition that's under the dealer's registration. They'll bring it to you at the mall in twenty minutes."

"I'm in the hotel bar. I'll meet them outside."

"I have a place for you to stay where you'll be safe and tended to by the best doctor I know."

"I don't want to get Anya involved in this, Pakhan."

"She insisted. It'll only be until you recover and we can figure out how to solve this."

"Okay, but tell the men with the car to bring some prescription pain killers, a weapon, and some food and water."

"I've already arranged for that and more."

Dimitri finished his sandwich and went outside to wait for the car, which arrived in minutes. A tall man got out of the car and approached him.

"Are you Dimitri?"

"Yes."

"Marat sent me. There's some blankets and a winter coat in the back seat and a tote bag with other items. Here's the keys."

"Thanks," Dimitri said as he quickly got into the car. He opened the tote bag and found sandwiches, a bottle of Oxycodone, antibiotics, two large bottles of water, and a Baby Glock 26.

Dimitri drove until he was exhausted before stopping at a truck stop on I-95 in Virginia. He slept for seven hours with his car parked between two large rigs, and then he drove another eight hours to Anya's house in Stony Brook. Dimitri pulled the car into the driveway and limped to the front door, where Anya was waiting for him.

Anya looked like an angel as she guided him into the house and onto a couch in the living room. She then went and parked the car in the garage and removed all the bags, taking them to her bedroom. Anya looked at Dimitri and said, "I need to take off your pants to check your injury."

Dimitri laughed. "It won't be the first time you've taken off my pants, Anya."

"Yes, but that was a long time ago."

Anya examined his leg.

"There's no fracture, but you have a very serious contusion. You'll need to stay off your injured leg for at least a week or two. I'll help you to the master bedroom."

"I don't want to put you out of your bedroom, Anya."

Anya kissed him passionately. "Don't worry, you won't."

# 15

Kim visited Cai in the hospital after she was stabbed, as did Shen, Lian, and Mei. Cai's parents also visited from their home in Qufu and were staying in the Xiyuan Hotel on campus, courtesy of the university. She was informed by her doctors that she'd be able to return to school in a couple of weeks. In the meantime, her professors and classmates were recording her classes.

The story of the attack on Cai had made her a minor celebrity on local Harbin TV. All of the local news reports applauded Cai's bravery while trying to save her roommate from a Korean who was in the country illegally. The reports also stated that the Korean was arrested after suffering minor wounds during an apparent fight with some friends after someone called the police.

Kim laughed when he heard that the wounds were considered minor. He was also relieved after hearing that the police had closed the case. Kim called Shen to tell him the news.

"Hi, Shen. It looks like I'll still be available for the project and school."

"Yes, I heard the news. Unfortunately, the loss of Cai will be difficult, so I've decided to take her place."

"Can you manage the project and also do Cai's work?"

"I think so, but I'll need your help with both, Kim."

"Sure, I'll help with anything you need."

"Good. Meet me after our last class today. I'll drive us to my apartment where we'll have some privacy."

"Won't Lian be there?"

"No, she only stays at my place on weekends. She has her own apartment."

Kim always enjoyed riding in Shen's Mercedes and was even more impressed when he saw Shen's apartment. It was on the ninth floor of a high-rise in New Harbin City, one of the most luxurious areas of Harbin. Shen noticed Kim's reaction and said, "It's not mine, Kim. It belongs to my father's business. He's letting me use it as long as I'm in school."

"This place is huge, and your view is incredible."

"Yes, it's a two-bedroom suite. Follow me to the bedroom I use as my office."

"Wow, it's really well equipped," Kim said, as he looked around Shen's office.

"Thanks. You can set up your laptop on the small conference table. Here's a jump drive with a copy of the target network addresses that Sean Flaherty provided. Take a few minutes to copy and review them while I change my clothes."

"Thanks," Kim said as he began his review of the target information.

Shen returned in a few minutes wearing sweat clothes. Kim laughed. "I hope this review isn't going to be as strenuous as your clothing indicates, Shen."

Shen smiled. "No, I'm going to do my daily workout in the gym in the basement after we're done. You're welcome to join me."

"Thanks, but I have some things from school that I need to take to Cai after we're done. When does Flaherty want us to begin the probing of these addresses?"

"Two days from now."

"That's not a lot of time to prepare. What are these network addresses listed as special targets?"

"I don't know, Kim. Flaherty told me not to worry about them. He said they don't require probing."

"Why is that? They're in the range of addresses selected for the attack. It doesn't make any sense not to probe them, Shen."

"Yeah, I know. Flaherty said they were preselected for attack."

"That's crazy. How can we attack targets without first probing to identify the type and severity of their vulnerabilities? You need to ask Flaherty about that."

"I'll contact him before he leaves tomorrow night."

"Okay, let me know. How do I get to the hospital?"

"You can use the tenant car service. Here's my service card."

Kim took all the recordings for Cai's classes to the hospital. When he entered her room, he saw Cai's laptop on the hospital bed table.

"How'd you get your laptop, Cai?"

"Mei brought it from the apartment earlier. I think I'll be able to return to school and the project sooner than anticipated, Kim."

"Don't worry about that, Cai. Shen is taking your position until you get well."

"How are things going?"

"I'm not sure. We just got the target information, and it's very strange. There are targets that are preselected for attack, even though we're not allowed to probe them first."

"Why would they preselect targets for attack without probing for weaknesses, Kim? How would they know if the attack would be effective or not?"

"I have no idea. Maybe they have other sources of information on these targets that they plan to provide us before the exploitation phases. Shen plans to ask Flaherty that question before he leaves. He's also providing grades on all the students."

"Why would they want to grade us?"

"I don't know, unless this is just some crazy recruiting exercise."

"That doesn't make any sense, Kim. It would be an extremely expensive way to recruit."

Shen met Flaherty at the Shang Palace that evening and handed him his grading report. Flaherty looked at the grades.

"You're an easy grader, Shen. All As and Bs but no Cs or Ds? I'll also want grades after the probing phase is completed and again after the exploitation phase. From now on, I want number grades with a clearer differentiation, is that clear?"

"Yes, but what's the purpose of the grades?"

"I wasn't told, and I only do what I'm told. You should as well."

"I always have, Sean. But it's hard to plan if I don't know the goals. My team needs to know why certain targets are listed as special targets that shouldn't be probed, but are listed for attack during the exploitation phases. How do we know how to exploit them if we don't probe first?"

"You worry too much about things that aren't your concern. The vulnerabilities on those addresses are assigned to a separate group."

Shen wasn't sure what that meant. It almost sounded as if the vulnerabilities were being created as opposed to being discovered. He quickly discarded that thought; creating vulnerabilities on that many addresses would be impossible.

When Kim got back to his apartment, Lee Park was waiting for him. Kim knew that she had a key since she was the landlord, but up to now she'd always called first if she was going to meet him there.

"This is a surprise, Lee. Why are you here?"

"I'm sorry, Kim, but it couldn't be helped. I got a message from your uncle that you need to return to Nampo immediately and meet with him at his office. He said it had nothing to do with your family, but was related to your mission, and he needed to discuss it with you face-to-face."

Kim wasn't worried about his safety, since he knew his uncle would never put him in danger. He didn't like leaving Cai while she was in the hospital, and was concerned that he might be ordered to return to North Korea for some new assignment away from her. The very thought of that made him nauseous.

"How am I supposed to return immediately, Lee? Air China only flies to North Korea three times a week. The next flight is two days from now."

"The admiral has set up a special flight. It's been approved by the Chinese and your government."

"When's the flight, and how do I get to fleet headquarters in Nampo?"

"A military plane will fly directly from Harbin Taiping Airport to the air base outside Nampo. The admiral will have a car take you to his fleet headquarters. I have your authorization papers. Just take them to the Air China office by nine tomorrow morning and they'll direct you. I've arranged for a taxi to pick you up here at eight."

"How long will I be gone? I need to tell my professors and classmates."

"Don't worry, I'll take care of that. I'll tell the school that you had to visit a sick relative. The admiral said you should be able to return tomorrow evening at the latest."

A half hour after Lee left, Kim received a call from Cai.

"Hi, Kim. Some woman called me and said you had to return home tomorrow. Is everything okay? Are you in any danger?"

"I'm fine. It's a short trip to meet with my uncle. I'll be home tomorrow and will come by the hospital to see you."

"I hope you're not in any danger."

"Don't worry, Cai. My uncle would never let me be harmed. Get some rest."

"Okay, see you tomorrow."

Kim got up the next morning and packed a few toiletries in a small bag along with a change of clothing. The taxi arrived at eight and took him to Harbin Taiping International Airport. He was led to a gate at the far end of the airport by a uniformed policeman who stayed with him until the gate was opened shortly before nine. A young North Korean Air Force second lieutenant came through the gate and introduced himself.

"Commander, please follow me," he said as he led Kim onto the plane. "Please take any seat, you're our only passenger today."

Kim made himself comfortable in what was obviously the admiral's private plane. The two hour flight landed at the air base near Nampo. Kim sat in his seat until the lieutenant opened the exit door and led him toward a waiting car. He enjoyed the ride, which passed areas and landmarks that Kim remembered from his childhood.

When he arrived at the Western Fleet headquarters, Kim showed his authorization papers and military ID to the guard at the entrance, who saluted and directed him to the admiral's office. Kim hadn't visited his uncle since the Glorious Leader had promoted him to fleet admiral over a year ago. When Kim arrived at the office, he took a deep breath, opened the door, and introduced himself to the admiral's secretary.

"The admiral will be right out, Commander, he's just finishing an important conference call. Please take a seat and make yourself comfortable."

Kim sat on a black leather couch under the North Korean flag. He waited almost twenty minutes before his uncle appeared. Kim immediately stood at attention and saluted.

"At ease, Commander. Please follow me."

Kim followed the admiral into a small conference room with no phones and was directed to sit as the admiral closed the door. As he looked around the room, he realized that the lack of phones, windows, and electrical sockets was by design. He quickly glanced at his cell phone and realized it was being jammed. This was a room designed to prevent eavesdropping. He wondered why he was there and what the admiral was up to.

"How are you, Kim? You look well."

"So do you, Admiral," Kim said.

"Don't lie, Kim. I can see by your expression that you don't believe that."

"Are you okay, Admiral? You've lost a lot of weight."

"I'm dying, nephew. It isn't a fast death, but it's a certain one. The doctors here have no way to treat my illness. My doctor is an old friend who's keeping me alive, since the quacks in the navy are incompetent. I don't want our Glorious Leader to remove me, so we're keeping it secret. I'm just telling everyone that my doctor told me to lose weight for my health."

Kim was shocked. It took him a while to respond to what he just heard.

"I'm sincerely sorry to hear this, Admiral. You've always been like a father to me. You're the reason I joined the navy."

"And you've always been like a son to me, Kim. It was my honor to watch over your mother, sister, and you after my brother died at that incompetent shipyard."

"Thank you, sir."

"I'll not bore you anymore by talking about my health like old people do. I'm sure you're wondering why I've invited you here today."

"Yes, sir, I was. Am I in some trouble?"

"Not at all. The intelligence information you've provided has been highly appreciated by the leadership. I need to ask you a question that you need to keep confidential. Can you do that?"

"I can, Admiral. What's the question?"

"Do you feel any different about our government since I approved your assignment to Harbin?"

Kim took a deep breath. "Yes, Admiral, I do. It seems we treat our people like slaves while other countries place a higher value on their citizens' welfare and freedom."

"Good. I was hoping that would be the case. I wanted to improve your skills since I knew you were good, but I also wanted to improve your perspective. My plan is to save you from this oppressive regime by helping you defect to another country. China won't allow your defection because of their agreement with North Korea not to accept North Korean defectors."

"What about my mother and sister? Can we get them out as well?"

"Possibly. I'm working on a plan to do just that. But it may require some outside help from the American Navy. I also need to discuss something else with you of even greater importance. It has implications that go far beyond our family. In fact, it could impact the lives of everyone in China, the United States, and their allies."

"What is it, Admiral?"

"Our leaders have come up with a plan to use the information you provided to trigger a catastrophic war between China and the United States. They plan to amplify the current tension between them after their relationship is worsened by the project you're involved with. The Chinese plan to display their naval strength during an upcoming military exercise between the United States and its East Asian allies: Japan, Taiwan, and South Korea. That exercise will provide our leaders with the opportunity they've been looking for."

Kim was stunned. He realized his uncle was talking about the possibility of North Korea precipitating a disastrous nuclear war between the US and China.

"When is this exercise, and where will it take place, Admiral?"

"The exercise will take place less than five weeks from now around the disputed Senkaku Islands."

"I've never heard of those islands. Where are they?"

"They're uninhabited islands near Taiwan. Japan regained territorial rights to them from the United States in 1972, but China and Taiwan have also claimed title, which has created a political problem for the United States. The joint military exercise is being held about a month from now with all of the allied countries as a way to promote solidarity. The Chinese will also send their ships to the region to show their conviction for their ownership of the islands."

"How does this have anything to do with North Korea, Admiral?"

"Our leaders believe that a cyber attack on America by the

Chinese students you're working with could create a problem for the American president. His support for a law that would put penalties on Chinese trade based on their cyber attacks on American businesses has already worsened their relations. The attacks by your group of Chinese hackers will make it even worse. Our maniacs have decided to stoke that fire by sending some of our latest submarines to the exercise area. They'll launch anti-ship missiles while submergred at the ships of the allied countries from points very close to the Chinese surface fleet. The allied fleet will retaliate, thinking the Chinese surface fleet has launched the missiles. A state of war will exist that will benefit North Korea, since China will prop up the current North Korean regime with billions in aid that will help them fight the Americans and their allies."

"That's insane, Admiral. Our navy doesn't have the technology to pull this off. We don't have the submarines or missiles with the required stealth or targeting capabilities for such an operation. In order to confuse the allied fleet into thinking the Chinese had launched the attack, we'd need quieter submarines. They'd never get close enough to the Chinese fleet without being detected by the Chinese Navy. We'd also need a guidance system capable of accurately targeting individual allied ships to prevent hitting Chinese ships."

"You've been in cybersecurity and away from our navy too long, Kim. We now have all these capabilities. The Chinese have provided us several of their latest Russian Kilo diesel-electric submarines that are extremely quiet as part of our agreement with the Americans to denuclearize. These submarines are so quiet the Americans can't always find them. Some of the new submarines also have very accurate guidance systems that allows an operator to select the target and steer the missile toward it while submerged. It's much better than the guidance systems on our older submarines."

"I don't understand. Why would the leadership even consider this plan? If it doesn't work, our country could be destroyed."

"They know the risks, but they are desperate men. Our leadership accepted the help from the Americans to revitalize and modernize our economy. It's clear that it will not happen as fast as they would like, and they're worried about a possible revolution. This is all their fault, Kim. They have applied much of the US denuclearization revenue to our military instead of growing our economy. The only way they can stop a revolution is to start a war between China and the US to get financial aid and protection from China."

"Does this mean they'll restart our nuclear weapons program?"

"They don't have to, Kim. Our military has over two hundred nuclear warheads that were buried in a fortified storage facility within the Mantapsan mountain test site. The collapse of the mountain and all tunnels to the storage facility prevented the US inspectors from finding the warheads. That is why our government agreed to denuclearization. Now that the detailed on-site inspections of our other nuclear facilities have ended, our military has started digging a new tunnel to the storage facility."

"How long will it take to get to the warheads, Admiral?"

"At least six months, but the US recently detected the tunneling, and made inquiries to our government. All tunneling has been temporarily terminated. Our leadership doesn't want to put the US on alert. Nor do they want to antagonize China, which has populated areas near Mantapsan mountain. China is very upset by the release of radiation after the mountain collapsed and its potential impact on their country. I believe we shut down our nuclear program primarily due to China's concerns, as opposed to the concerns of the US. They no longer trust our leaders with a nuclear program."

"Admiral, should I return to Harbin and try to terminate the planned attack on the American businesses?"

"No, I think it's too late for that, and it wouldn't work anyway. The two agents you met in Harbin tracked your American contact to Beijing and Shanghai, where he met with students at universities in those cities. You cannot stop those attacks, since neither you nor I know who's involved there. Besides, the attack on the American businesses is just a pretense for the planned naval attacks, not a cause."

"How can we stop this, Admiral? You must have an idea, since you ordered me here for a reason."

"You must find a way to contact the Americans, and it must be before the naval exercise."

"I'm not certain how to do that. I have no contacts with the Americans."

"I believe the cyber attack on American businesses is inevitable. We know it's being financed by an American, as described in your report. You need to identify who that is so you can contact him and alert him to what's happening. Maybe you could do that through his representative, the American whom you interrogated."

"I'll talk with my friend Shen, who's running the effort in Harbin."

"Good. But you cannot tell your friend why you need to talk to the American. Before you leave, I have a special treat for you, Kim. Come, I'll show you."

As Kim walked out of the conference room, he saw his mother and sister, Hana, sitting on the couch. Both jumped up and hugged him. The admiral asked his secretary if she'd ordered lunch, and she said that the commissary was bringing it up now. They all went back into the conference room and reminisced until lunch arrived.

Kim asked how everyone was, and he could see the troubled looks on their faces.

"It isn't good," Kim's mother said. "The price of everything is higher while our wages are being cut. Hana can't find a job even though she had excellent grades in school."

The admiral interrupted.

"They know how I feel, and they're ready to leave. They also know we're working on a plan to make that happen. I may need you to return at some point to help implement their escape. You'll need to contact me when you're ready so I can bring you back."

"That's fine, Admiral. I'll be here when we're all ready."

After lunch was over, the admiral hugged Kim and said, "Be safe, my son."

Kim was driven back to the airfield and boarded the admiral's plane. He was back in Harbin by mid-afternoon, and took a taxi to the hospital to see Cai. As Kim walked into her room, he saw a surprised look on her face.

"I didn't think you'd be back so soon. Is everything okay?"

"Yes, everything's fine. My uncle just needed to talk with me about some issues related to my assignment in Harbin."

"They're not bringing you back, are they?"

"No, don't worry, it's nothing like that. We can talk about it more after you get released from the hospital. Did they say when that would be?"

"It could be as early as tomorrow. They say I have remarkable recuperative capabilities. Shen is going to take me back to my apartment, and Mei will watch over me like a mother hen. I'll also be able to help with the probes using my computer at the apartment."

"Are you sure you're up to it? I don't want you to overdo it."

"I'm fine. I'll go crazy with nothing to do other than school."

"Okay, I'll tell Shen."

Kim left Cai after about an hour and called Shen. They decided to meet at the Xuezi Restaurant on the HIT campus and have dinner. Shen told Kim about the conversation he had with Flaherty. He said that Flaherty was coming back to Harbin in less than three weeks.

"Why so soon, Shen?"

"They shortened the schedule for the probing phase. Flaherty hasn't told me why."

"That's crazy. How are we supposed to complete the probing in that amount of time? It was already too short. Did Flaherty explain why certain target addresses didn't need to be probed?"

"His answer didn't make sense. He said that those addresses would be assigned to a separate group."

Kim shook his head and said, "Why would they need a separate group of hackers for those specific addresses if we're probing all the others within the same range?"

"I have no idea, but do you think the separate group could be the hackers in Beijing and Shanghai?"

"That still doesn't make sense, Shen. We haven't been assigned any specific addresses within their assigned range, so why would they be assigned addresses within ours?"

"There must be something we're missing, Kim."

"Yes, and there's only one way to find out what it is."

"Yes, I know. Do you still have the truth serum?"

"It's in my refrigerator," Kim answered. "We'll need to use it on Flaherty again when he comes back."

"This project is getting a little too clandestine for me, Kim. The use of truth serum is beyond what I signed up for."

"I know. It's unfortunate that we'll have to use it again, but this time we'll need it to identify and monitor Flaherty's contacts in America."

"How are you going to do that?"

"I'm still working on that. I'll let you know."

"I'm sorry that I got you all involved, Kim."

"It isn't your fault, Shen. We all went along willingly, and the money has been great. It's been an adventure that I don't regret. After all, I met Cai because of this project, and she's the best thing that's ever happened to me."

# 16

James was going to have to inform two of the people he cared about the most that he was resigning as Federal Chief Information Officer. He thought about it all the way home, after dropping Rick off at his house in La Plata. James knew telling JoAnn would be difficult. It would mean they'd be living too far apart to see each other as much as they had before. He decided to tell her over dinner at Michelle's.

The president was even more difficult, since he was not only James's boss but also one of his closest friends. His district as a state senator included VSI's headquarters, and he'd helped the company greatly by providing contacts with potential customers and strategic business partners. James was worried he was letting the president down just when the president needed him the most.

James called Barbara on her cell to request a short meeting with the president.

"Good afternoon, Barbara, it's James. Can you get me in to see the president tomorrow?"

"Good timing, James. He was just talking about you. How about tomorrow after our meeting with the Chinese ambassador to discuss the foreign cyber-attack legislation? He'll want to talk with you about the outcome. I'll schedule it for four tomorrow afternoon. Is that okay?"

"Sure, Barbara. I'll see you then."

James winced as he thought about how the president had relied upon his advice on his most important legislative initiative. That would change after James went back to VSI.

Unlike with JoAnn and the president, telling George that he was reclaiming his position as CEO would be a pleasure. George wasn't someone to be trifled with, but James was furious over his threats to Ann. Still, he needed to be careful. He'd seen George lose his temper and seek revenge using scorched-earth tactics when provoked. Hopefully he would accept James's explanation for his change in plans and also save Ann from any more threats.

James called JoAnn after getting home. She sounded sleepy when she answered the phone.

"Hi, baby, how are you doing? I hope I didn't wake you."

"No, I'm fine. How are Ann and Jim?"

"They're okay, but Rick isn't. He was in a hit-and-run with a big pickup the other night."

"Is he okay?"

"He has some cuts and bruises, but should be fine. His part-time roommate is a doctor. A beautiful blonde doctor."

"Really? How convenient."

"Can we meet for dinner at Michelle's tonight? I have something important to tell you."

"Sure, as long as it isn't about breaking up with me so you can chase after a blonde doctor."

"Never. I have what I want. Also, Rick's a former US Navy SEAL and he carries a gun."

JoAnn laughed. "What time?"

"How about seven?"

"Okay, I'll meet you there."

James had one more call to make before going to bed. He knew George would still be up since he was a notorious insomniac. James called George's private line, and a woman's voice answered. He recognized the German accent.

"Hello, Astrid, this is James Jordan. You met me and my fiancée at Michelle's."

"Yes, James, I remember. I assume you want to talk with George. He's right here. I'll put him on."

"James, what can I do for you at this late hour? Is everything okay?"

"Everything's fine. I was wondering if we could meet tomorrow at your office."

"Sure, James, let's meet at noon. I'll have lunch brought in. Do you remember where my office is?"

"I remember. See you tomorrow, George."

James had a restless night thinking about his meetings the next day. He finally fell asleep but was awakened at nine in the morning by a call on his cell phone from Ann.

"Hi, Ann. What's up?" James said, while yawning.

"I hope I didn't wake you up, James."

"It's okay. I had trouble falling asleep. What can I do for you?"

"I just wanted to let you know that I found the key to Philip's desk, and I'm going to the bank to get Philip's combination to the safe from our safe deposit box."

"Thanks, Ann, that'll be a big help. How can Rick and I get into the development where the summer home is located?"

"I'll leave my spare gate entrance cards for you and Rick at the security gate and the key to Philip's desk on the kitchen table."

"Great. I'm planning on being there tomorrow morning."

James called Rick and told him that he was going to the Wu summer house and asked if he wanted to come.

"Yeah, just let me know when you're going. I also told Allison that you may be moving in. She approves; she says she never tried a ménage à trois."

"Neither have I, Rick, or at least not one that included another man. You're not my type."

"Yeah, ditto that. The important thing is that she has no problem with you staying at the house."

"Thanks. Now all I have to do is tell JoAnn at dinner tomorrow night. I'm not looking forward to that."

James got to George's office in Rosslyn five minutes early. He was escorted into the conference room by George's executive assistant, Nadya Murin. James really liked Nadya. She'd worked for George for as long as James knew him. Nadya was probably in her mid-fifties but was still very attractive with wavy red hair and beautiful eyes. He thought she must've been very striking when she was younger. Nadya was George's diplomat. She was there to soothe the feelings of those George had offended, which was a long list. James knew it was Nadya, more than anyone else, who knew where all the bodies were buried.

Nadya sat down across from James.

"George is late as usual. You know how he likes to make people wait."

"Yeah, I know firsthand, Nadya. Someday it'll backfire on him."

"It already has. He did it to the president right after he was elected. I think George was sending a message that he was still the most important person in the room."

"I haven't heard about that. What happened?"

"He was informed by Barbara Chang that the president wasn't available and he would have to reschedule in a few months."

George finally walked into the conference room.

"Hello, James. How are you and your lovely fiancée?"

"We're fine. How are you and Astrid?"

Nadya got up and left, and George ignored the question.

"Lunch will be right in. What can I do for you today, James?"

"I'm here to tell you some confidential information before I tell anyone else. I feel you deserve to know first, since it involves VSI."

"I hope you're not permanently resigning from VSI," George said, in jest. "That wouldn't be good."

That's what James was hoping George would say.

"No, just the opposite, George. I'm returning to VSI to resume my duties as CEO. Now that Philip is gone, I believe it's best for the company."

George looked dumbfounded. He didn't say anything as he just stared at James, deciding how to respond.

"This is a real surprise, James," he finally said. "I thought you promised the president you'd stay until the end of his first term."

"I did, and I sincerely regret that. But I believe he knew it was coming after I took a leave of absence. We all know that Philip's sudden death left a big hole that needs to be filled."

"Yes, it did. I thought we were going to select a temporary replacement at the board meeting next week. Don't you think we have competent people like Theresa, Tom, or Christopher who are capable of assuming the position? You may not realize it, but they've been taking on most of Philip's duties while he was working at Fort Meade. They're all very competent."

"They are. But I believe VSI needs my experience right now more than the president needs me as Federal Chief Information Officer."

"When do you plan to leave? Don't you think the president will want you to stay until his signature legislation is passed?"

"That could take a while, George, and I'm needed back at VSI as soon as possible."

George nodded, and suddenly changed the subject.

"What've you been working on lately?" George said quietly, as if he'd given up on changing James's mind.

"I'm helping the FBI investigate Philip's murder."

"Have you made any progress?"

"Not as much as I'd have liked, George, but we have some leads that we're following."

George suddenly raised his voice as he said, "That investigation is extremely important to all of us who knew and loved Philip. If you're making progress, then you need to continue helping the FBI. We all need to know what happened on that horrible night, especially Philip's wife and son. That should be the most important thing for all of us, especially you."

James was annoyed that George had just used Ann and Jim to try and convince him to not return to VSI, when he was, in fact, returning to protect them from George.

"I believe I can still help the FBI while also taking back my duties as CEO," James said, his voice filled with conviction.

"I'm sure you can, but you won't be as effective splitting your time, and you know it. If you really want to help, then the investigation should be your highest priority. I propose that you postpone your return to VSI until there's some resolution on Philip's murder. In the meantime, I'll agree to postpone the vote on the temporary CEO until the investigation is completed. We'll essentially leave things as they are. You could still advise Chris, Theresa, and Tom while continuing to assist the president and FBI."

James was puzzled by George's response. Why had he been so strident about controlling the vote on the temporary CEO and then suggest postponing it? He knew he was missing something, but he didn't know what it was.

"That's a great idea, George. I'll cancel my meeting with the president."

George walked James out after lunch was over. As soon as James was gone, he went into his office, closed the door, and made a phone call.

"You need to accelerate the plan. James is coming back as CEO after he finishes some work with the government. You have no more than a month to complete the job and remove the evidence."

James went back to his office and checked his email. There was one from Barbara saying the ambassador had postponed their meeting and the president wasn't available. Another was from JoAnn informing him that the senate was caucusing for the vote to select the next majority leader, so she couldn't make dinner.

*Well, that worked out well,* James thought. He didn't have to attend meetings he no longer needed and could leave for Ann's summer house immediately. James called Ann.

"Hi, Ann, I just met with George and I have great news. George has offered to postpone the VSI board meeting until the FBI investigation is completed."

"Jim is here, so I have you on speaker. Did he say why?"

"He said he wanted me to continue to work with the FBI on Philip's case."

"Did you hold a gun to his head?"

James laughed. "No, it was his idea."

"Tell him we accept."

"I already did. I'm coming down to the house tonight, Ann. Did you get my combination?"

"Yeah, you're all set. Call me when you need it. Jim already left the entrance cards for you and Rick at the gate and the key to Philip's desk on the kitchen table. Goodbye, James."

James went back to his condo and emailed Rick, asking him to bring a portable hand-held ground-penetrating radar. Rick had told him that the FBI used them to find bodies or other items buried underground or encased in concrete. Before leaving, he changed into some jeans, a sweatshirt, and boots and packed a few items that he'd need, including his laptop and a change of clothes.

There were reports of a big winter storm targeting the DC area including southern Maryland. It was a great opportunity to see if his new SUV was as good as advertised. When he arrived at the gated community, James picked up his gate card from the guard and drove to the house. While unpacking, he made a call to Rick.

"How are you feeling, Rick? Is your doctor taking care of you?"

"She's working tonight and I'm feeling much better. I have the radar and I'll bring it to the house tomorrow morning. Can you tell the gate to let me in, or should I just show them my badge?"

"Ann set up a gate card for you. The guards have seen enough FBI and police badges for a while. Don't forget to bring the FBI analysis of the safe."

"I will, but I don't think there's anything useful."

The next morning, James was awakened by the doorbell. He opened the door for Rick, and noticed the falling snow.

"Come in out of the snow, Rick. It looks like the weatherman may be right this time."

"Yeah, it looks that way. The weather report for this area is ten to twelve inches. I don't think that rear-wheel drive rental is going to get me home."

"Pull it into the garage next to my SUV, which may be our only transportation."

James ate breakfast and reviewed the FBI report.

"This report is useless, Rick. It's only one page and basically concludes that the safe is a high-end house safe."

"Yeah, I know. The radar should give us more information."

"We'll get to the radar later. Ann left me the key for Philip's desk. Let's go through it first."

James opened the desk, and he and Rick went through its contents. Rick found a jump drive in one of the desk drawers.

"You continue to search the desk, Rick. I'll plug the jump drive into my laptop to see if there's anything interesting."

"The papers in the desk all appear to be old designs and ideas that your partner wanted to keep," Rick said. "I haven't seen anything that has a date newer than three years ago."

"Yeah, Philip kept everything. They're probably just concepts that we never implemented. This jump drive only has a single folder listed as 'Bedroom Safe,' and it includes the design data, drawings, installation requirements, and warranty for the safe. There's also a separate Word file titled 'Safe Synchronization Code.' The code has ten numerical digits."

"Maybe it's a phone number."

"That's what I'm thinking. I'm writing it down, Rick."

"I'm going to get the radar to scan the safe from below the master bedroom. I'll also take some pictures."

"Good idea," James said. "I'll stay here and review the safe's design data and drawings."

About fifteen minutes later, Rick came back upstairs to the bedroom.

"I think you should see these pictures, James. The safe is embedded in a cement block and is installed on top of the main beam for the first floor. It's located between two vertical posts in the wall between the kitchen and living room. I took pictures from every angle."

"Let's load them onto my laptop," James said, as he connected the USB cable. "Okay, they're downloading."

"We also need to load the program from this disk," Rick said. "It scales the pictures, provides length, height, and thickness, and can display everything in three dimensions."

"Okay, I'm loading the software, Rick. Let's see what we've got."

"This software is amazing, James. I can see everything including their length, width, and depth by just moving the cursor."

"Yeah, I can see that. It looks like the safe is rectangular, about eighteen inches in length, twenty-two inches in width, and about thirty inches deep. There are two horizontal extensions that look like flanges that run the width of the safe on both sides."

"They're not symmetrical, James. One extends out two inches from the body of the safe, while the other one extends sixteen inches. They're both about three inches in height, and there are anchoring bolts on each side that connect it to the second floor main beam."

James moved the display cursor.

"Look at these wires from the house circuits leading into the longer sixteen-inch flange, Rick. There must be something in the flange that requires power. I think that flange on the long side might be more than just a flange."

"What do you think is in there, James?"

"It could be where the electronics that control the safe is located. The safe might have a microcomputer built into the long flange. It probably has Bluetooth capability to connect to the bedroom phone and possibly cellular network capability, like a tablet."

"So it can communicate with a cell phone or a computer?"

"Yeah, I'm pretty sure it can, Rick. It might also record and send audit files on when it was opened and closed or if there were attempts that failed. It could've sent messages to Philip's cell phone to alert him if it was opened. That's how I'd design it."

James and Rick walked up to the master bedroom and removed the carpet and floor panel covering the safe. James called Ann on his cell phone. When she answered, he asked her for her combination, which he punched into the phone. He then put the house phone in the bedroom and his cell phone in speaker mode that allowed her to answer the security challenge. The safe unlocked. James thanked her.

"I think we should measure the inside dimensions of the safe. Do you have a tape measure I can borrow, Rick?"

"Yeah, it's in my pocket. I thought we might need it."

"Okay, it looks like the inside dimensions are seventeen inches in length, twenty-one inches in width, and about twenty-four inches deep. I measured the safe walls as being a half-inch thick."

"That's strange," Rick said. "The length and width are what I anticipated based on external dimensions and wall thickness, but the depth isn't. There must be another compartment below the bottom of the safe that is about five inches in depth."

James thought for a moment. "I'll bet there's an electric motor in the wider flange. It probably retracts the bottom of the safe and opens a bottom compartment. It's probably controlled by the circuit board, which activates the motor after a second combination is entered. That's why Philip didn't need a duress code. All the important stuff is in a hidden compartment."

"I think your partner used that compartment for storing information that only he could access and his wife couldn't."

"Yeah, I'm sure Philip designed it so that only his combination for the main safe would enable access to the hidden compartment by entering a second combination only he knew. He obviously did it for security reasons. I bet that safe synchronization code has something to do with the hidden compartment."

After breaking for lunch, James called Ann.

"Hi, Ann, did you get Philip's combination from the safe deposit box?"

"Yes, I did. It's right here, James."

James copied down the combination on the same paper that he'd written the safe synchronization code.

"Thanks, Ann. I might need to call you back if I can't answer the security challenge."

"I just had a thought," Rick said. "What if the voice challenge has to be answered in Philip's voice?"

"I doubt that, Rick. Voice analysis is probably beyond the capabilities of the small microcomputer in the safe. Also, why would Philip leave his combination in the family safe deposit box if voice analysis was required? I know they were close, but I doubt either Jim or Ann could imitate Philip's voice."

James relocked the safe. He then entered Philip's combination and waited for the security question, which asked for Philip's nickname in high school.

"The Riddler," James answered.

James and Rick watched as the main compartment of the safe unlocked.

"How'd you know the answer to that question, James?"

"I gave Philip that nickname. He loved riddles, the more complex the better."

"Would Ann or Jim have known?"

"Probably not. It was a private thing between the two of us in high school, years before he met Ann. He abandoned it in college. Philip didn't want to be identified with a comic book villain. That wouldn't be good in our line of work."

"So what combination should we try first to open the bottom compartment?" Rick asked.

"I'm entering the safe synchronization code. Let's see what happens."

The hidden compartment didn't open.

"Well, that didn't work, James. Try it again slowly, in case you made a mistake."

"Okay, Rick. I'm entering it again, very slowly."

"Nothing happened. I don't think the synchronization code is the combination, James."

"You think?" James said, with sarcasm.

Rick grinned and said, "Just trying to be helpful."

"I know, and I'm sorry. I think I know why it didn't work. Synchronization usually refers to time. I think the synchronization code is a time code, Rick."

"You could be right, James. It's the correct number of digits for seconds, minutes, hours, and years."

"I bet it's based on the date and time the safe was installed. Ann told the FBI the safe was installed about eighteen months ago, that fits with the numbers in the synchronization code when converted to months, days, minutes, and seconds."

"How would that relate to the combination?"

"Maybe the combination is the difference in time between the sychronization code and the current date as calculated by the processor in the safe. Try that, Rick. Use your calculator to determine the difference, based on the time from the atomic clock on the nightstand."

Rick calculated the time difference for ten seconds ahead and showed it to James.

"Okay. I'll count from five, four, three, two, one, now."

Again nothing happened.

"Are you sure it's correct, Rick?"

"Yes, James, I checked it twice."

"What do you think we should try next?"

"I don't think it's what but rather who, James. You're the key."

"What do you mean?"

"Philip set this up for you in case something happened to him. It's a puzzle he wants you to solve. You're the only one who knew the answer to the challenge question. I think the synchronization time code is part of it. Philip knew the synchronization code could be found by anyone looking through his desk, so it's probably something based on it. He wouldn't hide the combination in plain sight."

"You're right. That would be too easy. The synchronization code is probably part of a riddle. That's what the challenge question was telling me. Philip is speaking to me from the grave."

"I agree. What's he telling you, James?"

"I'm not sure, but this is really fun. It's like old times when Philip and I used to challenge each other with puzzles and riddles."

"I'm glad you're having fun. Have you looked at the snow lately? If we don't get out of here soon, we may be stuck here tonight."

"Don't worry, Rick. My SUV will get us home."

"I hope so. I hate being trapped in an abandoned house when it's snowing. Did you ever see *The Shining*?"

"Relax and enjoy this, Rick. Give me some ideas."

"Well, if you believe you're on the right track, then tell me this. How would Philip have expressed the combination differently than what we've already tried?"

James thought for a minute or so and then looked at Rick with a huge Cheshire cat smile.

"Rick, you're a genius."

"Thank you. What'd I do?"

"You framed the issue perfectly. The combination is made up of numbers, right?"

"Yeah, that's obvious."

"True, Rick. But numbers can be expressed in different numerical systems than the decimal system we use every day. What system have information technology types like Philip, you, and I used, other than decimal, which only has ten base numbers?"

"Hexadecimal. It has sixteen base numbers and is used for identifying computer memory addresses. Do you think that's it?"

"I'm pretty certain not everyone is familiar with the hexadecimal system, Rick. Philip knew I was as familiar with it as he was."

"Yes, but it's difficult to use since numbers above nine require letters. Why would he do that instead of some type of number substitution or transposition? Cryptographers use that all the time. With Philip's background in cybersecurity, he'd have known that."

"Yes, but I worked with Philip for years. He knew I'd remember that he used this method before. He always hated the drudgery of having to change his network password every ninety days. All the employees would automatically get a warning beginning from ten days before the password expiration date. The password had to include numbers and letters and couldn't be the same as the last five passwords that were used. Philip wrote a program that generated a password based on the numbers representing the date when the password was first used. The next password was based on the next expiration date and each new one thereafter. That met all the requirements except the need for having numbers and letters, so he decided to generate his passwords in hexadecimal."

"That's clever. Hexadecimal uses zero through nine and then adds A through F to represent the six additional symbols. Any numbers larger than nine would usually include letters."

"Correct. In those rare cases when one didn't, Philip would've substituted a letter other than A through F. That would meet all the password requirements. I think Philip took the time difference we tried previously and then converted it into hexadecimal."

"That would make sense, since it probably also meets the safe's pass code requirements. The pass codes Ann and Philip used for opening the main part of the safe had numbers and letters. The requirements for the lower compartment must be the same."

"I've got an application on my laptop that converts base ten numbers to hexadecimal base sixteen, Rick. I'm going to convert the differences that fits with the numbers in the synchronization code when converted to months, days, minutes, and seconds."

James ran the calculations on his laptop.

"Here we go. I calculated the combination for thirty seconds from now. Tell me when the clock reads 15:30:26, and I'll enter it."

"Okay—five, four, three, two, one, now!"

James entered the code, and the bottom of the safe began to retract.

"It worked, Rick. It really worked."

"Yeah, and it looks like we hit pay dirt," Rick said, as he pulled two large-clasp envelopes out of the safe.

"I recognize Philip's handwriting, Rick. One envelope is labeled 'Backfire' and the other one is labeled 'Zeus.'"

"Looks like this trip wasn't a waste of time. I guess we have some homework to see what your partner thought was so important that he had to hide it in a safe that Sherlock Holmes couldn't crack."

# 17

Sun Yu was worried. He had just been called back to the embassy by the ambassador, who seemed upset. Sun was concerned that his absence could delay the documentary, which was going so well. He hoped he wasn't being summoned to address some minor concern. Still, there was no way he could ignore the ambassador, so he immediately booked a flight to DC.

The flight from Kennedy was crowded and unpleasant, which didn't help Sun's mood. He went immediately to the ambassador's office and waited while the ambassador talked on the phone with Zhou Ming. Based on their conversation, Sun knew something had happened, and it wasn't good.

"Hello, Sun Yu the producer," Ambassador Yang joked. "Your plan worked well and we did find Dimitri. Unfortunately, one of our agents was gravely injured and may not live. How long will it take you to wrap things up in New York?"

"What happened? The last I heard, we'd tracked Dimitri to Florida."

"Yes, but he escaped after being surrounded by our people. This man is very resourceful and dangerous. One of our agents is now in critical condition in a hospital in Orlando. Apparently, Vasin was also injured during the fight, but got away without a trace. Someone is clearly helping him. Could he still be working for the US government?"

"Dimitri Vasin worked for US Intelligence in the past, Ambassador. My information indicates that he's now working for someone in the private sector for a lot more money. It could be possible that he still occasionally works as a freelance operative, but we'd have no way of verifying that."

"I plan to go to the White House to meet with the president and his chief of staff tomorrow morning and ask them that question. I'll let them know that our agent was attacked by a former agent of the US government. If he doesn't dispute it, I'll ask him if Mr. Vasin is currently their agent."

"If he got away so easily, then he probably had help from someone he knows, Ambassador. Possibly in Brighton Beach, where we're doing the documentary. He may have contacts with the Russian Mafia, and they could've provided such help. I suggest that I return to Brighton Beach and see if there's any information I can find that might provide some clues. I might have to break into his house, Ambassador."

"Do whatever you have to, Sun, but don't get caught."

"I'll be careful."

Sun flew back to New York and visited the bar in Brighton Beach that evening. As he walked in, he saw the Chinese director of the documentary.

"How did things go today?" Sun asked the director.

"Not so well, Sun. None of the Russians we wanted to interview showed up."

"Have you seen Marat?"

"No, I was told he'll be here later."

Sun left and walked to Dimitri's house. He checked the outside of the house and found no evidence of any security system, such as cameras or external speakers to sound an alarm. Finding nothing, he walked to the back of the house and down the cellar steps, where he was out of sight. He picked the lock and let himself in while using a small pen light to navigate up the stairs to the first floor.

"I'm Putin," said a voice in the dark. "Who are you?"

Sun was rattled until he scanned the room with his flashlight and saw Putin in his cage. He snickered, and then continued to check the first floor, but found nothing of interest.

"Dimitri will be right back," Putin said repeatedly, as Sun climbed the stairs to the second floor. He found what appeared to be Dimitri's bedroom and office. Sun began searching a desk and found some Russian books, DVDs, and CDs, but no papers or any pictures of family or friends. He searched the end table next to the bed and found an envelope containing pictures with inscriptions on the back. The pictures were mostly of Dimitri and a very attractive girl, probably his girlfriend, based on some of the poses. One picture included Dimitri and his girlfriend with three other people, one of whom he recognized as Marat. It had a very long inscription in Cyrillic that he couldn't read. He took a picture of the inscription with his phone, put the envelope with the pictures back in the drawer, and quickly left.

Sun returned to the bar, and as he came through the door, he saw Marat. He could tell something was wrong, because Marat ignored him, which was unusual. Sun went up to the bar and ordered a beer. He called to Marat, who walked over.

"I haven't seen you for a while, Marat."

Marat leaned over and whispered into Sun's ear in Russian.

"I know who you are, Sun. I suggest you finish this farce you've been working on and leave, or someone might get hurt."

"We'll wrap it up as soon as possible, but the project is real," Sun whispered. Then in a loud voice that everyone in the bar could hear, Sun said, "It's going to be a great documentary, Marat. I'm very excited about it, and I'm sure you are, too."

Marat looked around the bar and saw many of the locals smiling and celebrating after hearing Sun's words. He then stared at Sun for what seemed like forever.

"Come back tomorrow at noon and we'll talk," Marat said.

Sun nodded and then walked out of the bar. He took a taxi back to his hotel and called Zhou Ming.

"Zhou, what happened in Florida? Do you know the agent who was hurt?"

"I know him. He's young, enthusiastic, and inexperienced."

"That's a deadly combination."

"Thankfully, not in this case. It looks like he's going to live."

"That's the best news I've had all day. Is there any permanent damage?"

"No, and it looks like Mr. Vasin wasn't trying to kill him at all. In fact, he probably saved him. Apparently our young agent was injured when he was tripped and fell on Mr. Vasin's knife."

"Are you certain?"

"Yes, the agent told us while being questioned in the hospital earlier today. Vasin also left his phone next to the agent's body, which allowed us to find him and get him to a hospital before he died."

"So the Russian apparently has a conscience. Does the ambassador know?"

"I'm not certain. I just found out less than an hour ago."

"You need to let him know before he meets the president tomorrow."

"Okay, I'll tell him."

"Thanks, Zhou. I'm going to email you an inscription. It's in Cyrillic. I need it translated and sent to my email account no later than tomorrow morning."

"Everyone's gone at the embassy. I'll need to send it to Beijing. You should have it by tomorrow morning."

"That's fine. Goodnight, Zhou."

The next morning, Sun checked his email and saw the translation of the inscription: "Anya and Dimitri with Papa, Dimitri's mother and sister, and Milena at Grozny College."

The search of Dimitri's house had paid off. Sun now knew that Dimitri's former lover was Anya Chubais, the daughter of Marat

Chubais. He went online and searched for Anya Chubais in New York City but found no matches. Sun broadened the search to the entire state and found one match in Stony Brook. He called Zhou again.

"I need you to find out as much as you can about Anya Chubais. She lives in the town of Stony Brook in New York State. At the very least I need her current address, phone number, and occupation, and get it back to me as soon as possible."

An hour later, Zhou called back.

"I sent the information to your email. Anya Chubai is a doctor. Do you think she's treating Vasin?"

"Possibly. She and her father apparently knew Vasin from their time in Russia."

Sun called the ambassador later that morning and asked how his meeting with the president went.

"I informed the president that Zhou Ming was set up by a man named Dimitri Vasin. I also told him that we know he was an American intelligence agent and that we hoped he wasn't still working for US Intelligence. The president said he'd find out if we provided evidence of our accusations against Vasin."

"You know we can't provide any evidence without revealing our sources. I'm sure the president also knows that."

"Yes, but at least he'll make some inquiries, and if he finds out what I said is true, I'm sure he'll take action on his own. All we really want is to prove that none of our personnel were involved in the death of the senator, and I believe he wants that as well."

"I assume Zhou informed you that Vasin didn't try to injure our agent, and that he was merely defending himself?"

"Yes, but we still need to find him, Sun."

"I think I know where Dimitri Vasin is located. Will you authorize the use of one of our private investigators to confirm my information, Ambassador?"

"I will, but I don't want another violent confrontation. We need someone who's very professional. I recommend Jeffrey Turner. But only to find him, Sun. When you have his location, provide it to me immediately. I'll provide it to Barbara Chang. We need to let the Americans handle this, Sun. It's their problem, not ours."

Sun called Turner after he got off the phone with the ambassador. He provided the location of the house where he thought Dimitri Vasin was staying.

"All I want you to do is find out if Dimitri is in the house. Don't confront him or the owner of the house, Anya Chubais. Mr. Vasin is very dangerous, Mr. Turner."

"Do you need proof that he's there?"

"Yes, I need actual evidence that he's in the house. Just let me know when you have it so we can inform the FBI."

"Okay, I'll fly up to Long Island and begin the surveillance tomorrow."

After his conversation with Turner, Sun left the hotel and took a taxi over to Marat Chubais's bar in Brighton Beach. Marat waved him over as soon as he arrived.

"Follow me to my conference room where we can have a private conversation."

"Good idea. I want to settle this today."

"So do I," Marat said, as he led Sun down the stairway.

"Do you want anything to drink?"

"I'll have one of your illegally imported Russian beers," Sun said. "Did you have anything to do with canceling our interviews?"

"What do you think?"

"I think you did, but I'd like to know why."

"You violated my trust, Sun. A man in my position can't tolerate that. That's why."

"How'd I do that? What'd I do?"

"You came here to Little Odessa, where my friends and family live and where I have my business, and claimed you were making a documentary. You lied to me. You're actually looking for a man who's like a son to me."

"We're making a genuine documentary, Marat. It's the most important thing in my life right now. Yes, I know others have motives that are based on using this production to find someone, but I just want to finish this film."

"Who are these others, and why do they want Dimitri? Is it the police or the feds?"

"It's the Chinese government. They want to find him to prove he framed one of their agents for murder. Your friend almost killed another Chinese agent in Florida."

"Do they know where he is?"

"No," Sun lied. "They've abandoned the search. Your friend is too dangerous. They'll let the US authorities track him. It's their job and not China's. I just want to finish this documentary."

The pakhan wasn't sure he believed everything Sun told him. He did believe that Sun wanted to finish the documentary, and trying to impede his effort wouldn't be popular with the mayor and the authorities. Marat also knew that the sooner they left, the sooner things would return to normal. The NYPD would also leave and allow him to resume his real businesses.

"Okay, Sun, I'll make sure you can complete your interviews. When do you think you'll be leaving?"

"We'll be done within a couple of weeks, after all the interviews are completed. Most of the crew will be gone before then."

Marat agreed, and they shook hands.

After Sun left, Marat called Anya.

"How is Dimitri doing, Anya?"

"Much better, Papa. I think he'll be able to leave in a week."

"Have either of you noticed anything different or out of place, such as new cars or people you haven't seen before, especially Chinese people?"

"No, everything seems normal. Is Dimitri in a lot of trouble?"

"I'm not certain. The Chinese have been looking for him, but there's no information that anyone knows where he is. Still, it's best to be cautious."

Jeffrey Turner flew into MacArthur Airport and rented a car. He brought everything he needed for surveillance, including a small telescope, a long-range parabolic microphone, and night-vision binoculars. The Chinese had also provided him with a laser surveillance listening system that could pick up conversations inside a house from the sound vibrations on the windows.

Turner drove from the airport to the address for Anya Chubais and slowly cruised by her house. He noticed a vacant house across the street from Anya's that was for sale as a foreclosure and thought it would be a good place to operate from. Turner picked up some things at the local stores, including blankets and some small battery-powered lanterns. He packed everything into a duffel bag and parked his car at a small playground close to the vacant house. It was a cloudy, cold night and it was starting to snow, so he doubted anyone would see him.

Turner walked to the back door of the house, easily picked the lock, and entered. There were several electric space heaters throughout the house to keep the water pipes from freezing, so he knew there was electricity. He set up the parabolic microphone, unpacked the laser surveillance listening system, and went outside wearing night-vision binoculars until he found a location directly across from Anya's house. He hid the laser surveillance system in a tree and adjusted it until his laser receiver picked up the reflection off the picture window in Anya's house. Turner then turned on the audio transmitter and adjusted it until his portable wireless receiver was working.

After everything was set, Turner returned to the house. He unpacked the blankets, and made himself comfortable while listening through the earphones connected to the portable receiver. At first he heard nothing, but around ten that evening he heard voices.

"I hope we still have some of those pastries left, Anya," said a male voice.

"You shouldn't eat too much of that, Dimitri," said a female voice. "That's how Papa got fat."

Turner recorded the entire conversation and then went to the bathroom where there were no windows and turned on the light. He opened his laptop and sent the recorded audio file to Zhou Ming and the ambassador as an email attachment. The email said, "Dimitri is at Anya's house in Stony Brook. It's snowing hard, so he's probably not leaving soon."

After retrieving all his equipment, Turner packed everything in his bag and watched Anya's house. After all her house lights went out, Turner packed his car and drove to a hotel near the airport. He then called Zhou Ming and the ambassador to confirm they'd received the email with the audio file.

Later that evening, the ambassador phoned Barbara Chang.

"Ms. Chang, I hope I didn't wake you up."

"No, I'm still up. What can I do for you, Ambassador?"

"I have positive evidence that the man who framed our diplomat is located in a house in Stony Brook, New York. I've sent the address to your email account, and I'd like to meet with you tomorrow morning at nine to discuss this."

"Okay, Ambassador, I'll see you then."

The meeting at the White House included the Chinese ambassador, Zhou Ming, Barbara Chang, and Shelly Brockner. Zhou talked first.

"Good morning. My name is Zhou Ming, and I'm the diplomat who was framed by Dimitri Vasin and was beaten and detained by the police for something I didn't do."

"Mr. Ming, the FBI director and I would like to apologize for how you were treated, but the federal government had no involvement."

"Thank you for your apology, Ms. Chang. I want to play an audio file from my cell phone that was recorded last night. The female voice is Anya Chubais, a doctor and the daughter of Marat Chubais, a tavern owner and an influential leader with the Russian population in New York. The male voice is Dimitri Vasin, who fits the description of the man who poisoned Senator Thompson's aide the evening of the senator's death. Mr. Vasin is a former and possibly still current intelligence agent of the US government."

"Excuse me, Mr. Ming, Dimitri Vasin hasn't worked for the US government in over three years."

"I apologize, Director Brockner. Nevertheless, Dimitri Vasin is dangerous, and he should be apprehended before anyone else is hurt."

"Can you tell me how the recording was obtained, Mr. Ambassador?"

"Certainly, Barbara. It was obtained by a private investigator and former FBI agent who is working for the embassy."

"Has anyone identified the recording as Dimitri's voice?"

"No, we haven't done a voice analysis, Director. But the recorded conversation indicates that a man named Dimitri is in the house. We're certain that a number of people could identify his voice, including the deceased majority leader's former aide, Carla Allen. She already identified Dimitri Vasin as the man who poisoned her. I'd be happy to provide all this evidence to the FBI."

"That won't be necessary. The recording should be legally sufficient for a search warrant to determine if Mr. Vasin is in the house. We'll apprehend and detain him for questioning in the poisoning of the senator's aide. While he's in custody we'll also question him about the majority leader's death—which, I want to remind everyone, hasn't yet been determined to be a murder."

That afternoon a team of FBI agents waded through a foot of snow to surround Anya's house. There was nowhere for Dimitri to go after they announced their presence, so both Dimitri and Anya surrendered without a fight. They were both taken to the local FBI office for questioning.

The FBI agent in charge of the local office entered the room where Dimitri was being held.

"Have you been read your rights, Mr. Vasin?"

"Yes, I have."

"How do you know Anya Chubais?"

"She's a friend and a doctor who was treating my wounds. Anya knows nothing about what I'm being charged with."

"We know that; she's leaving with her attorney. On the other hand, you're being charged with two counts of assault and attempted murder. One count is on a federal employee, Carla Allen. The other is on the Chinese agent you assaulted in Florida. Apparently the Orange County police in Florida are also charging you with assault on a parking valet, as well as grand theft auto."

"I'd like to talk to an attorney."

"Do you have an attorney?"

Dimitri thought about it. Given the situation and the deal he was going to propose, he knew it wouldn't be wise to involve the Big Man's attorneys.

"No, I don't have an attorney, but I'm officially requesting one," Dimitri said.

"All right, we can call for a lawyer from the Legal Aid Society of Suffolk County. Given the weather, it'll be a while."

Dimitri smiled. "I'm not going anywhere," he said.

The assigned attorney finally made it to the FBI office about two hours later. As Dimitri entered the conference room, his lawyer stood up and introduced himself.

"I'm Sylvester Irving, Mr. Vasin, and I'll be representing you."

"How long have you been with the Legal Aid Society, Mr. Irving?"

"Actually I'm not with them. I'm taking this case pro bono under an agreement my law firm has with the Legal Aid Society. I read the case file. What do you have to say about the charges?"

"I'm innocent. There is no irrefutable evidence, and a trial would be a waste of everyone's time. I also have some information to trade that I know the government will want."

"What are you asking in return?"

"The dismissal of all charges."

"It better be very good information."

"It is," Dimitri said. "I can provide the names of two individuals located within the US who are currently involved in espionage for China. One appears to be a high-level executive in a technology company in Virginia, and the other is a US Army soldier stationed at Fort Belvoir. In addition, I have photographic evidence that links them to a Chinese intelligence agent in DC. I can also provide embarrassing evidence of a sanctioned murder by a US intelligence agency against a high-level official in Afghanistan several years ago."

The lawyer stared at Dimitri for a few seconds.

"If you truly have this information, I sincerely hope it's well protected, Mr. Vasin."

"I have several copies in safe deposit boxes."

"Okay, Mr. Vasin, let's make an offer for the government to drop all charges in return for your identification of all the individuals involved in espionage. If they don't agree, then we'll use the information on the murder in Afghanistan."

The lawyer called in the FBI special agent who led the team that had apprehended Dimitri and explained the situation. What came next was predictable: the offer went up the chain of command until it reached Shelly Brockner and Barbara Chang. Barbara had already checked out Dimitri Vasin's background. The president's director of national intelligence told her that Dimitri had been involved in some very sensitive intelligence missions. She knew what that meant. He probably had knowledge of US operations that could be extremely embarrassing and potentially harmful to other intelligence operations if disclosed.

Barbara set up a meeting at her office with Shelly Brockner.

"This Dimitri is very dangerous, Shelly, and if he was involved with the murder of Senator Thompson, he should be brought to justice."

"I agree, Barbara. But if the autopsy report says the evidence is insufficient to show that the senator was murdered, any charges would disappear. If the administration brought charges against him now, it would presuppose a murder that may never have happened."

"Okay, I hate the idea, but identifying and stopping an espionage ring would be a feather in the administration's cap."

"Good. Let's make a deal with the stipulation that Dimitri tell us who he's working for."

Dimitri reviewed the deal with his attorney.

"I'll agree to the deal with one modification. I'll tell them what I know about my employer if the government agrees to take no action against my sources."

"Okay, anything else?"

"Yes, if the government decides they can't or won't prosecute my employer, I want the government to provide me protection from any retaliation. That includes any efforts necessary to obtain legally sufficient evidence to support a future prosecution of my employer."

"Okay, I'll let them know."

After informing the president, the deal was agreed to by the Department of Justice. Dimitri and his attorney were flown to FBI headquarters in DC. Both Barbara and Shelly were there for the interrogation.

"What can you tell us about the espionage, Mr. Vasin?"

"The intelligence agent is a man named Zhou Ming who works at—"

"We know where he works," Barbara said. "Are you certain?"

"Here are the pictures and videos," Sylvester Irving said. "The US citizens involved in the espionage are also in the pictures. One is a corporate vice president named Alexander Buehler, and the other is a young enlisted man at Fort Belvoir named Koenig."

"How'd you identify your employer?" Shelly asked.

"I've never met my current employer, but his representatives called him the Big Man. A Russian friend informed me of an individual who was called the Big Man by the KGB. He said the Big Man was a Russian diplomat who defected in 1978 while working at the United Nations. His real name was Sokurov, but he changed it after the US government relocated him and modified his appearance. An associate identified Sokurov from the information I provided to him. His current name is George Solomon."

Barbara smiled. She'd always suspected that George Solomon had criminal connections. Shelly Brockner also had no trouble believing Dimitri's story, since she had independent evidence that George and the senator had a very contentious meeting days before he was killed.

"Do you think George Solomon wanted Senator Thompson killed, Mr. Vasin?"

Dimitri grinned. "I absolutely know that he did."

Shelly knew what that meant, and she also knew that there was nothing they could do about it based on their deal. She had an idea.

"Dimitri, the deal you agreed to says that the government has to provide protection against any retaliation from your employer. It included any efforts necessary to obtain legally sufficient verification that will support a future prosecution of your employer. The only way we can obtain evidence to support future prosecution of George Solomon is if you help us. No one knows of your arrest. There was no story released to the news media because of its sensitivity with respect to our future relations with the Chinese. We'd like you to continue working with George until we can obtain independent evidence that will support his arrest. If you choose not to, then our deal with you is nullified."

Sylvester Irving jumped to his feet and said, "That's an outrageous interpretation of our deal, Director Brockner."

"I haven't heard any protest from your client, Mr. Irving."

"I accept your offer, Director," Dimitri said. "I'd love to help you put him away, the sooner the better."

# 18

James called Ann to tell her about what he and Rick had found in the safe at her summer house.

"Hi, Ann. We found something interesting in your safe."

"Does it relate to my husband's murder?"

"We're not sure. There were two large envelopes in a hidden compartment that only Philip could access. One envelope was labeled Backfire and the other was labeled Zeus. Both labels were in Philip's handwriting. Would you know anything about that?"

"No, I don't, James. But that doesn't mean anything, Philip was great at keeping secrets."

"I know. Rick and I just saw evidence of that while trying to crack the hidden compartment in your safe. Thanks, Ann."

"I take it from your conversation with Ann that she knows nothing about the envelopes," Rick said, while staring out the window.

"No, she doesn't," James said.

"The snow's coming down harder than ever, James. I sure hope your SUV can get us out of here."

James walked to the large window at the front of the house.

"Yeah, there's at least ten inches of snow. The only thing moving out there is that big SUV with a snow plow. It's strange that he's only plowing this street over and over."

"We need to go now, James. Do you know anyone who can retrieve my car and bring it back to my house in La Plata?"

"Sure, Rick, I'll have VSI take care of it."

"Which route are you taking home?"

"I plan to take the main roads to my condo in Crystal City. Those back roads to your house probably won't be plowed."

"I hope you don't mind me staying at your place, James."

"No problem. My rates are well within the government per diem." Rick smiled. "Could you load the SUV? I need to call my boss."

Rick called Director Brockner to tell her what they'd found in the safe and that he would be at James's condo.

"That's great, Rick. I expect most government offices in DC to be closed for a few days. I'm staying in DC, since I'm tied up with some new evidence relating to Senator Thompson's death. Call me if you find something."

It took more than three hours to get to Crystal City on the main roads. James walked into his condo and saw that the lights and television were on. JoAnn walked out of the bathroom wearing just a towel and a surprised look that matched the ones on James's and Rick's faces.

After several seconds of silence, James said, "Hi, baby. What're you doing here?"

"I couldn't drive home from the Capitol. The Key Bridge was closed due to an accident, so I took the metro here. I hope you don't mind."

"Of course not. I hope you don't mind that we have a guest. This is Rick."

"Not at all. It's nice to finally meet you, Rick."

"Same here, Senator. Congratulations on your engagement."

"Thank you. Let me leave the two of you to your work so I can get dressed."

James took the folders out of his bag and dumped the contents of the one called Zeus on the dining room table. It included a USB flash drive.

"Let's start tomorrow with this one, and then we can look at the Backfire folder later, Rick. It'll take us a few days to go through all of this."

"That works. The director said that the government offices in DC will be shut down due to the storm for at least a day or so. She doesn't expect me to come in."

"Sounds like a plan."

The next morning, they began their analysis of the contents of Philip's safe. James copied the contents of the flash drive onto his laptop and his backup laptop so he and Rick could work together. The drive contained a number of folders. They started with one labeled "Design Specification."

After they spent most of the day analyzing the information on the flash drive, James said, "I know what Zeus is, Rick. It's a design specification for a sophisticated computer worm. Each of the Word files defines the specification for the individual worm components. There's a separate file for the target locator, propagator, command and control, payload, life-cycle manager, tracker, and update interface. This is Philip's design, Rick. I recognize his style."

"You seem to have an enthusiasm for malware design."

"Not all malware, just worms. Both Philip and I found worms much more interesting than viruses. Unlike a virus, a worm has mobility that allows it to move through a network and its systems on its own. A virus relies on the media it's embedded in. It can only move when the host program or application it's in is downloaded or transferred by human interaction. A virus is like a bomb: it explodes wherever it's dropped or placed. A worm is like a missile that can track targets and destroy them."

"It's still malware, James."

"Yes, but just like a missile, it can be used for offense or defense, and the components are analogous. The worm's target locator compares to the targeting system on a missile; the worm's propagator to a missile's rocket engine; the worm's command and control to the same mechanism on a missile; the worm's payload to the missile's warhead; the worm's life-cycle manager to the missile self-destruct mechanism; the worm's tracker to the telemetry identifying the missile's trajectory; and the update interface to a missile's electronic interface that supports software updates."

"I think you have seen such worm technology before."

"I have, but this worm specification is more sophisticated than anything I've ever seen, Rick. It has a completely autonomous command and control system that can identify and track targets."

"What kind of targets?"

"Virtually anything with software or firmware, including programs, applications, or malware such as other worms or viruses. The design can use specific code within the target software or firmware as a target signature. It can also use sophisticated artificial intelligence from internal or external sources to identify and track malware behavior and also attack and destroy it. It can even exchange information through a network protocol with other worms to share target information and coordinate attacks. This worm can also either destroy viruses or envelop them into its payload for infecting targets."

"That's one hell of a worm, James."

"More like the worm from hell, Rick."

"Yes, and you seem to have such advanced knowledge about it. I get the impression that you're not just familiar with this technology but have actually designed and used it before."

"Why do you think that, Rick?"

"I'm somewhat knowledgeable on computer viruses and worms, but it's clear to me that you're an expert. You've picked up on the technology in the specification and its application very quickly. Much too quickly to have never seen it before."

James hesitated.

"You're right. I have seen it before, but I need your promise to keep what I'm about to say absolutely confidential."

"I promise."

"Philip was designing a very sophisticated defensive worm. It was designed to hunt down and destroy sophisticated malware using a technology that we developed at VSI years ago. It's what we called our 'secret sauce.' We used it as a defense mechanism in our boundary protection systems."

"Why was it kept so secret? You could've put it in your patents."

"We decided when we started VSI that using malware as a defense was too controversial for a security system. No one would buy it. The design could also be modified for attacks, which is what Philip and I were afraid of. The concept isn't new. It's like an antiworm."

"Like the CodeGreen antiworm I read about in school? Wasn't it used to attack and destroy the CodeRed worm?"

"Yeah, that's the one. But this one is infinitely more sophisticated."

"How are you so sure that Philip designed it?"

"I recognized his programming style and the basic design as one we've used before."

As Rick went through the papers in the Zeus envelope, he came across a letter-sized envelope with the words, *For James Jordan Only*. He handed it to James.

"I think this may be another message from the grave," Rick said.

James opened it and found a letter that was witnessed and stamped by a notary public. He quickly reviewed it.

"This letter is signed by Philip and is notarized by his attorney, Rick. It states that Captain Kinsley requested VSI to sell its products to the federal government and that Philip denied the request. The letter also references a contract that Kinsley awarded to a defense contractor's commercial division to procure VSI technology and test it. That's a direct violation of the VSI product licensing agreement and federal law. Unless Philip agreed to work with the government, Kinsley threatened to reveal the test results that showed VSI's technology was based on malware. Philip references a copy of the official test report provided to him by a whistleblower involved in the testing that Kinsley sponsored."

"Here's the complete test report, James. It has the contractor's letterhead and is addressed to Kinsley. It seems to validate Philip's letter."

"Let's go through the other envelope tomorrow, Rick. It's getting late, and I'm tired and disgusted."

The next morning, James opened the Backfire envelope. It included a DVD and another flash drive. Both contained a folder identified as Hypervisor Patch 0215-3a.

"This looks like the documentation for a patch of the latest VSI firewall and intrusion prevention system product," James said. "It's an update to the threat signatures in the VSI intrusion prevention system that we send to customers to update their system software. This is just normal stuff that Theresa's product support team handled. I wonder why Philip had it in the safe."

"Why don't you call Theresa and ask her about it?"

"Good idea."

James called Theresa, but was told she wasn't in. He asked to talk to Tom instead.

"Hi, Tom. I need some help."

"What do you need, boss?"

"Actually, I need two things. Could you send two guys to pick up a car at Philip's summer house? It's in the garage, so they'll need to get the house keys from Ann. I'll send you an email with the address I want it taken to. If nobody's home, tell them to leave the keys in the glove compartment. I also need you to look up a patch on the current firewall system and pull all the relevant information from the VSI configuration management system. The patch ID is 0215-3a. Send all the data to me by email."

"Okay, I'll take care of it."

Two hours later James got a call from Tom.

"Hi, Tom. Did the guys you sent to get the car get stuck?"

"I don't think so," Tom said. "Could you check that patch ID number again? I can't find it in our system."

"The number is 0215-3a. Is that what you have?"

"That's it, but I'll be damned if I can find it. Are you sure it's correct? I asked some of the lab techs if they knew what it was about and they haven't a clue."

"It's on the patch description document I removed from Philip's safe. It has the VSI logo and a representation of Philip's digital signature."

"I have no record of it, and there are no references to it in any of the documents in our files. Can you fax a copy of what you have to me?"

"I'll do it right now, Tom."

James and Rick continued reviewing the files in both folders on Backfire and Zeus for the rest of the day.

The next day, the government offices in DC were open, so Rick and JoAnn took the metro to work. Later that morning Tom called James.

"I got your fax and I'm still searching our files, boss."

"I hope VSI's configuration and patch management isn't screwed up, Tom."

"I don't think it is. Maybe someone sidestepped the required process."

"That would be even worse."

"I need to ask you something, boss. Did you leave the front door of Philip's house unlocked when you left the other day?"

"I don't think so, why do you ask?"

"The guys I sent to pick up the car just called me and said it was unlocked. They didn't need Ann's keys to get in, so they checked the house to see if anyone was there. The house was vacant and there was no apparent damage. They also said a carpet and a piece of flooring were lying on the bed in an upstairs bedroom, and there was a safe in the floor that was open."

"When you say open, do you mean the safe was unlocked, or the door of the safe was open?"

"They said the door was open and there was nothing in the safe."

"Thanks, Tom. I'll contact Ann."

James called Ann and described his phone call with Tom.

"Do you think someone broke in? Maybe teenagers who knew the house was vacant?" Ann asked.

"It could be that. You should call the police and tell them your house was broken into so they can investigate. I'm sure they'll ask you to be there when they check the house. Don't go there before the police arrive so you don't disturb any evidence. If you need me, just call me on my cell, Ann."

"Thanks, James."

James knew it wasn't teenagers. Someone had targeted the safe and might've been monitoring the house while he and Rick were there. He called Rick to let him know what happened.

"Good afternoon, James. I'm glad you called. Our meeting with the director is set for tomorrow morning at ten."

"That's fine, Rick. I called to let you know that Ann's summer house was broken into after we left. The guys from VSI who got your car said the front door was unlocked and the safe door was open. I think someone was watching the house, just waiting for us to leave. It might've been the guy in the SUV plowing the street."

"Yeah, someone seems real concerned about that safe. Let's talk tomorrow. I'm late for a meeting."

Rick and James showed up for their meeting with Director Brockner, and she personally invited them into her private office.

"Good morning, gentlemen. I have some information that needs to be kept confidential. We've identified a suspect who might be responsible for the murder of Senator Thompson. He's been identified by a former US intelligence operative named Dimitri Vasin who currently works for the suspect. The suspect's real last name is Sokurov. He worked as a diplomat for the Soviet government before defecting to the United States in the 1980s. His current name is George Solomon."

James was stunned by what he had just heard and said nothing. He just stared at the director until Rick asked the director a question.

"Who determined that Senator Thompson was murdered? Has Walter Reed completed their evaluation of the autopsy evidence?"

"Yes. They claim that they cannot accurately determine the size of the needle that was used. They suspended their analysis, and I've declared the evidence of foul play inconclusive. The body was released to the senator's family for burial."

"Then, how do we know he was murdered, Director?" James asked.

"I don't want to dwell on this since the information is very sensitive, James. I can tell you that Dimitri Vasin identified George as his employer and provided sufficient evidence to convince me that George contracted for the murder. Unfortunately, there isn't sufficient evidence to prosecute. Mr. Vasin has agreed to help us obtain such evidence. I'm requesting your cooperation in working with Mr. Vasin to obtain the evidence we need, especially you, Rick."

"Yes, Director. When will James and I meet him?"

"I'll let you know. Now what news do you have for me?"

"We found a secret compartment in the safe at Philip Wu's summer house that contained some interesting documents."

"What kind of documents, James?"

"Design documents for a very sophisticated antiworm that can find and attack any type of software, firmware, or malware. I recognized the design as being based on work Philip and I'd done at VSI. It's clearly Philip's design. I recognized his programming style."

"So was this the work he was doing with Fort Meade?"

"Yes, he was developing an antiworm."

"So you think that's what got him killed?"

"I don't know, but there was a notarized letter signed by Philip that indicates he was coerced by Captain Kinsley into performing the work he was doing. The letter states that Kinsley threatened to reveal VSI trade secrets that he obtained by illegally procuring VSI technology and testing it. Philip included documentation that validates his assertion against Kinsley and the government. This is the original copy of the information I described. I plan to keep it, but you can make a copy."

"Thank you, I'll take you up on that offer. I may need the original to prosecute Captain Kinsley."

"I'll certainly make it available. I also plan to place a claim on any of the technology that Philip developed for the government on behalf of VSI and Philip's family."

"I'll need to see what the claim entails, but if it's reasonable, I don't believe the government will object. Anything else?"

"Yes, there was another envelope in the safe that relates to a patch for the software in one of VSI's products, but VSI has no record of it. I'm investigating it."

"Do you think it's important?"

"Philip must've thought so, but I don't know why."

"Okay, keep me informed."

Shelly had several copies made of the documents and returned the originals to James.

"I'm going home to work, Rick. Do you want to come?"

"Might as well. I still don't have a car."

Later at James's condo, he and Rick were reviewing the material on Backfire when Rick got a phone call from Admiral Mancini.

"Hi Rick. I just called to let you know that the FBI and NCIS showed up at Fort Meade and took Captain Kinsley away in handcuffs. Can you tell me what this is about?"

"I can't, Admiral. If I did they might take me as well. Take care."

"What was that about, Rick?"

"Captain Kinsley was arrested by FBI and NCIS agents. I'm surprised they did it so quickly. I just got an email from the director that the FBI is getting a subpoena for all government documents related to Zeus. They're contacting all the contractors and government personnel involved, and warning them that any use or release of VSI data will result in criminal prosecution. They'll probably settle very quickly."

"That's great, Rick. Do you mind if I tell Ann?"

"No, but ask her to keep it quiet."

James called JoAnn.

"Hi, baby. I need to tell you that Rick may be staying at the house again this evening."

"That's okay. It looks like I'll be spending a lot of time at the Capitol until the vote for the new majority leader is over."

"When do you think it'll be over?"

"I'm not sure, but it could be a couple of days. The caucus is really divided."

"Okay, I guess I shouldn't make any plans."

"Sorry about that. I promise I'll make it up to you. Did you know there are rumors flying around the Capitol that Walter Reed found no evidence that Senator Thompson's death was suspicious? Have you heard anything about that?"

"Yes, but I can't talk about it under threat of imprisonment."

JoAnn laughed. "I guess Shelly Brockner scares you more than I do."

"She does. I don't think I'd look good in an orange jumpsuit."

"Yes, and I don't think it'd look good if I married a felon."

# 19

Cai had been doing well since being released from the HIT campus hospital. She'd provided significant support from her apartment during the probing phase of the project. Kim visited her every day and really appreciated Mei's help in looking after Cai. Mei was a new person now that her tormentor was gone, never to be seen again.

Kim planned to meet with Shen that evening after class to discuss their progress and the next meeting with Flaherty. His top priority was to contact the Americans and warn them about the North Korean plan. He confided in Cai about what his uncle had told him, and she offered to help.

"How do you plan to make contact with the Americans, Kim?"

"I need to find an American at a high enough level."

"How about Sean Flaherty?"

"I don't think he's at that level, but he might know someone who is. If he does, I should be able to monitor their email communications. I'll find out when he comes back to Harbin."

"How will you monitor their email, Kim?"

"I'll install some software on Flaherty's laptop after we interrogate him and he falls asleep."

"What'll the software do?"

"It'll modify his email software settings to send copies of his incoming and outgoing emails to an account I'll set up. It also allows a script to be sent within any email from Flaherty, which can be used to take over the email accounts of anyone he communicates with."

"So the script automatically installs the software on other computers?"

"Yes, Cai. All I need to do is wait for it to install on someone's account at the contact level we need."

"You'll need to show me how to do that, Kim."

"Why, do you plan on monitoring my email?"

"Only if I thought you were unfaithful."

"That will never happen, Cai. I need to meet Shen to discuss the results of the probes and the upcoming meeting with Flaherty. I'll see you later."

Kim and Shen met at the pub at the Shangri La and found a quiet area to talk.

"The probes of the American targets are essentially complete, Kim. All I need to do is finalize the report on identified vulnerabilities for all of the targets and the grades for my team. The vulnerability report is on my laptop. I want you to review it with me before we leave."

"Sure, no problem," Kim said.

"What's your plan for interrogating Flaherty?"

"The same as last time, but after he falls asleep I'll install some software on his laptop to monitor his communications. Make sure he brings it to your suite and that it's up and running before I arrive."

"That shouldn't be a problem. He always brings it to review my reports from the jump drive I give him. Am I still asking the questions?"

"Yes, Shen. I have some new questions that'll focus on Flaherty's contacts in America. We need to know who's running this project and what the real goals are."

Shen nodded and said, "I'm going to stay at the Shangri La with Lian. Do you want me to arrange a suite for you?"

"Yes, but let me ask Cai first."

Kim called Cai. "Shen has offered us a suite at the Shangri La tomorrow night. Do you want to go?"

"Of course I do."

"Cai says yes, Shen."

"Okay, I'll set up two suites. Let's go through my vulnerability report."

Shen powered up his laptop and showed Kim his vulnerability analysis. Kim agreed with most of it, but identified some additional vulnerabilities that Shen had overlooked.

"This is great analysis, Kim. You should be leading this project."

"No thanks. I have enough to worry about right now."

"Yeah, me, too. I'm really worried about the grades I'm supposed to give everyone and what they're for."

"I'm also worried, Shen. We need to ask Flaherty about the grades and his contacts again, in case he learned something new."

Kim met Cai the next day in the lobby of the Shangri La and they went to their suite. He felt awkward around Cai in their hotel bedroom. They hadn't been intimate since her operation. He wasn't certain if she could or even wanted to. The issue was settled quickly when Cai decided to take a shower before dinner and asked Kim to join her.

"Are you staring at my scar, Kim?"

"I can hardly see it. The surgeon did a great job. It's a lot smaller than the scar I have from when I had my appendix removed."

"Yes, I saw that scar. I thought it was from an injury. I guess the surgeons in North Korea aren't as good as those in China."

"That's for sure. They're butchers. It still hurts sometimes."

"Let me kiss it and make it better, Kim."

"Go ahead," Kim said with a smile.

After the shower they got dressed and met Shen and Lian for dinner at the Shang Palace. Dinner was great, and Kim happily watched Cai eat her entire meal and all of their shared passion fruit tart dessert.

After dinner, they talked about how the attack would go during the exploitation phase.

"What do you think will happen, Kim?" Shen asked. "You have more experience than the rest of us."

"I think we'll successfully hack into at least ten percent of the targets. The size and breadth of the exploitation will definitely get the attention of the Americans. I just hope it doesn't also get the attention of the Chinese government."

"The Chinese government won't care," Lian said confidently. "America is on the verge of passing a law aimed at implementing penalties on the Chinese government for using cyber warfare against their businesses. Our government will never accept bullying by the Americans. There's no possibility they'll go after us."

As they were leaving the restaurant, Kim handed Shen a copy of the interrogation questions.

Shen quickly read them. "Thanks, Kim, I hope we get the information we're looking for."

The next morning, Kim called Shen.

"Have you heard from Flaherty?"

"No, but the front desk said he had checked into his room right before midnight. I don't expect to hear from him until after noon. I'll call you when he contacts me."

Kim looked at Cai and saw that her eyes were open and she was smiling.

"Do you want breakfast?" Kim asked.

"Yes, I'm really hungry. Please order the American breakfast, but ask them if they could include one of those passion fruit tarts that I had last night."

"So you need more passion? Did I disappoint last night?"

"Not at all, but that joke sure did."

"Yeah, I guess it was pretty bad."

A little after one, Shen called Kim.

"Flaherty called. He's going to meet me in my suite in about an hour. I told him I'd order room service for lunch."

"Fine, call him back at one thirty and ask him what he wants so I can place the order before he gets there."

The order was delivered to Kim's room, and he dosed Flaherty's food and drink like before. He then took the food cart over to Shen's room and waited outside the door until Shen let him in. Kim saw Flaherty's laptop on the dining room table. It was powered on and displayed Shen's vulnerability report. He watched as Shen began to ask the questions.

"I need to ask a few questions about the project, Sean, so that I understand it better."

"Sure, whatever you need, Shen."

"Who do you report to?"

"Nadya Murin. She works for Whitey."

"Where's Nadya's office?"

"She works with Whitey in Rosslyn, Virginia."

"Do you have her email address?"

"Yes, it's in my address book on my laptop. We exchange emails frequently."

"Does your address book include Whitey's email address?"

"No. I was told I couldn't have that information."

"Do Whitey and Nadya communicate by email?"

"They do when he's out of the office."

"Do you have any contact information for US government officials or politicians?"

"No, my work doesn't involve the US government."

"Does Nadya have any contacts with the US government?"

"I don't know."

"Does Whitey know any US politicians?"

"Yes, Nadya says he owns many of them."

"Why do I need to provide grades for the students, Sean?"

"Nadya said it was for the vacation Whitey is arranging."

"Is the vacation for the students?"

"Yes. I'm really tired, Shen."

Flaherty suddenly fell asleep and Kim walked back to Flaherty's laptop and inserted his flash drive. He loaded the monitoring software onto Flaherty's computer, which took less than five minutes. Kim also downloaded Flaherty's address book. He asked Shen to call him after Flaherty was gone and then left with the food cart.

When Kim got back to his suite, he briefed Cai on the answers he got from Flaherty.

"We have the complete name of a woman as a point of contact this time. Her name is Nadya Murin, and she works in Rosslyn, Virginia, for Whitey. There was also something strange about what Flaherty said this time."

"What'd he say, Kim?"

"He said that the grades were for a vacation that Nadya Murin was arranging. When Shen asked if the vacation was for the students, Flaherty said yes."

"Why would the students need a vacation, Kim? Where would the vacation be?"

"He didn't say, Cai. But I'll be able to monitor Flaherty's email so maybe I can find out."

"Did Flaherty say who he exchanges emails with?"

"Yes, he's been exchanging emails with Nadya Murin, but not with Whitey. Nadya communicates with Whitey via email when he's out of his office. She also told Flaherty that Whitey 'owns' many American politicians."

"What does that mean, Kim?"

"I think it means Whitey has a lot of political power. Maybe he knows the president."

Just then Kim got a text from Shen. *Flaherty about to leave. Lian and I will be there in fifteen minutes to discuss answers.*

After they arrived, Shen began by describing the conversation he'd had with Flaherty before he was dosed.

"I provided the report on the results of the probing and the grades. Flaherty seemed more interested in the grades. He asked for that first. He didn't seem very interested in the results of the probing at all. What do you make of that, Kim?"

"Maybe it's because he doesn't understand it. After all, he's a lawyer, not a hacker."

"What do you think of his responses to the question on grades? How would the student's grades be related to a vacation, Kim?"

"Maybe the vacation is a bonus based on good performance, and the students with the best grades get a vacation somewhere."

Kim changed the subject.

"I'm going to monitor Flaherty's email to see if I can get any additional information."

"What are you looking for?" Shen asked.

"Contacts that might be of value if something goes wrong."

Lian rolled her eyes.

"Nothing is going to go wrong as long as we get paid," she said. "Speaking of that, when are we supposed to get our final payment, Shen?"

"Flaherty already deposited it in the bank and told me to withdraw the funds after the exploitation phase ended. He said there'd be bonuses for good results that I could distribute as I want. I asked if it had to be based on the grades. He said it didn't."

"How are you going to distribute the bonuses?" Lian asked.

"I plan to divide it equally between the four of us."

"No, Shen," Kim demanded. "We need to divide it equally between the entire team so there are no bad feelings that might create problems."

"I agree with Kim," Cai said.

"Okay, I hadn't thought about that, but I guess you're right, Kim. Flaherty also mentioned that there was a cybersecurity conference in Munich that all the students could attend, all expenses paid."

"Maybe that's the vacation Flaherty was referring to," Kim said.

The exploitation phase began the next day, and after they were done, Shen briefed Kim on the results.

"Our success rate was almost twenty percent, better than we anticipated. I was very surprised that it was almost ninety percent on all the network addresses that were designated as special targets and weren't probed."

"There's something wrong, Shen. The success rate shouldn't be that high on the systems that weren't probed. The only way that could happen is if those systems had their security disabled somehow."

"How could that be possible, Kim?" Shen asked.

"I don't know. Corporate insiders with security training could disable a company's security, but not at this many sites. Finding and organizing insiders at scores of different businesses throughout the US would be impossible. I have no idea how it was done."

"I checked the proxy server you set up at HIT to store the captured data, and it had more than seven hundred gigabytes of data, much more than we'd anticipated. I just hope the proxy servers adequately masked our network addresses so we can't be traced."

"They should have," Kim said. "I configured the high-density physical servers with a maze of virtual servers, switches, and firewalls that would make such a trace almost impossible during the attack. Did you download the data to the USB drive?"

"Yes, and then I erased any trace from the servers. I'll provide it to Flaherty this evening at six. I have our final payments and bonuses. Tell Cai to join us at the Shangri La at seven."

Shen arrived at the Shangri La shortly before six and asked the desk clerk to call Flaherty's suite.

"Mr. Flaherty has already checked out, sir. He left last night, but he left a letter for you."

Shen was confused, but calm, since he had already received their payment. When Kim, Cai, and Lian arrived at the pub, they found Shen sitting in the back drinking a beer.

"How'd your meeting go with Flaherty?" Kim asked. "Did he provide any further instructions?"

"We didn't meet. He left an envelope that I want to open with everyone here."

Shen opened the envelope and read the letter inside. It contained the number of a post office box in the state of Virginia where Shen was to send the drive. They were also officially invited to the Munich Cybersecurity Symposium, all expenses paid. Everyone was ecstatic about their bonuses and the symposium except Kim.

"Why are you not happy, Kim?" Cai asked.

"I'm concerned that Flaherty has suddenly left without notice. Don't send the drive yet, Shen. I have a feeling we may need it. I'm going to see what's going on with Flaherty."

Kim pulled his laptop out of his bag and checked Flaherty's email account. The last email from Flaherty was from the previous day saying that the mission was complete and that he was coming home. Kim went through some previous emails and saw several about the grading of the students. There were others about arrangements that would need to be made for them after *the event,* which Kim assumed was the exploitation of the American businesses. He found one email in which Nadya said her boss had met with James and *the event* needed to be implemented sooner than planned. There was also an email from Nadya to Flaherty saying they needed to set up arrangements for Munich before *it hits the fan in China.*

"I'm not very familiar with American slang, Shen. What does that mean?"

"I don't know. Let's ask our favorite bartender. He spent a lot of time in America."

Shen waved him over to their table. After ordering more drinks, Shen asked him the meaning of the phrase. The bartender laughed.

"The complete phrase is 'before the shit hits the fan,' and it means before a disaster." The four of them looked at each other with fear in their eyes and wondered what disaster was going to hit China.

# 20

Washington, DC, was digging out of one of the biggest snowstorms in years, and Rick was on his third day at James's condo. He was homesick and especially missed Allison. When Rick met with James after work, he saw a big pile of documents on the dining room table.

"What's going on, James?"

"I've been reviewing all the patches for VSI's latest firewall and intrusion prevention system product. I led the development effort before leaving VSI."

"Is there something wrong with the design?"

"Not that I know of. The technology is solid, but I can't find the patch that Philip described in the Backfire file. Tom also hasn't been able to find any reference to it in the VSI data management systems."

"Could Philip have made a mistake? He was human."

"No, I'm certain the patch exists. Philip left a copy of it in his safe. There's just no documentation for it at VSI."

"That's strange, all right. Why don't you just analyze the patch Philip included in the Backfire file and see what it does?"

"I plan to, but to do that I'd have to install it on the test hypervisor firewall system in the VSI laboratory. That laboratory is always booked solid. I asked Tom to reserve some time for me tomorrow. I'm waiting to hear back from him."

"I'd like to go with you, but I have a meeting with Dimitri Vasin tomorrow morning at nine."

"The guy who identified George Solomon as his boss?"

"Yeah, that's him. Do you want to come along? You know George better than me, so your presence could be helpful."

"Sure, and then you can come with me to VSI. I can drop you at your house on the way back."

"Sounds like a plan. Let's get some dinner."

They'd just finished dinner when both their cell phones rang. James saw Barbara's phone number and answered it.

"James, a serious cybersecurity event is hitting businesses all over the country. It looks like it's originating from three cities in China. The president is having a meeting with the Chinese ambassador as we speak to express his displeasure."

"Do you think this has anything to do with what happened to their agent and their opposition to our cyber-attack legislation?"

"We aren't sure, but the president wants you at the White House for a meeting tomorrow morning at seven. I'll be there with the director of national intelligence and Shelly Brockner."

"Okay, I'll be there, Barbara."

Rick was just ending his call as well.

"Was that your girlfriend on the phone, Rick?"

"Not hardly, it was Director Brockner. She told me about some Chinese cyber-attacks and wants me to accompany her and the head of the FBI Cyber Division to a meeting with the president. I need to go back to the office to get my spare suit."

"I'll drive you. I'm also going to that meeting."

James and Rick showed up for the meeting at the White House the next morning, and Barbara briefed them on the discussion between the president and the ambassador.

"Ambassador Yang denied any involvement by his government in the cyber attacks. He said the US shouldn't blame the Chinese government every time our commercial sector is attacked. The meeting ended when he said that we should provide more support to help secure our businesses instead of passing laws to penalize China."

The president arrived and described the attacks.

"The attacks originated from Beijing, Harbin, and Shanghai and were directed at banks, financial institutions, and commercial research organizations throughout the country. A lot of data was downloaded, but there's no evidence of any disruptions in business. I've gotten calls from the CEOs of these businesses, many of whom are friends who supported me during my campaign. They're demanding action, including quick passage of the foreign cyber-attack legislation."

"The initial evidence shows the attacks are originating in China," Shelly said. "I have a hard time believing the Chinese weren't involved, Mr. President."

"I met with Ambassador Yang, and I believe he may not have been aware of the attacks, Shelly. It doesn't mean the Chinese didn't do it. He was defensive based on the recent events involving their agent, and he referred to the foreign cyber-attack legislation as the 'anti-China legislation.' We need help from all our cybersecurity experts to determine what happened, before things get out of hand."

The president adjourned the meeting but asked James and Barbara to stay. James told Rick he'd meet him later at the FBI.

"We need to analyze the data we've gotten on the attacks from the FBI. I want you to postpone your leave of absence and take the lead on this, James."

"What about the DNI, Mr. President? Shouldn't he be leading this effort?"

"I invited the DNI as a courtesy since he should know what's going on. This was an attack on our businesses, not our military. You know our business environment better than the DNI or anyone else in the intelligence community. Having the DNI lead the investigation would also raise the stakes with the Chinese."

"Okay, Mr. President, I'll do it. What resources do I have?"

"Any resources you want outside of DoD, unless I'm convinced they need to be involved. We're treating this as a crime, not a military attack. I've put the FBI director and the attorney general on notice to provide any Department of Justice resources you might need."

"In that case, I'd like to have FBI Special Agent Rick Tanner assist me. He's an expert in cybersecurity and we work well together."

"Use whoever you want, James. Just get me some answers."

James called Rick after his meeting with the president and informed him of his new assignment.

"I already know, James. The president told the director that you're in charge. She wants to meet with the both of us in her office as soon as you get here."

"Okay, I'm on my way."

Director Brockner, Rick, and the head of the FBI's Cyber Division were waiting in the director's office when James walked in.

"Welcome back, James. I'm sure you're getting tired of seeing me."

"I'm happy to be back, Director. The FBI has become like a second home to me."

"That's good, because it looks like you'll be here until we solve this problem. I'm having all the data from the attacks collected and compiled so that you and your team can go through it. You can have access to anyone in the Cyber Division. Rick can help you identify the personnel and their capabilities. Can you please tell James about the data collection process, Rick?"

"Certainly, Director. The evidence boxes on this conference table are what we have so far. It includes the source network addresses where available, as well as the network addresses that were attacked. We're collecting any audit data that the businesses were able to provide on prior attacks and probes. In addition, we're working with the target businesses on identifying the types of systems that were victimized and the security systems used by each victim. It isn't entirely complete since we're still gathering data, but as we get more we'll provide it to the team."

"How are you correlating the audit data from all the sources?" James asked.

"That's our main problem," Rick said. "The data that's available varies widely as to accuracy, completeness, format, and consistency, which makes comparisons very difficult. We'll need to correlate much of the data manually and at a lower level of detail than is ideal. This is very much an exercise in finding the lowest common denominator."

"I'm setting you up in an office near Rick's. You'll have access to any personnel and facilities that the Cyber Division can provide. Is there anything else you need, James?"

"Not yet, Director. I'll let you know if I do."

Rick took James back to his new office, which was quite large and had a separate conference room.

"Who did they fire to get me this office?"

Rick laughed. "It's been vacant for a while. The last person who had it died of a heart attack while sitting at that desk. Some people claim it's haunted."

"You're kidding."

"No, I'm not. I used it for a while and heard some noises. Probably just problems with the heating and cooling vents."

"Well, if I see any ghosts, I'll send them to you."

As they started going through the data, James suggested they use a geographical map.

"We need to see where all the source and destination network addresses are located both in China and the United States."

"The FBI has a system that will provide that information on a big screen, James."

"Let's see it."

Rick led James to a large room that looked like a small movie theater with a panoramic screen. The large screen depicted the geographical source of the attacks. As they looked at the map, they both saw a pattern.

"All of the source addresses are either on university campuses or nearby in three Chinese cities, James."

"Yeah, I see that. This indicates to me that the attackers were probably students attending the universities near the source locations. I'm familiar with many of these schools, and they all have highly rated cybersecurity and cyber warfare programs. We need to make a list of the universities so that we can provide this information to the president when he sees the ambassador again."

"This data on the organizations that were attacked in the US seems to have no pattern. They're all over the country."

"Every state in the United States was attacked. That's a pattern in itself, Rick. In addition, the number of attacks seems to be in proportion to the size of the population in each state. This looks more like a targeting map for a public relations campaign than a cybersecurity attack. Have we gotten any information on the nature and goals of the attack?"

"Yeah, and it's very strange. It appears that all of the attacks that were successful resulted in data being downloaded. None of the attacks have disabled IT systems or inserted malware for long-term attacks used to deny service, destroy data, or modify and report on system operations. There was also no attempt to conceal the attacks, and the files that were downloaded appear to be random."

"Why do you think they were random?" James asked.

"The analysis we have gotten so far indicates that the attacks don't appear to be directed at specific companies, specific industries, or specific types of data. In fact, most of the data that was taken is relatively trivial, with no or little commercial value. We have no idea what the overall goal of the attack was."

James smiled. "That's because you're not looking at the big picture, Rick. It appears that the goal was to attack every state in proportion to its population without doing any damage. The attacks seem to be designed to annoy people and companies as opposed to really damaging them. It looks like somebody used a lot of resources just to piss off a whole bunch of Americans, including the president. The question is, why?"

"I think we should look at the audit data to see which of the targets that were probed were also attacked. That might tell us something."

"I agree, Rick. We should also identify any IT systems and cyber-security systems that had an abnormal number of breaches. The system audit data will tell us if there are systems with vulnerabilities that are being exploited."

"The review of that much audit data will require more resources than we currently have, James. I'll ask the director for more people to help scan and review the audit files."

The first group showed up almost immediately from the FBI's Cyber Division. They were supplemented by FBI contractor person-nel from the DC area. All had experience in reviewing audit data at various FBI data-processing, data-center, and security-operations center sites.

"We're starting to get some meaningful audit analysis data from our FBI personnel, James."

"I see that. However, your analysis data is revealing a very strange pattern. Slightly more than ten percent of the network addresses that were probed were successfully attacked. I would expect that, but the success rate on addresses that were successfully attacked without first being probed was about eighty-seven percent. That's impossible."

"What do you think it means?"

"I'm not sure, Rick. We need to see which security systems were experiencing such poor performance. Let's have your analysts do a sort on that while I check on some things with Tom."

When James returned, the results were compiled and waiting for him and Rick. As James was reading the analysis, he suddenly stopped and blurted, "Oh my God! This can't be right."

"What can't be right, James?"

"This analysis, Rick. It says the latest VSI firewall and intrusion detection technology was the culprit in over ninety percent of the attacks that resulted in the loss of large amounts of data. That tech-nology has been the industry leader since it was first released two years ago. It was the culmination of more than ten years of research that Philip and I led. It's based on our ideas."

"Do you think someone sabotaged the VSI systems?"

"How could that be done at all of the sites that were breached? There are too many sites in too many locations all over the country for this to be an insider attack. That would require a huge well-organized conspiracy. None of what we've seen indicates that's even possible."

"What else could it be?"

James thought for a moment.

"If it isn't an insider attack, then there would have to be a flaw in the VSI technology that someone discovered. Maybe someone who knew the technology very well and found a way to implement what is commonly referred to as a zero-day exploit. There may be a way a zero-day exploit could be implemented on such a large scale. But to prove it we'll need to travel to VSI."

As James left the Hoover Building with Rick, he turned on his cell phone and saw several calls from JoAnn. He called her and she answered immediately.

"Hi, James. Guess who's the new chairman of the Senate Finance Committee? I'll give you a hint: it's someone you've slept with."

"How many guesses do I get? There are so many possibilities."

"Very funny, James."

"That's great, baby! I'm really happy for you."

"Where've you been all day? I've been calling all afternoon."

"I'm sorry. I've been locked up in the FBI."

"What'd you do? Do you need bail money?"

"Where are you?" James asked, ignoring her joke.

"I'm at the Hawk 'N' Dove, celebrating the election of the new majority leader, Senator Domingo."

"Well, don't celebrate too much. You might want to take a taxi home."

"Why, do I sound drunk? I only had a few martinis."

"Please take a taxi home, JoAnn. I'll call you tomorrow."

When they got back to the condo, James pulled the DVD for Hypervisor Patch 0215-3a from his briefcase and made several copies.

"Here's a copy of the VSI hypervisor patch, Rick. Put it in a safe place."

"What're you doing with the other copies?"

"I'm putting one in my safe and taking the remaining one with me. I'm also taking the original DVDs of the patch and the Zeus worm to VSI for storage in their vault."

"Why are you making so many copies of the hypervisor patch?"

"I think the patch on this DVD is what enabled many of the cyber attacks from China. I'll find out for certain when we get to VSI tomorrow. I just want to make sure the evidence is safe in case it's needed."

The next morning, James called Tom before he and Rick left for VSI.

"Hi, Tom. Rick and I should be there by ten."

"The lab is ready, boss. It wasn't really a problem, since Chris and his development team are off-site at a customer facility and Theresa is on vacation."

"When you get a chance, could you find out who has been working in the lab recently? I also need some engineers and techs to set up the test on the patch."

"Is there anyone in particular that you want?"

"Just enough technical support to load the patch I'm bringing on the VSI test system. I'll also need you to set up the attack simulations."

"Okay, I'll have everything ready by the time you get here."

"I'm also bringing a folder with data on what Philip was working on, as well as a guest from the FBI. So watch your language."

James and Rick arrived at the VSI facility. They signed in at the reception desk and were given VIP visitor badges. An escort took them to the VSI system development laboratory, where Tom was waiting.

"Hi, Tom. This is FBI agent Rick Tanner."

"Nice to meet you, Agent Tanner."

"Nice to meet you as well. You look younger than I expected."

Tom smiled. "Thanks. Working at VSI keeps me young."

James laughed. "Here's the patch DVD and the Zeus folder, Tom. Let's load the patch and see what we've got."

Tom loaded the files from the DVD.

"The files are loading, boss. It's very strange. I've never seen a patch this large, and it has some unusual files. I'll have the techs start the simulator. Okay, guys, bring the simulator up and select the 'end of days' attack scenario."

"Nothing's happening, Tom. The simulation screen is blank."

"I know, boss. None of the files on the patch are loading, and the test firewall and intrusion protection system are working fine."

"That's not what I expected, Tom. Damn it!"

"This is the first time I've ever seen you disappointed that one of our systems worked perfectly, boss."

"Very funny. Why wouldn't the test firewall and intrusion protection system load the patch?"

"I have no idea. The simulator checked all the files on the patch and didn't indicate any problems. It should have loaded."

"Let's discuss this in the cafeteria. I need some breakfast and coffee."

James felt better after eating.

"You know, Rick, I can't figure out why those patch files didn't load from the DVD."

"Maybe it's not a valid patch or it's corrupted."

"I guess that could be it."

"What time do you plan to leave, James? I need to meet with the director this afternoon."

James looked at his watch to see what time it was. Suddenly, a big smile appeared on his face.

"That's it, Rick! Time is the trigger! The patch was probably set to be enabled at a certain time, and I'll bet that it was set to be disabled at a set time. Call your boss and ask her for the date and time based on

Coordinated Universal Time that the attacks began and how long they lasted. Tell her it's important."

Rick made the call to the director and suddenly realized what James was up to.

"Your boss is a genius, Tom," Rick said, as he made the call.

"Yeah, I've always known that, Agent Tanner. I just wish he'd stop playing detective and come back to work."

"Maybe he can do both."

After a few minutes, Shelly Brockner called Rick back and provided the requested information. Rick wrote it down on a napkin and gave it to James.

"Let's go back to the lab and see if this works," James said. "Tom, I want you to set the network time protocol for the lab to the date and time on this napkin."

Tom entered the information from his lab console and said, "Okay, I reset the date and time."

"Run the simulation again, Tom."

"Okay, here we go. Keep your fingers crossed. The test system is up and the attack scenarios are running, boss. Something's happening. The files from the DVD are loading, and the test firewall system is being reconfigured. Holy shit, everything is getting through our defenses! It's like the firewall and intrusion protection system disappeared. There's something else going on, as well. I'm seeing additional traffic on the network that the simulator isn't generating."

"Record the traffic and download it to the forensics sandbox so you can analyze it later. Get the report to me as soon as you can."

"Okay, boss."

James and Rick left VSI and drove back to Rick's house, where they stopped to make some calls. A new Mustang sat in the driveway.

"Hey, look at that, Allison must've picked up my new Mustang. Well, I guess I have transportation again, James. You're no longer my chauffeur."

"That's great, Rick! Try not to get in any more accidents."

As they walked into the house, Rick was greeted by Allison, who gave him a big kiss. James called Shelly Brockner and told her what they found.

"Good afternoon, Director. It appears that the patch that was sent out to all the VSI customers disabled their VSI security systems. It also seems to be generating some additional network traffic."

"What kind of traffic?"

"I'm not sure. I've asked VSI to do a forensic analysis and give me a report. They should have it to me by tomorrow morning."

"That's great. I want to thank you and Rick for determining the nature and source of the attack on the businesses. Can I talk to Rick?"

"He's right here," James said, as he handed Rick the phone.

"Great work, Rick. Take the rest of the day off."

"What about our meeting, Director? I thought you wanted to tell me something."

"I do. Captain Kinsley confessed to being responsible for your accident."

"Did he identify the driver of the pickup and the shooter?"

"No, he wants witness protection first. We're working it, Rick."

"Thanks, Director."

"What's up with your boss, Rick?" James asked.

"She said it was Kinsley who was responsible for my accident."

"That's progress. I hope I can find the bastard who developed that patch."

"Any ideas on who it could be?"

"It had to be someone at VSI with advanced technical knowledge of our products. Do you have a place where I can lie down? I have a monster headache."

"Sure, use the bedroom at the top of the stairs. We'll have dinner when you wake up."

James got about two hours of sleep and was awakened when Rick knocked on the door.

"James, I have the president on the phone."

"I'll be right down."

James put on his shoes and went downstairs. Allison handed him the phone with a surprised look on her face.

"Hello, Mr. President. What can I do for you?"

"Can you meet me tomorrow at the White House at nine? We have another crisis."

"Can you tell me what it is, so I can be prepared?"

"The Chinese ambassador just called me and said that his government's websites were under attack. He said it appeared that the attacks were designed to embarrass the Chinese government and to promote dissension within the Chinese population. I think he believes that we had something to do with it as retaliation against the attack from China. He's bringing proof when we meet tomorrow. I need you to be at the White House for a meeting at nine tomorrow morning."

"Can I bring Rick Tanner from the FBI with me?"

"Bring whomever you need. I need to put this fire out as soon as possible."

"I understand, sir," James said, as he ended the call.

"What'd the president want?"

"Can we talk in a more private location, Rick?"

Allison overheard them. "Don't worry, I'm leaving."

"I apologize, sweetie, it's just business."

When Allison was gone, Rick asked James what was going on.

"We need to meet with the president tomorrow at nine, Rick. The Chinese think we attacked their government web pages, and the president is upset that things are spinning out of control."

"What can we do?"

"I'm calling Tom. Hi, Tom. How are you coming with your forensic analysis on that traffic we downloaded from the patch?"

"I'll have it done by tomorrow, boss."

"I can't wait that long. Use any resources you need, but I need a full report before I meet with the president tomorrow morning."

"Okay, we'll work through the night, if necessary."

"Call me as soon as you know anything."

After hanging up, James saw a text from JoAnn asking him to call.

"Hi, baby. Did you get home from the Hawk 'N' Dove okay?"

"Yes, I took a taxi like you suggested. What's going on with the Chinese, James? The media is all over a story about how American businesses have been the target of a cyber attack from China. Now there are reports that we've retaliated with a cyber attack on them."

"I can't tell you much, baby, since I'm leading the investigation. Don't worry. I'm certain we didn't attack the Chinese. I don't think we're going to war."

Allison had walked in to tell them dinner was ready and overheard the end of James's conversation with JoAnn. Rick saw the look of fear on Allison's face.

"Don't worry, honey, this is just a normal day at the office for us," Rick said with a smile.

"You need to find another job, Rick," Allison replied, with a grim look on her face.

When James got home, he poured himself a scotch and watched the late-night news reports on the cyber attacks. The reporter made it seem as if China and the United States were on the verge of war, which James hoped wasn't the case. James fell asleep on his couch and was awakened by a call from Tom.

"I hope this is good news, Tom. What'd you find?"

"The traffic being generated by the patch is a very sophisticated worm. Its payload is designed to modify Chinese government web pages. It looks more like a prank than an attack to cause any real damage, but it could easily have done so if that was the plan."

"Thanks, Tom, that's great work. Fax me the complete report."

"Who do you think did this, boss?"

"I'm not sure."

"It would have to be someone who used the VSI development laboratory to develop that patch."

"I agree, Tom. After you get some rest, I want you to review all the audit logs for the systems in the lab for the last two weeks. I need you to identify the audit logs for that patch and then correlate them against the laboratory log book. See if you can identify who was in the lab when the patch was being developed and tested."

"Will do, boss."

James went back to sleep, but was awoken by the fax machine in his office. He got up and retrieved the report from VSI. The forensic analysis indicated that the structure of the worm was similar to a design James had seen before. James made copies of the report and put them in his briefcase. He then showered, dressed, and waited for Rick. They arrived at the White House and were led to a small conference room. The president showed up a minute later with Barbara Chang.

"What do you have for me, James? I hope it's good news."

"Yes, sir. I have a complete analysis and forensics report."

"Thanks. Can you just give me the highlights?"

"We believe that the attack was initiated by Chinese hackers at several universities in Beijing, Harbin, and Shanghai. A security system made by VSI was modified by a maintenance patch that disabled the security system at a preset time. That allowed the attack to have a much higher success rate than it should've had. The attack also triggered malware sent from the patch to preselected Chinese government websites. This malware was designed to seek out Chinese web pages using a specific type of software and inject text to modify their content with slogans that would embarrass the Chinese government. None of the malware was designed to steal or modify data or cause denial of service attacks. In addition, all of the malware had a lifecycle of forty-eight hours, which means it should end shortly."

"I'm very sorry to hear that it was initiated from VSI, James. Do you know who's responsible?"

"Not yet, Mr. President. We're reviewing the VSI laboratory logs to see if we can identify who developed and tested the patch."

"VSI has already suffered significant damage due to the actions of a military officer. I'll order that no information be released on VSI's potential compromise to avoid any additional damage. This will also have no impact on the compensation owed to VSI."

"Thank you, Mr. President, but my primary goal is to find out who's responsible for the cyber attacks."

"So as it stands right now, we believe Chinese students were probably responsible for the attack on American businesses, but the Chinese government is denying it. Is it possible the Chinese government wasn't involved in the attack on our businesses and knew nothing about the students, Barbara?"

"It's definitely possible, and if that's the case, the Chinese would never admit that the attack was initiated from within China without their knowledge. The only way they can save face is to pin it on us."

"Thanks, Barbara. That makes their motivation less ominous. I still can't ignore it, however. American citizens are scared and angry about what happened. We must identify who was responsible for this."

As they drove to the Hoover Building, James and Rick discussed the recent attacks.

"These attacks are definitely linked, Rick. There had to be some coordination between the Chinese attacks and the response from the VSI security systems in the United States. It can't be a coincidence."

"I entirely agree, James. Someone or some group set up this attack using resources in China and the United States."

"It's a sophisticated attack that had to be expensive. Yet, the data taken wasn't valuable. I have no idea what their motive was."

James turned on the news on the car radio. The cyber attacks had caused the stock market to plunge over four thousand points in two days. James suddenly realized who might be responsible.

# 21

Kim was extremely worried about what was being reported on the Chinese national media. There were news reports of cyber attacks from America that were changing Chinese government websites. Cai sensed his anxiety and asked him what was wrong.

"I think the cyber attacks on the Chinese government websites are related to our attacks on the Americans and the disaster discussed in Nadya Murin's email to Flaherty. I'm worried we could be in trouble."

"What can we do?"

"I need to check my laptop to see if the software I loaded onto Flaherty's computer is letting me monitor any useful email accounts."

"If you load your email account on my laptop, I'll also be able to see the emails."

"That's a good idea. I'll do it now."

"Good, I'll make us some tea. Where is it? I'm not familiar with your kitchen yet."

"It's in the cabinet next to the stove."

Ten minutes later Cai returned with the tea and saw Kim smiling.

"You seem happy, Kim. Is your program working?"

"It is. I can see the emails that Nadya Murin is receiving and sending. She seems to communicate with Flaherty a lot. The software I loaded on your laptop will let you see their emails, too. Take a look."

Cai looked at her laptop display and saw the emails sorted by their date and email account name. She began reviewing Nadya's emails.

"Nadya is forwarding many of Flaherty's emails to the account of *gsolomon*," Cai said. "It has the same domain name as Nadya's account. Do you think they work for the same organization?"

"Yes, I looked at some of them while you were in the kitchen. Many of her emails with *gsolomon* include information that seems to relate to the project. I haven't seen any emails between *gsolomon* and Flaherty. Flaherty said he had no contact with Whitey. Maybe Whitey is *gsolomon.*"

"I think you're right, Kim. Here's an email between Flaherty and Nadya that she forwarded to *gsolomon* in which Nadya describes a security problem in China as if it's ongoing and was related to the recent crash of the American stock market."

"I saw that. There are also more recent emails where *gsolomon* is copied. I found one between Nadya and Flaherty in which she says, 'the Chinese could identify the students as being responsible for the event.' There's a response from Flaherty saying, 'we need to implement the vacation.' Her response to him says, 'Whitey is dragging his feet on the payments.' I think the event isn't just our attack on the Americans, Cai. It also includes the attack on the Chinese web pages."

"I'm doing a web search on *gsolomon*. Look at this, there's a George Solomon of the Solomon Group investment firm. It says he's a billionaire and president and chairman of the board of the Solomon Group. Look at his picture, Kim."

"Yeah, I see it. With all that white hair, he could be the 'Whitey' that Flaherty talked about in the interrogations. Probably a code name to protect his true identity."

"Do you think George Solomon could be the American contact you're looking for?"

"He could be. But based on how Flaherty described him and on some of the emails we saw, I'm not certain he'd help us."

"Yeah, that last email said he's dragging his feet on the vacation for the students. I'm worried, Kim."

"Let's see if we can find someone else as a contact."

After an hour of searching through emails, Kim found what he was looking for.

"I found an interesting email from Flaherty to Nadya," Kim said. "Flaherty told Nadya that George asked him to cancel the VSI board meeting because James Jordan wasn't resigning his government CIO position. There are other emails referencing George's concern that James's return as the CEO of VSI might disrupt the project. He also recommended that the project schedule be shortened so it can be completed before James's possible return."

"That explains our compressed project schedule, Kim."

"Yes it does, and I think we might have found our contact. Do a search of Flaherty's address book and see if there's an email account for James Jordan."

"Here it is, Kim. He's listed as James Jordan, CEO of VSI with a VSI domain name."

"I know that corporation, Cai. VSI builds cybersecurity products. I think we need to share this with Shen. I'll call him."

"Okay. I need to go back to my place to change into some clean clothes. I'll be back."

Kim called Shen and invited him to his apartment. When he arrived, Kim showed him the relevant emails on his laptop.

"What do you think this means, Kim?"

"I think our attack on the American businesses triggered the attack on the Chinese government web pages."

"How?"

"I believe the addresses we didn't probe were probably preset to release a worm that attacked the Chinese government web pages."

"So when we attacked those addresses the worm was released?" Shen asked.

"Yes, the worm was probably very sophisticated, like the Stuxnet worm that targeted the specific software used in the servers that controlled the Iranian nuclear centrifuges. I think this worm must have targeted unique software on the Chinese web servers."

"If we could prove that, then we'd have the evidence that we weren't involved in the attacks."

"Yes, Shen, but to do that we'd need to access a Chinese government web server. I doubt there are any we'd have access to."

Shen smiled. "I'm not so sure. There's a server at HIT and other universities that the Chinese government installed. It provides a web page that foreign students can access to apply for information about the university. It collects prospective student information, such as name, address, occupation, education, and family background that our Ministry of Intelligence uses to influence the admission process. They use it to find students who might be beneficial to China."

"How do you know this?"

"Lian and I are part of a team of HIT students that install security upgrades to the web server as part of a student project. It's how we met. I know the unique web software they're using, and I still have a current copy on a DVD. It's proprietary to the Chinese government."

"Do you have access to the server?"

"Yes, the government still uses students to make security upgrades to the server. It's faster and cheaper, and the web server has no classified information."

"Good. Let's check out that web server and see if it has any malware on it."

"And if it does?"

"We'll need to download it to those remaining USB drives Flaherty gave you."

"Why do you want to remove it? We should just leave it there, Kim. What if we get caught removing the data?"

"I'm certain the attackers used malware with a time-based self-destruct mechanism. That's what I would do," Kim explained. "Once the target time is reached, the evidence will be destroyed, preventing forensic analysis and destroying our alibi. We have to download the evidence before that happens."

Kim and Shen went to the server room at HIT. Shen logged into the web server from his laptop.

"There are some unusual files on the server, and the web page for foreign students is corrupted, Kim."

"Good, that means the malware hasn't been erased yet. Download everything onto two of the USB drives and reinstall the uncorrupted web software from your DVD. I've got to meet Cai."

Kim walked into his apartment and saw Cai hunched over her laptop.

"Have you seen any more interesting emails while I was gone?"

"Yes, there's an email from earlier today between Nadya and Flaherty. Flaherty says they need to finalize the plans for the vacation in Munich. There's one from George Solomon that says they need to recruit the best students for VSI, since they need new talent after the death of Philip Wu and the resignation of James Jordan."

"That's really good work, Cai."

"Thanks, what's next?"

"I think we should do a web search on Philip Wu and James Jordan and see what we get."

After a brief search, Kim and Cai compared their results and found that both men were longtime friends and cofounders of VSI. The most interesting information was that James Jordan had been the CEO of VSI before being appointed by President Meredith to the position of Federal Chief Information Officer. It was described as a high-level position that gave him direct contact with the president.

"Looks like we just found our contact, Cai."

"What're you going to do?"

"I'm going to draft an email from Flaherty's account directly to

James Jordan's VSI account. I'll then delete it from Flaherty's folder to eliminate any record of it. The email will identify me as a student from HIT who was involved with twenty other students in hacking the American businesses. I'll also state that the hackers were paid by George Solomon through a point of contact named Sean Flaherty."

"You should also let him know that none of the hackers knew anything about the attacks on the Chinese websites. That's important, Kim."

"Yeah, that's good. I'll add that and also say that we were used by George Solomon and are in desperate trouble. The next part will definitely get his attention. It relates to something my uncle told me about a planned attack on the US fleet. I'll include my email address at HIT. The school doesn't monitor student accounts."

Several minutes later, Kim had completed a draft of the email and showed it to Cai.

"Mr. Jordan seems like a very important person, Kim. I bet he gets a lot of emails every day that he doesn't even read. We need to make sure he notices this one and reads it."

"I know. I've checked the high importance tag. But I need a title that will catch his attention. Do you have any ideas?" Kim asked.

"Use 'George Solomon and Chinese Cyber Attack.' That should get his attention since he obviously knows Mr. Solomon."

"That's good, Cai. I'm thinking we should also forward some of the emails we captured from George and Nadya that indicate his involvement. That will give us credibility as hackers and also provide background information on the project and George's involvement."

After their meeting with the president at the White House, James and Rick drove to the Hoover Building. Rick led James to a conference room where he saw a man in his thirties dressed in an ill-fitting suit.

As James walked in, the man stood up and with a slight Russian accent said, "Hello, Mr. Jordan. I'm Dimitri Vasin."

"I understand that you know George Solomon, or rather know of him," James said.

"That's correct. Although I've never met him personally, I'm certain he's the man who employed me over the past few years."

"That's very interesting. I've known George for twelve years and never heard him mention your name."

Dimitri smiled. "I doubt that he would. I've been employed by him for the last three years to perform special tasks of a private nature."

"What kind of tasks did you do for George?"

"I can't go into any detail."

James frowned. "We're looking to find out exactly what George has been up to and whether he's done what you say he has. The FBI wants to get sufficient proof to have him arrested and put in jail. I myself don't work for the FBI, but I know George pretty well. He helped me and Philip Wu start our business."

James noticed Dimitri shift in his chair slightly when Philip's name was mentioned.

"Did you know Philip Wu, Mr. Vasin?"

"No, but I recognized the name. He was your partner and was killed during a burglary at his house. It was all over the news about two months ago, wasn't it?"

"That's correct, he was my best friend. If you know anything about his death, I'd like to know."

Dimitri changed the subject.

"Do you think George was responsible for your partner's murder?"

"I never even considered that and I'm not sure I'd ever believe it. George and Philip knew each other even longer than I've known George."

"I didn't know that. What would you like me to do with respect to Mr. Solomon, Agent Tanner?"

"You're to provide surveillance on George through any legal means available. I want regular reports with photos on who George met with and where he went. Do you understand?"

"Yes, Agent Tanner."

After Dimitri left, Rick asked James what he thought.

"I think he knew Philip somehow. His posture changed when I mentioned Philip's name."

"I noticed that too," Rick said. "It's something to keep in mind. Let me ask you something: Have you found any information on who implemented that bogus patch?"

"Not yet, but I have some candidates. The problem isn't so much 'who' as it is 'why.' I think this was more than just an attempt to piss off our businesses and the Chinese government. Did you see the drop in the stock market?"

"So you think someone was trying to manipulate the stock market?"

"Yes, I really do, Rick. We should look at who was buying as the stock market was crashing."

"I know who might be able to help us with that. The new chairman of the Senate Finance Committee."

"Maybe, but I have someone else in mind, Rick. How'd you and Allison like to join us for dinner tonight at Michelle's?"

"Sounds great. I'll text her."

James called JoAnn.

"I have reservations at Michelle's for tonight at seven. Are you up for it?"

"Definitely. What time should we meet?"

"Meet me at my place at four."

"Why so early?" she asked, and then realized why. "Forget that last comment, baby."

"Great, see you at four—all of you."

Rick laughed. "You're a dog, James."

"Is Allison coming?"

"Yes, she's looking forward to meeting the senator."

"I'm heading home, Rick. I need a nap before JoAnn arrives."

"Yeah, I know. It's been a tough few days and you need to be rested for the main event."

James got home and was asleep in seconds after lying down on his bed. He slept soundly until JoAnn arrived, and then started removing his pants after taking off all her clothes. James let her continue and enjoyed the experience of JoAnn leading. After an hour of passion, JoAnn took a nap, while James got up and took a shower. He then woke JoAnn so that she could shower and dress while he checked his email.

James saw some emails from Sean Flaherty, listed as high importance. He assumed it was about the postponed VSI board meeting and almost ignored them until he saw the subject.

JoAnn came out of the bedroom and then walked into his office after hearing him say, "Oh my God," several times.

"Is everything okay, James?"

"I'm not sure, these emails are incredible. There's one from George's attorney, but it was actually sent by someone else."

"Someone probably hacked his account. I know people who had that happen, and their contacts get ads for Viagra or something."

"This isn't the same, baby. This email is from a student in Harbin, China, claiming that he was one of twenty hackers paid by George to hack American businesses. He says that none of the hackers knew anything about the attacks from America on Chinese government websites. His knowledge of Nadya, George, and his attorney Sean Flaherty makes him credible. He says they were all used by George and might be in serious trouble with the Chinese."

"Do you think he's telling the truth, James? It might just be a hoax."

"I don't think so. He forwarded emails between George, George's attorney, and Nadya that discuss plans to get the students out of China. He also says he has critical information about a planned military attack on the US fleet that he needs to get to the president. The email includes his email address at the Harbin Institute of Technology. If this is a hoax, it's a very elaborate one."

"What're you going to do?"

"I'm asking him for some additional proof. I have the list of network addresses that had the highest rate of exploitation. The ones that made the VSI security products look like Swiss cheese. I'm asking him if he knows which ones they are. If he answers correctly, there's no doubt about his credibility. I'm also forwarding the emails to Rick."

"So I guess this will be a working dinner?"

"Sorry, baby, but a possible attack on the US fleet takes priority."

"As a US Senator, I have to agree."

"Could you drive, baby? I need to text Rick that we're on our way and also check my email."

"Do I have to drive your rocket?"

"No, we can take your car."

As James walked into the restaurant with JoAnn, he could see the look on Rick's face and knew he'd seen the emails.

"Do you think it's real?" James asked.

"It sure looks like it, but we need to wait for his response on those addresses before we know for sure."

"Does anyone know what time it is in Harbin?" James asked.

Allison responded. "It's seven thirty in the morning tomorrow. I spent two semesters in China when I was in undergraduate school."

"That means we could get our answer while eating dinner."

Michelle seated them and brought them their drinks. James tried to keep the conversation light, but he could see everyone was holding their breath each time his phone buzzed. He looked at his email five times with no luck.

They'd finished dinner and were ordering dessert when the phone buzzed again. James looked at the email and nodded his head. He took the piece of paper with the addresses out of his pocket and handed it to Rick.

"He says he only has the ones that were attacked from Harbin. Check them off as I say them, Rick."

After Rick had checked them all, James said, "He's for real, and his name is Kim. I'm sending an email back to him saying we authenticated the information. I'll also send an email from my government account letting him know that we'll meet with some people in the US government who could help, such as Barbara Chang."

"When are you going to contact her, James?"

"Right now," James said, as he dialed his phone.

"Barbara, sorry to bother you at this hour, but I need to discuss something urgent that just came up. It involves the Chinese cyber attacks. I don't want to talk over the phone. What's the earliest you can meet me? It's really urgent."

"I'm in DC. Do you still live in Arlington?"

"Yes, Crystal City. I'll text you my address."

"I'll be there in thirty minutes."

James texted his address and said, "We all need to go. Barbara's going to meet us at my condo."

They all were at James's condo in twenty minutes.

"What a view of the Potomac. This is really nice, James."

"Thanks, Allison. Does anyone want a drink or something?"

James's phone rang and Barbara said she was at the front desk. He went down to the lobby to escort her up.

"I'm sorry you had to leave your party, Barbara."

"I should thank you, James. It was a boring fund-raiser, and the food was horrible. Can you show me the emails?"

"They're on my laptop on the table."

Barbara read the emails and said, "My God, have you confirmed this as being accurate, James?"

"Yes, I have. Kim knew details about the cyber attack that only the hackers would know."

Barbara called the president as she walked toward a more private area. James heard her say, "Okay, we'll be right there."

"The president wants to see you and Rick immediately, James. Bring your laptop. I'll drive."

As Barbara drove, she went into a tirade about George.

"I warned the president about George. He can't be trusted. The old bastard thinks he's bulletproof because he was the largest financer of the president's campaign. I'm just glad I limited his access to the president, or this could've been worse. As it is, I know the opposition will still try to use this to discredit the administration. We need to get out in front of this and make sure George is held responsible for his actions. I'll bet he put those students in jeopardy and created the conflict between the US and China just to manipulate the stock market and pad his bank account."

"I've known George for a long time, Barbara. We may need more proof than an email from a hacker in China and a statement by a Russian expatriate to bring him down."

"Yeah, I know. Okay, we're here. Follow me. We're going to the private residence."

James had never seen the president wear anything other than a suit and was surprised to see him in jeans and a Washington Nationals sweatshirt.

"James has some emails to show you on his laptop, Joe. It's rather alarming."

After looking at the emails, the president asked, "Are you sure these emails are real?"

"Yes, sir, I checked the information on the addresses that were attacked. His response was completely accurate."

The president shook his head several times while saying, "I'd never have believed George would do something like this. This isn't going to be enough to convict him. George has some very good lawyers. We need to get some real proof to nail him. I also need to get those students out of jeopardy without having the federal government directly involved. The Chinese could think we're behind all of this."

"Maybe we could put some pressure on George to get the students out, and I believe I know how to do it, Mr. President. I'll contact him first thing tomorrow morning and set up a meeting."

"You'll need to light a fire under George's ass, James. The Chinese will eventually figure this out. That could end any hope for the students, including Kim. My primary concern is this attack on our fleet referenced in Kim's email. This makes Kim the highest priority. No matter what happens, we need to get him out of China to find out what he knows."

"I understand, Mr. President."

Barbara arranged for a White House limousine to drive James and Rick back to the condo. When they walked in, both JoAnn and Allison were wearing pajamas and bathrobes and having a nightcap. James and Rick said hello before going back to James's office.

"I'll schedule my meeting with George for tomorrow. Can you arrange for me to be wired, Rick? I'll also need a small listening device I can leave in his office."

"Not a problem, James."

# 22

George Solomon was having a great week. He'd just humiliated the Chinese government in front of its own people while using Chinese students to do it. In addition, the attacks on US businesses from China had moved public opinion almost fifteen points in favor of the foreign cyber-attack legislation. He'd accomplished this with no real damage to the United States or China.

The attacks on US businesses, while widespread, hadn't caused any serious harm. George had ordered all the data that was collected to be destroyed. The attacks on the Chinese websites did no permanent damage in China other than harm the population's respect for their government. George was happy that the Chinese were upset. If they were going to sponsor cyber attacks against America, then that attack dog could come back and bite them in the ass, like it just had.

The decline in the stock market had caused a panic on Wall Street, which resulted in a temporary drop of more than four thousand points, but it was quickly returning to normal. He was sure that his investment companies had done well, since his philosophy was to buy whenever there were sudden drops in the market based on panic. That was a bonus, but it wasn't part of his plan. The only thing left was to make certain no one found out.

He was awakened from his pleasant daydream by Nadya.

"You need to move on getting those students out of China, George. They may have evidence of what you did. If the government figures out what happened, you'll be prosecuted. You could be wearing an orange jumpsuit."

"I'm not going to pay four million dollars to the Chinese government just to expedite the student's travel permits, Nadya."

"You're being childish, George, and your fiancée agrees with me. If you don't move quickly, we won't be able to make the final arrangements for the chartered flights or the hotel reservations for the students. There is also a payment due today to secure the reservation of the International Congress Centre in Munich as the symposium site."

"The Chinese are bluffing. Once they give in, everything else can be handled. This is just poker, Nadya, and it's a game I'm good at."

"Yeah, and the stakes are the students' lives and your freedom. You need to fold, George, or this could be your last hand."

As they were talking, George got a call from James Jordan.

"James, what can I do for you today?"

"I'm nearby, George, and I'd like to meet you at your office."

"Sure, James, looking forward to it."

When James arrived, Nadya escorted him back to George's office. As he sat down, James attached the listening device to the underside of his chair while his hand was hidden from George's view.

"What can I do for you today, James?"

"We have a problem, George. Someone in China sent an email to my VSI account last night. They informed me that our VSI flagship product had been compromised during the recent cyber attacks by a group of Chinese students. He also claims that our product had supported malware attacks against Chinese government websites. I verified the email by using my government position to identify the network addresses that were attacked. They matched perfectly with

the ones he provided. He identified you as being involved and provided copies of emails from you, Nadya, and Sean Flaherty that prove
your involvement. The students are very concerned that they might
be caught by the Chinese government. VSI could be ruined if this got
out, George. Why would you do this?"

As George listened, his face slowly transitioned from joy to concern and then to outright fear.

"I'm not going to insult your intelligence by lying about this,
James. I need to know what you intend to do with this information."

"I'll take it to the FBI and the president, unless you fix this. Why'd
you do it?"

"To discredit the Chinese government and increase public support
for the foreign cyber-attack legislation. Have you seen the news about
the impact on public opinion? Believe me, I had no intention of hurting VSI or those students. In fact, I'm making plans right now to get
them to Munich, and I guarantee that I'll make good on any revenue
VSI loses because of this."

"This was reckless behavior, which is uncharacteristic of you. How
did you ever believe that you'd get away with it?"

"I was told the connection to VSI couldn't be discovered."

"Who told you that, George? Was it someone who worked for VSI?"

"I can't tell you that, but I can fix this. Just give me a little time."

"I'll give you until tomorrow to solve this, and then I take it to
Barbara Chang and the FBI."

With that, James walked out, leaving the listening device in place.

George Solomon had just seen his day and possibly his life go
from the highest ecstasy to the deepest depression in the course of
a two-minute conversation. He knew he was probably not going to
recover unscathed, but he at least had an opportunity to minimize the
damage if he acted quickly.

He called Nadya into his office.

"Give the Chinese anything they want to process the travel permits for the students, Nadya. I also need you to charter their flights to

Munich within the next twenty-four hours, and make sure all of the students have a hotel room and transportation."

"You never finalized the payments to the hotels, George. I'm certain that at this late date, the only rooms available will be in the high-priced five-star hotels reserved for VIPs."

"Tell the symposium manager that these students are the VIPs. Have him move the others to whatever is left or I'll withdraw my support for this symposium."

"I may need your help with this. What are you going to do?"

"Hire an attorney."

George called Jason Fisher of Fisher and McGowan.

"Jason, this is George Solomon, how are you today?"

"Fine, George, what can I do for you?"

"I want to have Mr. Sean Flaherty elevated to partner and transferred to your Washington DC office as my personal attorney."

"I can't do that without getting the approval of the other partners, George."

"Last time I checked, our annual fees with your firm were in excess of eight figures. If you want to keep my account, I suggest you do whatever you have to so that Mr. Flaherty is a partner by close of business. I also want him in my office by nine tomorrow morning. Is that clear?"

"Yes, George. I'll take care of it."

Nadya came back into George's office and said, "Everything has been taken care of with the Chinese and the symposium manager."

"Good. I want you to email Mr. Flaherty and tell him he's just been made a partner in his law firm at my direction. In addition, tell him to send emails to each of his contacts in Beijing, Harbin, and Shanghai, ordering them to notify their students that they'll all be attending the symposium. I'm leaving for the rest of the day. If you need me, call me at home."

When George got home, he poured himself a vodka and made a phone call.

"Don't talk, just listen," George said. "James Jordan knows that the VSI systems were compromised and were the reason for the cyber attacks on China. I was able to control the situation by telling him I'd make good on any damages to VSI. It's just a matter of time before he figures out who sabotaged the VSI technology. You need to fix it."

James called Rick after the meeting with George.

"Hi, James. Did you enjoy your meeting?"

"Yeah, I really did, Rick. What're you doing?"

"I'm in my office listening to George. Looks like he's moving heaven and earth to get Kim and the rest of the students out of China. I guess your little discussion with him worked. George also called his law firm and asked for Sean Flaherty to be promoted to partner in the firm. He wants him transferred to DC to be his personal attorney. What do you make of that?"

"Well, I don't think it's gratitude for a job well done. I think he's trying to buy Flaherty's loyalty and keep him from talking. I'm not an attorney, but that would be my guess."

"Mine too. The director is thinking about using Dimitri to tail George. What do you think?"

There was no answer.

"Are you still there, James? Did you hear me?"

"I heard you, and I think it's a good idea. I was just looking at a text from Tom. He wants us to come to VSI and look at the log book and audit logs from the laboratory systems. You up for a road trip?"

"Sure, I'll meet you at the condo."

James and Rick made it down to VSI in a little over an hour. Tom met them in the lobby and took them directly to the laboratory. "I've seen more of you in the past week than in the previous year, boss."

"Yeah, I know. You're probably getting tired of my face."

Tom smirked. "Do you believe in ghosts?"

"No, but Rick gave me an office in the Hoover Building that everyone thinks is haunted. Why do you ask?"

"I think we may have a ghost in this laboratory. Come, I'll show you. After you left VSI, Philip changed the employee identification badges. The new ones are smart cards with the employee's identification information and other relevant data. We use them to get in the building after-hours and to log on to our computers."

"When did this happen?"

"About six months ago."

"You think he implemented it because of all the security incidents?"

"I'm certain of it. It allows us to control and log all employee operations while they're using the network and labs, including who made what changes to all VSI network and lab systems. Watch as I log into the test system we used the other day by using my smart card badge. I'm putting my badge in the smart card reader and entering my PIN and password. That's required for anyone who wants to log into the system as an administrator with elevated privileges. Now I'm logging into the audit files for the test system and searching the audit files from eight days ago at about three in the afternoon. You can see the names of everyone who logged in around that time. It shows the date, time, and operations performed for each name. All of the names are VSI employees whom we know had authorization to be in the lab and to access the test system. But watch what happens when I do a search for 10:12 p.m. that evening. What name do you see?"

"My God, it's Philip's name," James said. "That's impossible, he was already dead."

"Yeah, I know. Look at the operations he performed."

James quickly examined the log file.

"Philip's ghost reset the system clock forward to the same date and time that we entered the other day when we were testing the patch. So whoever logged in had Philip's ID badge, and was testing the patch that implemented the attacks on the Chinese websites. But how'd they have Philip's PIN and password, Tom?"

"I don't know, but that information is a lot easier to get than a badge from a person who's deceased. I'll bet half the people in this lab know other employees' PINs and passwords. I've even seen them ask others to enter it for them while they're working on something else in the lab. The lab is always less formal than the real world. That's why Philip required the use of smart cards. It's the only way to control and track who's doing what."

"So an imposter used Philip's badge?" Rick asked.

"Yes, but that's not all. Look at the lab entry and exit log book for that same date, for entry at 10:05 p.m. and exit at 12:22 a.m. What do you see, boss?"

"Are you kidding me? I don't believe it."

"I know, boss. It sure looks like Philip's signature, doesn't it?"

"Yes, Tom. We both are very familiar with that signature. But 'P. Wu' is only three letters. It would be easy to fake. Even so, it looks real. It would have to have been made by someone who knew Philip's signature pretty well, and that he generally just used his first initial."

James saw several people enter the lab. "Let's continue this conversation in a more private venue, such as my old office."

As James walked into his VSI office, he saw that nothing had changed since he left. Everything was still in the same place, and nothing was missing. He sat down behind his old desk and put his feet up like he had in past private meetings with his staff.

"You look good behind that desk, boss. It reminds me of our design meetings."

"Thanks Tom. I'll be back, so don't sell anything yet."

James looked at Rick and said, "So what would you conclude, G-Man?"

"G-Man? That word hasn't been used to describe FBI agents since J. Edgar Hoover was the director. In answer to your question, though, I would conclude that the badge was provided to the imposter by someone who was at the scene of Philip's murder, when his briefcase disappeared. The imposter had to know Philip's PIN and password and enough about how he signed his name to provide a pretty good forgery in the log book. The same person either developed the patch or knew enough about it and the laboratory equipment to test it. Ergo, it was someone who worked at VSI, had excellent technical skills, knew Philip pretty well, and had a connection to his murder."

James pointed at Tom. "Your turn, Tom. Who do you know at VSI that meets the first three of the four requirements Rick just stated?"

"It could be either Theresa, Chris, or me. We all work at VSI, have the technical skills, and knew Philip very well. I knew Philip's PIN, but I didn't know his password. Also, on the date and time listed in the log book I was at a bachelor party for Gary Hayden, one of our engineers. I already checked the date, since I did the same analysis before you got here."

"Thanks, Tom. I never really thought it was you, and I'm still not certain it's Chris or Theresa. There isn't enough evidence to prove it's either of them."

"True. But as the only law enforcement officer in the room, I believe they're good enough suspects to be questioned."

"I agree with that, Rick. Are Chris and Theresa still off-site, Tom?"

"Yes, Chris is with his development team. I talked with him yesterday. Theresa is on vacation, but I have no idea where she went. She just suddenly notified Chris and me by email that she was stressed and needed to take some time off."

"Can you give me their phone numbers, Tom?"

"Sure, Rick. I have them in my phone. I'll text them."

"I know I've kept you busy, Tom. But have you had a chance to review the Zeus folder I gave you during my last visit to VSI?"

"Yes, I evaluated the design, and my team implemented the code in the development lab. It's definitely based on VSI technology, but it has a target locator and command and control capability that's incredibly sophisticated. I'm having fun playing with it, and I've made some modifications to decrease the size of the object code. It's definitely

Philip's design, and it's one hell of an antiworm. We're going to integrate it into some of our current VSI technologies, boss."

"How does it compare to the Backfire worm, Tom?"

"Backfire is also very sophisticated, and it's designed to be offensive. Whoever developed it has talent, and there's enough similarities to Zeus that I'm certain it was developed by someone who knows our technology."

"I agree, Tom. It's getting late, and Rick and I need to leave."

Rick handed Tom his card and said, "Ask both Chris and Theresa to call me when you hear from them."

As they were walking to the car, James said, "I think Theresa is the more likely suspect. Her position gave her control over all product modifications, including all patches. Philip also didn't want her to be the new CEO. It was in his will. I think we should concentrate on her."

"I'll look at both, James. I've been trained to always expect the unexpected. Can you drop me at my house?"

"Sure, no problem, Rick."

When James got home, he immediately called Barbara. He described what they'd seen at VSI and told her that a rogue VSI employee could be involved in the cyber attacks.

"Thanks, James, I'll let Shelly know. That bug you planted in George's office was a great idea. It looks like all the arrangements for the students have been completed, and they'll be on their way to Munich. George is also going, and we recorded his itinerary as he was dictating it to his secretary."

"I think Rick and I should also be there, Barbara."

"I agree, and if Rick checks his email, he'll see that Shelly has already booked both of you on a flight to Munich tomorrow, with my approval. You'll also be accompanied by Dimitri, who's assigned to monitor George in case he tries to defect. Goodnight, James. Have a good flight."

Ten minutes later, James got a call from Rick.

"Hey James, did you hear the news? We're flying to Munich tomorrow."

"Barbara just told me. She said that Dimitri was also going to keep a close eye on George in case he tries to flee. I don't believe he'd do that, but I could see where it might be a problem, since he's not a US citizen."

"That's exactly why it's a problem. I've been given specific orders by the director to prevent that no matter what. I hope you understand what that means, James."

"I do, I just hope it doesn't come to that. It could get bloody, since George generally travels with bodyguards."

"I think I can handle it. I've been granted a right to carry weapons in Germany by the attorney general and the German government. I'm pretty certain George's bodyguards won't be armed."

"I wouldn't count on it, Rick. George is nothing if not resourceful. I'll see you tomorrow."

James was packing for the trip when his phone rang. It was JoAnn.

"Hi, baby. I'm packing for a trip to Munich tomorrow. Rick's coming with me. Where are you?"

"I'm at home. A woman called me on my personal cell phone about ten minutes ago. She said I needed to tell my boyfriend to back off or there'd be serious consequences. I'm worried, James."

James was upset, but he composed himself. "Don't worry about me. I'm traveling to Munich with Rick, so I'll be fine. Did you report the threat to the Capitol police? Maybe they can identify the caller."

"I did, but they said it was untraceable."

"I'll call Rick and see if the FBI can provide some protection for you while I'm gone. I'd like you to come over and spend the night."

"Okay, I'll be there in an hour. I love you."

"I love you, too, baby."

James called Rick and told him about the threat.

"Don't worry, James. I'll call the director and tell her what happened. JoAnn's a senator and you're a friend of the president. I'm sure she'll provide protection. I'll also ask Allison to watch over her until we get back."

"Thanks, but I wouldn't want to put Allison in danger."

"I don't think it's a problem. Allison is a really good shot and has her own arsenal. I pity anyone who goes after her."

# 23

Kim and Cai were meeting for lunch at HIT after their contact and communication with James.

"When are you going to tell Shen and Lian about our contact with Mr. Jordan, Kim?"

"Tonight. But I can't tell them anything about the attack on the US fleet. Even you shouldn't know."

"Don't worry, Kim. I won't say anything. I really don't know much anyway."

"Let's keep it that way. It's safer. I'm meeting with Shen and Lian at my apartment at six. Shen's bringing the USB drive with our collected data that was meant for Flaherty and the two USB drives with the malware."

"I'd like to be there also, Kim."

"That would be good. Maybe you can cheer up Lian. Shen says she's very unhappy about what was in those emails we hacked."

When they all met that evening, Shen handed Kim two USB drives as he entered Kim's apartment.

"Where's the third USB drive, Shen?"

"It's in a safe deposit box in Harbin. I gave you the USB drive with our downloaded data and one of the USB drives with the malware. How long do you think it'll take before the government identifies who's responsible for the attacks in China?"

"I don't know. It was a sophisticated attack, so it could take a long time. The exact source of the attack might never be discovered. It also may not matter, since I have some really good news. Where's Lian?"

"Lian's in the car. She doesn't feel well."

"You should get her, Shen. She needs to hear this news."

"Okay, I'll be right back."

Kim and Cai were shocked when they saw Lian. It looked as if she hadn't slept or eaten in a week.

"Kim says he has good news, Lian. Maybe it will cheer you up."

"What is it?" Lian asked.

"I found someone in the US government who's going to help."

"How'd you do that?"

"I used the software I installed on Flaherty's laptop to find an email address for a high-ranking official in the US government. He reports directly to the president and is an expert in cybersecurity. I told him of our situation and he sent an email saying he would help us."

Shen looked at Kim as if he was crazy.

"Are you sure he's who he says he is?"

"I'm certain of it. His name is James Jordan, and he was the CEO of VSI. He's now the US government's Chief Information Officer and reports directly to President Joseph Meredith."

"How do you know that this person is really James Jordan? The account might've been hacked."

"I sent my first email to his VSI account and he responded from his White House account. I don't believe a White House email account can be easily hacked. Do you, Shen?"

"No, probably not. When do you think we'll know if it worked?"

"I'm not sure, but I made it clear that the situation was urgent. He said he was going to meet with some people in the US government who would help us."

"How?"

"I think they'll provide us a way to get out of China."

Lian began to tremble. "I wish everyone would just forget about this so we can continue with our lives the way things were before the project."

"I doubt that'll happen, Lian," Shen said. "We may have to leave China, at least for a while."

Lian started to cry.

"I don't want to leave my family and friends. Where will we go, Shen?"

"It won't be forever; things will return to normal and we'll be able to come back. Just think of it as a vacation in another country, maybe America. At least we'll be together and we'll be free. I love you, Lian."

Lian kissed Shen and said, "I love you, too."

After Shen and Lian left, Cai hugged Kim.

"I'm worried, Kim. I'd like you to stay at my apartment tonight. Mei is away on vacation, so we'll have the place all to ourselves."

"Sure, Cai. Let me put a few things together while you call a taxi."

The next morning, Kim was awakened by his phone ringing. It was Shen, and he sounded out of breath.

"Kim, you'll never guess what happened. I was just informed by HIT that we've all been selected to attend the Munich Cybersecurity Symposium. We're all leaving this afternoon on a chartered flight out of Taiping Airport."

"What do you mean by 'all,' Shen? Who does it include?"

"All of the students in the project. I got an email from Flaherty and I just confirmed it with HIT. We're all going and we're staying at a really nice hotel in Munich for four days. I'll see you and Cai at the airport."

Kim quickly got dressed and told Cai the news.

"I'm going to my apartment to pack. I'll get a taxi to take us to the airport. See you in an hour, Cai."

Kim and Cai met Shen and Lian at the airport, and the flight left with all the students on time.

"I got an email from James Jordan before we left, Cai."

"What'd he say?"

"He's traveling to Munich with some people from the US government who want to talk with me. He included his cell phone number and said he'd meet us at the symposium."

"We saw his picture, so at least we know what he looks like. Did you see Lian before we boarded? The poor thing was crying, and so was Shen."

"Yeah, all the students were staring at them," Kim said.

"I know, the students think this is a four-day vacation. I wonder what will happen when they find out, Kim."

"I don't know, it could be bad. How do you feel about leaving China?"

"I'll miss my parents, but they'll be able to visit us in America. They've often talked about visiting, and they have the money to travel there. Now they'll have a really good reason."

After the plane landed, all the students were taken by bus to the Mandarin Oriental Hotel. As they checked in, they were given an itinerary and a schedule for the conference. Kim and Cai were assigned a junior suite, as were Shen and Lian.

"Do you think the room assignments were based on the grades?" Cai asked.

"Maybe," Kim answered. "I'm glad we got As."

"Did you see the itinerary? There's a presentation tomorrow morning by George Solomon."

"Yeah, it says all the symposium attendees from the universities in Beijing, Harbin, and Shanghai are required to attend."

"I can't wait to hear what he has to say," Kim said.

When they got to their room, Kim tipped the bellhop well and asked if the students from Beijing and Shanghai were staying at the hotel.

"No sir, the students from Beijing are at the Charles and those from Shanghai are at the Sofitel," the bellhop said as he left.

"I think the students from each city were intentionally assigned to different hotels, Cai."

"Why would they do that?"

"Probably to cut down on the opportunity for sharing information before George Solomon's presentation."

"I guess we'll find out tomorrow what Mr. Solomon is trying to keep secret. I'm really tired, Kim. I was too excited to sleep on the plane, and they had some great movies. I'm going to take a nap."

"Okay. I need to check my email and prepare for the meeting with Mr. Jordan tomorrow."

Kim set up his laptop and sent an email to James that said they'd arrived in Munich and were staying at the Mandarin Oriental Hotel. He then documented the details of the North Korean attack plan, as described by his uncle, and saved it on a jump drive. As the adrenaline from the last few days started to diminish, Kim suddenly felt tired. He delicately got into bed with Cai and took a nap.

Kim dreamed of his mother singing to him when he was young. When he woke, he realized it was Cai singing in the shower. He decided to join her. After a passionate fifteen minutes, they both got dressed for dinner. Kim watched the TV as Cai was putting on her makeup. He found a horrible news report about the North Korean Navy intercepting and killing hundreds of North Korean refugees attempting to escape in small boats. The newscast said that several such incidents had occurred in the past month due to severe food shortages. It was clear that things were getting increasingly worse and that he'd need to get his family out soon.

Kim and Cai met Shen and Lian in the main hotel restaurant. Although the food was great, they were virtually silent during the meal. They all felt out of place, and Kim didn't think it was because

of jet lag. Their lives had just changed in the blink of an eye, and they
were trying to cope with the uncertainty of their future.

James, Rick, and Dimitri were notified on the morning of their flight
that they needed to meet with an assistant director of the FBI at eleven.
They arrived at the assistant director's office, and he gave them a copy
of George's itinerary and that of the students.

"You and I are assigned to the same hotel as Kim," Rick said.

"Yeah, Dimitri is assigned to the Hotel Konigshof, where George
is staying. Let's listen, the assistant director is explaining the goals of
our trip."

"I'm here to brief you on your mission," the assistant director said.
"There are two primary tasks. The highest priority is the interrogation
of Kim, which will be conducted by James and Rick. There will also be
intelligence agents present from the Central Intelligence Agency and
the Defense Intelligence Agency, who will identify themselves at the
airport in Munich. They will take you to the International Congress
Centre in time for George's presentation to the students. You will also
be provided with photographs of Kim secretly taken by our agents
when he checked into his hotel. A separate room has been set up for
the meeting with Kim after Solomon's presentation. Dimitri, you will
monitor Solomon and report to Rick regularly on his activities, and
immediately if he tries to flee. Good luck."

James, Rick, and Dimitri were driven to Dulles Airport in an SUV.

"I'm glad the director is taking the security threats seriously, James."

"What do you mean by that, Rick?"

"This SUV is armored. It's the same model they use for the president."

"I guess we should all feel honored," James said, as both Rick and
Dimitri laughed.

The plane landed ahead of schedule in Munich. They were met at
the gate by their CIA and DIA contacts, who introduced themselves

as Terry and Don. After getting through customs, Terry and Don took them and their luggage to a waiting SUV, where they were given photographs of Kim.

James and Rick got to the International Congress Centre by 8:30. At 8:40, several small buses pulled up in front of the center, and the Chinese students entered through the front doors.

"I see him," Rick said. "He's the tall guy walking with that gorgeous woman."

"I see him also. He kind of walks with a military gait."

"Yeah, his eyes are also scanning the room. Definitely a spook."

"You think he was an intelligence operative? He's a hacker, Rick."

"He may be a hacker now, but I'd bet a week's salary that he has intelligence training."

James and Rick walked quickly toward Kim, and when they were within two feet of him, James said, "Hi, Kim. I'm James Jordan."

Kim turned and smiled. "I'm Kim Kwon-Mu, and this is my friend Cai Chan Li," he said.

James thought that Cai was probably more than a friend.

"This is Rick Tanner, Kim. He works for the FBI. Can we talk for a few minutes?"

"Sure, let me signal our friends." Kim waved at Shen and Lian, gesturing that he and Cai would join them inside.

"Kim, we have a room set up to talk with you after George speaks to the students," James said. "We need to discuss the North Korean situation."

"I'll tell you what I know, Mr. Jordan, but I'll also need some help from the US government. I'll explain after Mr. Solomon's presentation."

"We can only talk with you, Kim. Cai can't be present, since what we'll be discussing is very sensitive."

Cai nodded and said, "I understand, Kim. I'll wait for you outside the room."

Rick handed Kim a small listening device the size of a cell phone.

"I'd like you to carry this into the presentation. It will record and transmit George's presentation."

"I'm familiar with the technology. I'll see you after the presentation, Mr. Jordan."

Kim and Cai quickly entered the auditorium after showing their symposium badges. As they found their seats, they saw a tall man with white hair standing at the podium: George Solomon. There was a large screen behind the podium that displayed the words "Welcome Students" in Chinese.

"Good morning, students. I'm George Solomon, the man who financed your trip to Munich and this symposium."

A translation of what he was saying was displayed on the screen behind him. Many of the students started to applaud, but George quickly waved them off.

"I'm here today to thank you for your efforts and the excellent work you've done. All of you should take pride in your accomplishments. You're here today and for the next several days as an expression of my appreciation. Your trip from China is also intended to remove all of you from danger."

The room suddenly got very quiet. George could see he had everyone's attention and continued with his presentation.

"Unfortunately, not everything went as planned. Some members of the Chinese government may erroneously believe that you could be responsible for the attacks on the Chinese government web pages."

There was suddenly a lot of conversation among the students, and George asked them to listen to what he needed to tell them. After the room became quiet, George continued.

"I arranged for this vacation to get you out of China until this matter can be settled. We're working on a solution and hope for a favorable result. Those who don't want to return to China will be given full scholarships to any school in Europe or the United States, including all living expenses. After graduation, I will guarantee you jobs with companies I own. No one is prevented from returning to China. If you do want to return, I'll try to help, but I can't guarantee I'll be successful. I'll need to know what each of you want to do by the end of the symposium."

After he was done, George quickly left the stage and walked out the door with his bodyguards, Dimitri following him from a safe distance. As the students left the auditorium, James and Rick saw many emotions. Some were crying, some were stunned, some seemed disaffected, and there were more than a few who were happy.

"I don't think George incriminated himself with that speech, Rick."

"Yeah, I bet it was put together by his new personal attorney."

"Probably; it was cleverly worded so that he admitted no guilt."

"It looks like my boss won't find anything from George that she could use to indict him."

Kim and Cai and two other students walked toward James.

"These are our good friends and classmates, Shen and Lian."

"It's very nice to meet you," James said. "I'm impressed how well you all speak English."

Lian laughed. "The number of Chinese who speak English is three times the number of Americans who speak our language."

"We need to go, Kim," James said.

"What about Cai?"

"She can't go in the room during the briefing, but she can wait outside. There's snacks and drinks in the room we're going to. If Cai wants anything, she can ask the guards and they'll get it for her."

Kim and Cai said goodbye to Shen and Lian.

"Okay, Mr. Jordan, we're ready," Kim said.

They were led to a conference room where the CIA and DIA agents were waiting. Kim got Cai some energy bars and water and kissed her as she left the room. He then began his briefing.

"I want to thank you for meeting with me today. I'll tell you everything I know about my country's plan to attack the American fleet, but I need your help in getting my family out of North Korea."

"We will provide any help you need," James said. "I'll guarantee that as a representative of the president of the United States."

Rick was surprised. He was sure the president hadn't said that.

"Thank you, Mr. Jordan. I'm Lieutenant Commander Kim Kwon-Mu, a cyber warfare officer in the KPN and a former KPN SEAL and submariner. I was sent to China to learn advanced cyber warfare tactics at HIT. While attending school, I became involved in the project funded by George Solomon. I'm also the nephew of a North Korean fleet admiral who commands the North Korean Western Fleet. It was he who informed me of the North Korean plan in a meeting at his headquarters in North Korea. I have a short description of the entire plan on this jump drive. Please download it and read it before we begin talking. It's the only file on the drive, and it's in English."

After everyone downloaded and reviewed the two-page description, Kim asked if anyone had any questions.

"What does the North Korean government believe will be gained by this attack?" asked Terry, the CIA agent.

"More financial and economic support from China during the war that could result from the attack, if it is successful. North Korea is starving, and the leadership is afraid the food riots could turn into a revolution that America will support."

"Good morning, Kim. I'm Don. We're familiar with the North Korean submarine-launched anti-ship missile. My understanding is that it doesn't have the capability to target individual ships. This is especially true if they're within the small area where this exercise will be taking place. It could hit a Chinese ship by mistake."

"That's no longer true, Don. The old guidance system has been replaced with a new data link guidance system. This system allows an operator to select the target and steer the missile to it via a video display while submerged."

"Can you tell me why your uncle, a fleet admiral who is part of the North Korean leadership, wants to betray his country?"

"Yes, Terry. My uncle is a patriot first. He loves his country, but he knows, as I do, that the leadership is corrupt and becoming increasingly unstable. He is also ill and has less than three years to live, so he doesn't fear death. The admiral intentionally assigned me to China so that I might have more of an opportunity to contact someone who could help. As it turns out, that's exactly what happened."

"Can you tell us what you need from us to get your family out of North Korea and who that would include?" James asked.

"It includes my mother and younger sister who live in Nampo, and me. My uncle is working on a plan, but he says he might need the assistance of the American Navy. I'm not certain what he meant by that. However, the only feasible method of getting anyone out of North Korea is by boat, if you can get past the naval patrols. If I were to guess, I believe his plan would require us linking up with a US Navy ship or covert assets such as US Navy SEALs."

"How do you know about the SEALs?" Rick asked.

"I was a North Korean SEAL, and I know that the American SEALs have performed some covert operations in North Korean waters. In fact, our SEALs, including myself, specifically trained for intercepting their operations so we could capture one or more of them. The government wanted to display them to the world media for propaganda purposes and as hostages they could trade for a large bounty. The US SEALs were too good, however, and we never got the opportunity."

"Thank you, Kim. As a former US Navy SEAL, I appreciate the compliment."

"It's an honor to meet you, Rick."

"I agree with your analysis, Kim. Our navy SEALs are trained for exfiltrations like what might be needed here," Don said. "If the United States was to agree to assist you with the exfiltration of your family, would you agree to provide intelligence information? It would include information on the North Korean military and intelligence units, including cybersecurity operations."

"I will, but only after we get my family out."

"That's fine, but aren't you worried the North Koreans might find out you're in Germany?"

Kim smiled. "I don't believe my country would have any way of knowing where I am. Even if they did, I could simply tell them I was here for a cybersecurity conference with the other students in my school. My school could easily verify that, since it's the truth. Besides, I'll return to China after the conference is over in two days, probably with some of the other students who won't accept Mr. Solomon's offer. When I get back, I'll send my uncle a report on Mr. Solomon's treachery. I'm sure he'll insist on my recall so he could be personally briefed on what happened. The trip to Germany, although unanticipated, actually works into my plan. It gives me a reason to return to North Korea to initiate my family's escape."

James asked if there were any more questions. After not getting a response, he said, "Can you give us a minute to discuss the situation, Kim?"

After Kim left the room, James said, "I believe Kim is the real deal, and I plan to tell the president."

"I agree," Terry said. "He'll be very useful in our understanding of the political situation in North Korea."

"The exfiltration could be problematic," Don said. "Getting past the patrol boats to get close enough to a US ship will be difficult, and our ships won't violate the twelve-mile limit. The North Koreans are very aggressive in protecting their territorial waters as we saw with the Pueblo Incident back in '68. Even if an American ship got anywhere near the North Korean coast, it would create such attention that Kim would never get past the patrol craft."

"It can't be a surface ship," Rick said. "It would have to be a submarine, and the exfiltration would need to be off the east coast of North Korea where the waters are deep enough for a submarine to effectively operate. I know those waters from when I was a SEAL. The SEALs have a new electric mini-sub that's designed to operate from our attack boats. It has a range of forty-five nautical miles, requires a crew of two, and can carry six passengers. If Kim can get his family within twenty nautical miles of where the submarine can safely operate, then the mini-sub could pick them up and take them back to the submarine."

"I think that's our best option," James said. "Does anyone disagree?"

With no objections, James called Kim back into the conference room.

"We have a preliminary plan, Kim. We'll need to meet again over the next two days to provide you with more information before you return to Harbin."

"I'll need a secure means to communicate with you from North Korea. Can you provide that?"

"I can arrange that," Terry said. "We'll get you a special encrypted satellite phone by the end of the conference."

"Let Rick and I know if you have any questions, Kim. Here's our contact information. Enjoy the rest of the conference," James said. "After all, it's on George's tab."

# 24

Dimitri was given the keys to an SUV, and he followed George to his hotel after he left the presentation. He watched as George and his bodyguards took the elevator to his suite. Dimitri went back to the garage, found George's SUV, placed a GPS tracking device inside the rear fender, and then called Rick.

"I put the tracker on Solomon's car, Rick. I'll be able to track him using the tracking app on my phone."

"Okay, Dimitri. Let me know if he leaves the hotel."

Dimitri was tired from the flight, so he went up to his room and took a nap. At about three, he was awakened by the alarm that indicated George's car was moving. He went down to the garage and followed the limousine as it traveled toward the southwest section of the city before entering the Munich Waldfriedhof Cemetery. The Waldfriedhof seemed more like a park than a cemetery, since it was in the middle of woodlands that prevented anyone from driving to the burial sites. George's car stopped in the cemetery parking lot, so Dimitri parked a discreet distance away and called Rick.

"I just followed Solomon to a cemetery."

"Okay, let me know what he's doing there."

"It's a cemetery, Rick. I assume he's visiting a gravesite. His file said he lived in Munich at one time. He's probably paying his respects to a friend."

"Find out who it is. It could be helpful."

Dimitri watched from the car as George walked through the woods while carrying a large white box. His bodyguards stayed behind in the car. Dimitri got out of his car and entered the woods without the bodyguards seeing him. He quietly followed George as he made his way to a gravesite with a very large and elaborate tombstone.

George stopped and knelt while making the sign of the cross. He opened the box and removed a single flower that he delicately laid on the grave. George remained at the gravesite for twenty minutes, then kissed the tombstone and walked back to the car.

Dimitri waited for George's limousine to leave before going to the gravesite where he read the name on the tombstone: *Christina Hoffman.* He also read the inscription, *She joins the angels from whence she came. May her memory be eternal.* Dimitri took a picture of the gravestone and emailed it to Rick from his phone with a message saying that the person seemed very important to George.

Dimitri returned to his hotel and got a call from Rick.

"I got the picture. See if you can do some research on who Christina Hoffman is."

"That won't be easy. She died more than thirty years ago."

"See what you come up with and send it to me. I'll call Director Brockner to see if she can also provide some help."

Dimitri unpacked his laptop and did a web search on the name Christina Hoffman, using additional criteria including Munich and Waldfriedhof Cemetery. The only thing he found was a small news reference about the drowning of Christina Hoffman in Lake Starnberg and a local criminal investigation of her death. Dimitri emailed the information to Rick, who called the director.

"Director, I need some detailed information on a person whose gravesite George visited. The person's name is Christina Hoffman, and she drowned over thirty years ago. The local police did a criminal investigation of her death. Can you get someone to research this and send it to Dimitri and me?"

"Do you think it's important?"

"Apparently George did. Her grave was the first place he visited in Munich, and Dimitri said he seemed pretty emotional."

"Okay, I'll get our National Crime Information Center on it. They have the most comprehensive historical database on criminal investigations."

Later that day, Dimitri was checking his email when saw a new one from the FBI director. He opened it and saw an embedded news article on the death of Christina Hoffman. The article said Christina Hoffman drowned in Lake Starnberg while vacationing with her sister Frances at her boyfriend's summer house. There was no mention of the boyfriend's name, which Dimitri thought was odd, given that everyone else was identified. The article concluded by stating that her boyfriend and sister were both questioned by the police, but her death was ruled to be accidental.

Christina Hoffman was obviously someone who meant a great deal to George. Dimitri thought George was possibly the boyfriend in the article. If he could confirm that, he might have some information that could be useful. Christina Hoffman might be the key that opened the lock on a great many mysteries related to George Solomon.

When George returned to his hotel, he found an email from Sean Flaherty, his new attorney. It said Flaherty had some information on the Chinese hackers and that he needed to talk with him. George called him.

"Mr. Flaherty, so nice to talk to you for the first time. What can I do for you today?"

"I have some information provided to me by Jason Fisher."

"What is it?"

"Mr. Fisher was at dinner the other night with a friend who's an FBI assistant director. The assistant director told Jason that our most prominent client was going to be indicted by the FBI. He said that a Chinese student had some evidence of your involvement in the hacking and was going to provide it to Shelly Brockner."

"Don't worry yourself about that, Sean. I doubt they have any legally sufficient evidence to bring charges. Even if they did, I doubt the president would allow his justice department to proceed with such a high-profile case. The publicity from a trial could damage the already fragile situation between the Chinese and the Americans based on evidence that we could present in court. It could also reveal cybersecurity issues that the administration wouldn't want publicized."

"I hope you're right, Mr. Solomon. The agent said that the president was furious about your involvement. He made your arrest a top priority."

"I'll worry about that when it happens. That's why I have high-priced lawyers like you, Sean. Keep in touch."

George knew that his relationship with the president was forever damaged. The administration would be looking into every aspect of his businesses until they found something they could use. If they did, he planned to negotiate a deal that would allow him to retire. He would sell off his businesses and possibly move to another country. His fiancée, Astrid, was from German aristocracy, and she'd probably love to move back to Germany. Maybe he would buy a European soccer team and lead a life of leisure. George might even start a family with Astrid. He knew he was still capable at sixty-five and didn't even need those blue pills.

Before he did anything, however, George knew he'd need to return to the United States and tie up a few loose ends with James Jordan and the administration.

President Meredith was going through one of the most difficult weeks of his administration. He'd seen the stock market tumble over four thousand points in two days after the media exaggerated the impact of the cyber attacks from China. He believed that George Solomon was responsible, as did Barbara Chang, who was in his office to discuss it.

"What do you think we can do about George, Barbara?"

"We're in a difficult situation, Joe. There's no airtight legal evidence that George was involved. In addition, if he publicly acknowledges that he funded the attack, the media would have a field day, since he's your biggest financial supporter."

"It will be even worse if George is really responsible for Senator Thompson's death, as you and Shelly believe."

"Shelly believes George could also be involved in Philip Wu's murder, Joe."

"I find it hard to believe that George is involved in murder. George is a great schemer, but I can't believe he's capable of two high-profile murders until I have real evidence of his guilt. He'd have to be a criminal genius, and that'd be giving him more credit than he deserves."

"I hope you're right, Joe, but there is also the issue with VSI. The FBI determined that the attack on the Chinese websites was due to a technology developed by VSI. That hasn't been publicized, per your order. I know that it wasn't their fault, but VSI's former CEO is the current Federal CIO who reports directly to you. It wouldn't look good if the press found out."

"I'm not going to sell out James after all the help he provided to identify the problem. He and the company were obviously betrayed by a former VSI employee. The FBI needs to find out who it is."

"I would never suggest we betray James. The extortion committed by Captain Kinsley against Philip Wu could be related to the VSI problem. I hope Shelly figures it all out so we can get this behind us."

"So do I, Barbara. But my biggest concern is the possible attack by North Korea. I'm happy that James was able to alert us, but I'm frustrated that I can't warn the Chinese."

"I know, they'd never believe you without real proof. Especially now that our relations with them have deteriorated due to the cyber attacks and the pending passage of the foreign cyber-attack legislation."

"That legislation is currently sitting on my desk, waiting to be signed. I've delayed signing it as a courtesy to the Chinese ambassador, but I will sign it, Barbara. It was a campaign promise, and I believe it's necessary."

"I hope you can explain that to the ambassador at your meeting tomorrow, Joe."

"I know the Chinese are upset by the legislation, but maybe this will finally get their attention and change their attitude."

"I just hope they don't overreact during that naval exercise."

"Speaking of that, I just approved the covert mission to remove the North Korean agent and his family from North Korea. The CIA and DIA briefed me on how dangerous it is, but they claim it's worth it. Apparently the agent may be the best intelligence asset on North Korea that we've ever had. They say the information he provided could help prevent a war."

"I hope they're right, Joe. If this doesn't work, then this time next week we could be at war. A lot of ships could be sunk, with military personnel killed and injured."

Kim and Cai had spent the entire first day at the symposium listening to technical presentations and seeing exhibitions of the latest cyber-security technologies. During the breaks, Kim noticed groups of students discussing George's address and what they planned to do.

"From what I'm hearing, a lot of the initial hysteria is beginning to subside," Kim said. "Many of the students are discussing new schools outside of China."

"I know. Many seem to be discussing schools in Europe or the United States. Some have already contacted schools in Munich. I saw the school catalogs they had with them."

"I haven't heard many of them say that they were going to return and take their chances."

"I wonder what Shen and Lian are going to do, Kim?"

"I talked to Shen, and he said he thought they'd try California or New York. He met a senior from Shanghai Jiaotong University named Hakim who is going to a university in New York. It was arranged by an oil company in Saudi Arabia that George Solomon does business with. Hakim tried to convince Shen to join him and also go to New York."

"Where do you want to go?"

"I'll go wherever you go, Cai."

"I guess we're going to America then."

When they got back to their suite, there was a message from Rick asking Kim to come by his room to meet with him and James. As Kim entered Rick's room, he saw maps and two laptops on the dining room table.

"The president has approved the plan, Kim. The SEAL team is already preparing."

"That's great, Rick. How will my family and I rendezvous with the SEALs?"

"The navy's going to use a Virginia class submarine that's currently based in Japan. It'll carry a mini-sub with a five-man SEAL team."

"Have they selected the rendezvous site?"

"We can't use Nampo. As you know, the water is too shallow in the Yellow Sea, and especially in the Bay of Korea, for a submarine to operate. The east side of the Korean peninsula is a much better choice. Will it be difficult to get your family to the east side?"

"It shouldn't be a problem. There are many naval bases on the east side that the admiral could justify as sites for us to visit. One of the bases is in Wonsan, which is also a popular tourist destination for foreigners and locals. The admiral could justify going there as an opportunity to both visit the base and have a little vacation with my mother, sister, and me. There are also boats we could rent to rendezvous with the SEALs."

"Are you planning on taking your uncle with you?" James asked.

"I'm not certain he'd go, but I think it's a great idea. Do you think it's possible, Rick?"

"The mini-sub has the room if we use only two SEALs as operators and the other two to retrieve Kim and his family. I'm more worried about the weight, since that determines how much oxygen is needed. How much do you think the combined weight of all four of you'd be in pounds?"

"I weigh about 190 pounds. I'd guess that my mother and sister probably weigh a total of 200 pounds or less. My uncle has lost a lot of weight, and based on his height, I'd say he probably weighs between 140 and 150 pounds. That would make the total about 540 pounds."

"That shouldn't be a problem. The vehicle can carry eight passengers with a total weight much higher than that. I'll pass this information to Don and Terry to see if it's possible. The admiral would be a high-priority asset, so I'm certain they'd find a way if you can get him to go. The question is, can he handle the trip?"

"When I saw him a month ago in Nampo, he was moving fine."

"Okay. I'll notify Washington about the possibility of an additional passenger for the Yellow Submarine ride."

Kim was confused, "Why is the submarine yellow?"

James and Rick laughed. "The submarine isn't yellow. It was just a joke based on an old song from a famous British rock band."

"I have some technical questions," James said. "It sounds like the design of the new command and control system used on the Korean submarine-launched missiles isn't totally self-contained like the previous system. My guess is that the data-link system would require a network interface with an external source to get information for targeting. Am I correct, Kim?"

"Yes. The submarine's computer would need to send the target coordinates to the missile based on the selected target."

"So if we were able to inject a worm into the sub's computers, could it overload the computers through rapid replication?"

"Sure, the worms would reproduce so fast that they would use all the computer's resources and crash it."

"That could disable the targeting system through a massive denial-of-service attack, couldn't it?"

"Yes, James, but there are two problems with that plan. The first is getting the worm into the system, and the second is the trigger for the replication."

"I'm assuming there are no USB ports on the sub's computers."

"Yes, that's correct." Kim was starting to see where James was going with this. "However, there are shore-based systems that interface with the Kilo's onboard computers via a network to provide communications, navigation, and mission-planning information before each mission. That includes the exact time, which is necessary to determine latitude and longitude and to set the communication encryption codes. The information is provided by the servers at fleet headquarters, and those do have USB ports. If we can get a worm into the servers that provide the mission-planning information, it will likely be transmitted to the submarines. But what do we use to trigger the worms to replicate and take down the computers?"

"That's easy, Kim. Latitude will be the trigger. To get to the exercise area, the North Korean subs will need to travel south to the Senkaku Islands. The trigger will be a point of latitude we know they'll need to cross. It'll need to be close enough to the Senkaku Islands to prevent them from returning to North Korea to fix the problem. Once their subs reach that latitude, the worms will be triggered by the navigation coordinates processed by the onboard computers and crash them. You'll need to write the code to make that happen, Kim."

"In order to do that, I'd need to see the software on the onboard navigation system. It's in fleet headquarters in Nampo. I'd need a day or so to review it, modify the code for the trigger and targeting system, and then load it into the servers. I'll also need a worm with very sophisticated targeting capabilities, James."

"I can provide the worm, Kim. I also know some people at VSI who can provide you with the resources and information to integrate the trigger with the worm and program its targeting system. Do you think you can do that?"

"I'm sure I can. When can you get the worm and the information to me?"

"I'll have it and any required support software to you before you return to Harbin. When's your flight back?"

"I plan to fly back the evening the symposium ends. I've reserved a flight at about eight that gets me to Harbin at seven the next day. I plan to notify my uncle immediately after I return, and hopefully he can arrange a flight the next morning into Nampo."

"That's a lot of flying, Kim. How long do you think it'll take to get the information for the trigger and the target?"

"It should take less than a day. The difficult part will be getting into the server room at headquarters and loading the worm into the servers without being detected. Hopefully the admiral can help me with that. I'll keep you updated through my satellite phone."

"You'll have the satellite phone by tomorrow, as well as a few other items Rick scrounged from the FBI."

Before he left, Kim handed Rick a package.

"These are the hard drives with the data we downloaded from the US attack and the malware that attacked the Chinese web pages. I labeled them so you'll know what is on each drive. I'm guessing the malware had a time-based self-destruct capability."

"You're correct about the self-destruct feature, Kim. We'll set the time to before the attack on the Chinese websites to ensure the malware isn't erased. I'll personally take them back, so the FBI can maintain the chain of custody that will allow them to be used as evidence."

After Kim left, James called Tom at VSI, while Rick checked his email.

"I was just getting ready to call you, boss. I haven't heard back from Theresa, but Chris called me a half hour ago. I verified that he's with his development team at the customer site. He called to tell me that he was taking leave due to a family emergency involving his father. Chris said he might be gone for a week or so, but could be reached by phone or email."

"Thanks for the information, Tom. We need to find Theresa. I've never known her to be so inaccessible, even when she's on vacation. I also need you to do something else for me."

"Sure, what is it?"

"I'm sending you instructions by email on modifications that I need implemented on that Backfire worm you've been playing with. It's urgent—I need it completed by four this afternoon your time. I also need you to send any support software necessary for modifications to the worm."

"It shouldn't be a problem, I know that worm pretty well now. But this type of information is very sensitive, boss. We don't usually allow it outside the company."

"Don't worry, I know what I'm doing. Just get it ready and I'll make sure it's in good hands. Call me when you're done."

James called Barbara to arrange the delivery.

"Hi, Barbara. I have a very special package that I need picked up at VSI from Tom Allen and delivered with the highest security to my hotel in Munich by tomorrow afternoon. It'll be in an envelope."

"Why so urgent?"

"It's for Kim."

"Okay, I'll have it delivered to the naval base at Patuxent River and sent by military jet."

James got on his laptop and sent Tom the information on the required changes to the worm. He then checked his email.

"When did you come up with the idea to take down the North Korean attack using malware?" Rick asked.

"I considered it the day we first met with Kim. Due to my past naval experience, I'm familiar with the command and control systems, communications systems, and navigation systems used on submarines."

"Yes, but these are Kilo subs modified by North Korea. How'd you get that information?"

"I asked the president to get it from DIA. Their mission is to gather technical information on foreign military systems like the Kilo. DIA provided it to Don, who provided it to me this morning. I reviewed it, and I just sent some instructions to Tom for modifying the Backfire worm."

"So as I understand it, you're substituting date and time data used to trigger the Backfire worm used to attack China with navigation data."

"Yes. It makes no difference to the worm what the data is. Instead of monitoring time, this worm will monitor navigation position and will trigger when the target data is processed within the navigation server."

"And that target data is the navigation coordinates for the Senkaku Islands?"

"Yes."

"Clever, very clever, James."

"Hey, Rick, have you heard from Allison? Because I haven't heard anything from JoAnn via email or phone."

"No, but the FBI is monitoring them. We'd know if something was wrong. If you're worried, you should call her."

"I'm calling her now. I'll put the phone on speaker. Hi, baby. I haven't heard from you. Is everything okay?"

"I'm fine, James. I was just busy in my new job."

"How are you and Allison doing? Any more threatening phone calls?"

"No more phone calls, and everything is fine between Annie Oakley and me. She's something else. Did you know she owns a fully automatic AR-15? They're illegal."

James laughed. "You're on speaker, and Rick is listening."

There was a pause for a second. "Rick, I hope you never upset your girlfriend. It might be the last thing you ever do."

"We need to go, baby. I'll call you later."

"I'm going back to my suite and wait for Tom's call, Rick."

"Okay, see you at breakfast."

At about ten thirty, Tom called to say that everything was completed and ready to go. James thanked him and called Barbara so she could get it to Munich the next day. He thought it was ironic that the worm technology that had been misused to create the current tension between China and the United States might now be used to address it.

# 25

Rick wasn't happy about having to go to dinner with Dimitri, but James was busy, and he hated eating alone. He was surprised that he was actually enjoying his dinner partner's company.

"You seem so relaxed ever since we got to Munich. Why is that, Dimitri?"

"I like being back in Europe. I was born in Europe, and I feel more comfortable here."

"What's wrong with America?"

"Nothing. I like it also. It's a great country, but it's also a young country that doesn't seem to have an established culture of its own."

"That's because we're a nation of immigrants with a mixture of ethnicities and cultures."

"Yes, and it's reflected in your lifestyle. Your architecture is a mixture, and so is your food. European cities, like Munich, have a style all their own. The restaurants serve real food."

"So you don't like our food?"

"No, I've actually developed a taste for American fast food. It tastes good, and it's fast. Look around, Rick. The restaurant we're in operates at a slower pace than those in America. America has no traditions that encourage the relaxed enjoyment of the simple pleasures. It's rush, rush, rush all the time. It's probably why you have a much higher rate of coronary disease and mental health issues."

"You might be right. I do enjoy it here, but I miss my country when I'm gone too long."

"So do I. Damn, my alarm is buzzing. George must be on the move."

"I'll get the check. Pick me up out front."

Dimitri and Rick followed George's limousine to the airport, where he picked up an extremely attractive redhead.

"That's Astrid, George's fiancée," Rick said.

"They're not going back to the hotel, Rick. They're heading in the opposite direction. I think they might be heading to the Rathaus."

"What's the rat house?"

"It's the Munich town hall. It's where the city politicians work."

"Well, it's aptly named."

"They're parking. Let's follow them."

The Rathaus was huge and crowded with tourists, so Dimitri and Rick had little likelihood of being noticed while following their target. George and his fiancée entered the Ratskeller restaurant. Rick and Dimitri watched as George and Astrid were joined by a very tall, thin, young man with curly blond hair. Dimitri moved closer and took a picture of three of them while they waited for their table. There was an empty table near where George's party was being seated, so Rick bribed the waiter to seat them there.

"I can't hear what they're saying, Rick, but it doesn't look cordial."

"Yeah, it looks like George and the young guy are really getting into it."

Rick and Dimitri watched as the young man suddenly stood and said, "Drop dead, George," and then began to walk away. Astrid also stood and said, "Chris, please come back," as she started to go after him. George grabbed her arm and said something that made her sit back down.

"Let's follow the young guy, Dimitri."

The young man drove away in a Porsche as Dimitri followed him out of the city.

"My GPS says we're approaching Lake Starnberg, Rick."

"Yeah, I see that. He just took the road that goes around the lake toward those houses. It looks like he's entering the driveway leading to that three-story Bavarian-style house."

"I'll take some pictures and then we'll go back, Rick. My tracker shows George returning to his hotel."

"Okay, drop me off at my hotel, and we'll call it a night."

Back in his hotel room, Dimitri checked his email and saw one from the FBI with several attached photographs. He downloaded the attachments, which were obviously older photos of a beautiful, tall redhead. One of them showed her standing next to a man identified in the email as George Solomon.

Dimitri was struck by the photos. The tall young man at the Ratskeller looked very similar to the thirty-year-old picture of George. The nose was different, as was the chin, but the mouth, eyes, facial structure, height, and build looked almost identical. Dimitri knew that George had undergone plastic surgery after his defection from Russia, which could explain the chin and nose. There was no doubt in Dimitri's mind that Chris was George Solomon and Christina Hoffman's son.

Dimitri downloaded the pictures he'd taken earlier at the Ratskeller and Lake Starnberg, then emailed them to the FBI director and assistant director with descriptions. When he finished, he noticed an email from a familiar source. It requested a meeting at his earliest convenience in Manhattan to discuss an assignment. He replied, saying he was on vacation in Europe and would like to arrange the meeting for several days from then. The reply was immediate, and it stated that Dimitri's response was acceptable.

James went to bed after arranging the delivery of Kim's package and slept until Rick called him the next morning.

"Hi, sleeping beauty. I'm having breakfast downstairs in the Mandarin Bar. Why don't you join me?"

"Okay. Anything happen while I was asleep?"

"Not really, but we have a meeting in my suite at one to talk with Terry and Don about Kim."

"I'll be right down, save some for me."

James met Rick just in time to watch him finish a breakfast of white sausages and a large pretzel with beer.

"It's a little early for beer, isn't it? I believe there's a navy rule that the sun has to be over the yardarm, Rick?"

"Yeah, but I'm in the FBI now, and we can drink anytime. You should order this. It's listed under traditional Bavarian breakfasts."

"I think I'll pass. Coffee and strudel look fine to me."

"How's your plan coming?"

"Tom finished his work, and Barbara sent the finished package. I just got an email from her saying it was delivered to Don this morning. He'll bring it when we meet with him and Terry at one."

"Eat fast. That's less than an hour from now."

Don and Terry arrived at Rick's suite. Don gave James a jump drive with the modified Backfire worm, while Terry gave Rick two boxes, each containing a small encrypted satellite phone.

"These phones sure have gotten smaller, Terry. The ones we had when I was a SEAL were a lot bigger."

"What's in the envelope, James? It must be important if it came by military jet courtesy of the White House."

"It's a network worm and some support software, Don. Kim will use it to disable the North Korean submarines when he goes back. I think it's worth a try. Kim also thinks there's a possibility of including the admiral in the escape."

"I did the calculations, and the additional weight shouldn't be a problem," Rick said. "Kim says he's healthy enough to make the trip."

That caught Don and Terry's attention. After viewing the additional weight estimates, they thought it was possible.

"We'll run this by the SEALs and get back to you," Don said. "I also need to contact the navy so they can determine the exact coordinates for the rendezvous with the mini-sub."

James called Kim after Don and Terry left.

"Hi, Kim. When will you be back from the symposium?"

"We should be back by four."

"Good. Rick, and I have a few presents for you. I also want you to install the program you're using to monitor George's and Nadya's emails on my laptop."

"That'll only take a few minutes. Cai wants to know if you and Rick want to join us for dinner tonight."

"That sounds great. See you later."

"Looks like we're having dinner with Kim and Cai tonight, Rick. Speaking of dinner, how was your dinner with Dimitri?"

"We ended up following George to the Ratskeller restaurant where he met this guy who cursed him out. Astrid was also there."

"Who has the balls to curse George out?"

"Dimitri sent all the pictures to me. They're on my phone. Here, look for yourself."

James looked at the photos.

"That's Chris Hoffman, Rick. What the hell is he doing in Munich with George and Astrid?"

"Didn't you say that he called Tom and was taking leave due to a family emergency?"

"Yeah, I did. Tom said it involved Chris's father."

"How old is Chris?"

"Thirty-two. Why do you ask?"

"Dimitri followed George to a gravesite the first day he was here. Here's the picture of the gravesite. Look at the name on the tombstone."

"Christina Hoffman? Do you think she was related to Chris?"

"Make it larger so you can see the date she died."

"Thirty-one years ago. It could be Chris's mother."

"The assistant director also sent me some pictures of George from when he was in his thirties standing next to his girlfriend, Christina Hoffman. Take a look."

"Oh my God. George could be Chris's father."

"I'm certain of it. You said he'd taken leave due to a family emergency involving his father. That explains why he's in Munich, James."

"I'd like to talk to him to find out why meeting George was such a family emergency. Maybe he found out about what George did to VSI, and that's why he was so angry."

"Maybe he has evidence. Dimitri has a car, and we know where Chris is."

"Okay, but we need to get your boss's permission."

"I just texted her."

"Your phone is dinging. What'd she say?"

"She said yes and is notifying Dimitri to coordinate with me."

Five minutes later, Rick got a phone call.

"Hi, Dimitri. I assume the director called you."

"Yes, she said the man in the Porsche was Chris Hoffman, and he's the VSI CTO."

"That's true. He used to work for James when he was the VSI CEO."

"I didn't know that. Let's meet at seven tomorrow morning. On the way to the house, I'll tell you and James something about George Solomon that you may not know."

Kim arrived at Rick's suite with his laptop. James gave him the package with the worm, and he downloaded the software files onto his laptop. They went through the files together and James answered Kim's questions, including those on the integration of the targeting information and the trigger. James was very impressed with Kim's skills and how fast he picked up on the technology. He knew Kim could succeed as long as he had the information he needed on the North Korean submarine navigation and communication systems and got access to their servers.

After completing his work on the worm, Kim inserted a flash drive into James's laptop and loaded the same software he'd loaded on Cai's laptop. He gave James a one-minute tutorial on how it was used and its capabilities, but it was unnecessary because James was familiar with the concept.

"Thanks for the software, Kim. Have you seen any interesting emails on any of the accounts you've been monitoring?"

"I'm not sure. There were several emails yesterday involving George, his attorney, and someone who claimed that George owed them money due to some large stock transactions. I don't understand it. Do you think it's important?"

"It might be. Can you find it for me?"

"Sure, here it is."

James read the emails.

"Look at this email, Rick. It says George put a hold on this person's trading accounts. He's threatening George unless he removes the hold. George responded by claiming the trades were illegal because they were based on insider knowledge of the stock market crash. What do you make of it?"

"It looks like someone was using George's firm for insider trading, and he caught them."

"It looks that way to me, too. Maybe George wasn't in it for the money."

"Maybe not, but I don't believe he's going to win any humanitarian of the year awards. Before I forget, your new satellite phone and night vision binoculars are on the kitchen table, Kim."

"Thanks, Rick. Are there instructions?"

"They're in the box. Where do you and Cai want to go to dinner?"

"One of the students at the symposium told us about a place that had great Cantonese food. I'd like to try it."

"Sounds great. Do you have the address?"

"Yes, it's not far. I'll call Cai to meet us in the lobby."

"Okay, I'll call for a taxi."

After finishing some excellent Chinese food, Kim asked about the best technical schools in America and whether James and Rick thought he and Cai could get accepted at one.

"Since George is picking up the bill, I'd think you'd have your choice. There are a lot of great schools in America, but if you want one that specializes in cybersecurity, I think Carnegie Mellon, MIT, University of Maryland, USC, and George Mason have some of the best programs. Just tour the country to find the area and school you like the best. As I said, it's on George's tab."

At the end of the evening, the waitress bought them all a small glass of mint schnapps courtesy of the restaurant. It was a great evening, even though James knew there was no guarantee that they'd be able to repeat it. Kim was definitely going in harm's way. They returned to the hotel and said goodbye.

As Rick shook Kim's hand, he said, "Good luck, Commander. As we used to say in the SEALs, the only easy day was yesterday."

Kim wasn't sure what that meant, but he knew his life was about to get a lot more dangerous.

The next morning, James and Rick met Dimitri in the lobby, and as they drove out of the city, James said, "Okay, Dimitri, what do you know about George that I don't?"

"Christine Hoffman drowned in Lake Starnberg thirty-two years ago under mysterious circumstances. I also know that George was there when Christine died and that the police questioned him about her death."

"Are you implying that George was responsible for her death?"

"I'm not sure, James. I do believe someone was covering for him."

"What do you mean?"

"His name was the only one left out of the newspaper article. The article said there was no evidence that it was anything other than an accident."

"Do you also believe that George could hire someone to kill for him?"

"Yes, I do. And I don't just believe it, I know it."

Dimitri pointed to Chris's house.

"It looks like he's home. His Porsche is still in the driveway."

Dimitri drove the SUV up the driveway and parked it behind the Porsche. They got out and walked toward the house, but Dimitri stood farther back so he had a clear view of the entrance and the windows at each of the three levels. Dimitri saw a curtain on one of the windows move. He knew they'd been seen.

The door opened, and a very muscular young man stood in the doorway. ⟋ *should be lower case A*

"*Was wollen Sie?*" the man said.

"He wants to know what you want," Dimitri said.

The man then said in English, "Who are you looking for?"

"Christopher Hoffman."

The man turned and yelled, "Chris, there's some people here that want to talk to you."

James heard Chris Hoffman's voice.

"Tell them to wait until I find my clothes. Do you remember where I took them off?"

About five minutes later a very hungover Chris Hoffman came to the door wearing a bathrobe and said with a shocked look on his face, "James, this is a surprise. How'd you find me?"

Chris invited them in, but Dimitri decided to wait outside.

"Chris, I know that George Solomon is your father and that you had a big fight with him the other day. Can you tell me how it relates to the family matter you cited for your leave?"

"It's a very personal issue, James. Why do you want to know?"

"George is suspected of criminal activity that involves VSI, and I want to know if you know anything about it."

"No, nothing like that, although I hope you nail the bastard."

Then Chris started to laugh.

"What's so funny?" James asked.

"Biologically, George isn't the bastard, I am. In fact, he was responsible for making me one by not marrying my mother before he let her die."

"I'm sorry, Chris. Is that what your argument was about?"

"No, we don't talk about that anymore. As you might've guessed, Klaus here is more than a friend. George has never accepted me as gay and is trying to bribe me into being straight."

"I'm sorry. I had no intention of intruding into your personal life."

"That's okay. Is there anything else you want to ask?"

"Yes. Do you have any idea where Theresa is?"

"No, I don't, James. All I know is that she's on vacation. She notified Tom and me by email, which I thought was strange. I knew she was unhappy at VSI. You did, too, James."

"She hasn't answered any calls or emails. Tom told me you were fighting with her over access to the lab."

"Yes, but that's no big deal. We were always fighting over resources. I needed the lab for design, and she always had some emergency with product support. She seemed really stressed about some patch she was working on."

"Thanks for your help, Chris. You have a beautiful house."

"Yeah, I inherited it from my mother's family. It's a lot more than I'll ever see from George."

"See you back at work."

"I'll be back in a few days. Oh, if you see George, tell him I said to go screw himself."

They left and Dimitri drove them to the Hotel Konigshof. James went to the front desk and said, "Please call George Solomon's suite and let him know James Jordan is in the lobby and I'd like to meet with him." The desk clerk made the call, and after talking on the phone for a few seconds, told James he was invited up to George's suite.

James took the elevator, while Rick and Dimitri stayed in the lobby. He knocked on the door and was let in and frisked by one of George's bodyguards, who then led him to the living room area. George was there drinking coffee while reading a newspaper.

"Come in, James. This is a real surprise. How long have you been in Munich?"

"Since the symposium started."

"If I knew you were going to attend, I would've asked you to be one of the speakers."

"I'm not here for the symposium. I came to make sure you were following through with your promise to help the Chinese students."

"So you're here to spy on me. Well, what have you discovered?"

"That you really screwed those Chinese students and took advantage of them to address your own interests. The president has lost all trust in you, Ann Wu detests you, and I'll never forgive you for the damage you did to VSI. I also know your son Chris Hoffman hates you and claims you're a homophobe."

James could see that his remarks had slowed George down a bit, since he was thinking before he responded.

"I believe you're guessing about my relationship with Chris. But since you and I are old friends, I won't deny it."

"I know that Chris is your son from a relationship you had with Christina Hoffman more than thirty-two years ago. I also know that she drowned and that you were questioned but never charged."

"I guess you know it all, so why are you here?"

"I'm here to tell you that I intend to have you voted off the board and to force the confiscation of all your stock via a civil suit for malicious actions against VSI. I'll also ask for damages."

"I won't fight you, James. I'll give my stock back to the company and will pay any damages your lawyers reasonably request. My life as an investment banker is over, and I plan to retire and live the good life with Astrid, possibly here in Munich. My lawyers are currently discussing the evidence with the Department of Justice regarding my involvement. They tell me that the government might have enough for an arrest but not enough to support a conviction."

"Maybe not, but you're not going to walk away from this. There are people in the Justice Department who believe you're responsible for the murders of Philip Wu and Senator Thompson. They're working very hard to prove it."

"I never killed anybody. They'll never prove it because it isn't true."

"By the way, your son has a message for you. He says to go screw yourself."

# 26

James and Rick flew back to DC the day after the symposium ended. Both JoAnn and Allison were at the airport to meet them and drive to James's condo. JoAnn asked how the trip went, and James filled them in on Kim and his girlfriend, Cai. He also told them about his meetings with George and Chris. JoAnn was shocked to learn that Christopher was George's son.

"Poor Chris. I'd hate to have George as my father. I've been thinking about introducing him to a friend who just went through a bad breakup. I think he and Chris would be good together."

"You knew Chris was gay? How'd you know?"

"Just a feeling, James. I can't explain it."

"I've known Chris for almost twelve years and never would have guessed. Why didn't you tell me?"

"Why, would it have made a difference?"

"No, but I can't believe I didn't know. He said his father was a bastard, and I agree. George believes his lawyers will make sure he'll only get a slap on the wrist. Unfortunately, he may be right."

"That's terrible, but maybe it's something I can investigate as the chairwoman of the Senate Finance Committee."

"I'm sure George would just love that. He'd claim he was being persecuted by the fiancée of the VSI CEO whose failed products were the cause of this entire problem. I don't think either one of us wants that kind of publicity."

"There are also angry investors who physically threatened George," Rick said. "He put a hold on their investment accounts because of insider trading. Was that a common practice when you worked for him, JoAnn?"

"Yes, Rick. George never tolerated it when I was there."

"What if his firm profited due to prior knowledge of the attack?"

"I'm sure it did profit, Rick. But George probably had nothing to do with it. The policy at the firm when I was there was to buy during panic sell-offs. I'm sure his firm made tons of money."

"I agree with you, baby. George didn't do this for the money. He offered to release his stock ownership in VSI and to work out a settlement with me for any damages that his actions may have caused."

"Isn't his offer an admission of guilt, Rick?"

"Not really, Allison. There's no proof George was responsible for sabotaging VSI products. He could say he was just helping the company recover from the actions of the Chinese students. I'm certain his attorneys would insert a clause saying that he wasn't admitting to any guilt by agreeing to help VSI."

"So there's nothing you can do?"

"No, Allison. The government will have to do something. There are sixty students who know about George's relationship with the cyber attack on the United States. At some point, that information will surface, and the press will find out. The administration has to get in front of the story and appear as if they want to bring the responsible parties to justice. Otherwise they'll lose the confidence of the country, and the Chinese government wouldn't be very happy either."

"Rick's right. This will turn into a political show, and the media will eat it up. Well, at least I'll have some time with James now that you're back."

"Yeah, about that. It looks like I've been activated as a commander in the US Navy at the president's request. I ship out to Yokosuka to join the crew of the USS *Washington* in three days. I'm sorry, baby."

"What? Why did the president do that? Is this punishment because of VSI?"

"No, baby, I volunteered. I'm still a commander in the naval reserve, and I wanted to be involved in Kim's rescue mission. I had to convince the president that my training could be valuable."

The first thing George did after flying back to the United States was to meet with Sean Flaherty.

"Mr. Flaherty, have all the Chinese students identified what they plan to do?"

"Yes, Mr. Solomon. About thirty percent of the students decided to remain in Munich, forty percent decided to go to America, and more than twenty percent to other countries. Less than ten percent elected to return to China and take their chances."

"I'm sure that'll piss off the Chinese government. Please make certain that the best students are recruited by companies we invest in."

Dimitri took a flight back to New York after he watched George's plane leave. When he returned home, he immediately sent an email to the Big Man's representatives saying he was available. They scheduled a meeting for the following afternoon in Manhattan.

The next day, Dimitri took a taxi to the building where the meeting was scheduled to take place. After going through security, he was escorted to a conference room, where a woman was waiting for him. They exchanged greetings, and as she handed Dimitri an encrypted flash drive, she told him that everything he needed to know was on the drive.

Dimitri returned home and began reviewing the file while drinking a beer. It was another assassination. While reviewing the description of the target, he nearly choked. The target was George Solomon. He read it again just to make sure. There was no mistake, but it didn't make any sense. He couldn't figure out how he'd been wrong about George.

He immediately called Director Brockner.

"Director, I need to meet with you as soon as possible."

"What's it about?"

"A threat on George Solomon's life."

"Okay, tomorrow in my office at nine."

Dimitri arrived at Shelly Brockner's office and was led to her conference room, where she was waiting. He powered up his laptop as he said, "Director, I had an interesting meeting in Manhattan yesterday with my former employer's representatives. They gave me this flash drive. It provides information on a target that they want removed."

"I assume that means killed, Dimitri. Is this the kind of job you normally were assigned?"

Dimitri ignored the question, and entered his eight digit code to decrypt the drive.

"This is all the relevant information on the target. I think you'll find it startling. I know I did."

Dimitri turned the computer screen toward her and sat back in his chair as he watched her reaction.

"I don't understand. The target is George Solomon, but you told us George was your employer."

"Apparently the information I was given was inaccurate."

"Or you might've been purposely misled. Have you considered that possibility?"

"I have, but the sources for the information were people I've known for years. I've trusted them with my life. I believe they may have been misled or misinterpreted the information, but I can't believe they'd intentionally mislead me."

"I don't think this changes my plans with respect to George, but the information is appreciated. Thanks for coming here today."

After Dimitri left, Rick walked into the direc
his trip to Munich. He briefed her on the meetin
man and the emails indicating George wasn't man
market for profit.

"It doesn't matter, Rick. The FBI is going to arres
We have sufficient evidence for an arrest even if we can't get a conviction.
An arrest would take the pressure off the FBI, and it could also save
George's life. Dimitri just briefed me on a new contract that he received
from his previous employer. The contract was for George's murder. Dim-
itri had it wrong. George isn't the Big Man, and we have no clue who is."

Rick was taken aback by the director's revelation. After considering the news, he said, "Arresting George would be a good idea if we
could keep him in jail, Director. His lawyers will certainly get him out
on bail, and we have no conclusive evidence that he was involved."

"I agree, Rick, but I'll ask for a house arrest and the surrender of
his passport. George would be confined to his home with an ankle
bracelet that monitors his location. He'd agree to that if we showed
him evidence that his life was in danger."

"That could work, as long as the location is secure so he can't be
targeted. We'll also need to minimize his staff and check everyone who
would have any direct contact with him."

"Okay. I need to discuss this with Barbara to make sure she agrees.
You should tell James."

"I'll call him."

Shelly called Barbara and briefed her on h... the FBI's plan to arrest
George.

"He needs to be in a real jail, Shelly, not in his house."

"We can't do that, Barbara. Dimitri showed me evidence that he
was just offered a contract by his former employer to murder George."
After a long silence, Shelly said, "Did you hear me, Barbara?"

"Yes. I was just thinking that might be a better solution."

"What?" Shelly screamed.

"Okay, okay, go ahead with the house arrest."

"Thanks, Barbara. I also want to let you know that Theresa Killian is our primary suspect as the VSI employee that sabotaged their security systems. She had access to all the required VSI resources, and she had the skills. She was also the employee in charge of developing all VSI patches, including the one that supported the attacks on our businesses and the Chinese web pages."

"Do you plan to interrogate her?"

"I would if I could find her. We're looking for her, but so far we have nothing."

"What about Mr. Hoffman?"

"We no longer believe he was involved."

"When will you arrest George?"

"If the president agrees, I'll inform the attorney general and draft the arrest warrant."

"I suggest you do that immediately, Shelly. The president is meeting with the Chinese ambassador this afternoon. He could certainly use this information to ease the tension existing between us."

George was in a good mood as he read the *Wall Street Journal* on his way to his office. The stock market had completely recovered, and the White House was blaming the press for blowing everything out of proportion. George knew the White House was right; in fact, his plan had depended on the media doing just that.

As George entered his office, he was met by Rick Tanner, who showed his badge and said, "George Solomon, you're under arrest."

"On what charges?"

"Violation of the Federal Computer Fraud and Abuse Act."

"I'd like to call Sean Flaherty, my attorney."

"Sure, tell him we're taking you to the Hoover Building."

George called his attorney.

"Sean, the FBI has just arrested me. They're taking me to the Hoover Building. Rick Tanner is the agent in charge."

"Don't say anything until I get there."

"Don't you think I know that?"

As George was being led out of the office, he turned to Nadya and said, "Tell Astrid I might not make lunch."

George was taken to a conference room where Director Brockner, Rick, and James were waiting. Ten minutes later, Flaherty arrived.

"Director Brockner, I'd like a list of the charges against my client."

"Certainly, Mr. Flaherty. Here is the arrest warrant. It cites hundreds of counts under the Federal Computer Fraud and Abuse Act, including unauthorized access to computers, theft of proprietary data and information, malicious denial of service, and theft of property."

"Where is my client being arraigned?"

"We'd like to avoid a public arraignment process, since we believe your client's life is in danger. Instead, we'd like to have the arraignment here with a federal judge on the phone and place your client under house arrest at his home in Virginia."

George smiled. "This is just an attempt to avoid the publicity from an arraignment in a federal court. I know lots of people who dislike me, but I doubt any of them would try to kill me."

"George, I've known you for a long time," James said. "You know I've never lied to you. I've seen the proof that the FBI is going to show you. The man who was contacted to kill you is here and will explain it to you. You need to listen to him."

"All right, let's get this dog and pony show over with. Bring my executioner in."

Dimitri walked into the room with his laptop. He showed George the evidence, including pictures and locations of his homes and businesses, his friends, and all his clubs and favorite restaurants. George was stunned. There was information in his profile that he thought was totally private.

"How'd you get this information?" George asked.

"I was the one who was contacted to complete the contract, Mr. Solomon. The information was provided by my former employer. When I saw who the target was and what they wanted done, I contacted the FBI and showed them this evidence."

"Someone had to go through a lot of trouble to get this information. I guess they really want me dead. How will this house arrest and the FBI protect me, Director Brockner?"

"Dimitri will tell his contact that you're being heavily guarded and that there's no way he or anyone else can complete the contract. That will lead to either of two possibilities. They'll either give up, or attempt to find a way to get to you. I believe it'll be the latter, and we'll be there to stop them."

"Okay, I'll agree to this as long as my fiancée, business manager, and attorney are allowed to visit whenever I want. I also want my current household staff and bodyguards to remain at my home."

After a quick phone discussion with the attorney general, Shelly said, "The government agrees as long as we have the names of everyone who's to have access so they can be vetted."

After the meeting, George was arraigned and taken back to his residence, where he was fitted with the ankle bracelet. Shelly called Barbara.

"We've got him, Barbara. George Solomon is officially under house arrest."

"Thanks, Shelly, I'll let the president know so he can inform Ambassador Yang when they meet today. Please make sure no mention is made of the words 'house arrest' in any communications."

The White House press conference was very short. President Meredith announced that George Solomon had been arrested for his support of the recent cyber attacks. He told the reporters that he couldn't answer any questions about the case while it was pending. He was thankful that no one asked where George was being held.

*So far so good*, thought President Meredith. He wasn't looking forward to meeting with the Chinese ambassador, because he knew there might be questions he couldn't answer. The Chinese had traced the attacks on their web pages to the United States, but the Chinese media hadn't identified the Chinese students as being culpable. The president knew that if the Chinese government was aware of it, they would refuse to publicize it either for political reasons, or possible embarrassment, or both. James had briefed him on the difficulty the Chinese might have in finding the true source of the attacks. Maybe they really didn't know.

Ambassador Yang arrived slightly early, and the president greeted him in the Oval Office.

"My government is very gratified by the news that one of the persons responsible for the cyber attacks has been arrested. I'm also saddened by the fact that it was a close friend of yours."

"I wouldn't call George Solomon a close friend, Mr. Ambassador. He might've thought that, but I certainly didn't. George was arrested for helping to disable some security systems that allowed the hacking of our businesses to succeed. Has your government identified who was responsible for the attacks on the Chinese government web pages?"

The ambassador was flustered for a second, and the president thought he was about to blame the United States, but instead he simply said, "No, we haven't. My government is still very upset with the passage of the foreign cyber-attack legislation by Congress. It's a bad law that will ultimately damage both our countries."

"Sixty-five percent of the country is in favor of the legislation, Mr. Ambassador."

"Yes, Mr. President, that's true. But you could veto it, and there wouldn't be enough votes to overcome your veto. That would certainly be appreciated by my government as a gesture of friendship."

"I can't do that. The bill was a campaign promise. If I veto it, I'd be going against my own policy and be seen as a hypocrite and a weak president. Some of the more onerous provisions that the late Senator Thompson wanted have been removed. I believe the legislation is necessary, especially in light of recent events."

The president could see that the ambassador wanted to say something in response, but instead he said, "I'll inform my government. We believe Mr. Solomon should've also been charged with kidnapping."

"On what basis, Mr. Ambassador? There's no evidence under US law that George Solomon kidnapped anyone."

"George Solomon tricked my government and our students into believing the cybersecurity symposium was an educational experience. He lied to the students about being in jeopardy if they returned to China. There was no threat to the students from my government. The threat was from George Solomon, who scared the students so that he could recruit them for his businesses. Has the educational system in the United States become so poor that you have to kidnap Chinese students to obtain talent you can no longer get from your own citizens and universities?"

President Meredith's face reddened, but he composed himself before responding in a calm and careful manner.

"The United States had nothing to do with that symposium. You could solve the problem yourself by formally inviting the students back. Your government could simply issue a public statement that said none of the students would be punished. In addition, the educational system in the United States is still very productive and has generated numerous technologies that many countries still seem intent on stealing."

The president knew the Chinese government would never publicly invite the students to return. It would be an admission that Chinese students were involved in the attacks. He concluded by saying, "The United States had nothing to do with any actions taken by George Solomon. I'm intent on his prosecution for the crimes he may have committed that have damaged both our countries."

The ambassador agreed, and the meeting ended with his reminder of the upcoming Senkaku Islands exercise. "The Chinese Navy will be watching," he said.

James visited George in his jail cell, which was a 35,000-square-foot mansion on one hundred acres of land in Warrenton, Virginia. He was led through the front door and then a metal detector as George waited for him with a big smile on his face.

"Welcome to Alcatraz, James. How are things in the outside world?"

"Things are fine, and I'm sure you know what's happening better than I do."

George led James into the library and poured himself a vodka and tonic.

"Can I get you a drink, James?"

"It's a little early isn't it, George? It's only eleven in the morning."

George smiled. "As Jimmy Buffett says, it's five o'clock somewhere."

"Actually, it's five o'clock in Munich, but I'm sure you knew that, George."

"So what can I do for you today, James? I know you didn't drive all the way out here for my stimulating conversation."

"I want to apologize for accusing you of murdering Philip and Senator Thompson. Dimitri was certain it was you, but after his revelation, we know you had nothing to do with it. I always had a hard time believing you could be involved in murder."

"Thank you, James. I appreciate that."

"I also wanted to ask you if you've heard from Theresa."

"No, why do you ask?"

"The sabotage of the VSI patch would have had to be done with the support of someone at VSI. There were only three realistic possibilities, and both Tom and Chris are no longer suspects. She's the prime suspect."

"Why do you believe it's her?"

"Theresa had the skills and the access, and maintenance patches fell under her responsibility. She also suddenly took leave right before the cyber attacks and hasn't been heard from since."

"I didn't know that. She's a close friend and a beautiful and intelligent woman. I really hope she's okay."

"Was she involved in your plan?"

"You know I can't talk about that and you can't ask me without my lawyer being present. Nice try, though."

"This has gotten very personal for me, George. JoAnn got an anonymous call from an unidentified woman warning her that I needed to back off my investigation."

"And you think it was Theresa?"

"I don't know."

"I doubt she'd be involved. I know her better than I know my own son."

"What happened between you and Chris?" James asked.

"Christopher hates me and has for a long time. He thinks I killed his mother, which isn't true."

"What happened to her?"

"She was with me at my summer house on Lake Starnberg. I was on the beach reading a newspaper while she was on a pontoon raft with her sister Frances. Christina slipped as she was getting ready to swim back to the beach and she hit her head on the raft. Her sister completely froze and did nothing. I jumped in and tried to save her, but by the time I got there, it was too late. She'd already drowned. Frances never accepted her sister's death and blamed me."

"How'd Chris find out?"

"When he was fourteen, he found some pictures of his mother and me at Lake Starnberg and asked his Aunt Frances about it. She told him about the accident and that I didn't try to save her. He believed her and never listened to my side. He trusted her, since she raised him while I was gone building my financial empire. Chris has hated me ever since."

"I'm very sorry, George. I have one last question. I know you put a hold on some accounts with your firm after the stock market crash. Can you provide me with any information on who owned the accounts?"

"No, but I know who can. A senior account manager at one of my offices informed me of some very large trades made right before the crash. The trades were identified by our automated monitoring systems.

Whenever that happens, we automatically place a hold on the accounts to determine whether there was illegal insider trading. My lawyer has all the information. Technically you need a warrant, but I'll have him give it to you as a favor. Remind the FBI that I'm cooperating."

"Thanks, George, I'll do that. Goodbye."

As James was driving back to DC, he saw a pickup truck coming up behind him as if it wanted to pass. It was a two-lane country road, so James slowed down and moved to the side of the road to let the truck get by him. As the pickup passed, he saw the passenger-side window open and a rifle barrel pointed at him. James hit the brakes on his SUV and quickly pulled off the road as he heard a shot that destroyed his windshield but missed him. He stopped and jumped out of the passenger side of the SUV to shield himself as the pickup made a U-turn and started to come back.

James thought about running, but then saw a blue sedan about a quarter mile away moving quickly toward the pickup in the same lane. When they were less than a hundred yards apart, the truck swerved into the other lane as its passenger fired several shots at the car. That was followed by a half dozen loud bangs from the passenger side of the car. The passenger side of the truck was shredded as it flipped and rolled several times before coming to a stop.

The blue sedan pulled up behind James's SUV. He saw the passenger door open and heard a familiar voice say, "Looks like I got the SOB with those twelve-gauge slugs. Are you okay, James?"

"Not that I'm not grateful, but what the hell are you doing here, Rick?"

"I'm protecting your ass at the insistence of the president. You're needed for an important mission, Commander."

"Thanks, Rick, but why did you get in the same lane as the truck? Were you going to ram it?"

"Of course not. I like you, but this wasn't a suicide mission. I needed him to move over so I'd have a shot at the shooter on the passenger side of the truck."

"Oh, I see."

"Let's go see who's in that pile of rubble."

As they approached the pickup, James saw the unconscious male driver and dead female passenger with a rifle lying at her feet.

"Look, Rick, the shooter has a bandage on her left hand and wrist. She's probably the person who shot at you a few weeks ago."

"Yeah, I guess I didn't miss. I thought I might have to give back my navy marksmanship medal."

# 27

Kim had flown back from the symposium, arriving in Harbin about seven in the evening. He immediately called Lee Park, and asked to meet with her that evening. Lee consented, and she arrived at about eight.

"Thanks for coming on such short notice, Lee. I just got back from a cybersecurity symposium in Munich that was set up by HIT. I discovered something while there that I need to talk to the admiral about. It's very important, and I need to fly back to Nampo as soon as possible."

Lee looked at him sternly. "You should have informed me before you left China, Kim. What would I have thought if I needed to find you and you were gone?"

"I had no warning, Lee. The university didn't inform the students until the morning we were leaving. I'm sorry, but I really need to meet with my uncle."

"Okay, I'll contact him immediately and see if he can meet you tomorrow."

"Thanks, Lee."

Kim began packing for the trip. In addition to his clothes, he took the remaining truth serum. He thought he might need it.

Lee Park called before midnight and said that his trip had been approved and that she was coming by with his authorization papers. She arrived about a half hour later.

"They set up a special flight like the last time, Kim. You need to take your papers to the Air China office by nine. There will be a car waiting when you land in Nampo."

Kim was shocked when Lee suddenly kissed him on the cheek. "Good luck, Kim. Say hello to your uncle for me."

After Lee left, Kim placed a call to Rick on his satellite phone.

"Hello, Kim. I was waiting for your call. Where are you?"

"I'm still in Harbin. My flight to Nampo is tomorrow morning at nine. Have you heard anything from Cai?"

"Not yet. I'm sure she's getting settled in New York. I need to tell you that James will be on the attack sub to help with the mission."

"That's great, but has he ever been on a submarine before?"

"Yeah, he's a reserve naval officer. He spent some time on subs after graduating from the Naval Academy. Some of it wasn't so great, but you can ask him about that when you see him."

"Thanks, Rick."

"Good luck, Kim."

Kim arrived at the North Korean Western Fleet headquarters in Nampo the next morning. He immediately went to the admiral's office, where he was escorted into the secure conference room by one of the secretaries. The admiral, who was sitting at the conference room table, looked up from a document he was reading.

"Close the door, Commander. Is everything all right?"

"Everything's great, Admiral. I've done as you asked, and the Americans are aware of our plan. They've also developed an escape plan that will allow them to take all four of us."

"Three is risky enough, Kim. Four will be too dangerous."

"You need to tell the Americans about our country's nuclear capabilities. It can work, Admiral. Let me explain what we have to do."

Kim briefed the admiral on the plan.

"I still think it's risky, Commander. But if the Americans think it's possible, I'll agree to it. Tell me more."

"All of us will need to get to Wonsan and find a boat to get out far enough so that the SEALs can get to us. I'll have very precise coordinates for the location we'll need to get to. Can you help with the boat, Admiral?"

"Yes, I know someone in Wonsan who can provide us with a boat."

"Good. I have a plan to disable the command and control system on our Kilo submarines so they won't be able to fire their missiles. It'll require access to the program code for the navigation system on the Kilo to make it work. Can you help me?"

"That information is located in the software support department in the basement of the headquarters building."

"How can I get access to it?"

The admiral thought for a few seconds. "We've had security issues in our computer and server rooms. I could ask you to do an inspection, since you're a security expert. I'll set it up."

The admiral called his aide on the phone.

"I want you to draft a memo that says I'm assigning a security expert to evaluate the security of the fleet headquarters starting tomorrow. The security expert is Lieutenant Commander Kim Kwon-Mu. Everyone is to provide him with their complete cooperation. Distribute the memo by this afternoon."

"We need to talk with my mother and sister this evening, Admiral. I need to tell them about our plan."

"I'll invite them to dinner at my residence."

That evening, Kim was reunited with his entire family over dinner. Under normal circumstances, it would have been a celebration. This occasion was different.

After dinner, Kim instructed them on how their escape plan was going to be implemented. The idea of leaving on a fishing boat wasn't a problem. When Kim explained they'd be met by a mini-submarine that would take them to a larger submarine underwater, his mother and sister thought Kim was joking.

Kim made it clear that he was serious. He then explained in detail how the plan would work. When he was certain everyone understood all the details, Kim looked directly at his mother and sister and said slowly and clearly, "No matter what happens, everyone will need to stay calm. You will need to maintain your poise regardless of the situation. Is that clear?"

Everyone nodded, including the admiral.

The admiral had Kim's mother and sister driven back to their home outside Nampo but asked Kim to stay at his residence so they could talk.

"How's Lee Park, Kim? Is she still attractive?"

"Yes, she is. She told me to say hello to you for her. I didn't know you knew her."

"We've known each other for a long time. I was in love with her once. My dear departed wife knew it, and she threatened to leave if I didn't send her away. It's hard loving two women, Kim. I think of her more since my wife passed away."

"Maybe you can see her again after we leave. I'm sure she could find a way to get out of China."

"Maybe. I'm tired. I'll see you in the morning."

The next morning, Kim put on his dress uniform and went to the fleet headquarters building with the admiral. He was introduced to the admiral's staff as an expert in cybersecurity.

"Do you need any assistance, Commander?" the admiral's aide asked.

"I appreciate the offer, Lieutenant. It'll go faster if I do it myself. Can you escort me to the basement?"

"Yes, sir. You'll need a diagram of the room. I'll get one."

After his escort left, Kim went directly to the software library and located the information on the Kilo onboard computer software, including the navigation program. He found a small unoccupied maintenance room and started to review the information. After about fifteen minutes, he found what he needed. Kim made some notes on the required modifications in the worm's trigger and targeting system. He also removed several critical pages from the loose-leaf binder, folded them, and put them in his pocket.

Kim left and started to walk through the other areas of the building, asking questions and making observations as if he was doing an actual inspection. He completed his inspection and put together a quick two-page report that identified the security deficiencies he'd found so far. He took it to the admiral.

"Admiral, I need to return to your residence to complete my work in private."

"I'll have my driver take you," the admiral said.

Kim worked for more than seven hours and had almost completed the required changes to the worm's configuration when his uncle returned home. He looked pale and seemed upset.

"What happened, Admiral? You look exhausted."

"I was in a teleconference with some of the senior officers involved in the Senkaku Islands plan. The maniacs have decided on a backup plan in case the new anti-ship guidance system on the missiles fails. Recent tests have shown a much higher than expected failure rate. As a backup, one of the three Kilos will be carrying torpedoes. It's an older model that doesn't have the sophisticated electronics on the two newer Kilo submarines."

"That doesn't make sense. Our torpedoes don't have the required range and the American navy has excellent sonar. The Kilo could easily be detected before it gets within the effective range of the torpedo."

"You don't understand, Kim. The backup plan is to fire at a Chinese ship so that the Chinese will think it was launched by an American submarine."

"But the Americans aren't planning on using their submarines or aircraft carriers in the exercise so that they don't antagonize the Chinese government. Also, the Chinese ships have sensors that are almost as good as the Americans'. It's possible they could detect the Kilo and sink it."

"We both know that, but the maniacs are desperate."

"I'll need to call my contact in America to let him know about the change in plans. Tomorrow morning I need to get to the server room on the first floor of the headquarters building to load the malware. Could you please let your aide know that I'm going to perform an inspection of that area?"

"I will, but we need to get there early to ensure the server room is vacant."

"Do you have access to any weapons that we can take with us on the boat?"

"Follow me, Kim."

The admiral took Kim to a maintenance shed behind the residence.

"Is this what you need?" the admiral asked.

Kim was amazed to see explosive and phosphorous grenades and a small arsenal of weapons, including AK-47s, rocket-propelled grenades, a Russian RPG-7 rocket-propelled grenade launcher, and a .50 caliber semi-automatic special-applications scoped rifle.

"What's all this for, Admiral? Were you planning an invasion?"

"I've been putting this together for the last six months. It was for your escape, which I guess is now our escape."

"Where'd you get the .50 caliber rifle?"

"I got it three years ago from a former Russian colonel who specializes in the sale of exotic weapons. He owed me a favor."

"Did you tell your staff about your trip to Wonsan?"

"Yes, I told them I was going to visit Eastern Fleet headquarters in Wonsan and might also do some fishing. I also bought a large cooler like fisherman use, to store the weapons in the trunk of my car."

"Have you made plans for where we're staying in Wonsan?"

"Yes, we're staying in one of the luxury hotels on the waterfront, right near the Wonsan fishing pier."

Kim's satellite phone rang, and he knew it was Rick. He informed Rick about the North Korean contingency plan.

"They must really be desperate to try something like that," Rick said. "If they get caught sinking Chinese ships, they'll be annihilated by their only ally. I'll inform the navy that the mission just got tougher."

"I hope your navy can detect the Kilo. My uncle says the new Kilos can evade your attack boats."

"I doubt that; our latest subs are really good. Oh, I almost forgot. Your uncle was approved. We have room for him on the mini-sub."

"That's great. We're leaving for Wonsan tomorrow."

"Good. I'll call tomorrow night. Goodnight, Kim."

Rick hung up, and Kim resumed his work on the worm.

The next morning, Kim met with the admiral's aide.

"I'm going to inspect the servers on the first floor today, Lieutenant. I don't need you to escort me. I've got a map."

"Yes, sir."

Kim found the servers that were used to load the time and navigation data for the Kilo submarines. It was early, and the facility was virtually empty, with the exception of a single sailor performing maintenance on some of the routers on the other side of the room. He found the server he was looking for and inserted the flash drive in the server port. It took less than a minute to complete the malware insertion. He hoped the worm would find its way to the servers at Eastern Fleet headquarters in Wonsan.

Kim then walked through the entire room and did a security inspection and completed his report, which he provided to the admiral's aide. He met the admiral in his office and briefed him on what he did.

"The malware was inserted, Admiral. It should find the servers in Wonsan that connect with the Kilos. I just hope it works."

"Is there a problem, Kim?"

"No, but I think we'd have a higher probability of success if I could get access to the servers at the Eastern Fleet headquarters where the Kilo submarines are located."

"The commander of the Eastern Fleet is a good friend of mine. I'll tell him about the work you did here and recommend that you also inspect his facility. We were classmates at the naval academy and have always been competitive. I'm certain he'd want his facility to be as secure as mine. I'll arrange a meeting for tomorrow morning."

Kim awoke at about seven and loaded the admiral's Mercedes-Benz with the luggage and the cooler with the weapons from the shed. He tried to hide the cooler by covering it with the luggage, but he knew that even a casual search of the car would be a death sentence for everyone. He and the admiral then drove to Nampo to pick up Kim's mother and sister.

The trip to Wonsan was 150 miles from the west coast of North Korea to the east coast. It was a scenic trip through forests and over mountains that normally took about two and a half hours. Kim was familiar with the journey due to his service with the North Korean Reconnaissance Bureau, which monitored traffic on the road at several military checkpoints. He could sense the tension within the car rapidly increase every time they approached a checkpoint, and then quickly subside after they went through it without being stopped. Kim realized that the checkpoint's guards were being intimidated by the military insignias on the admiral's car that signified his rank.

They pulled into the parking lot at their hotel in Nampo, and took their luggage to the lobby. The admiral had arranged for two rooms on the sixth floor, the top floor of the hotel. All of the rooms had spectacular views of the waterfront and the walkway to Jangdok Island.

"Let's unpack and then we'll all meet in the lobby," the admiral said. "I want to show all of you the waterfront."

After stopping for barbecued clams at one of the stands, Kim pointed at the lighthouse.

"I want to see the lighthouse on Jangdok Island and take some pictures, Admiral."

"Good idea, Kim. Let's all go."

"Are you sure, Admiral? It's a long walk."

"I'm sure. Do you want to go, Hana?"

"Yes, uncle. The lighthouse looks like a white candle on a big green dumpling."

"You're right, Hana," the admiral responded. "The island is round and covered with trees. It does look like a green dumpling with a candle on top."

The walk was fairly long and it gave Kim a chance to see whether the admiral was healthy enough for the coming ordeal. He was no longer worried when he heard Hana say, "Slow down, Uncle, my feet hurt and I'm tired."

Jangdok Island provided a spectacular view of the harbor and beyond. It was a great place for scrutinizing the area where they were going to escape. Kim used the high-powered binoculars Rick had provided.

"Do you see anything out there, Kim?"

"Yes, Admiral. I see a corvette and some patrol helicopters. I hope your nautical patrol maps and schedules will help us evade them."

"We can't rely on the schedules, Kim. The navy changes them frequently. Let's meet in the hotel basement when we get back. There's a sauna and a swimming pool, and I've arranged for privacy."

"I'm ready to go back now. I'll meet you there."

Kim was enjoying the sauna when the admiral joined him.

"I rented a fast boat from a fisherman I know. He's being paid well, but we might have to subdue him to secure our escape, Kim."

"How do you plan to do that, Admiral?"

"I obtained an intravenous general anesthetic from my doctor. It should last up to four hours, which will give us enough time. We're meeting with the fisherman tomorrow evening. He'll provide directions to a fishing spot less than two miles from the rendezvous point."

"Good, I'll bring the night-vision binoculars to detect possible threats."

That evening they were all finishing dinner at a local restaurant.

"We're leaving tomorrow," Kim announced to his mother and sister. "Be ready by five in the afternoon, and wear your dark clothes."

"Let's all go to the hotel bar," the admiral said. "We should have a final celebration."

The admiral ordered soju, a sweet, clear liquor, for everyone, and offered a toast. "To family and freedom."

"This is really good, Kim. Can I have another?"

"No, Hana. Soju is very potent. I need everyone to be at their best tomorrow."

The next morning, Kim and his uncle drove to the fleet headquarters and were taken to the office of the fleet commander. Kim saluted the fleet commander, who said, "I finally get to meet you, Commander. Your uncle has told me great things about you. I hope you can help us with any security problems we might have. My adjutant is waiting for you in his office down the hall. He will give you a tour of our data-processing facilities."

"Thank you, Admiral," Kim said as he saluted.

Kim walked down the hall to the adjutant's office, who stood and saluted when Kim walked in.

"At ease. Lieutenant, I need you to take me to your data-processing facilities."

"Yes, sir, they're in the basement. I'll show you."

Kim could see that the facility was much larger than the one in Nampo.

"Can you show me where this facility interfaces with the ships?"

"Yes, sir, it's in this next room where the application servers, network routers, and switches are located."

The adjutant explained where everything was and what it did.

"How is mission data transported to the ships and submarines, Lieutenant?"

"The data is loaded from the servers in these two racks. The servers in this first rack are for the ships, and the rack behind it is for the submarines. Each server cabinet within a rack is marked by ship or submarine type. The servers in each cabinet are designated by function, such as navigation, communications, command and control, fire control, and sonar."

"I'm going to be doing an inspection of the security status of this facility at the fleet commander's request, Lieutenant."

"Yes, sir, I was briefed."

"I'll provide you a copy of my report after I'm done, and we can review it before I provide it to the fleet commander. Your presence isn't needed. My inspection needs to be totally objective."

"Yes, sir. You know where my office is, and the cafeteria is right down the hall. The food is okay, and they have great tea. I recommend the red ginseng."

"Thanks, Lieutenant. I'll meet you later."

The adjutant saluted and left, and Kim went immediately to the submarine rack and found the servers for the Kilo submarines. Kim inserted the flash drive with the malware into each server's USB ports. After he was done, he removed the drive and put it in his pocket.

As Kim walked through the facility, he saw several security issues that needed to be addressed. The most obvious was his easy access to the USB ports. He found pieces of paper taped to some of the systems with PINs and passwords, probably left by administrators or maintenance personnel. Kim also observed personnel coming and leaving the processing facilities without signing the log book.

Worst of all was a network access port in a public area. Kim connected his laptop to the port and found that it was active. The security at this facility was poor compared to the one at Nampo. Kim hoped their coastal security was equally as poor.

When Kim described what he'd seen, the adjutant became visibly upset.

"Please, Commander, don't put that in your report."

Kim had an idea.

"Don't worry, Lieutenant. We can discuss this after I get back from lunch."

Kim told the admiral about his plan and borrowed his car to drive back to the hotel. He found the bottle of the SP-117 and put it in his pocket. He drove back to fleet headquarters and purchased two cups of the red ginseng tea at the cafeteria. It was after lunch and the cafeteria was almost empty, so he found a quiet spot and dosed one of the cups with the SP-117 before taking it to the adjutant's office.

"Lieutenant, I brought you some tea to calm your nerves before we discuss what I found. Relax for a few minutes before we begin."

The lieutenant thanked him and began sipping his tea as Kim described the problems he found.

"My staff is very young and incompetent, Commander. The best technicians are grabbed by state security and we get what's left."

Kim knew that was probably true. After a few minutes of tea and sympathy, Kim could see that the lieutenant was ready for some questions.

"Do you have any knowledge of the Eastern Fleet coastal defenses, Lieutenant?"

"Yes, sir, it's all defined in the Coastal Security Plan for Wonsan."

"Do you have a copy here?"

"Yes, it's in my safe."

"Please show me."

The lieutenant opened his safe and provided Kim with the latest copy of the plan. Kim looked through it and made detailed notes on the placement of the patrols, the patrol craft being used, and the scheduled routes and times. He realized almost immediately that the mini-sub rendezvous point was directly on the patrol line of one of the patrol craft. Kim also asked questions about the armament on all the patrol craft and their sonar and anti-submarine warfare capabilities.

The lieutenant finally dozed off, and Kim looked through his office for additional information. He found a memo about how recent exercises had found holes in the security plan that were in the process of being corrected. The lieutenant showed signs of waking, so Kim quickly shoved the memo in his pocket, returned the security plan to the safe, and locked it.

When the lieutenant awoke, Kim reprimanded him for dozing off.

"I'm sorry, Commander. We've been working long hours preparing our Kilos for an important mission."

"Okay, I'll give you a break this time, but you need to correct all the deficiencies in the manner we just discussed."

The lieutenant looked confused, "Could you send me a summary of what we discussed, Commander?"

"Sure, Lieutenant. I've got to go."

Kim quickly walked out of the headquarters building to the admiral's car. He got in the passenger seat, and made a satellite phone call to Rick.

"Rick, I just saw a copy of Wonsan's Coastal Security Plan. You need to move the rendezvous point farther in. The eight-mile point from the coast is right on one of the patrol lines. I suggest a new rendezvous point six miles from the coast, between the four-mile and eight-mile lines."

"That's good info, Kim. Anything else?"

"Yes, the patrol boats at the twelve-mile point have sonar and might be able to detect the mini-sub."

"I don't think that's a problem. The mini-sub is electric and is very quiet. I doubt they'd hear it, but I'll inform the navy. I'm more worried about the increased distance that the mini-sub will need to travel based on your new information. The extra distance leaves no margin for error."

"I know. I'm texting you the times that the patrol boats at the four-mile, eight-mile, and twelve-mile lines will be closest to our route."

"Thanks, I'll inform the navy. By the way, James arrived in Japan yesterday morning. Hopefully, you'll see him soon."

Kim returned to the fleet headquarters building just as the admiral completed his meeting with the Eastern Fleet Commander.

"Did everything go well, Admiral?" Kim asked, as they walked to the car.

"Nothing has changed in the plan, but I was briefed on the capabilities of the new Kilos. I'm not certain the Americans will be able to track them. The fleet commander seemed certain they couldn't, and he explained why. We need to inform the Americans."

Kim got another call on the satellite phone from Rick.

"I passed that information you gave me to the navy, Kim. You'll be getting a call in the next twenty minutes from Lieutenant Aiden, the operations officer for the SEAL team. He wants to make sure everything is correct."

"Thanks, Rick."

When they got to the hotel, Kim immediately went to his room and waited for the call. His phone rang, and the voice at the other end said, "Is this Kim?"

"Hello, Lieutenant Aiden, what can I help you with?"

"We've moved the new rendezvous point two miles closer to the coast. I'll text you the new coordinates. I've also moved the rendezvous time back thirty minutes so that you'll have sufficient time to stop in each patrol zone to reconnoiter before moving on. It's my understanding that the patrol boats farthest out have sonar, but it probably has very limited range. I suggest you take a slightly lateral heading to the northeast. When you're four miles from the shore, take a direct course toward the new coordinates. Is that clear?"

"Yes. Is the mini-sub quiet enough to avoid the sonar?"

"We aren't certain, we don't have a lot of experience with the mini-sub. If they do detect it, we have some noisemakers to distract them and take them away from its location. The team is already traveling and should be there in about eight hours. Good luck."

Kim saw the text with the new coordinates from Aiden, and looked at his watch. If everything went well, Kim and his family would be free in eight hours.

# 28

Rick had just completed his last satellite call from Kim when Director Brockner phoned.

"George is missing, Rick. He isn't at his house, and we have no idea where he is. Can you find out if James heard from him?"

"I doubt he could have, Director. James has been out of the country since yesterday."

"He was one of the last people to talk to George. Do you know what they talked about?"

"George talked about his involvement in the cybersecurity attack. How did he get away and disable the tracking bracelet?"

"He didn't disable the bracelet. Instead, he found a way to remove it sometime last night and sneak out of the house. We're still investigating how he got out without being seen."

"George is resourceful, but he doesn't have the skills to remove the bracelet, Director."

"I've been told it's not that difficult. All you need to do is insert a metal rod between the bracelet and your leg and twist until the rivets pop. It would be hard for him, but a bodyguard could've done it. The bigger issue is how he got out of the house and past the guards, and who helped him. Someone must have; all his vehicles are at the house."

"I know we monitor his phones. Has he had any unusual communications?"

"None, but we don't monitor his corporate email. That was in his agreement with the government. His lawyer claimed it could provide proprietary information that the government shouldn't have access to, and we agreed."

"James left his laptop with me and showed me how to monitor George's corporate account. I'll check it if you want, Director."

"Yes, please do, and let me know if you find anything."

Rick reviewed George's recent email and found one from two days ago. The subject line was "Tragedy," and it was from Chris Hoffman's account. The email stated that Chris Hoffman was in the sender's custody.

The email also had a link to a news article and warned that the same fate described in the article would befall Chris if George didn't follow their instructions. Rick accessed the link and found an article from an English-language Munich newspaper about Klaus Schmidt, whose nude body was found floating in Lake Starnberg. The article said that the deceased had been brutally murdered, and that the police were looking for his roommate, Christopher Hoffman.

Rick found George's reply email, in which he agreed to follow any instructions. There were no other related emails, so Rick had no way to determine how George received his instructions. He forwarded the emails to the director, who called back an hour later.

"I think we found out how George got his instructions, Rick. He received a letter yesterday that looked like it came from George's attorney. It was given directly to George without being opened, since it was considered to be privileged communications. Our agents found the envelope in George's bedroom, but no letter. We determined that law firm letterhead on the envelope was forged. It's pretty obvious that the missing letter was the instructions."

"So where do we go from here? Are there any other leads?"

"We're checking to see if Chris Hoffman re-entered the United States. That's all we have right now."

Later that morning the director called Rick again.

"Now Dimitri is missing, Rick. Have you heard from him?"

"No, I haven't. Do we have any new information on Chris?"

"Yes, we got a facial recognition hit for Chris at Newark Airport. It looks like he arrived from Munich about six thirty yesterday evening. He was traveling under his passport."

"Was he with anyone?"

"We can't tell. The camera footage from the airport shows him walking with a limp in a small crowd of about four men and two women. There are also some bruises on his face."

"We should run facial recognition on the crowd."

"We're doing that now, Rick. There's no record of Chris renting a car at Newark or any footage of him being picked up. It looks like he could've gotten into a car in the parking garage out of camera view."

"Do you think George is also in that area?"

"We don't know, but we've issued BOLOs for both of them. I need you, Rick. Are you done playing with the navy?"

"Yes, Director. I'll put my FBI hat back on."

Dimitri knew this would happen. A man like George Solomon isn't someone you can ever have total control over. He has too many resources to find a way out of his house, if he wanted to. And apparently he did.

Per Director Brockner's orders, Dimitri monitored George like he was a cheating spouse. It was Dimitri's responsibility to deliver all letters to George from his attorney unopened. They were privileged communications not to be seen by anyone other than George. In performing this duty, Dimitri became very familiar with the law firm's letterhead and recognized the forgery on the envelope. He had also delivered the latest letter to George, but not before opening it first.

The escape plan described in the letter was simple. George was to wait until his normal bedtime, and have one of his bodyguards pry off the bracelet. Everyone's guard would be down, but not Dimitri's. He'd found the dumbwaiter in the basement when he'd inspected the house after George's arrest. He knew it was intended for deliveries of alcohol to George's bedroom, but it was big enough for a person. Even one as big as George.

It was a simple task to stake out the pickup point on the main road near the house, as identified in the instructions. Dimitri waited in his car and watched as George made his way from the basement to the pickup point. A black stretch limousine soon arrived to pick George up. Dimitri had to admit, George definitely had style.

Dimitri followed George all the way to New York City. When the limousine stopped for a restroom break, Dimitri placed a GPS tracker on it, allowing him to track the car during daylight without getting too close. He followed George all the way to the Plaza Hotel in Manhattan.

Although Dimitri knew the FBI would go crazy when they found out both he and George were gone, he wanted to determine what George was up to before turning him in. Once he told the FBI, they'd have agents all over the hotel. He knew from recent experience that this approach didn't always work.

Whatever was going to happen wasn't going to take place that day, since the limousine remained parked in the garage. Dimitri checked into the hotel and bribed the clerk to find out George's room number. He checked the tracker app on his phone to see if the limousine moved and then called Rick.

"Dimitri, where the hell are you? Director Brockner is livid that both you and George have disappeared. Is he with you?"

"You might say that. We're staying at the same hotel in Manhattan. However, we came separately. George in a limousine, and me following all the way up here. Where are you?"

"I'm in my office booking a flight to New York as we speak. Do me a favor and reserve me a room at whatever hotel you're at."

"Sure, but this isn't any hotel. I'm staying at the Plaza in Manhattan. It's very expensive."

"The director will approve it. I'll be there in about four hours."

"No problem, but I don't think we need an army of agents. Could you please limit the troops so we don't spook the locals and draw attention to ourselves?"

"Okay, but we'll need some technical support from the local FBI office."

Rick arrived at the Plaza Hotel and took a room two floors below Dimitri's. He immediately called the FBI office in Manhattan, identified himself, and asked for the agent in charge.

"This is Agent Casella, what can I help you with, Agent Tanner?"

"I need help from your office on a BOLO issued on George Solomon. We'll need at least two agents and electronic surveillance support. I need them to meet me at the Plaza Hotel in three hours. The director has made this case her highest priority, Agent Casella."

"Okay, I'll be there with Agent Miller."

Rick called Dimitri.

"I need your assistance. Meet me in my room. We're about to take George into custody."

"I'll be right there."

Dimitri arrived five minutes later, followed by the two FBI agents. Rick briefed them on how they were going to take George into custody.

"George is a fugitive who was under house arrest in Virginia until he escaped. He's in the Royal Terrace Suite on the top floor of the hotel. We believe his son Chris was kidnapped and is being held somewhere in this area. I'll contact hotel management and notify them that George is a fugitive. We'll then go up to his suite with management's assistance and take him into custody."

"Is he armed, Agent Tanner?"

"I doubt it. George is sixty-five years old and isn't considered dangerous, unless you're playing poker with him. I just notified hotel management that they had a fugitive in their hotel and that we're going to apprehend him. They're on their way up to check our credentials and the arrest warrant."

"I assume you'll announce yourselves first," Dimitri said.

"Yes, and if George doesn't open the door, hotel management will open it with their key."

After a hotel employee arrived, they all took the elevator to George's suite. Rick knocked on the door.

"George Solomon, this is the FBI. Open the door."

George opened the door and raised his hands.

"Four armed young men for little old me. You flatter me, Agent Tanner."

"Stop with the humor, George. This isn't the least bit funny. I need to know what's going on. If I'm not satisfied with your answers, I'll immediately take you back to DC, and your house arrest will be terminated. You'll be assigned to a solitary cell in a real prison without any possibility of bail."

"Please, Agent Tanner, you can't do that," George pleaded. "My son was kidnapped. If I don't meet with the kidnappers, they'll kill him."

"What do they want, George?"

"I don't know. I was told to come up to New York City and stay at the Plaza Hotel. They said they'd contact me via the disposable cell phone in the limousine they arranged for."

"Did they pick this hotel, or did you?"

George smiled faintly. "They picked the hotel, but I upgraded my room to this suite."

"You have two options, George. You can either be escorted back to DC, or you can meet with the kidnappers. If you choose the second option, we'll monitor your location and communications via a wireless microphone. You'll need to have them confirm their guilt. We'll then arrest them and get your son back. Which option, George?"

"Can you conceal the microphone so they won't find it?"

"Yes, but we'll need something you'll have on you, such as a piece of clothing," Agent Miller said.

"Will a dress shirt work?"

"Yes, that would be perfect."

George went to the bedroom and got one of his shirts. Agent Miller examined it. "This will work. I'll have it back to you in an hour."

"Okay, George, tell me about the communications you've had so far with the kidnappers. Start with the limousine service's name."

"I don't know the name."

"How do the kidnappers communicate with you?"

"The cell phone they provided in the limo."

"I need to see the phone, George."

"Here, it's in my pocket."

Rick examined the phone.

"Yeah, that's what I thought. It's a burner. Dimitri, go to the garage and get the state and license plate number from the limo."

"No need, Rick. I remember the number and it had DC plates."

Rick sent the plate number to the FBI to find out who it was registered to. He also called Director Brockner to tell her that George was in custody and had agreed to help them get the kidnappers.

"Who do you think is behind all this, Agent Tanner?"

"I don't know, George. You have lots of enemies. The timing suggests it might be someone involved in the recent cyber attacks."

"I only funded and managed the recruitment of the Chinese hackers. That's all. I knew that VSI was involved, but I had no information on who at VSI was involved or how it was being done."

"So you sabotaged VSI? How could you do that, George?"

"That wasn't my intention. They said there'd be no long-term damage and no one would get hurt. I was only interested in the political damage to that godforsaken corrupt regime in China."

"Who are *they*?"

"I have no idea. They offered a service I needed to achieve my goal, and I bought it. I buy special services all the time. May I ask how you plan to protect my son and me when I meet the kidnappers?"

"We'll monitor all communications via a wireless microphone. If either of you is in danger, we'll intervene. If you see anything you don't like, then use a word or phrase we'll recognize as an alarm signal."

"How about Virtual Security?"

"That works. I'm going to leave Agent Casella here in your suite. Agent Miller will return shortly with your shirt. Any questions?"

"Yes. Shouldn't I have a weapon for protection?"

"No, they might search you."

George agreed with Rick, but he knew that he wasn't going in unarmed. He had learned how to hide his weapon of choice and had been trained by Russian experts in how to use it.

Rick got a call from the FBI about the limousine and was told it was registered to MC Enterprises, LLC.

"Can you determine the corporate owners?" Rick asked.

"We'd need a court order, and we can't get that until tomorrow."

"Forget it. That's too late," Rick said.

Agent Miller returned with the shirt and briefed George.

"The new buttons on your shirt are wireless microphones, and they're activated by the sound of voices. You'll need to remove your overcoat when you meet the kidnappers. If you don't, your coat could block the sound. The microphones have three hours of battery life."

As George was putting his shirt away, his burner phone rang. He answered and grabbed a pad of paper on which he wrote a time and a location: ten the next day in Fair Lawn, New Jersey.

"Did you recognize the caller, George?"

"No, Agent Tanner. It was a man who said the limousine driver had the address and would drive me."

"That complicates things, but we'll be able to follow you from a safe distance with the GPS tracker. We'll be watching in the lobby when you leave tomorrow, but don't acknowledge our presence."

Rick looked at Dimitri. "We'll be armed, but I have no authority to tell you what to do for self-protection. It's up to you, Dimitri."

Dimitri smiled. "I know that, Rick."

Rick returned to his room and was in bed when his phone rang.

"Hello, who is calling?"

"This is Nadya Murin. Am I talking with Rick Tanner?"

"You are, Ms. Murin. What can I help you with?"

"I just got a call from Davis Fielding, an investment manager for our company. He said the name of the company whose account was put on hold is Big Man, LLC, out of New York. They provide concierge professional services. James told me you wanted this information."

"The company was called Big Man? Are you certain?"

"Yes, I am."

"Did Mr. Fielding know the name of the owner?"

"He didn't. However, Mr. Fielding said one of the owners of Big Man came to his office and threatened him if the hold on their accounts wasn't removed. He said it was a woman."

"Did he describe her?"

"Yes, he said she was very attractive, medium height, dark hair, and in her late twenties to early thirties."

"Thanks, Ms. Murin."

Rick thought the woman could be the missing Theresa Killian.

The next morning, George had breakfast in his room and asked the limo driver to have his car out front by nine fifteen. Rick and the two FBI agents rode with Dimitri in his car. Each of them had a radio so they could listen to George's conversation with the kidnappers.

The black limousine drove to New Jersey, where it pulled up to an ordinary-looking house. George exited the car and followed the driver to the front door. The door opened, and George and his driver were let inside. Dimitri saw the limousine and parked behind the house, where it couldn't be seen.

George was immediately searched after he entered, but nothing was found. He took off his coat and asked to see Chris.

"Your son is here," said one of the men sitting at a table.

"Who are you?" George asked.

"I'm Marat."

"Why have you kidnapped my son, Marat?"

"No one was kidnapped," Chris Hoffman said, as he entered the room. "We just want to discuss the accounts that you put on hold."

"So that's what this is about," George said, as he sat at the table across from Marat. "You want the money from your insider trading?"

"Yes, we want the money we earned."

"You didn't earn it, Chris, and neither did your friends. What you did was illegal. How did you know about the cyber attack?"

"You might say that I'm very close to the person who designed and programmed the patch that caused the attack," Chris answered.

"Did you kill Philip, Chris?"

"I've never killed anyone, George. I have friends that can do that. Unfortunately, Philip was working in the lab at the wrong time. He saw a printout of some test code on the Backfire patch that I worked on and realized what was going on. Philip new it was the work of Theresa's team, since they were in charge of patches. He said he was going to confront Theresa, which would have ruined everything. I told her, and she took care of it."

"It's hard to believe that any woman would kill for you, Chris."

"She didn't do it, George. It was someone else."

"It's the same thing. You're all guilty of killing a great man who many people loved and respected. That includes me. Did you also kill Senator Thompson?"

"You were responsible for his death, George. When you called your contact after your meeting with the senator and told him that you wanted to cancel the project, he contacted us. We had no choice, so she also had the senator removed. That killed the senate bill and allowed our project to continue. She also put a contract out on you, when you put a hold on our accounts. When we realized there was no way to get to you while you were under house arrest, we staged my kidnapping."

"I know that Theresa enjoyed the finer things in life, but it's hard to believe she would do all that for money, Chris. On the other hand, I know you'd do anything for money."

Chris glared at his father before saying, "I guess I'm like you in that respect, George. She also came to visit me in Germany while I was there."

"So that's where Theresa went when she disappeared."

Chris smiled and said, "She visited me at my home in Munich because she knew I was depressed after my meeting with you at the Ratskeller. Unfortunately, she caught me in bed with Klaus. He got jealous and angry when he found out who she was, and he attacked me. My injury and bruises are real. Klaus could've killed me. She had no choice; she killed him with a butcher knife. We've had a relationship for a long time. She loves me, which is more than you ever did."

George smiled and said, "You're gay, Chris. I've never seen you with a woman."

"I've played on both teams, George."

"How'd you two come up with this plan?"

"She saw an article about your relationship with VSI and hatred for the Chinese and their cyber attacks on American businesses. We used that information to plan it together. She wants to talk with you face-to-face. You've never met any of my lovers. Here's your chance."

"Yes, I'd prefer talking to the person in charge. I can't believe that the Theresa I knew would do this, or why she'd have any interest in you."

Chris smiled and said, "Why don't you ask her about that, George? I'll bring her in, so you can talk to her yourself."

George was stunned when he saw a beautiful woman walk into the room with Chris, and it wasn't Theresa.

"Hello, Mr. Solomon."

"Who are you?"

"My name is Anya Chubais, Mr. Solomon. I'm the CEO of Big Man."

"So you're the one that planned all this. You look too innocent to hatch such a diabolical plan. What'd you ever see in Chris?"

"Chris is very nice, and he always treated me well. I knew he had issues, but I seem to be drawn to men like that. Unfortunately, his issues were more than I could deal with, but we have remained friends and occasional lovers. He's a brilliant engineer, and he helped with a great many problems on this project. We want the money that we earned and that you're keeping from us, Mr. Solomon."

"So Theresa wasn't involved?"

"Theresa was involved, but not in a manner she'd have approved of. She introduced me to Chris a number of years ago."

"What happened to her?"

"The same thing that'll happen to you if we don't get our money," Anya said angrily. "I have killed before to make this happen, and I have no problem doing it again."

"You're a psychopath, my dear. You belong in a mental hospital."

"You shouldn't condemn me without having walked in my shoes. I was very young when I saw my brothers and friends slaughtered by the Chechens. My father, who's sitting across from you, knew I had the temperament for killing, and he taught me the skills. I was a natural, and no one believed a pretty but demure young woman like me was capable of it. But I actually enjoyed the excitement of it. The blood and gore were no more than I'd already seen in medical school."

"I know your type, Ms. Chubais," George said haughtily. "Putting a contract on me was stupid. Your emotions got in the way of making good business decisions. You'll always fail."

Rick watched Dimitri as he kept repeating, "How could she do this?" while Anya was talking. Rick remembered Anya from the FBI raid that arrested her with Dimitri. It was obvious that Dimitri wasn't prepared for what he was hearing. Anya had used him as her personal tool for the murders of Philip and Senator Thompson with no regret.

Suddenly, Dimitri burst from the car and sprinted toward the back of the house. Rick and the other agents followed, watching him slowly move through the foliage toward the front of the house.

Rick knew that the conversation in the house had created a distraction: no one inside the house saw them. He sensed an approaching climax.

George looked hard at Anya. "Will you let Christopher live if I remove the hold on your accounts?"

"Argue for your own life, George," Chris said. "I'm in no danger here."

Anya smiled. "If you agree to release the hold on our accounts, Chris will go free unharmed."

Chris was startled by the response. He looked at Anya pleadingly. "Is my life really in danger after all I've done?"

"Chris, you've always been so naive. Did you really think I came to Munich because I loved you? I needed you to bring George here."

"You ungrateful bitch. Without me none of this could've happened!"

George moved closer to the edge of his chair and worked his right foot out of his shoe.

"Shut up, Chris," George screamed. "I'm your father, and I'm trying to save our lives and prevent any more damage to Virtual Security."

Christopher turned to George with a puzzled look. He was about to say something when Dimitri crashed through the front door. He immediately shot two men before taking cover behind a large sofa. Almost simultaneously, Rick and his men came through the back door and shot another two men. George flipped the dining room table on Marat, and using his knife, fatally severed Marat's aortic artery. Anya screamed—"Papa!"—then turned, as she pulled a gun and fired several rounds into George Solomon's back, and two more into Chris as he ran to help his father.

Rick ran toward Anya and was getting ready to fire. Anya aimed at Rick and pulled the trigger, as Dimitri ran into her line of fire, and was hit twice in the chest. Rick fired back at a stunned Anya, both rounds exploding through her head, painting the wall with her blood and brains.

"Call an ambulance," Rick yelled to Agent Casella as he knelt next to Dimitri, who was lying on his back and barely breathing.

Dimitri looked up at Rick.

"This is my final act," he whispered. He closed his eyes and died with a peaceful smile on his face.

# 29

Kim was exhilarated by the possibility of freedom for him and his family. He also knew that he needed to prepare his mind and body for what was coming in a few hours. After doing some hapkido exercises to loosen his muscles and break a sweat, he then took a long, hot shower and sipped some hot ginseng tea. It was a routine he had used in the past on difficult assignments. This was going to be the most difficult assignment he'd ever have, since the lives of his entire family were at stake.

He got dressed in his black jeans, sweatshirt, jacket, and black slip-on tennis shoes, the same outfit the rest of his family would wear. There was a crescent moon and the skies were cloudy, so black camouflage face paint would not be needed. They all met in the lobby at five and went to the garage.

The admiral drove to the boat owner's business office and parked. Kim asked his mother and sister to wait in the car. The admiral greeted the owner.

"Hello, old friend. How's the fishing business these days?"

Kim was struck by how similar the boat owner and the admiral looked, and then he realized why.

"Hello, cousin. It's been a few years. Everything is in the boat, so you can leave any time. Did you bring the anesthetic?"

"Yes, I have it my pocket. Don't worry. We'll tie you up and make it look like you resisted."

"What's going on, Admiral?"

"My cousin is repaying a favor he owes me. He has agreed to provide his boat, but he insisted that it look like he was overpowered and drugged. His son will come by in four hours looking for him and will report it to the authorities. We should be long gone by then."

The admiral took his cousin's identification and thanked him for his help. Kim helped his uncle tie him up. They gagged him and gave him the anesthetic. It took effect almost immediately. The admiral broke his cousin's nose with a quick kick to the face to make it look real.

They walked to the boat and loaded the cooler with the weapons. Kim went back to the car and led his mother and sister to the boat, while the admiral started the engine. The boat was painted black, and the engines were very quiet for a fishing boat.

"This is an unusual fishing boat, Admiral."

"Yes, it is. My cousin has supplemented his income through smuggling. He was caught by the patrol boats a few years ago and I interceded on his behalf. It probably saved his life."

Kim took the wheel of the boat and took it past Jangdok Island and the lighthouse. He then turned to starboard toward the rendezvous point.

"The water is very calm, Admiral."

"It'll get rougher when we get past the breakwater. What do you think of the boat?"

"It's very responsive to the rudder and handles remarkably well."

"Yes, my cousin claims it'll do more than thirty knots. We're approaching the first patrol line. You should slow down and use your night-vision binoculars to see if there are any patrol craft."

"I don't see anything," Kim said. "I'm going to take the lateral starboard heading recommended by the SEALs."

After two miles, the admiral said, "Change your heading toward the rendezvous point and decrease your speed to ten knots."

Five minutes later, Kim said, "We're within one hundred yards of the rendezvous point. I'm going to idle the engine when we're there."

"We're ten minutes early, Kim. I'll pass around the rice cakes and the thermos of tea."

"Okay, I'm going to set up the .50 caliber rifle on the engine enclosure. Could you get me the clips?"

The admiral handed Kim the ten-round clips with high-velocity ammunition designed for destroying lightly armored vehicles. Suddenly, Kim heard a familiar sound. He immediately ran to the cooler where he removed the RPG launcher and loaded a grenade as he yelled, "Everyone down, now!"

Kim felt more comfortable as the noise diminished, but was instantly blinded by a light that made it seem like it had gone from night to day in a split second. A 500 MD surveillance helicopter must have spotted the bioluminescent wake from the boat and followed it until it found them. Kim didn't like the idea of killing his countrymen, but he had no choice. He aimed the RPG at the source of the light and pulled the trigger.

The helicopter exploded in a huge ball of flame. As some of the shrapnel from the explosion hit the boat, Kim heard a scream.

"Admiral, my mother's hit. Help her!"

Kim's mother was badly injured by a piece of shrapnel that had almost severed part of her foot. She was bleeding profusely. The admiral took a bungee cord and tied it tightly around her lower leg, which helped to stop the bleeding.

"Kim, I see bubbles near the boat. It must be the mini-sub surfacing," the admiral said.

"Get everyone into the sub, Admiral. There's a spotlight from a patrol craft closing on us. The helicopter must've gotten a message off."

"That patrol boat has machine guns that can destroy this boat from a mile away. You need to take it out, Kim."

Kim positioned the .50 caliber as two navy SEALs arrived in a rubber raft. They took his mother, sister, and uncle to the mini-sub. Kim maneuvered the boat so that it shielded the mini-sub from the approaching patrol boat, which was accelerating. It would be within range of the boat in about thirty seconds. Kim aimed the .50 caliber and fired all ten rounds in rapid sequence. He knew it was a long shot, since the craft was head-on and presented a very narrow target, but he hoped it was close enough to slow them down. He saw some fires on the patrol boat, so Kim knew he'd hit something. He loaded a second clip and aimed toward the fires. As soon as he'd finished the clip, he dove over the side and swam to the mini-sub.

One of the SEALs grabbed him and pulled him in just as he heard the explosion. The patrol boat had disintegrated. The mini-sub dove to over a hundred feet. One of the SEALs gave him some dry clothes as Kim asked, "How's my mother?"

"She's doing fine," said one of the SEALs. "We have a medical officer on the attack boat who'll take good care of her. That was some impressive marksmanship with the .50 caliber. Have you used it before?"

Kim smiled. "I was trained in its operation during SEAL training."

"Yeah, I could tell you knew what you were doing," said the master chief. "Nice to have you on board, Commander. Relax, it's going to take about two hours to get to the attack boat. It's almost eight miles beyond the twelve-mile limit."

They could see the bottom getting further through the transparent bow shield of the mini-sub as they moved farther out. The pilot yelled, "We have company. I'm taking it down to two hundred feet."

"I can hear the ship propellers. What do you think it is, Admiral?"

"From the sound of the propellers and the RPMs, I think it's a corvette. It has some anti-submarine warfare capability, but the corvette's sonar is probably too primitive to track the mini-sub's electric motors. They'll probably attempt to track us from our last reported course based on estimated speed."

Just as the admiral spoke, they heard the sound of depth charges exploding a quarter mile in front of them. The SEAL pilot said, "They have our course and will be dropping in a pattern as we move toward them. I'm changing course."

Kim knew that would extend their distance back to the attack boat, which could be a problem. They heard the North Korean ship drop another pattern.

The pilot laughed. "If we hadn't changed course, that last pattern would've ruined our day."

A minute later they heard another pattern farther back. The admiral smiled. "The corvette has taken its best shot."

"Do we have enough power to get to the submarine?" Kim asked.

The pilot responded. "We're not out of the woods. That diversion we had to take used up a lot of our battery power. We'll be riding on battery fumes by the time we get to the mother ship."

The mini-sub got very quiet as everyone stopped talking.

A while later, the silence was broken by the pilot. "Thank God Almighty, there she is. We have battery power for one pass to connect with the sub's air lock."

Kim looked out the bow shield and saw the submarine. It was huge, and it was just hanging there like a big balloon. The pilot maneuvered the mini-sub over the rear deck of the submarine. He then gently dropped it over the hatch behind the submarine's conning tower. Kim heard a metallic clunk followed shortly by the opening of the mini-sub's hatch by the SEALs.

"Not bad for the first time," the pilot said.

"Was this really the first time?" Kim asked.

"No," said the master chief. "We've had some training missions in the mini-sub, but it's the pilot's first time linking with a sub."

The first person off the mini-sub was Kim's mother. One of the SEALs had given her a pain killer, and she was groggy. The ship's doctor examined her in the sick bay and then met with Kim and Hana.

"Your mother is very lucky," he said. "There's no nerve damage. She has a fractured ankle, and some blood vessels were severed."

"Will she need surgery?"

"Yes, they'll do that in Busan. She's in excellent condition, which will speed her recovery."

Kim and his uncle were taken to see Captain Ortega, the submarine's commanding officer.

"The SEALs say you're a piece of work, Commander. That's high praise from that team. If I could award you a medal I would. Your actions saved this mission."

"Thank you, Captain. I'm just happy to get my family out of North Korea."

"I hope my boat meets with your approval."

"It does. My uncle and I are very impressed. We'd like to see the rest of it."

"I'll give you a tour later, but first I need to ask some questions about the capabilities of your navy's submarines. Does your uncle speak English?"

The admiral smiled. "I speak it as well as my nephew. I taught him."

"Great. Please follow me to the officer's wardroom where the four of us can have a private conversation."

As they walked in, Kim saw a familiar face.

"Hi, James. It's great to see you again."

"I'm glad you made it, Kim. I hope your mother will be okay."

"She will," said the captain. "I hate to spoil this reunion, but let's get down to business. I was provided a copy of the attack plan, so I know about the new North Korean anti-ship missiles and the contingency plan if they're disabled. Can you tell me about the capabilities of your two newest Kilo subs, Admiral?"

"They're the latest Project 636.3 models, and they're extremely quiet. I found out a few days ago that our engineers have made some modifications to the propellers that have made them even quieter. We know that when they're operating on electrical power while submerged, they have been able to evade your 688 class submarines. It's doubtful the Chinese will be able to find them."

"Thanks, Admiral. Can you tell me about their surface and submerged speeds and their maximum operating depth?"

"They have a maximum surface speed of seventeen knots and a maximum submerged speed of twenty-five knots. Their crush depth is about twelve hundred feet. At speeds over twenty knots while submerged, they lose much of their stealth capabilities, and the batteries are depleted at an accelerated rate."

"What about the older Kilo, Admiral?"

"It has basically the same performance but the electronics are not as sophisticated, which could make it immune to my nephew's worm."

"That's very helpful. My mission is to safely extricate you and your family and then rendezvous with a navy helicopter that will take you to South Korea. A second helicopter will remove the mini-sub and fly it back to Yokosuka Naval Base. Commander Jordan will remain to advise us on the likely effectiveness of the worm he developed. Gentlemen, I know you had a long day, so I suggest you get some sleep."

Captain Ortega directed one of his junior officers to show them to their quarters. The admiral was assigned to officer's quarters, while Kim was assigned to bunk with the navy SEALs. As Kim made up his bunk, the master chief asked him a question. "Did you ever run into any US Navy SEALs when you were a North Korean SEAL, Commander?"

"No, but we knew they'd visited on occasion. There was a bounty for capturing them."

The master chief laughed.

"What was the bounty?"

"A larger food ration and additional leave."

"That's all a US Navy SEAL is worth? That's not much," the master chief said. All the SEALs laughed.

"In North Korea it's an incredible luxury," Kim said.

The laughing stopped as they realized Kim was serious.

"I met a former US Navy SEAL last week. He's now an FBI agent," Kim said.

"Let me guess—was his name Rick Tanner?"

"Do you know him?"

"Yeah, I know Rick. He was the best SEAL I ever served with. Everyone called him Super SEAL because he was great at everything."

"What do you mean?"

"He was an incredible swimmer, sniper, and his martial arts skills were off the chart. He was a fourth-degree black belt in tae kwon do."

"Did he learn all that during your SEAL training?"

"Hell no. Rick's father trained him from the time he was small. It was just him and his dad after his mother was killed in a car accident when Rick was four."

"I guess you and Rick were close."

"We were. It's too bad about his injury."

"How'd it happen?"

"He tore up his shoulder when his rope snapped while rappelling down a cliff in Afghanistan. I heard he fell almost twenty feet onto some rocks. It ended his career. He went to school and then became an FBI cybersecurity geek. Why did you leave your SEALs, Commander?"

"I ruptured an eardrum during a mission and was sent to school to be a cybersecurity geek."

All the SEALs laughed.

"That isn't a joke," Kim said. "I really was trained in cybersecurity after my career ended, just like Rick."

"Do you get as much satisfaction with what you're doing in cyber-security as you had when you were a SEAL?"

"It's a different type of combat, Chief. But the rewards and feeling of accomplishment are just as great."

"What do you mean?"

"I inserted a worm in the North Korean weapon systems a day ago that could disable their onboard computer systems. If it works, two of the Kilos won't be able to launch their missiles and the third Kilo only has torpedoes with limited capabilities."

The master chief smiled and said, "Any worm that can disable an enemy sub's weapons is okay with me."

Captain Ortega sent a message to COMSUBPAC about the success of the mission and the intelligence information the admiral had provided. He then went to his quarters to get some sleep. Several hours later the executive officer woke him.

"Sorry, sir, but this message was listed as urgent. It's the response from COMSUBPAC."

"That all right, Smitty. I was expecting it. It looks like our mission has changed. We've been ordered to the Senkaku Islands to counter the North Korean attack by any means necessary. The report on the capabilities of the Kilo probably shook them up a bit. Send a message asking if we can keep our two North Korean military advisors. Tell them their knowledge is crucial to the success of the mission and that I need their answer quickly. They're scheduled to be transferred to Busan in less than two hours. I'll wait for the response in the wardroom."

"Yes, sir."

Twenty minutes later, Captain Ortega was informed that his request was approved. The captain summoned the admiral and Kim to his quarters.

"I've gotten a change in orders, gentlemen. This boat has been ordered to intercept the North Korean subs. Do either of you have any objection to remaining onboard the *Washington* and participating in the new mission as advisors?"

Both of them smiled. "We wouldn't miss it for the world," Kim said.

"Great, glad to hear it, gentlemen. We're surfacing in about an hour to transfer your family and the mini-sub. After that, I'd like to discuss the new mission plan with the both of you."

Captain Ortega had performed personnel-transfer training

exercises between a submarine and helicopter, but he'd never actually performed a real transfer in the open sea. He received direction that the transfer would occur twenty miles off the east coast of South Korea. The *Washington* surfaced at seven thirty in the morning and was met by an SH-60 Sea Hawk helicopter five minutes later.

Kim was on the forward deck of the submarine with his sister, mother, a medical corpsman, a boatswain's mate, and James, who wanted to watch. Several SEALs were also on the rear deck preparing the mini-sub for transfer.

"Wait for the basket to come all the way down," shouted the boatswain's mate. "Don't jump for it."

The helicopter lowered the rescue basket, which was swinging back and forth due to the wind. The corpsman saw it swinging in his direction and yelled, "I got it." He tried to grab the basket before it was in his reach. The boatswain's mate yelled, "Let it go, it's swinging out over the water." The corpsman caught it with one hand, and the basket swung him over the side as he lost his grip and fell into the sea.

James saw what had happened. He immediately grabbed a line and dove in after him. He swam toward the corpsman, who was having trouble swimming with a life vest in the rough seas and was rapidly drifting away from the submarine. James finally reached him and attached the line to the corpsman's vest. He held on to him as several of the SEALs on the deck began to pull them both in. James spotted three fins cutting through the water toward them and yelled to the SEALs, who also saw the fins and pulled harder. He suddenly recalled all his nightmares about sharks from when he was young. The fins turned toward James and he just closed his eyes and prayed. When they were within ten feet of him, he started laughing. They were dolphins. He was still laughing when the SEALs pulled him out of the water.

During the next attempt at lowering the basket, Kim and the boatswain's mate were successful in grabbing it. Kim placed his mother in the basket, strapped her down and said, "I'll see you soon, mother," as he gave her a kiss. She was raised to the helicopter, followed by Kim's sister, and then the helicopter slowly disappeared from sight.

The *Washington* remained on the surface as an SH-53 Sea Stallion helicopter arrived. Several SEALs connected chains from the huge helicopter to the mini-sub. The SH-53 rose very slowly until the chains were tight. It then lifted the mini-sub off the deck and departed for Yokosuka.

After the transfers were completed, the *Washington* submerged and took a course toward the Senkaku Islands. James, Kim, and the admiral were summoned to the officer's wardroom where Captain Ortega was waiting.

"The US Navy appreciates the information you provided on the new North Korean Kilos, Admiral. The 688 class boats may not be able to consistently track the Kilo, but Virginia class submarines like the *Washington* can. This boat has an extremely advanced sonar system that can scan in every direction simultaneously. Based on what you know about North Korean tactics and the capabilities of the Kilo, how would you plan this mission?"

"Kim and I believe the Kilos will take the shortest possible route from Wonsan to the Senkaku Islands in order to save fuel. That will take them through the Korea Strait between Japan and South Korea, past the island of Cheju-Do. They would then take a straight-line course to the Senkaku Islands."

"How long do you think it will take them to get to the latitude where Commander Jordan's worm should disable their combat systems?"

"We think it'll take about two days. Maybe less if they make most of the trip submerged. They're slower on the surface, but they have to come up to recharge their batteries. They'll stay submerged during daylight so they can't be seen."

"When were they scheduled to leave, Admiral?"

"They left about five hours ago while it was still dark. We should take the same course as the Kilos toward the latitude Kim programmed for triggering the worm. I suggest that we just wait for them there using your passive sonar. If the worm works, they'll stop and contact headquarters for direction and probably implement the backup plan with the older Kilo that only has torpedoes. If the worm doesn't work, all three Kilos will proceed without stopping. Either way, we should follow any Kilos that take a heading toward the Senkaku Islands."

"What if they take a different course?"

"If we somehow miss them at the intercept point, we should use the plan for the joint exercise to determine where the allied fleet will be each day. From that information, we can plot a position where the Chinese fleet would have the best chance to obtain visual, radar, and sonar data from the exercise. The Kilo submarines would need to be close to the Chinese fleet to make their primary plan work. That's where this submarine should be positioned to destroy the three Kilos."

"Our passive sonar should pick them up, so I doubt we'll miss them. What if Commander Jordan's worm disables the two Kilos and they implement their backup plan with a single Kilo, Admiral?"

"If the worm disables two of the Kilos, we should position this submarine between the allied fleet and the Chinese ships. That's where the single remaining Kilo will be."

"Thanks, Admiral. I agree with your analysis. Our best chance is to find the Kilos while they're still north of the Senkaku Islands. I have one more question: How talented are your Kilo commanders?"

"They're not very experienced, Captain. We've only had the Kilo for less than a year. Most of our tactics aren't very sophisticated. They're usually predictable, since deviating from training and using initiative isn't encouraged. Occasionally, you may find an officer with initiative and intelligence who will separate himself from the pack. Sadly, such characteristics aren't encouraged. It's thought of as being too individualistic, especially for a country that needs its population to follow a single leader who thinks of himself as a god."

"Who in the allied fleet is aware of the North Korean threat?" Kim asked.

"It's my understanding that only the US commander and his ship captains are aware. It was decided that the Japanese, Taiwanese, and South Korean fleet commanders wouldn't be notified. They have a very nationalistic attitude about this exercise. It's in their waters, and they'd be easily provoked. They're all definitely cocked and loaded when it comes to the Chinese and North Koreans."

"Is there anything else you would like us to do to help, Captain?"

"Yes, Admiral. I'd like you and your nephew and Commander Jordan to plot the likely intercept point with the Kilos at the latitude where Commander Jordan's worm would disable their missiles. I'd also like you to plot the likely attack locations of the three Kilos for their primary plan, as well as the location of the single Kilo for their backup plan. Thank you, gentlemen, you can leave now. I need to talk with Commander Jordan alone."

After the admiral and Kim left, James said, "What do you need, Captain?"

"I need you to not kill yourself, Commander. There were three SEALs on deck who are trained for pulling people out of the water. I don't need the notoriety of losing a good friend of the president and the fiancé of a US Senator while you're on my boat."

"I'm sorry, Captain, but the SEALs were at the other end of the deck and I was much closer. I understand your concern, and I won't do it again."

"Thanks, James. It's been a while since we had a confrontation."

"Yeah, not since my second year at the academy when I caught you with that left hook."

"Yes, I remember. It still hurts. I was Brigade champion for two years running until you beat me. I would've beaten you the next year if I hadn't graduated."

"Maybe."

"How do you like my boat?"

"I hope it's as good as advertised. I guess we'll find out pretty soon."

"Don't worry, I'll get you home to your senator in one piece."

"I hope so. My last submarine mission didn't go so well."

"Yeah, I heard about that. I'm about to give Kim and his uncle a tour of my boat later. I'd like you to join us."

"Yes, sir, I'd enjoy that."

The admiral and Kim were in the junior officers' quarters to discuss the required mission planning when James joined them.

"How does it feel to be on a submarine again, Admiral?"

"This doesn't feel like a submarine, Commander Jordan. There's no smell of diesel fuel, and everything's so clean. This is more like a submerged luxury hotel."

They began their planning by reviewing the exercise schedule and the locations of the allied fleet during each day of the exercise. They'd been at it for about two hours when Kim was informed that the captain wanted to see him in the officer's wardroom.

"Kim, I was just informed that your mother underwent surgery at the hospital in Busan and is doing well. She should be released in the next week and will join your sister in temporary base housing. Now, are you and your uncle ready for the tour I promised you?"

"Yes, Captain."

"Good. Commander Jordan is also joining us."

Captain Ortega called James and the admiral to the officer's wardroom and began his tour.

"This is the engine room, gentlemen. Nothing special here unless you like to see a lot of nuclear reactor plumbing. The primary innovation in our propulsion system is our pump-jet propulsor rather than regular propellers. It makes us very stealthy and quiet. Quieter than your Kilos, Admiral."

"I hope so, Captain."

"Our next stop is the command center, which isn't located directly below the deck since there's no periscope. The surface view is provided by telescoping photonics masts with high-resolution cameras, infrared sensors, and a laser rangefinder. All images and data are displayed on flat-screen monitors in high definition."

"I've never seen anything like this technology, Captain."

"Thank you, Admiral. We'll skip the torpedo room. I'm sure you've both seen torpedoes, and the vertical-launch Tomahawk missiles are highly classified. The best part of the tour is our sonar system. We have a bow-mounted spherical active and passive sonar array, a wide-aperture lightweight fiber-optic sonar array, and two high-frequency active sonars mounted in the sail and keel under the bow. The system enables safer operations in shallow coastal waters, like the ones we were in for your exfiltration, Kim. Our ASW performance is vastly improved by the continuous scan of the waters surrounding the boat."

Kim was impressed and could see how advanced the *Washington* was compared to the Kilo. He also knew that if it was detected, however, it would be just as vulnerable as their prey.

# 30

The *Washington* was on course to make it to the Senkaku Islands thirty hours after receiving their new orders. Captain Ortega had set up James, Kim, and the admiral in the officer's wardroom to work on their intercept plan with the Kilos.

"Good afternoon, gentlemen. What do you have so far?"

"We've looked at the nautical maps of the five Senkaku Islands and the plans for the military exercise," James said. "The exercise will take place over four days to the east, north, west, and south of the islands, in that order. We've marked areas on the maps where the *Washington* could intercept the Kilos and where the Chinese Navy would most likely station their ships to monitor the exercise."

"Where's the intercept point for determining whether the commander's worm worked?"

"It's right here, fifty miles north of the islands," James said. "The admiral believes the Kilos will approach the Senkaku Islands from the northeastern side of the islands. The water is deeper there and would make the Kilos more difficult to detect. As the Kilos approach, they'll need to be outside of the Chinese fleet to avoid their sensors. The

Chinese ships will have their sensors directed inward, toward the allied exercise area, which is close to the islands."

"When do you think the Kilos will implement their attack?"

"We believe their ideal time will be on the second day when the ships are to the north of the Senkaku Islands. They'd be closer to North Korea and it would be easier to escape the target area. If the worm works, the two Kilos with the missiles would no longer be viable. The admiral was briefed on that scenario in North Korea, where it was decided that the disabled Kilos will be ordered to return home to lessen the chance of detection."

"What would happen if your worm failed, Commander?"

"Three Kilos will proceed to the target area and attack the allied fleet as planned. Our suggestion is to take out all three Kilos immediately after you're certain the worm failed. That way the Chinese fleet would not know what happened, since all their sensors would be pointed toward the allied fleet."

"I agree. We're authorized to destroy the Kilos if the worm fails."

"What are your orders if the worm succeeds, Captain?"

"That's where it becomes less clear, Kim. My orders are to follow and monitor the remaining Kilo, since we know its mission will be to sink a Chinese ship. Your report indicated that it's possible the Chinese fleet might detect the Kilo. If they do, my orders are to monitor the exercise, but take no action against the Kilo. It's no longer our problem. I don't agree with that, but I have my orders."

"Why don't you agree?" James asked.

"We all know what can happen when you have a desperate enemy. The Kilo could make a mistake and sink an allied ship or be detected and attack both sides. The panic and confusion might achieve exactly what the North Koreans want, the allied fleet and Chinese fleet shooting at each other. I guess we'll find out soon, as we're about to be at the intercept point. I'll need your help, so please follow me to the control room."

As they entered the control room the executive officer said, "We're at the intercept point, Captain."

"Thanks, Smitty. Okay, all stop. Let me know if we pick up anything on the sonar."

"How effective is your passive sonar?" the admiral asked.

"We can hear a sardine fart twenty miles away. Seriously, we're like a black hole in the ocean. In this mode nobody can hear us, but we can hear and analyze anomalies at one-tenth the decibel level that a 688 boat can. We're much quieter, faster, and can dive much deeper than any Kilo, and we never have to surface unless we want to. We also have more firepower than any class of attack boat in the world."

"We're picking up some anomalies along the predicted target track, Captain," the sonar officer said. "It's definitely surface traffic."

"It's two in the morning, so it could be the Kilos charging their batteries on the surface," Captain Ortega said.

Thirty minutes later the sonar officer said, "The ASW identifies the target signature as Kilo subs, sir. They're coming directly toward us."

"Let me know when they get within five hundred yards."

Ten minutes later the sonar officer said, "I just lost them, Captain."

"Okay, take her up to fifty feet and raise the photonics mast. Set a course toward the last point of contact."

"There they are, Captain. All three of them. They're totally stationary and at almost the exact position that we predicted."

"I see that, Commander Jordan."

"We're copying some unencrypted voice radio traffic, Captain. Can one of our guests interpret it?"

"Good idea, Smitty. Can you help, Admiral?"

The admiral listened for a few minutes and then he smiled.

"Apparently the worm worked. They're requesting new orders from headquarters."

"Why don't they encrypt their radio communications, Kim?"

"The encryption systems were probably disabled by the worm, since they need accurate time to operate properly."

"Well, it looks like they're following their orders," the captain said. "Two of the subs are turning around, and the third is now headed toward us. That must be the sub with only torpedoes. Ahead one-third and maintain our distance at one thousand yards."

Captain Ortega was beaming as he walked over to the admiral, James, and Kim. "Great work, gentlemen. Your efforts just made our mission a lot easier."

"Thank you, Captain. We all appreciate that," James said.

"You're welcome. Excuse me, I need to make a phone call."

Captain Ortega approached his executive officer.

"I need you to send a message to COMSUBPAC, Smitty. Tell them that there is only one Kilo approaching the exercise area and the *Washington* is tracking it."

"Yes, sir."

"The Kilo's diving, sir."

"Yes, I can see that, Chief. I'm sure they want to avoid detection by surface ship radar. Okay, set our depth to be the same as theirs and maintain distance."

"They've leveled off at three hundred feet, sir."

"Thanks, Lieutenant."

Two hours later the sonar officer said, "The Kilo's slowing down and his depth is decreasing, sir."

"He's probably coming up for a look-see. Take us up to fifty feet and raise the mast."

"Yes, sir."

"What do you think of our panoramic display, Admiral? The photonic mast lets us see all around us at once. It's a big improvement on a periscope."

"It's very impressive, Captain. We can see both the allied and Chinese fleets at the same time."

"Yes, it's like having a ringside seat at a prize fight."

"The Kilo seems to be closing his distance on one of the Chinese ships, Captain."

"Let me know if he opens his torpedo doors, Lieutenant."

"It's turning away and it looks like it's moving toward a second ship."

"It's probably checking to see how close it can get before being detected. How close did it get, Lieutenant?"

"Five hundred yards, sir."

"Gutsy SOB, isn't he, Admiral?"

"They don't have much confidence in their torpedoes, Captain. The Kilo was probably ordered to get as close as possible."

"He just got caught, Captain. One of the Chinese ships must've detected the Kilo at about three hundred yards and has turned around and is moving toward it. The Kilo is trying to move out of their sonar range."

"Thanks, Lieutenant."

"He's at dead stop, sir."

After almost an hour, Captain Ortega told the executive officer that he was going to take a nap.

"It looks like the Kilo has gone silent and is probably saving his batteries. Let me know if anything happens, Smitty."

Five hours later, the executive officer woke him.

"Captain, we just picked up a sonar bogey, it's another submarine."

"Another Kilo?"

"No, sir. This one's a Chinese attack boat, one of their newest. It went right past us and the Kilo toward the allied fleet at ten knots."

"Okay, send a message to COMSUBPAC about the contact. Tell them we think the Chinese detected the Kilo during a practice attack run, and it might've incited them to monitor the exercise with one of their new submarines. I'm going to the control room."

As Captain Ortega walked into the control room, he saw the admiral, Kim, and James sitting at a small table.

"Don't you guys ever sleep?" the captain asked.

"We heard about the Chinese submarine," James said. "What do you think it means?"

"I think the Chinese believe they detected an American sub and sent one of their latest nuclear attack boats to find it, Commander."

"The new Chinese boats are almost as good as our latest 688

boats, Captain. Their ASW could detect the Kilo. If they think their fleet is in danger, they'll use their active sonar and might also detect the *Washington*."

"Yes, I know, Commander Jordan. Do you have any ideas?"

"We could transmit the recorded sonar data on the Kilo doing its practice runs and the sonar data recorded on the Chinese boat to COMSUBPAC via the SATCOM. You could suggest that it be provided to the Chinese government as evidence of North Korean intentions."

"Great idea, Commander, but I'm not sure COMSUBPAC would do it. It would disclose classified information on our operational capabilities. But at this point it's worth a try."

The *Washington* sent the recorded tracking information to COMSUBPAC who forwarded it to the Pentagon and the secretary of defense. After evaluating the information with his staff, the defense secretary met with the president, who requested an urgent meeting with the Chinese ambassador.

Ambassador Yang was contacted on his cell phone at a local restaurant and took his embassy limousine to the White House. The president briefed him on the recorded data and its source.

"This sonar data was recorded by one of our ships in the Senkaku Island exercise a few hours ago, Mr. Ambassador. It shows the sonar signature of a Chinese nuclear attack boat and a North Korean Kilo operating near the exercise. You can see from the visual display that the Kilo is making targeting runs on a Chinese ship. We also have intelligence information from a very high-level North Korean military source that the Kilo intends to sink one of your ships within the next twenty-four hours. The North Koreans will then blame it on America."

"This is very shocking, Mr. President. You're accusing the North Koreans of planning an attack on its closest ally."

"Yes, Mr. Ambassador, that's exactly what I'm saying. If your government doesn't verify this information, we could soon be at war."

The ambassador didn't know what to think. Recent events made it hard to trust the president. If he ignored the president's warning, and a military clash between the United States and China occurred, his life would be over. Not to mention the lives of many Chinese and Americans. He decided it was best to kick this problem upstairs, as the Americans would say.

"I need some privacy to make a call, Mr. President."

"Certainly. Do you need a private room?"

"No, I can call from my limousine. It's very secure and very close."

The Ambassador called Beijing and requested that he be put through to his cousin, the Chinese president. He described the situation and the proof as provided by President Jordan. The Chinese president said he'd call him back.

Twenty minutes later the Chinese president called Ambassador Yang and said, "The Koreans denied it. I also talked to our National Minister of Defense, who acknowledged that one of our submarines was in the area of the exercise. I think the Koreans are lying. They seemed very nervous and evasive when I asked them about the Kilo. Ask President Meredith what he proposes to do and call me back."

The ambassador returned to his meeting with the president and asked some additional questions.

"Mr. President, how do you propose we handle this delicate situation?"

"I suggest we disable the Kilo so that it can't sink one of your ships."

"How do you propose we do that? Our submarine hasn't been able to find the Kilo."

"We know exactly where it is, Mr. Ambassador, and we've been monitoring it for almost forty-eight hours. We could provide you with its location, or we could handle it ourselves. The decision is yours, but I need to know as soon as possible."

"I need to make another call, Mr. President."

The president nodded.

The ambassador called the Chinese president and relayed the president's offer.

"Let me talk with the Koreans one last time. If they deny the situation again, you can tell the president to go ahead. I'll call you back."

In ten minutes the Chinese president called.

"They're lying to us again. It's time to teach them a lesson. Tell the president to go ahead with his plan, but tell him we need some time to contact our ships, so they know what's happening. I'll call back when I know it's been taken care of."

Three hours had passed since the *Washington* had transmitted its information to COMSUBPAC, and there had been no response. Captain Ortega and his executive officer were drinking coffee in the control room.

"I'm getting tired of this waiting, Smitty. But at least they're considering the information we sent. We would've known by now if they weren't."

"What do you think we should do, sir?"

"I think we need to ready in case they want us to take out the Kilo. Load two Mk 48 torpedoes and prepare for launch. Maintain distance to target at one thousand yards."

"Yes, Captain."

Several minutes later the sonar officer updated Captain Ortega on a change in the current situation.

"Captain, the Chinese ships are using their active sonar. With all that pinging we can't hear a damn thing, sir."

"Okay, Lieutenant, take us out of range of the sonar and try to maintain our track on the Kilo."

"Yes, sir, I've still got him. He's also moving away."

"What about the Chinese boat?"

"He took off before they started pinging. He was probably warned and was expecting it. I have no idea where he is."

"Okay, maintain our distance from the Kilo."

"Captain, we have a VLF message coming in from COMSUB-PAC," the executive officer said.

"Thanks, Smitty, validate the message and bring it to me when you have it all."

"Yes, sir. It'll take a few minutes."

Several minutes later the message was received and validated.

"Here it is, Captain. It says the Chinese forces are aware of the Kilo and its probable intentions. We've been ordered to destroy it if it takes any hostile actions against the allied fleet."

"Does it say anything about taking action against the Kilo if it takes hostile actions against the Chinese fleet?"

"No, sir."

"Captain, the Kilo is moving toward the allied fleet at about ten knots."

"He's probably trying to avoid detection by the Chinese active sonar. Follow him and maintain distance, Lieutenant."

"I found the Chinese boat, Captain. It's moving toward the Chinese fleet at about twenty-five knots."

"It's probably joining their surface fleet to protect them from the Kilo."

"The Kilo stopped when the Chinese boat passed it, Captain."

"What was the Kilo's distance from the Chinese boat when it passed?"

"About eight hundred yards, sir."

James approached Captain Ortega.

"The Kilo had to have detected the Chinese boat as it went by. At the speed it was moving, the Chinese boat wouldn't detect the Kilo or the *Washington* as it passed."

"My thoughts exactly, James. Is the Kilo still stationary, Lieutenant?"

"Yes, sir, it seems like it's confused."

"I'm sure it is, Lieutenant."

"Captain, it just turned 180 degrees and is following the Chinese boat at a distance of about 1500 yards."

"Thanks, Lieutenant. Continue to maintain distance on the Kilo. Can I see you for a minute, Admiral? I need some information."

The admiral walked over and said, "What do you need, Captain?"

"Are the sonar-detection systems on the Kilos sophisticated enough to determine the type of sub it's tracking?"

"Not beyond whether it's a diesel-electric or a nuclear boat and the approximate size. The Kilo commander wouldn't know if it was an American 688 or a Chinese nuclear attack boat. I assume that's the information you're looking for, Captain?"

"Yes, it is, thank you. I think the Kilo misidentified the Chinese boat as an American 688 class attack boat. They're very similar in size and acoustic characteristics, and that's not by accident. My guess is that the Kilo captain assumed that the Chinese surface fleet had detected an American boat and were using their active sonar to find it."

"I agree," James said. "The Kilo may be reverting to the original plan to sink an American ship or, in this case, what he believes is an American submarine."

"Yes, Commander. The Kilo captain believes it's an American sub that's approaching the Chinese surface fleet. I'm sure he believes that if he sinks it, the destruction of the sub will be blamed on the nearby Chinese fleet. The North Koreans will erroneously believe that they have achieved their goal. I assume you see the irony in this situation, Commander Jordan."

"I do, Captain. The North Koreans will sink a Chinese submarine, while thinking it was an American submarine. The Chinese will know why they did it, having already been warned about the North Korean plan by the US government. The North Koreans would think they'd succeeded. Instead, they would've actually triggered a potentially catastrophic response from China, their only ally and benefactor."

"Exactly, and to make it even worse, the sinking of the Chinese submarine would've been done by a Kilo submarine that was provided to North Korea by China. That would make the Chinese furious. It might almost be worth letting them do it, but I can't let that happen."

"I admire your humanity, Captain."

"Thanks, James, but my humanity could get me court-martialed. I have no orders to sink the Kilo if it tries to sink a Chinese ship."

Captain Ortega knew what he had to do. He called over his executive officer.

"I need you to send a message to COMSUBPAC on the VLF, Smitty. We need permission to sink the Kilo before it sinks that Chinese submarine."

"The SATCOM would be faster, sir."

"No, we could lose the Kilo if we came up to a depth that would allow us to use the SATCOM."

"Okay, I'll send it immediately, Captain."

Captain Ortega walked over to the admiral.

"Admiral, can you give me a quick briefing on North Korean torpedoes?"

"Yes, Captain. The torpedo used on the Kilo has a speed of about thirty-five knots and uses both active and passive acoustic homing. It's only effective at ranges less than five miles. This torpedo is more accurate when the submarine is stationary, so the Kilo will probably come to a complete stop before firing."

"Thanks, Admiral. Let me know if the Kilo reduces its speed, Lieutenant."

"Will you shoot if he stops, Captain?"

"No, James. But if he opens his torpedo doors I will. The Kilo is not my main concern. I'm more worried about the reaction of the Chinese fleet after we sink the Kilo. If they assume their own submarine was sunk, they might go into an all-out attack mode against any underwater targets. That could make both the *Washington* and the Chinese attack boat potential targets. I just hope the Chinese boat quickly identifies itself to the Chinese fleet after the Kilo is sunk."

"So do I, Captain. But we both know that in panic situations, even well-trained personnel will shoot first and ask questions later."

"Yes, and if that happens, I'll be concerned about the Chinese

Yu-7 ASW torpedo on their surface ships. It's based on our Mk 46 torpedoes that the Chinese purchased from us back in '85. This model has been deployed on their destroyers and frigates right above us, and it's very good. It's deadly at distances up to ten miles. The only defense we have against it are our acoustic countermeasures."

"Captain, the Kilo is reducing its speed as it approaches the Chinese fleet."

"Maintain our distance to target at one thousand yards, and generate a target solution on the Kilo. What's the status of the Chinese boat?"

"It seems to be changing course and is moving toward us and the Kilo."

"Was the turn slow or sudden and has its speed changed?"

"No change in speed, and the turn was wide and slow. The Kilo is slowing down and is opening its torpedo doors, Captain."

"You're right about your officers, Admiral. The captain on the Kilo thinks it was discovered by the Chinese boat. An experienced officer would know that the slow, wide turn is not an attack maneuver. The Chinese boat was just moving back toward the allied fleet."

"The Chinese boat must've heard the sound of the opening torpedo doors. It's transitioning to active sonar. He'll find the Kilo and us, sir."

"I know, Lieutenant. Fire one!"

"The Chinese submarine just fired one of its torpedoes at the Kilo too, sir."

"Shit!" the captain shouted. "Let's get out of here. All ahead flank. Come left to course one six zero and ten degrees down bubble."

"You're heading toward that deep trough we passed over yesterday?" James asked.

"Yes, Commander. I intend to get this sub to some dark blue water."

"Lieutenant, has our torpedo hit home?"

"Five more seconds, Captain . . . yes! Scratch one Kilo, sir."

"Thanks, Lieutenant."

"I just picked up a second explosion, sir. It was definitely an impact from a torpedo."

"Thanks, Lieutenant. If we're lucky, that was the Chinese Yu-7 torpedo impacting with the wreckage of the Kilo as it was sinking."

"Captain, I just picked up three sonar bogeys. The ASW identifies the biggest one as the Chinese submarine. The two following it are torpedoes, sir!"

"Are we in their path, lieutenant?"

"No, sir, but they're heading to that same trough that we're moving toward."

"Damn! Sometimes I hate being right, James. The Chinese surface fleet just fired two torpedoes at their own submarine."

"How far are the torpedoes from the Chinese boat, Lieutenant?"

"It's about six thousand yards ahead of the closest torpedo, Captain."

"Can the Chinese boat make it to the torpedo's maximum operational depth in the trough before the first torpedo catches it?"

"No, sir."

"I want a firing solution on the Yu-7 torpedoes chasing that Chinese boat, Lieutenant. Launch two Mk 48s when you have it."

"Yes, sir."

"What are you planning on doing, Captain?" James asked.

"Have you ever heard of a torpedo being used to destroy another torpedo?"

"No."

"Neither have I, but I know it's theoretically possible. It would require an extremely fast torpedo with a proximity fuse and a warhead large enough so that it could destroy the target torpedo without having to hit it. Luckily we have such a torpedo. The Mk 48 has a speed of almost sixty knots, a proximity fuse, and a 650-pound high-explosive warhead. It was recently upgraded with a new sonar tracking capability to make it effective against smaller and more agile submerged targets such as torpedoes, but it's never been tested. I plan to test it now."

"Launching now, sir."

"Thanks Lieutenant, keep me updated."

"You realize that if you take out either Yu-7 torpedo and miss the second, the one that survives could go into search mode and possibly target the *Washington.*"

"Yes, I know that Commander Jordan."

"The Chinese boat is approaching the trough, but the first Yu-7 torpedo is only a thousand yards behind and closing at a rate of 550 yards per minute, sir."

"If this doesn't work, that Chinese boat has less than two minutes to live, Captain."

"Let's hope it does work, Commander."

"The first Mk 48 is closing on the first Yu-7 torpedo, sir. It's about a thousand yards behind. Nine hundred, seven hundred, five hundred, two hundred . . . it's going to be close. Son of a bitch, I think it worked! It did, the Mk 48 annihilated it!" the sonar officer shouted.

Captain Ortega smiled and then ordered, "All ahead flank, let's follow the Chinese sub to the deep end of the pool."

"I just picked up another explosion, Captain."

"Was it the second Mk 48?"

"Yes, sir, but it's too soon for it to have caught the second Yu-7 torpedo. It must have triggered on the explosion and wreckage of the first Yu-7 torpedo."

"Is the second Yu-7 torpedo still tracking, Lieutenant?"

"No, Captain, it seems to have broken its lock on the Chinese sub, which is beneath the Yu-7's maximum operating depth. Oh my God, it's now tracking us."

"All ahead flank. Twenty-five degrees down bubble. That's one persistent SOB. What's the distance, Lieutenant?"

"About a thousand yards, and closing at about 370 yards per minute."

"That's too close to launch another torpedo. How long before we get past the Yu-7's maximum depth?"

"Two and a half minutes, sir. But that's based on the capabilities of our current Mk 46. If the Chinese version is faster, we could have a problem."

"Let's pray it isn't."

"This is a hell of a way to analyze the capabilities of their weapons, Captain."

"I agree, Commander Jordan."

The tension on the boat was thick as the sonar officer ticked off the distance to the Yu-7.

"How soon before we're at the torpedo's maximum depth, Lieutenant?"

"A little over a minute, Captain, and the torpedo is less than a minute and a half behind us and closing."

Captain Ortega grabbed the microphone for the 1MC to talk to the crew. "This is the Captain, ready the countermeasures and rig for impact."

"We're at its maximum depth, Captain, and there's no sign of it slowing down."

"Thanks, Lieutenant. Sound the collision alarm!"

"We're at five hundred yards and I believe, yes it's definitely slowing. The speed has dropped to about eighty percent, but it's still closing. We're now at four hundred yards and its speed is dropping, but it's still closing, sir."

"Deploy the countermeasures."

"Three hundred, 200, 150 yards! It seems to be moving away from the boat, Captain. I think it's tracking the countermeasures, sir."

"Great, let's hope it's moving far enough away."

Suddenly there was an explosion and the entire boat shook.

"The torpedo missed, Captain!" James shouted. "The son of a bitch missed!"

Captain Ortega was silent as the rest of the crew cheered. He looked down and wiped his brow as he slowly grabbed the 1MC.

"This is the captain. It looks like we live to fight another day. Okay, Smitty, let's take this boat back to Yokosuka and to a depth where I can use the SATCOM to make a phone call. I'm going to my quarters to write my report, and I don't want to be disturbed unless it's absolutely necessary."

Captain Ortega was exhausted and exhilarated at the same time. The only thing he was concerned about was the sinking of the North Korean submarine without authorization. About thirty minutes later, the executive officer called his quarters.

"Sorry to bother you, Captain, but we just got a message from COMSUBPAC."

"Read it to me, Smitty."

"It says that the USS *Washington* is authorized to take any measures necessary to protect any ships participating in or legally monitoring the naval exercise in the Senkaku Islands. I think you're off the hook, Captain."

"Well, I guess I get to keep my stripes. Thanks, Smitty."

That evening Captain Ortega invited the admiral, James, and Kim to have dinner with him in his quarters.

"What do you plan to do when you get to America, Admiral?"

"I plan to go fishing. I may even start a fishing charter business."

"How about you, Kim?"

"I'm going to find my fiancée and celebrate our new life in America. But first I need to visit my mother in the hospital in Busan to make sure she's okay."

"Is there anything you need to make this journey easier?" the captain asked.

Kim smiled. "There's one thing, Captain. Do you have any American adventure movies?"

The captain laughed. "Haven't you had enough adventure, Kim?"

# EPILOGUE

Kim and his uncle arrived in Yokosuka and were provided housing and food allowances on the navy base. That evening, the DIA contacted them to let them know that they had arranged for a car to take them to the airport in Tokyo for their flight to Busan the next morning. Their flight arrived in Busan at about noon and they were provided housing at the Lotte Hotel. After checking in, Kim and his uncle took a taxi to visit his mother in the hospital.

As he entered her room, Kim's mother smiled and said, "I'm so glad you're okay, Kim. Both your sister and I were very worried."

"Where is Hana?"

"She's staying in base housing and is getting fat from eating such good food."

"I can't imagine Hana ever getting fat, mother. Where are you going after they release you tomorrow?"

"I plan to stay with Hana in Busan for a while. She says it's really pretty, and the officer who visited me said we can stay in base housing until we find a place of our own. How long will you be here, Kim?"

"I'll be traveling to the United States tomorrow. I'm meeting with some government officials to discuss the situation in North Korea. What are your plans, Mother?"

"I want to get a job as a secretary, and Hana is making plans for college. She wants to be a doctor."

"That's great. I'll contact you when I get settled. Maybe you can visit me and my fiancée, Cai. I'm sure you'll both love her."

Kim then hugged her and kissed her on the cheek. He could see she was starting to cry.

"Don't cry, Mother. We're free. I'll see you again soon."

Kim and his uncle went back to their hotel room and found two new suitcases and some new clothes, compliments of the US government. Everything fit perfectly.

"I wonder how they got the sizes right. I never gave them my measurements."

His uncle laughed. "You're wondering how a country that builds luxury submarines can get our measurements right? I think they're capable of a lot more than that."

"I can tell you're really enjoying yourself, Uncle. Let's go out and celebrate."

"Okay, but we need to be back early. We have a long flight tomorrow. I hear Hawaii is paradise."

"We're only going to be there for one day, and then we fly to Washington."

"Yes, I know. We fly for nine hours, but get to Honolulu only fifty minutes later than we left, on the same day. That's a long day for an old man like me."

They arrived at the airport in Busan at eight. The flight was full, and Kim couldn't sleep. He was exhausted by the time they arrived in Honolulu. As Kim exited the plane and entered the Honolulu airport, he couldn't believe his eyes. Cai was standing in front of him. She had tears in her eyes as she ran to him and jumped into his arms so hard she almost knocked him over. Cai kissed him all over as Kim's uncle watched with amusement.

"I guess you know this girl, Kim. If not, the people in Hawaii are even friendlier than I was told."

"This is my fiancée, Cai. Cai, this is my uncle, the admiral."

Cai hugged him and said, "I'm very glad to meet you, Admiral."

"Please call me Kwan," he said. "I'm fairly certain that I'm no longer an admiral."

"We have a suite at the Hilton on Waikiki Beach, and so does your uncle. James flew in last night from Japan. Rick and his girlfriend flew in yesterday afternoon, as did James's fiancée."

"That's great. I'm really tired, Cai. It's been a long week."

"I understand. I missed you so much, but I'll leave you alone until you regain your strength."

"I'll be okay by tonight. I recover quickly."

Cai smiled. "Yes, I remember."

After Kim and Lee got their luggage, Cai led them to a red Camaro convertible.

"I rented it with my new credit card, provided by Solomon Enterprises. I also have a New York driver's license. Mr. Solomon's company is keeping all his promises." On the drive to the hotel, Cai told Kim that George and his son had been killed by a crime syndicate.

After getting to their suite, Kim took a long warm shower. When he came out of the bathroom, there were Hawaiian shirts and shorts on the bed.

"I went shopping, Kim. I hope you like them."

"I do, they look very colorful. Wake me up around two. I'd like to get some sun after being cooped up in a submarine for a week."

Cai joined him in the bed. About two hours later they were both awakened by pounding on the door.

"Open up, this is the FBI. I hear you have a woman in there."

Cai ran to the door. "Hello Rick. Where's Allison?"

"Downstairs at the bar with James and JoAnn. We'll see you at the Rainbow Lanai in about fifteen minutes, okay?"

When Kim and Cai arrived, James, JoAnn, Rick, and Allison were enjoying tropical drinks.

"What would you guys like?"

"Mai Tai, Blue Hawaiian, or Lava Flow, it's on me," James said.

"He means that," Rick said. "As of two days ago, he's one of the richest men in the world."

"No, Rick. I don't want to discuss that. Three men I worked with and cared about died. I take no joy in that."

"I'm sorry, James. But I've already spilled the beans. You're going to have to share the news with your friends."

"Okay, you tell them."

Kim and Cai looked confused.

"What happened, Rick?" Kim asked.

"George Solomon left most of his fortune and corporate ownership to Philip Wu's widow and James. The rest went to charities, his fiancée, Astrid, and Nadya Murin, whom the board appointed as the new board chairman and CEO of George Solomon Enterprises."

"Are you leaving your job at the White House?" Kim asked.

"Absolutely not. I plan to stay as long as the president wants me. Rick is getting a promotion. Why don't you tell them about it, Special Agent Tanner?"

"I've been selected to be the Special Liaison on Cybercrime with the FBI director and the attorney general."

"I hope one of you has a job for Cai and me after we graduate."

"Have you decided on a school?" Rick asked.

"No. We plan to tour the United States to find one, courtesy of George Solomon."

"Where's your uncle, Kim?" JoAnn asked. "I thought he'd be joining us."

"He's meeting with some American intelligence officers at Pearl Harbor to discuss my country's nuclear capabilities. The US Navy is also going to have him examined by their best doctors at the Bethesda Naval Medical Center when we get back to Washington."

"That will be a week from now. I worked it out so we all get to spend a week in paradise," James said.

"That's great. I can't believe how my life has changed. Nine months ago I was a North Korean. Now, I'm going to be a US citizen and marry the woman of my dreams."

"I know what you mean," James said. "I'm engaged to a gorgeous US Senator, have a great job working for the president, and wonderful friends. It can't get any better than this. What a country!"

# AUTHOR Q&A

Q: Your novel spans the globe and probes deeply into computer tech and military maneuvers. What inspired you to write this novel? Would you say the creative spark came more from wanting to write about politics, or international relations, or computer tech?

A: I've had an interest in writing since high school, when I wrote some science fiction short stories that many of my friends and teachers liked. I never took it seriously until much later, after I had graduated engineering school and started working as an electronics and software design engineer for private industry and then the federal government. My interest in politics and international relations was fostered by some of my classes while I was in law school and by my youth in New York City and by my current life in the Washington, DC, area. Both areas are political hotbeds. After graduating law school, I took a job with the US Patent Office, and after a year or so, I decided that I was more interested in designing and patenting my own digital electronic and IT systems and software rather than representing designers who were seeking patents for their technology. I started my own company in the DC area providing consulting and design services for electronic systems, information technology, software, and artificial intelligence for the US Navy and other Department of Defense and federal agencies. I saw cybersecurity as an evolving business, and I decided to provide cybersecurity support and services and design cybersecurity systems for industry and the federal government. Over the years we were very successful and won many large contracts for both our cybersecurity services and systems. After retiring at too young an age, I needed something to do, so I started providing individual consulting support to companies and writing articles on cybersecurity. My wife encouraged me to expand that into writing books on cybersecurity. I decided to use my knowledge to write fiction based on my past experiences in cybersecurity and my knowledge of the political and international environment based on time in New York and Washington DC.

Q: You clearly have a fascination with the inner workings of cybersecurity. Where did you learn so much about it? Was it more through experience or research?

A: Actually it was both. I love cybersecurity and AI since they both have a technical and personal element that most technologies don't have. To implement a successful cyber attack, the hacker must understand both the technology involved and human nature. Many, if not most, successful attacks exploit human error that only a knowledgeable hacker might understand based on their understanding of the technology and how a system architect, software/hardware designer, production engineer, test engineer, support engineer, help desk support, or shipping clerk perform their duties. Many hackers study all the operations that a company performs to design, develop, test, produce, maintain, and ship a software or hardware IT product to find a weakness they can take advantage of. They might even try to get some of the attack team's personnel into the organization to obtain the necessary information. That's not necessary if the attacker is an insider who understands the technology and its potential weaknesses.

In the book I describe the Information Systems Security Assessment Framework. One of the components of the framework is social engineering, which requires a smooth talker to trick someone in the target organization into providing information that will support a penetration attack (aka "hack"). You'll also see a reference to a penetration tester, which is an individual who attempts to hack a system to find vulnerabilities that need to be fixed. Hacking is very much a cat and mouse game that is often more psychology than technology. I love the game and the technical and psychological challenges.

Q: What about your descriptions of military actions—for example, the skills of navy SEALs and the capabilities of various submarines. Did you do a lot of research? Did that research involve actually being in a submarine?

A: I spent a lot of years working with the navy, mostly the aviation side. I had the opportunity to fly in a lot of naval aircraft at the Naval Air Warfare Center in Patuxent River, including the F-14, F/A-18, A-6, S-3B, P-3C, EA-6B, and EC-130. I also got the opportunity to spend time on the USS *George Washington* during naval tests with the EC-130 aircraft. The *George Washington* was cramped, which isn't the case with the latest US Ballistic Missile submarines (SSBNs), which are large and comfortable. The *George Washington* class submarines were the first class of SSBNs. They were originally designed as attack subs, but were changed prior to production to incorporate a section for the first submarine-based Polaris ballistic missiles. The section that was added became known as Sherwood Forest since it contains a forest of vertical launch tubes. While I was on that boat, I used to walk through that forest regularly and found it spooky to know that in those tubes was enough power to destroy several large countries. There were things I had to research, including the latest US Virginia class submarine; the North Korean Kilo submarine and its torpedos; the Chinese submarine and its torpedoes, and the SEAL Swimmer Delivery Vehicle.

Q: You weave a lot of plotlines through this novel. Did you start out with the end in mind, meaning did you know who was "guilty"? Or did that change as you wrote the story?

A: There were definitely aspects of the plot that evolved as I wrote the book. Rick became a major character that I used to play off of James. In the next books, he takes on a role of his own but still works with James. My "guilty" characters were intended to be George and Dimitri. However, at the end I softened both characters a bit in their final chapter. I have this belief that most people are not villains, although they can seem that way if circumstances force or encourage them into doing something that is terrible. I guess you could say that Anya was the ultimate villain but she wasn't really a major character until the end. Like a lot of evil people, she used those she knew to get what she wanted based on her desire for wealth and power. Chris, Dimitri, George, and Marat all died because of her, and she finally got what she deserved.

Q: Do you have a favorite character? If so, what do you most appreciate about him or her?

A: James is my favorite character since he is based on my experiences with the navy designing cybersecurity and AI systems. We have a number of similarities, which makes it very easy to write about him. One of our differences is that he didn't patent his cybersecurity systems, while I did patent mine.

Q: Was there a character that gave you the spark for telling this story?

A: No. The idea of depicting malware as a counter-weapon was based on a technical paper I wrote almost twenty years ago.

Q: Apologies if you don't want to reveal this, but are any characters in this book based on real people you know?

A: Some of the names I used are from real people. James, JoAnn, President Joseph Meredith, and Michelle are all based on people I know well. James is a slightly taller and younger version of me. JoAnn is based on my wife, whose name is also JoAnn. President Meredith is named for my son, Joseph, and his wife, Meredith. Michelle is my daughter, and she is an excellent chef who will probably own her own restaurant someday. I can also say that the personal characteristics of James, JoAnn, and Michelle are based on the people they're named for. The characteristics of President Meredith are based on John F. Kennedy, one of my favorite presidents.

Q: Several of the characters end up surprising the reader. Did they also surprise you? Did you have to adjust the actions or backgrounds of them as you wrote?

A: Yes, I modified some of them as I wrote the book. Dimitri was a character who was originally designed to be entirely evil. I decided to moderate that to make him more interesting and complex. George was another character who had many conflicting character traits, but it was easy to understand both his hatred of the Chinese because of his brother's death and his guilt concerning Chris. He's not a likable character, but he isn't evil like Anya. Rick took on a larger role as James's sidekick and he also added some comic relief.

Q: This novel is timely, given current international relations and the shifting alliances between countries, especially the United States, North Korea, China, and Russia. You treat your characters from these countries with equanimity rather than bias. Did you hold yourself back from injecting personal feelings about these countries?

A: No. I think I described North Korea and China in a way that most sane people would see them. My depiction of Russia in the book was based on various descriptions of the Chechen wars.

Q: Your characters travel the globe. Have you been to all of the places you describe? Even North Korea? If not, how do you create such convincing descriptions of these locales?

A: No. I did lots of research, especially for Harbin, China, and the locales described in North Korea. The scene in Germany was much easier since I know the city very well, having visited it a number of times. The description of the university in Russia that was destroyed by the Chechens was based on information from the internet.

Q: This book covers so much ground that it's not easy to label it simply "cybersecurity" or "political thriller," because it also has elements of romance, family drama, and of course international espionage. If you had to pick one genre to slot your book into, what would it be?

A: Cybersecurity thriller. The following books in this series will also contain elements of romance, family drama, and international espionage.

Q: Who are your favorite writers? Did a specific writer or book inspire you to write this book?

A: Kathryn Casey, Tom Clancy, Harlan Coben, John Connolly, Clive Cussler, Gillian Flynn, Vince Flynn, James Patterson, Ann Rule. I met Tom Clancy at an event in Maryland many years ago. Both he and his first book, *The Hunt for Red October*, influenced me greatly.

Q: Did you create your novel by using an outline, or did you sit down and follow wherever your imagination took you—and then come back and revise the first draft?

A: I outlined the chapters to decide where I wanted to go. The book had too many characters and too many moving parts to free-lance the chapters and scenes.

Q: What was your favorite scene to write in this story, and why?

A: There were really two. The battle scene in Chapters 29 and 30 at the end of the book and the shootout in Chapter 28 in which Dimitri gets killed.

Q: What was the most difficult scene to write, and why?

A: The shootout in which Dimitri, Anya, George, Chris, and Marat are killed was very difficult. The timing needed to mesh so that the shootout was easy to track and understand. I also needed to keep Anya's identity as the villain secret until the end of the chapter. However, the final scenes in the book involving the American, Chinese, and North Korean subs were definitely the most difficult because of the research required on the subs and their weapon systems. The setup for the final battle and the strategy choices and reactions by the characters was also very complex.

Q: Do you have a favorite character in the story? If so, what is it about this character that you most appreciate?

A: Other than James, Rick is my favorite character. He has a great sense of humor, which is also misguided at times. He is the source of most of the comedic scenes in this book and the next ones. Kim and Cai are also favorites due to their ability to handle difficult situations while maintaining a zest for life.

Q: In a similar regard, which character in *Cyber Countdown* do you most identify with, and why?

A: James. We both have a background with the navy. We both worked for the federal government in high-level positions. We both were successful at cybersecurity because we loved it. Finally, we both have gorgeous wives named JoAnn who are from Minnesota and are very good with finances.

Q: Have you ever been a hacker?

A: I was a penetration tester for the Department of Homeland Security and the Department of Defense, which is essentially a "white hat" hacker. White hat hackers find vulnerabilities in order to fix them, while black hat hackers take advantage of them to attain wealth or power or for political reasons.

Q: If someone came to you for advice on how to get started writing, what would you tell them? What is the best—and the worst—advice you've ever gotten about writing?

A: I would advise anyone who wanted to start writing to write about what they know and love. The other requirements with respect to when to use dialogue and narration will come later. Spelling and grammar are important, but with good spelling and grammar checking software and accomplished editors, that shouldn't be a big problem. Best advice: Write about what you know. Worst advice: You need the sex scenes to be more graphic and explicit.

Q: What's next for author Terence Flynn?

A: I've completed a second book titled *Cyber Apocalypse* that includes many of the same characters that appear in this book. I'm also writing a third book in the series, which is currently titled *SCADA Red*.

# READING GROUP GUIDE

1. This book contains many plot twists and turns. Which one(s) surprised you the most? Why?

2. It wouldn't be easy to leave one's homeland, yet many characters in this book do just that. Discuss which characters leave their countries of origin, and why. Would that be a difficult thing for you to do? Why or why not? What would you do in their situation?

3. This book is filled with intricate details of cybersecurity, cyber warfare, worms, malware, and hacks. Which of these new technologies did you find the most intriguing?

4. Do you have any experience with hacking someone else's information or being hacked—perhaps having your identity stolen? How does this kind of invisible theft feel different from old-fashioned theft? Why?

5. Perhaps the most surprising turn comes near the end, when a character makes the difficult decision to leave the homeland. Did this surprise you? Why or why not? Would you have made the same decision?

6. Dimitri is at times a thug and at other times a gentleman. Discuss how he changes, and why he makes this change.

7. Why do you think George Solomon and his son have such a difficult relationship? Did this come as a surprise to you?

8. There's a lot of romance in this story between James and JoAnn, Kim and Cai, and others. How are these couples good for each other? Do you think these relationships will last?

9. There's an old saying about "honor among thieves." Did you see examples in this story? What characters do you think acted both honorably and dishonorably, and what examples do you have of their behavior?

10. North Korean student Kim Kwon-Mu and American cybersecurity expert James Jordan share many of the same traits, yet are different in obvious ways. Discuss what they have in common, and how they're different.

11. Does Kim see his uncle, whom he calls "Admiral," as a father figure, or more as a military superior? In what ways are the two roles—parent and superior—the same, and in what ways are they different?

12. Did any of the technology described in this book—from military capabilities to intricate computer worms—surprise you?

13. If you could have access to one of the incredible technologies described in this book, what would you choose, and why?

14. Do you think cyber attacks like those described in this book will play a greater role in warfare in the future?

15. There are good and bad aspects to using computer technology in harmful ways, such as inserting a "worm" or virus to disable someone's access or information. In addition, there's a lot of harvesting of our personal data without our knowledge, such as we've seen

in recent news about Facebook selling our information. What do you think about these threats? Are there times computer hacking is acceptable? How does a person or government make such a determination?

16. Who was the real villain in this story, and why? Did that come as a surprise to you?

17. What was your final assessment of George Solomon? Do you think he acted honorably, or did he never overcome his selfish ambition?

18. Which character was your favorite, and why? Which character did you change your mind about, and why?

19. If you could spend an afternoon with one of the characters in this book, who would you choose, and why? If you could spend an afternoon in one of the scenes in this book, what place would you choose, and why?

20. Have you ever been in a submarine? Do you think you would enjoy being submerged for weeks at a time?

21. If this book were a movie, who do you imagine in the roles of: James Jordon? Senator JoAnn Young? President Meredith? Kim Kwon-Mu? Kim's girlfriend, Cai Chan Li? Dimitri? If you were invited to play one of those roles, who would you like to portray, and why?

22. If you could write a sequel to this novel, which characters would you want to write about? If you could send a message to the writer about a possible sequel, what would you tell him you want to read more about?

# ABOUT THE AUTHOR

The author grew up in New York City and went to school at Queens College and State University of New York at Stony Brook graduating with a B.S. in Electrical Engineering and an M.S. in Computer Science. He also received a Juris Doctor from American University in Washington D.C. while working for the Departments of the Navy, Justice, and Commerce in Washington DC.

After leaving the government, the author started his own engineering consulting company providing Information Technology and Cybersecurity support services and products to the Federal Government and commercial businesses and has U.S. patents in both technology fields. He provided cybersecurity support to DoD, DHS, NASA, NIST, and NSA. He continues to lead his company into new technology areas including Big Data and Artificial Intelligence and is on the Board of Directors of several cybersecurity organizations.

The author has been happily married for 24 years and has a son and daughter. He currently lives in Southern Maryland and enjoys sailing, traveling, and all water related sports and activities including fishing, scuba diving, surfing, swimming, and water skiing. His interests include science, history, politics, and technology and enjoys reading books about history, science, science fiction, technology, and especially adventure novels based on new technologies and scientific and technological research.